Dear Reader:

Every now and then y you away.

That's what happened when I read Tara Harper's first Wolfwalker book: It grabbed me and didn't let me go until I had read the very last page . . . which left me begging for more. Her descriptions of the action had me on the edge of my seat—especially when the heroine, *who was afraid of heights,* desperately picked her way up the side of a sheer cliff (see Tara's bio at the end of this book to learn why her action reads so realistically!). And the telepathic bond between the heroine and her wolf was as beguiling, as satisfying, as the relationship between a rider and her dragon in Anne McCaffrey's beloved Dragonriders of Pern books.

I love Tara's books. (So does Anne McCaffrey, for that matter!) I want to share them with as many people as possible.

And that's why I'm thrilled that Tara has returned to the world of the wolfwalkers with a brand-new heroine, a brand-new wolf, and a brand-new adventure: The perfect introduction for those who missed the earlier books, and another great reading experience for her growing legion of fans. Read it: You'll like it!

In fact, I'm so sure you'll like this book that I'm willing to bet on it. This book is GUARANTEED to be a great read (see last page for details). From where I sit, it's a sure thing!

Happy Reading!

Shelly Shapiro
Executive Editor
Del Rey Books

By Tara K. Harper
Published by Ballantine Books:

Tales of the Wolves
WOLFWALKER
SHADOW LEADER
STORM RUNNER
GRAYHEART

LIGHTWING
CAT SCRATCH FEVER
CATARACT

GRAYHEART

Tara K. Harper

A Del Rey® Book
BALLANTINE BOOKS • NEW YORK

A Del Rey® Book
Published by Ballantine Books

http://www.randomhouse.com

Library of Congress Catalog Card Number: 95-96187

ISBN 0-345-38053-3

Manufactured in the United States of America

First Edition: August 1996

10 9 8 7 6 5 4 3 2 1

For my brother, Kevin Harper,
who saved me from losing my leg to that
bull sea lion with the broken tusk

A special thank you to Kevin Harper; Dan Harper; Richard Jarvis; Sandra Keen; Marc Wells; Ed Godshalk; Thomas Moore, University of Arizona; Dr. Howard Davidson; and Dr. Ernest V. Curto, University of Alabama, Birmingham.

I

Steel gleamed. It was night, but even with the lack of light, the blade shone in her eyes like a flat of polished glass. The hand that held the knife was draped with shadow; the body, hidden by the dark, was tense as ice before it breaks. Behind her, the warehouse labs were nearly lightless; the floors glowed only faintly to outline the paths of the open rooms and halls. Outside, the nomoon night shrouded the warehouse walls, and the streets themselves were black. And yet the steel knife in the doorway gleamed.

Rezsia did not blink. She did not move. She barely felt the absence of the pulse that should have pounded in her throat. Then, finally, the heartbeat rolled through her body like a kettledrum in a canyon. One beat, and an hour of staring at that blade. Another pulse, and a night and a day, while her lungs forced a hundred warnings to her racing, feverish brain. Something harsh swept through her teeth, and she realized she was breathing.

Could he see her clearly in the shadows? Did he know just where to strike? If he shifted—even fractionally—there was no movement to her night-adjusted eyes. She thought a cold breeze touched her spine, but her skin did not dare shiver. Deep in her mind, an echo howled, and blocks away, from beneath the stable, a lone, gray shape leaped up.

The flat, glass vials in her pocket were cold against her frigid fingers. She was going to die, she told herself in a kind of absent horror, for a fungus in her pocket. NeGruli's man would gut her like a rabbit. Skin first, then her innards, then up under her ribs to her heart. And when her bones were bare to the moons, and her blood steamed hotly in this chill, spring night, he'd find the glass containers in her pocket; and with them, take the rest of her family to the trial block, and condemn them to join her in death.

One hand clenched with futile strength: she had no sword to grip. Her bow was on her riding beast, along with the war bolts she had borrowed from an older brother. The sheath and long knife that had hung from her belt—her eldest brother had them. Each awkward length of steel or sinew that could have protected her here would have made her clumsy inside the darkened warehouse, and she had left them behind. And false confidence from carrying the blades at all could have crippled her in the space through which she stole. No sword or bow; no steel at her waist; no throwing knives close at hand . . . Item by item, her mind took stock of every weapon on her belt or body, and when it was done, she still stared at the guard before her, because the only blades she carried that night were the two boot knives, securely in place, a meter from her fingers.

The doorway breathed with the chilling breeze that slid along the street. Damp, glowing roads pooled their shadows between the trees. Few outside lights were needed in the city—not with faintly luminescent streets to outline the buildings, and nine moons to shine through the night. But the moons did not help her on this night. Not one of them clung to the backsides of the clouds above the county. The long, thin bed of rootroad trees, whose glowing roots stretched out in hardened avenues, threw such faint light that Rezsia could barely define the outline of the guard against the doorway. The pale streets were sentinels of silence; and the night itself seemed to wait with neGruli's man for her movement.

The silent man shifted once, a hair closer—her eye exacted the distance—and she smelled the dust on his clothes. Not warehouse dust, or lab dust, or the smells of fungal gels or spores. His jerkin was like the pelt of a wolf—heavy with the scent of the woods and trails—and his breath was sweet with the same. She could almost feel his body before her as the wind curled around his frame; could tell he was taller than she. His hair was hidden beneath a warcap, and his face disguised by darkness. She didn't know if she saw or felt the way his weight balanced on the balls of his feet. But she knew that, even with the dark that hid them both, he did not miss the way her skin flinched over her ribs, away from the point of that knife.

She took a breath so gently in that it barely shifted her lungs.

"How about you put down that knife, and I won't have to hurt you."

Even to herself, her low—almost whispered—voice was steady. She did not know that her lips curled back from her teeth like a wolf, and the flash of fear that lay deep in her eyes looked more like the gleam of a hunter.

The knife did not waver.

"If you're waiting for the others, they won't be coming. They went to the Iron Bar for a grog." Her voice was cool as the steel of that blade. Yet, steady as she sounded, her muscles had somehow lost their heat and now clamped like stone to her bones. Her throat could barely push the words between her frozen teeth. Chilled, her hands seemed iced onto the glass vials. And in her mind, still thin and distant, the heat of the wolf who raced through the streets left her sea of fear untouched.

Did the knifeman slant his head to hear her? She turned her right palm up as if in entreaty. The blade flicked in response—its warning clear: don't move. But she was already closer to that gleaming blade—closer now by a hand. Her voice was so soft it was almost lost in the breathing of the wind. "Give me your name, blader."

Was it his breathing she heard or hers? She stretched her fingers and gained another inch. Her balance crept to the balls of her feet. "What would you do with my body, anyway? Stuff me into one of the kilns and put my ashes out in the morning—"

A slight sound broke the pale silence of the road. A footstep—a voice? For an instant neither moved. Then Rezs's hand shot out. She followed her own movement with a violent lunge. One hand grabbed the knifeman's wrist, the other grasped his elbow. She yanked him toward her. His ribs hit hers. She didn't notice when his elbow jammed into her side, half twisting her body around him. She threw her slight weight on the bend of his arm and wrenched it back toward his gut. His grip on the blade seemed to loosen. And just before the knife went in, she hesitated.

Like wind through a net, her leverage disappeared. His arm rolled up, not down and back. Hard muscles bunched beneath her grip. His thick wrist twisted; his iron fingers kept their grasp, and with an almost negligible flick of his body, she was turned like a doll and pinned against his chest.

She did not move. The frigid steel now pressed against her throat. One rock-hard arm circled her slender waist; the other crossed her chest from armpit to neck to hold that blade to her flesh. Eight blocks away the young Gray One's feet sped swiftly.

Her pulse beat against the hardened muscles of his forearm. Her breathing was harsh, yet her chest barely rose and fell, as if expanding her lungs might push her neck against the knife. Instinctively, her fingers dug into his arm, pulling it down and tight to her chest. The howl of fear that rose in her head deafened her to her thoughts. Her mental voice, even with control, was tinged with the fright that pounded against her ribs. She couldn't help her mental cry: *Vlen!*

Wolfwalker—I come!

Her nostrils flared. No weapons, she thought; she had only Gray Vlen and bluff—

"My dog doesn't like those who manhandle me."

The voice was low, but steady, and it took Rezs a moment to realize it was still hers.

"You've a wolf, not a dog." His voice was barely more than a breath. "If you value its life, keep it away. And be quiet."

But Vlen's shadow flicked along the city blocks. The low brush that grew between the rootroad trees broke beneath his weight and sent the night creatures skittering to avoid his feet. His link to Rezsia, new and thin in both their minds, strengthened with his urgency. Rezs's breath was suddenly caught in Vlen's, so that her lungs pumped with his, shallow and fast; and her nose was clogged with odors. She tried to separate the scents—to remember that it was her own hands that smelled of fungus; her clothes that smelled of the labs. It was the night that smelled of muggy dust and fog. And the knifeman, with that steel on her throat, smelled of trails and sweat. And blood. There was blood upon his hands, his knuckles. Faint—as if it had been clotted. It made her dry mouth water as if she had bit her own lip to taste the same sweet, tangy fluid.

His hands shifted; the blade indented her flesh. "Keep him back," the knifeman breathed.

How did he know? Could this man feel the wolves as she did? *Vlen*— She couldn't keep the fright from her tone. *Wait! For moons' sake, stop! Come no closer.*

The wolf pulled up, uncertain, his limbs almost trembling with eagerness. Another sound drifted down the rootroad, and this time it was clear: footsteps in the nomoon night. Rezs jerked, and the steel seemed to slide on her neck. She froze again.

"Be still," the blader whispered. "And very, very quiet."

Rezs's hearing, heightened by the sense of the cub, caught the sound of the steps like a slow, unrhythmic pounding. She didn't think she could tense any further, but somehow she tightened like a coil. The arm that crushed her chest pressed down upon her breathing. The steel that laid its line of ice along her neck seemed to slice her flesh. And the howl that echoed in her mind was closer now, and louder: Vlen was two blocks away.

Wolfwalker! The fang is at your throat—

Stay, she forced herself to command. *The guards that come this way—follow them—stalk them. Tell me how close they come. I'll deal with this one myself.*

She didn't know if her surge of aggression was a result of her fear or his. But it heightened her adrenaline rush until she felt as if her muscles were so ready to strike that they would snap her bones if she did not release their tension. She inhaled in shallow breaths and formed a picture of the guard. Blood . . . The scent of the scabs on his hands . . . And the odor of the forest . . . The jerkin and belts that pressed on her ribs— they weren't the clothes of a guard, but a scout. She felt the thoughts rattle through her skull. Her eyes, frozen forward, caught the shadows of the guards the same instant the blader moved.

But the knifeman did not shout to bring the other guards more quickly. He shifted back, taking her with him. It was the last thing she expected. She stumbled, and he caught her like a dancer and lifted her from her feet so that her boots didn't scrape on the building's stone.

Her brain did not seem to be working. She didn't struggle; instinctively, she let her body melt into his. Some tiny thought noted sardonically, as she shrank against his hard chest, that the drive to hide from new, unknown dangers must be stronger than that of fighting known ones.

He set her down as he felt her body balance against him. Then they moved, together, out of the doorway and along the wall, deep in the shadow of the eaves, his steely grip changing only its hold, not its strength upon her flesh. Behind them, the dark door swung almost silently shut, but to Rezs's urgent ears, its tiny click was like the first fall of an ax at dawn. She gasped. The steel pressed hard against her throat. The arms urged her back more quickly. Gray Vlen howled in her head, and Rezs choked silently as she tried not to answer out loud. Her body twitched as Vlen paced urgently back and forth, as if caught on a leash by the trees. She could feel the cub's feet hit the soft edges of the rootroad, then jump back into the line of darkness.

The formless shapes of neGruli's guards became sharper. Their voices, low and murmured, drifted like the fog.

". . . saw him in Ramaj Ariye."

"Yes, but he's thinking of coming back to Randonnen."

"NeGruli won't like that."

"How's he to know? The boss is off sucking power from the elders like a roofbleeder taking blood from its victims. By the time he gets back from the council meeting, he'll have other things on his mind. . . ."

Even in the dark, it was clear that all four of them were big—neGruli's guards were always broad and tall—and the long swords at their sides swung like batons to their steps. She would have walked right out into them, Rezs realized, had the blader not caught and stopped her at the door. She would have headed right out into the street where those guards and everyone else could have seen her, and then she would have had to run for it.

In her mind, Gray Vlen snarled at her. Head down, shoulders hunched; Vlen's shadow now barely brushed the shrubs as he followed the group of guards toward the warehouse. His yellow eyes gleamed at their movements as they passed his vantage point, and Rezs stared at the guards, not only through her eyes, but his.

Gray One, she sent urgently.

Wolfwalker, he returned. His mental voice trembled with eagerness that made Rezs's lips tighten. *I am here.*

She could feel the knifeman's pulse offset against her own; the tightness of her hands on him, and his on her waist and ribs, locked them in each other's arms like lovers. As one, they eased to the corner of the building, then paused. Rezs didn't have to look over the man's shoulder to see what halted their steps: she knew that wide alley as well as she knew the street beside her own home. It was not the clutter of kilns and fire-walls, crates and storage cabinets that made the knifeman pause. It was not the lack of pattern to the placement of the baths or drains. Instead, it was the rubbish of glass and paper, brittle reeds, and snapping seed pods, across every meter of that area. It was the mass of garbage laid down each dusk—a jumble that was swept aside each morning. And it was impossible to walk through without making noise.

". . . like to see his face when he finds out that Faure is back," said one of the guards.

"Turin, here, said she'd give her last sight of all nine moons to see the face-off."

"Who wouldn't? Faure neKintar has a way with words. If anyone could rouse the elders to realize neGruli's plans, it would be neKintar. Of course, neGruli pays as well as Faure talks. No matter what neKintar says, neGruli will have voting rights on the council by fall."

Another guard chuckled. "I'd hate to be in a Durn's boots when that happens."

"I'd hate to be in the boss's boots if he takes the west road—the Durn stopped three speakers last time they took that road out to the council meeting. You can bet the Durn would love to get their hands on neGruli."

"And I'd hate to be in your boots if you don't check the warehouse, by one . . ."

Rezs and the blader pressed back against the corner, but slunk no farther around it. Rezs knew there were shadows in which they could hide, but the knifeman did not shift toward them. NeGruli's men were so close now that Rezs could even hear their breathing. Her eyes, locked before on the knife-man's blade, now stared at the guards like a rabbit.

"Don't look at them," breathed the voice in her ear. Her start was swallowed by the tightening of the knifeman's grip.

"Close your eyes or look down." His lips brushed her earlobe. "Don't think of them. Don't think of us. Make your mind empty—as if you're not here. And keep the wolf away."

Gray Vlen, as if he could hear the man's voice, faded behind a tree. This time Rezs jerked for real. Instantly, the man's arms crushed her until she could not even gasp. If she had thought his grip was tight before, it was now like a cord of steel.

"You coming in?" It was one of the guards.

Another one—the tall woman—gestured toward the alley. "In a minute. Might as well do the outer rounds now."

The knifeman seemed to shrink back. "Close your eyes," he breathed sharply. Rezs obeyed: Vlen's sight was hers through the link.

Shadow shapes were suddenly lighter, but blurred in her mind's eye. The scent of the guards, of the knifeman, of herself clogged her nose through Vlen's. The knifeman's forearm moved over her mouth, loosely, so that even her breathing was muffled.

The woman's voice continued. "You check the doors. Roark and I will do the outer rounds. We can do the labs together."

The Gray One slunk along the edge of the rootroad on the other side of the street. His mind was hot with the scent of his prey.

Stay, she sent to the cub.

I can smell them. I can almost taste them on my tongue.

No! She made her mental voice hard and sharp. *Wait there.*

Closer—the two guards moved to the alleyway. The knifeman seemed to stop breathing. The urgency of the Gray One's whine pierced her so that she felt her mind go blank. The glass vials in her pocket seemed suddenly to glow like the streets, as if to say, Here we are. Come get us, and Rezs winced as if their light would hurt her closed eyes. She did not even recognize the absurdity of the gesture.

So close that she could have touched them, the guards moved around the corner and stared down the alley as if it held worlags, not kilns and storage cabinets. The guards' eyes never touched the corner itself, nor the shadows in which Rezs and the blader hid. Carefully, together, as if they had done it a thousand times before, the two guards moved down the wide space, ignoring the noise of their feet.

"Be better with lights," the one on the far side muttered. His voice was so soft that it barely carried to Rezs.

"If you want to be a target," the other one agreed softly. "Moons will be out again within the hour; the next round will be faster."

Five minutes for them to move the length of the alley. Five minutes in which Rezs tried to grow into the wall like a patch of flattened shadow. Then the guards were around the corner at the other end of the building, and the alley was clear and silent.

As one, Rezs and the blader breathed. She made to shift, and his arm dropped smoothly from her mouth to her neck, locking her back to his chest. The steel that had almost become part of her neck was cold again on her flesh.

"Don't try it," he breathed. "This steel would take the blood from your throat faster than you could call out for your wolf." His whispered voice grew harsh. "And never," he added softly, "hesitate in a kill. The result would feel like this—"

He moved like a whip, and the knife sliced across her carotid.

II

Rezsia couldn't scream. The cold steel seemed to slit open her pulse, and like a wind, Gray Vlen leaped across the road.

"Breathe," the man's voice echoed in her death-deaf ears. "And keep the wolf out of sight."

Her mind was blank. Her pulse seemed to thrust itself against her hands as she grabbed at her throat. The wolf cub launched himself from the ground; and smoothly—almost negligently—the knifeman twisted Rezs so that the cub hit her body instead.

"Hurry," he whispered. One of his muscled hands grabbed hers. He yanked her out into the rootroad. Gray Vlen lunged for his leg. Somehow, without losing his balance, he turned so that Vlen slashed at his boot rather than his thigh. He cast a single look at the cub: back off. Stand off. I'm more than a match for you—Rezs could almost hear the words echo in her head. Vlen, midleap, scrambled clumsily to halt his attack. The yearling's snarl, deep down in his throat, was almost too low to hear, and the shaft of subservience that the cub projected thickened Rezs's fear from fog into ice.

Now she fought. Silently, furiously, struggling like a madwoman. If she bled, she did not notice. If she caught a breath, she didn't care. She could not wrench her wrists free of the knifeman's grasp. She brought up her knees to find his soft groin or gut, but he turned his hips and slid her blows off as if he brushed aside a twig. She dropped her head suddenly, then forced all her weight up in a vicious lunge. He *knew*— He moved his head back and twisted, and she not only missed, but her body, pressed against the length of his, was suddenly thrust away and shaken. Brutally, violently—as if she were a jammed door that by dislodging he could get open. "Stop it," the man snapped, his voice still low.

"Vlen—" she choked out. "What have you done to him?"

"Nothing. He's fine. Now hurry." He set her down so hard her teeth clacked together, then took one of her arms in that viselike grip and shoved her into the dark line of trees that marked the middle of the faintly glowing road. With a single glance back at the warehouse, he shifted his grip and dragged her across to the other side.

She stumbled in his wake, her mind still frozen. Her neck was cold with the chill of night—cold and firm as if it had never been touched by steel of any kind. Her left hand clutched her throat. "What—"

"I used the back of the blade, you little fool." He yanked her hard into the darkness between the buildings on the other side.

One hand on her throat, and her mind still not quite working, the words he spoke seemed to roll over in her head: the back of the blade . . . Not cut, she thought. Not sliced at all.

On both of their heels, Gray Vlen snarled, but made no move toward the man. The blader's voice was still low: "Where's your riding beast?"

Anger flared in Rezs's stomach, and she felt it shake through her body like a wind. She clamped her lips shut before drawing a deep breath through her nose. The cub moved up beside her, his steps a wary lope, his eyes turning constantly toward the man. "Chankeny Stables," she bit out. "Eight blocks up, seven blocks west."

Without speaking, he turned along the blocks and dragged her roughly in his wake.

She touched her neck again. "Was it necessary," she demanded in a low voice, "to scare me like that?"

His own low voice was cold and harsh. "Yes."

She tried to wrench her hand from his grasp, but she might as well have tried to take a meal from a mudsucker. From shadow to shadow, he dragged her along like a dog. Gray Vlen, on her heels, merely laid his ears back and growled so softly that she heard nothing with her ears.

"Moonwormed root," she cursed abruptly as she jammed her foot on the uneven edge of the road.

"Keep quiet," he shot back.

She gave him a look as sharp as any blade, and as if he had eyes in the back of his head, he chuckled. As suddenly as it had swept through her body, the anger washed away. Her brain seemed suddenly cold and sharp. In the darkness, she stared at the man through Vlen's eyes, not her own.

Tall, yes—as tall as neGruli's guards always were, but the scents of this one's clothes were wrong. Strong, for sure; lean perhaps—she couldn't tell from the bulk of his jerkin. And the blood on his knuckles—she could feel the scabs when she grasped his hand back in her own. "Who are you?" she demanded, her voice as low as his.

He did not answer. Instead, he hauled her around the last corner. Even in the shadow cast by the light on the front of the stable, she could see her riding beast under the side overhang—her bridle ornaments and saddle silver glinted dully, delineating its front and back. Each of the beast's six legs stamped the ground in turn with patient irritation at the night flies. Like a cross between an oldEarth horse and an ant or centipede, the dnu's fat body gave it the look of a barrel on spindly legs. But it was fast and steady, and she had trained it well. And it didn't recognize the man. Its head swiveled around.

"Keep it quiet," he ordered in that still-harsh whisper as he yanked her to a stop beside him.

She balked, pulling with futile strength against his grip. "Dammit, who are you?"

He paused. Slowly, he turned to face her, and she stared at his features as though she could see them in the dark. For a moment neither one moved. Then, slowly, she reached up to touch his face. Without seeming to move at all, he was suddenly a meter away. Rezs's eyes narrowed, and deliberately, she followed him forward until her fingers made contact with the line of his jaw. Stubble, short and stiff, prickled against her skin. Beside her, Gray Vlen's low snarl grew subtly louder until it almost drowned the words of the man.

"Don't," he said softly.

She stared at the tiny glints in his eyes. She did not remove her hand. "Are you talking to me or the wolf?" she heard herself ask quietly.

"You're gutsy," he said softly. His words seemed to hang in the night. "But you have no idea what you're doing."

"Now or then?"

His eyes gleamed, and Gray Vlen snarled a challenge. The man didn't look at the cub, but his hand covered Rezs's and removed it from his face. "Are you always this forward with men you meet in the dark?"

"Only when they save my life," she returned.

"And if I hadn't?"

Now it was Rezs who tried to pull her hand back, but the knifeman's grip was like a clamp. She could feel the calluses on his fingers; the thickness of his hand to hers. She felt the mass of hard bumps on his bones where past blows had thickened them with calcium deposits and left his long fingers rough and scarred. His skin was warm on her chilled flesh. She wanted to pull back, but couldn't move. Fear or the thrill that caught her breath—or her curiosity of the man—one of them was compelling.

She no longer tried to move away. There was an echo in her mind—a haunting tune that slid away as she caught the sense of it—and a voice that rang with a timbre she could not hear with her ears. Gray Vlen pressed up against her thigh, nudged her softly, then whined and backed away. Neither one noticed.

"Gutsy," he repeated.

His other arm traced hers up until it rested on her shoulder. As his hand pressed against her back she felt her stomach tighten, and without thinking, she stepped up and into his arms. It was she, not he, who started the kiss, and as their lips met, the cub's growl grew until his voice became a soft howl. There was a sense in her head of double vision. Vlen's image of herself was sharp, and the man who held her no longer distant through the link, but a shadow shape that she could almost see—a figure that seemed to run beside yet somehow never quite with the wolf pack whose memories echoed in Gray Vlen's mind. Like a wisp of fog that hangs above a canyon, a melody floated above the shapes.

"Grayheart," she whispered.

The blader stiffened. For a moment neither one moved. Then he released her so suddenly that she staggered. She started to speak, but without a word, the man stepped back, then turned and strode away. Rezsia stood rooted. Too late she stepped forward. Her eyes strained to see him; her ears stretched to hear his steps, but only through Vlen could she do it. The light breeze brushed the trees along the rootroads, and the knifeman's form was gone.

Gray Vlen panted. His ears pointed, then flicked back toward Rezs. *Wolfwalker?*

She stared into the alley where the man had disappeared. *Your memories—that voice in the song of the wolves—you know him, Vlen?*

He sent her a jumbled mix of images, too fast for her to sort.

She clenched her fists and tried to clear her mind. "Again, Gray One," she said, projecting her question as she spoke. "I didn't understand."

This time, slowly, as though he, too, were concentrating, the wolf cub sent the images. Boys, men, shadows, wolves— shapes that moved in the forest at dusk and dark and dawn. A violence of rejection that clung to the images like that thread of music: ghosts in the Gray Ones' minds. *His scent,* said Vlen, *is in my memory like the sight of a deer far away in the fog.*

For a moment Rezsia stared down the alley. She could no longer feel the man's presence, even through the Gray One. But one thing he had left her: when she touched her throat, she could still feel his steel on her flesh.

III

Her dnu snorted softly, and Rezs turned to her riding beast. With the moons not yet risen, she untied the dnu by touch, then swung thoughtfully into the saddle. There was no way to soften the dull pound of the hoofbeats in the street, and she didn't try. Instead, she urged the beast into a smooth rolling canter, toward the western side of the city. The cub circled to lope just ahead of the dnu, and the eagerness he projected— for the ferns at the edge of the forest, for the wide rootroad that led to her home, for the thick, familiar musk smell in the hollow beneath her house—stole her attention until she rode more by instinct than with firm direction.

In ten minutes she was clear of the first city hub and out on the wide trade roads that radiated between the hubs. Fifteen minutes found her at the midpoint between the next two hubs. There, the outside lights hung far apart, and the night was filled with insect clacks and chitters, and the rustlings of the rodents who crept along the road. The walls of the clumps of houses were interspaced with the quiet dark of gardens. The chest-high lines of shadow she saw were the thin barrier bushes that defined the commons between the homes and workshops and gardens. Dnu didn't jump high, but they could find a way through almost anything. It was one of the reasons the Ancients had left their horses on oldEarth. Dnu had spindly legs, but they couldn't founder, hated barrier bushes, and were tough as rattan when it came to resisting most of the parasites.

Rezs urged her own dnu to keep to its pace while, unconsciously, she counted each block of trade and school buildings she passed: glassworks, builders, binders, cooks . . . The faint lights from a healer's clinic glowed four kilometers off to the right. Even at four kays, she could see that there were people still working there; shadows clouded the faint lights as healers moved hurriedly back and forth past the windows. A kay ahead, the luminescent, blue-green trees on a hill marked the biobuildings clearly. The trees seemed to writhe as she passed close by, and Rezsia grinned without humor. Part of that movement was the cloud of insects attracted to its flowers. The other part was the closing of the trees' carnivorous blooms.

She glanced up, following the light of the trees to the sky. The black, nomoon night, which used to frighten her as a child, seemed almost warm—like a blanket she could wrap around herself as she rode. She found her hand straying to her neck, as if by touch alone, she could make stronger the chill of the steel that had touched her. She started when Vlen sharpened his attention and shot her a sudden shaft of scent. Abruptly, her shoulders tensed, and her thighs tightened in the saddle to urge the dnu faster. *What is it?* she sent sharply.

She had projected wariness more than words, and the yearling responded with a surge of hunter intensity. Her mind filled with the odor of a dnu, leather scent and wood dust . . .

"Reszia?" came the soft voice from the shadows.

"Cal!" Her hands clenched on the reins, and the dnu abruptly slowed. As if her brother's voice had released the fear she had held within her, she slumped in the saddle. Her hands began to shake; the darkness blurred.

"You cut it close." Cal urged his dnu out of the shadows to pace her at her side. "Moons will be up in ten minutes. Did you get them?"

"I got them."

Some tremor in her voice must have betrayed her, because he leaned across the saddle and touched her arm for an instant when the two dnu matched steps. "You okay, little Lunki?"

She took a breath and let it out slowly. "Fine. We're both fine."

"Trouble?"

"No," she lied.

Cal peered at her in the darkness. His low voice took on a sharp note. "What happened?"

"Later," she said shortly. "I got what we wanted. Let's get out of here."

He bit back his questions and urged his dnu forward. He let her fall in after him. Together, the riding beasts slid into their smooth, six-legged lope, so that the rhythm of their hooves kept a syncopated time to the soft sound in her head of Vlen's padding feet. From behind Cal, Rezs felt her senses expand as the yearling breathed in. She could almost taste Cal's body scent in the air. It should have been a sweet odor, but it tasted acrid alongside the heavy pollens from the rootroad trees. The faint scent of caffiweed, which Cal had chewed to stay awake, came to her as a bitterness as she rode behind him. She savored the smells, separating them in her mind. When she tried to identify her own scents among the others, she projected her thoughts to Gray Vlen.

The cub flashed inside the treeline, startling her. *Your nose is as weak as a rock worm,* he sent.

She looked down and reached out along the bond between them until what seemed like a thin cord became a rope. Thicker, stronger—it caught at each one's senses, so that their minds turned in, and their eyes were blind. Vlen stumbled. Rezs cut a corner too wide, and her dnu's sharp hooves struggled to keep their footing on the dew-slick road. "Moonworms—"

Instantly, she thinned out the bond with Vlen. She'd already swung her weight instinctively to balance the dnu, and as the riding beast came out of the corner, she guided it to the center of the road where the roots had grown the hardest.

"Stay awake, Rezs," Cal called sharply.

She didn't bother to answer. Even though she had thinned out the bond to Vlen, through the wolf cub's eyes, she could feel the weariness in Cal's shoulders. He must have been waiting for her since soon after she left for the warehouse. Her tension softened. After a full day on the building sites, he should have been in bed, not out on the road this late.

The roads that radiated between the city hubs were wide and empty this time of night, and only the occasional lights or sound of someone working late in a private workshop disturbed their dark ride. When they finally passed through the next city center and reined up near their home, the fifth moon had risen, finally breaking the nomoon night. Its small glow shone through the breaking clouds, and it cast shadows that seemed almost too silent to Rezs. The eighth and first moons would not be far behind, she knew. And the second moon should crest over the labs within minutes, letting her own eyes—not just Vlen's—detail the grounds around her home. No nomoon night lasted more than nine hours. This one was only five.

For several minutes neither one spoke. Instead, they eyed the buildings carefully. The two stories of their house were quiet, with only one light in one of the upper rooms. The light shone dimly from one of the tapered arches—all the windows on that side had been allowed to grow into arches; it reminded their father of the home he'd had as a child, he'd told them once—though it was bright enough to light the courtyard.

Rezs used her peripheral vision to catch the movements of anyone who could be waiting. Though she strained her sight to find a hint of the watchers whom she had felt for days, no eyes other than Vlen's gleamed in the brightening night. No shadows shifted with anything other than wind. In fact, it was as quiet as if they had not risked her thievery at all, and that more than anything else kept Rezs's tension on edge.

She stretched along the bond to Vlen and let the flare of his nostrils affect her own. She didn't notice that she wrinkled back her upper lip like a wolf. As she breathed in deeply, the breeze that swept across the rolling ground of the commons carried the smells of the lemon-sweet ground cover. The sharp scent cut through the heavy smell of manure and masked the subtler scent of the flowers that lined the drive. Behind the lab, the changun trees were blooming—she could smell their sweetness like a faint taste of candy—and from two houses down, around the edge of the commons, she could smell the freshly turned earth from the Weller's work on their retaining wall. There was human scent on the wind, but her shoulders did not prickle, and Vlen's scruff lay flat.

Their own house stood on the peak of one of the gentle slopes. The shared barn stood behind the house, on the side of the slight hill, just above the terraced gardens, and between Rezs's home and their neighbor's. Like a timid child, the roof of the stable peeked out from behind a corner of the house. In front of her, the private corral and the gate to the commons stood out sharply in the moonlight. To the right of the gate, the lab was situated slightly below and along the side of what became a steeper slope.

From the shadows of the courtyard, Rezs blinked as a night insect batted against her eye, and Vlen shook his head as if it had struck his eye instead. Rezs murmured a reassurance. If her brother Lit waited for them in the labs, he did so quietly. No sounds indicated his presence; and the only light that shone from the long, low structure was faint and so dark as to cast no window shape on the ground.

Cal glanced at Rezs. His voice was low. "I don't trust my eyes and ears to find neGruli's men. They were here two days ago, and we never knew till they rode out through the gate."

She nodded. "Gray One," she said to Vlen. "The commons—the buildings around the edges—can you scout them? Look for anyone who watches us like a hunter."

Vlen snorted again, this time to clear his nose. When he turned his head to her, even in the dark, the yellow eyes seemed to gleam. Rezs could feel his excitement. *My nose is as good as any pack leader's nose. I could smell danger if it hid like a root in the ground.*

"Then go," she whispered. "And be careful."

Eagerly, he slunk behind the dnu and circled toward the house, so that the shadows swallowed him hungrily. Rezsia felt her limbs loosen in the saddle, as though his smooth movement relaxed her body. He was already past her sight.

Wolfwalker! he howled silently through the night.

Yellow eyes that were not Vlen's seemed to gleam through her thoughts. An echo wafted faintly through Rezsia's mind, as if the pack heard Vlen's mental call and shouted to her from a ridge. She tasted that sound. Savored it like the tang of a fresh-picked peach in winter. And then it faded, and only the tension of Gray Vlen's legs made her own thighs tight in the saddle.

She tried to stretch her bond with him to feel his feet on the ground. As if the fear in that night alone had strengthened their awareness of each other, his hot breath seemed to leap across her tongue. Her feet seemed to step automatically between the sharp roots of the barrier bushes where he trotted along the line. Head down, shoulders almost hunched, the cub loped to the far side of the stable, then out along the line of sharp-thorned shrubs, where the buildings hovered like guards. A night hare ducked into the light hedge at the fence; four moon-birds flashed overhead. But there were no odors of humans other than Cal and herself on the heavy air of the night.

She let her breath out in relief.

"Clear?" Cal asked softly.

"Around the house," she confirmed.

"What's wrong with your neck, Rezs?" he asked quietly.

Unbidden, her hand was hot on her neck, rubbing the spot where steel had touched flesh. Deliberately, she dropped her hand to the reins. "Nothing," she said flatly. "Just a scare."

Cal leaned over and caught her arm to hold her still as he peered at her neck. "What kind of scare?"

She shook her head. "It doesn't hurt."

"Who was it? A guard?" His voice was low, dangerous.

"No guard. And he scared me, that's all. Saved my life, I think. If I'd gone straight out onto the street as I had planned, I'd have run into neGruli's guards within a block."

Cal's voice grew cold. "This man met you inside the labs?"

She paused, her mouth half-open to answer him. It hit her suddenly that the chill she had felt before from the knife was as nothing compared with the coldness that settled in her gut. Inside the labs . . . The knifeman must have followed her. He must have seen—and known what she was doing.

Neither one spoke. Unconsciously, Rezs rubbed at her throat with her free hand. Cal watched her for a moment. "Wrench your neck?" he said finally.

Her violet eyes turned to his. "Thought he'd cut it," she answered.

Cal's grip tightened automatically, and Rezsia flinched. Her brother didn't notice.

Carefully, she pried his fingers off her arm. "Did it to teach me a lesson," she told him soberly. "I tried to disarm him, but I . . . hesitated right at the leverage point. He took me out with a single twist, then pulled the back of his steel across my neck. Right on the carotid." She touched her neck gingerly. "I can still feel it."

The set of Cal's jaw was clear in the moonlight. Rezs could feel the tension in his broad shoulders, and she knew that, had he not been mounted, he would have shaken her just as their father had done when they were young. "You're angry," she said flatly.

"Moonworms, Rezs, what do you think I should feel?" He bit back his anger, keeping his voice low. "I saw how you rode in from neGruli's—you were so tense in the saddle that the only reason you didn't fall off was your white-knuckle grip on the reins. It was obvious something was wrong—if for no other reason than I called you 'little Lunki' and you barely noticed."

"We knew tonight would be chancy," she said quietly.

"Chancy to get in and out without getting caught," he agreed. "And you said you were ready in case something happened." He peered again at her neck, as if he could see in the moonlight the line where she had felt cold steel cross flesh. "You've spent more years in the fighting rings than Biran. But when it counts—"

"Do you think I'm not aware of all of that?" she snapped back, her voice as low and intense as his. "That knifeman could have killed me. As easily as you take a breath in, I could have had my last. I screwed up, Cal—don't think I don't know that. I hesitated and lost my nerve. And if that blader hadn't actually been a friend, I'd be on the path to the moons by now, and my blood would be feeding the flies."

"You called him a friend—you know him?"

"No. There was nothing actually familiar about him. I only meant that he couldn't have been trying to harm me to do what he did."

"Would you recognize him again if you saw him?"

She hesitated. "I don't know."

"What was he wearing?"

"Not the gear of a guard, but other than that, I couldn't tell—"

"His voice—what did it sound like?"

"He was whispering."

"Did he have a specific walk? A stance? Any habits or movements you could recognize?"

"Dik droppings, Cal, he was dragging me down the alleys almost faster than I could jog. I was hardly in a position to analyze his posture. And once we got to my dnu, he took off."

Cal stared out at the commons. "So," he said softly. "You meet and attack a man in neGruli's warehouse, let this guy get a grip on you, threaten your life, drag you around for a while, locate your dnu so he'd have a chance to recognize your tack, and—"

"I get the point, Cal."

He said nothing. She could almost feel him thinking: How long before that man ran to the council meeting to tell neGruli? What if he didn't work for neGruli? Who else was involved in this? Should they burn everything now or wait to see what happened? The kilns out back were ready—just in case . . .

The night breeze rustled nearby in the trees, and thin branches clacked together. One of the moons climbed out of the new leaves and shone its light on the commons.

"I know his scent," she offered slowly after a moment.

Cal gave her an unreadable look. "Moonwarriors of all nine orbs above," he muttered, "save us from our sisters. Do you really think that man's going to smell the same after a bath or a change of clothes?"

The dark hid her flush. "What, by all nine hells, do you expect from me, Cal? I've never done this kind of thing before—none of us has. I did the best I could. I got the samples—there's nothing I can do about the rest of it."

"You know what Litten's going to say to me when he finds out what could have happened?"

"So that's why you were waiting for me? Lit sent you?"

"Mother made Biran, Lit, and I throw stars. I won."

"Isak is still with the council, then?"

He nodded. "And if he's not back yet, he could be there till dawn." Cal shrugged at her expression. "With neGruli just back from another of his trips, you know he's got at least one new thing to propose and one new idea to throw into the pot. When neGruli speaks, it's either up in arms against him or for him. Thank the moons that man's greed is consistent. Otherwise, his guards would never have risked a night at the pub, and you . . ."

You'd be dead. She heard the words as if he had said them, and the shiver that crawled from her memory of the knife made her spine shake like a rickety stool from the weight of her own latent fear. The tension she sent to Vlen made the cub lower his shoulders farther until he seemed to slink along the outer edge of the Borgeni-Reid shared barn. She caught just a glimpse of the gray cub's shape as he rounded the edge of the next house. As he circled the lab her nose wrinkled with the thick scents he breathed in. She snorted with him when he cleared his lungs of the odors.

Cal watched her until her expression relaxed and her posture returned to normal. "Still clear?"

She jerked, then nodded.

"How long did you have to wait to get in?"

"Not long," she managed. "The guards left as soon as it got dark—just as you predicted."

"All of them?"

"One stayed behind at the door. I snuck in when he left to relieve himself. He wasn't there when I left."

"Did he go to the bar with the others?"

She shrugged, but the blood on the knifeman's hands flashed into her mind. "Don't know," she said softly. "I had the feeling that the blader took him out."

A muscle jumped in Cal's jaw. "So at least two people know someone was in there tonight."

She shrugged. "I don't think it will matter. The blader had his chance to expose me, and he didn't do it. And even if a guard goes missing, none of the others dare admit they weren't at their posts—especially with neGruli's new fungi just brought into town. They'll cover the missing one's absence to keep their jobs. Better to do that than become unemployed and homeless, then indentured like a Durn. They might as well burn their homes and put themselves on the street as confess to neGruli."

"Why, Rezs," Cal mocked, "you sound almost bitter."

"Do you blame me?" she shot back.

"Count your blessings," he returned. "If neGruli were any less controversial, we'd have shorter council meetings. And if he hadn't gone straight to the council meeting, you'd never have gotten in the lab warehouse to find that sample before he stored it away, let alone had time to look at the records of his work."

"And his men would have been touching every shadow on watch, not just looking at them from the street."

Cal's voice, when he spoke, was carefully emotionless. "It was that close?"

She didn't answer, but her hands unconsciously tightened on the reins, and her dnu stamped its feet irritably.

"You've the luck of the moons, little Lunki. I just hope to god you got the right fungi, too."

"I checked the records carefully, Cal. If they're not the right ones, then he's not keeping his breeding stock anywhere in this city." She paused. "I could always go back again." She said it as a joke, but even to her own ears, her words sounded strained.

"We weren't planning on having to do this again, Rezs," her brother said sharply. "Just getting you in there tonight took forty-five days—five entire ninans of planning and setting it up, Rezs. Over a month for that, and four more months of waiting . . . If you didn't pick out the right samples, that's five months down the drain. It's not as if we can just do this again anytime we like."

"I'm not claiming I want to play thief again," she returned sharply. "I'm just telling you I won't make the same mistakes twice."

Cal watched her gaze flicker as Vlen rounded the labs, then slunk across toward the house. When the Gray One disappeared around the corner, Cal gave Rezs a hard look. "Gray Vlen was half the reason we agreed that you—not Lit—should go. Where was the wolf while all of this was happening?"

"I couldn't trust him to stay in the rootroad trees. He wouldn't settle down." She cut off his comment. "I had no choice, Cal. It was take him in and let him point every guard in my direction, or leave him with the dnu. So I left him with the dnu." She shook her head at his expression. "When that blader pulled the knife, Vlen was right there with me, Cal."

"But he didn't stop the man either."

"No," she agreed slowly. "There was something about him that made Vlen step back." She jerked involuntarily as the cub jumped the barrier bushes and cut across the commons. "The circle around the commons is clear," she added. "There's no one out here but us. If neGruli's set another man to watch us, that watcher isn't here now."

Cal eyed the shadow of the cub for a moment. He imagined he could see those yellow eyes gleam; then he dismounted. As he took the reins over the dnu's head, he glanced at his sister. "There's an ancient saying, Rezs—from the oldEarth colony that settled at Beta Canes: Each mistake you make is a jump in the grave, and only if god keeps throwing you out do you get to call that learning."

Rezs shot him a sober look. "We made a decision, Cal. All of us together."

"I'm not one to forget it. But what we agreed to do was to breed some samples, culture neGruli's fungi—copy his work—that was all. Make sure that it was his own, not something he was stealing from . . . someone else. Not all of us wanted to raid his warehouse or put all our work at risk. You made that decision—you and Lit and Mother alone. And you were caught, Rezs—we don't even know by whom. Now, even if the missing guard doesn't speak up, we have to assume that neGruli knows you were in there."

"It wasn't one of neGruli's men—"

He cut her off. "Can you be absolutely sure?"

She bit her lip. "No," she admitted slowly. "No, I cannot."

His quiet voice cut sharply across the night, and it took Rezs a moment to understand why. Gray Vlen was nearby, and he picked up the voice of her brother and doubled it in her ears. "I'm afraid for you, Rezs," he said softly. "Biran, Isak, Lit—we all are. Gray Vlen is changing the way you think—making you take risks that you've not got the training to judge—and each day your bond with that cub grows stronger. We're afraid . . ." His voice trailed off, and he stared at the second moon as it gleamed on the edge of the buildings.

"You're afraid you're going to lose me," she said softly.

He shrugged.

Absently, she slid from the saddle and fingered the reins in her hands. "Strange how, when we were growing up, you all egged me on to do everything you did, and Mother was the one who was screaming at me all the time not to kill myself. Now Father's terrified, Mother's calm, and the four of you are sweating like dnu in a hot spring."

"Hell, Rezs, we egged you on because you were so damned determined to keep up with the rest of us that we just knew we could make you do just about anything we asked. It wasn't because you were capable—" He shifted his dnu quickly out of range of her mock punch. "It was because you were stubborn. In a way, we were probably even proud of you. You've more than just the look of grandmother about you, you know."

"That's not necessarily a good thing, Cal."

"No, it's not. But every family has its burden, and you, dear sister, are ours."

"You bat-eyed, beetle-lipped field rat," she muttered. "If I'm a burden, how about you? It wasn't I who broke my leg just before stocking season."

He grinned without humor. "I wouldn't have broken it if you hadn't knocked me flying."

"If I hadn't sent you flying, that worlag would've torn your leg off."

"But who, Rezs, attracted the worlag?"

She shrugged philosophically, and the vials shifted in her pocket.

Cal followed her glance at the lab. "Litten's probably wondering where you are."

"I know. I'll turn the dnu out. Go on to bed. Your leg probably wants a rest."

"I don't like it, Rezs."

She didn't pretend to misunderstand. "I know." She hesitated, then leaned across and touched his arm lightly. "Thanks for waiting for me, Cal."

For a brief moment his hand covered hers. Then he handed her the reins. "Look in on Tegre before you turn in, will you? She's been . . . having the dreams again."

Rezs nodded. She watched him limp away in the moonlight, then glanced at the upper window. She had dreamed, as a child, not in nightmares, but of becoming a wolfwalker. It was said that, in Ramaj Randonnen alone, there were more wolfwalkers in the last fifty years than there had been in the last five hundred. She had wanted to be one of those wolf runners so badly that the night was an eager companion for her—one that would bring the wolves to her sleep as easily as day brought her studies or work. There were no night terrors that were not followed by the yellow, gleaming eyes and white, curved fangs that tore her fright apart and left her slumber peaceful. There were no dreams that did not carry the semblance of a thick gray pelt in the texture of sea or sky. She had wondered if the wolfwalkers looked after their own—if they watched distant family through those yellow gleaming eyes. Or if the wolves marked their wolfwalkers from birth so that, when it came time to bond, the chosen humans were already known to the pack and accepted as part of the Gray Ones.

Those lupine touches rode Tegre's nightmares—Rezs could almost feel them. The wolves ran through the girl's mind, calming her sleep, as they had done through Rezsia's and her brothers'. If it had been this way with Rezs's father or her grandmother, she didn't know, but those yellow eyes had never left her own dreams alone.

She rubbed her fingers together, and knew that Gray Vlen felt it. She wondered if she could somehow rub that pressure into Tegre's sleep—if she could reassure the girl that she was nearby. It was a futile gesture. Neither lupine eyes nor Rezs's voice was what the young girl wanted. And Tegre's mother, gone for two long years, was not likely to return. Gone or dead—Rezs wondered if the wolves would know. If it was one of the predator beasts that had killed the lighthearted woman, there might be little to identify even if they could find her body. By now, her bones would be cracked and splintered; her clothing torn to shreds.

Rezs shivered. She had seen the worlags twice as she traveled between the cities. She'd seen the lepa flocks once. All three times left her numb with fear. Had she been her legendary grandma, she would have felt no fear—she would have grabbed a sword and jumped to the fight like a rabid poolah. Rezs frowned at her hands. She had slender fingers, but they were strong; her skin was smooth and unscarred, but it was tough. She clenched her fists slowly, then let them unfurl. Then, thoughtfully, she led the two dnu past the house to the barn.

Cal's dnu nudged her hands as she turned it into the run, and she gave it a quick scratch under its chin. The scar tissue she found was healing nicely, but it still itched; she could feel the short hairs where the dnu had rubbed against the gate until its skin was bare. Cal still hadn't told anyone how he'd broken his leg. She might tease him about it, but if it hadn't been for him, that claw mark would have been across her chest, not the bony chin of his dnu.

Her own dnu trotted off without a backward look, as if glad to get to the softer ground of the commons. Rezs watched it for a moment. In the moonlight, it looked like a bloated demon. The two dnu joined the small herd on the slopes, and with their movements, the shadows writhed like living things.

Rezs shivered. That chill steel seemed to slide across her neck . . .

She shook herself. "Get a grip, Rezs," she told herself harshly.

She circled the house and crossed to the labs without another glance at the commons. She needed no light to see where she was going. Twenty-eight years growing up in this home gave her an intimacy with yard and courtyard that went beyond familiarity.

The outer door creaked as usual, and she let her fingers trail over the door seals. They needed to be regrown again; they had cracked in four more places.

"Rezs?" a voice called out softly.

"Got 'em, Lit," she returned.

"Thought you would."

She made a face in his direction.

"I heard that," he teased ungently.

She pulled the glass containers from her pocket as she moved around the cabinets and came into view. Lit had his tall frame bent over one of the counters while he added a touch of nutrient to the gels that filled his own flat, glass dishes. The small, directed light he used on the samples was bright and harsh in the near darkness of the lab; Rezs winced at the point intensity that struck her eyes. "Biran still here?"

"Went to meet Isak. Just in case."

She nodded. If neGruli's guards had caught her, Lit and the others would have been safe at the house—neGruli would never have risked a full-out attack in public. But Isak, alone on the west road as he returned from the council, would have been an easy target. "Any word from Father?" she asked as she set the vials on the counter.

He didn't look up. "Huh-uh," he grunted absently. His square jaw and high cheekbones were harshly lit by the lamp, and with the shadows hiding the jet black of his hair, he had the look of their father. Rezs's lips tightened.

As if he felt her expression, Lit looked up. "He'll come back, Rezs." He capped the nutrient bottle and set it aside in its counter slot. "It was nothing you said or did."

"Sure, Lit," she agreed, leaning on the counter. "The day I became a wolfwalker, he looked at me as if I'd changed into neGruli myself. Then he grabbed a pack, saddled a dnu, and took off. We haven't seen him since." She leaned against the counter. "It's been six ninans, Lit."

"Mother says he knows what he's doing." He opened one of the vials, cut out a thin sample, and scraped the fungi off on a slide. "It's not as if he hasn't taken off in the past."

She nodded reluctantly. "I know. It's just that the timing, with all this"—she gestured at the vials—"is . . . hard."

Lit shrugged without taking his eyes from the slides. "There are things Father has to do for himself." He put the slide in the scope and frowned as he adjusted the viewer. For a moment he was silent, then he sat back, rubbed his eyes, and looked through the viewer again.

"Well?" she asked finally.

He pursed his lips and stared at the scope. "Offhand," he said finally, "I'd say these look like the same end plants he passed off to the elders last fall. I can't see how this could be breeding stock for what he's selling now."

She bit her lip. "I spent the first two hours going over the records, but it was dark, and I had to quit every time the guards came by. I could have missed something."

"Maybe. Maybe not. Could be there's nothing to miss." He pulled out the slide, twisted to select an old sample from a rack of glass behind him, and put that in the viewer instead.

"You mean that Cal and Father were right, and there never was a local source of those fungi to begin with."

"He has to have a source, Rezs. New species don't just spring up from nowhere."

"Then he's holding his stock outside the city."

"Either that, or he's already bred enough to supply the elders with what they'll want this year. All he has to do is harvest the rest. His half-yearly trips could be a cover for gathering his final stock from wherever he's been growing them." He straightened up, pulled the old slide from the viewer, and tapped it absently as he stared off into the darkened lab. "But far as I can tell about these, there's no difference between old and new."

"You're sure." It was a statement more than a question.

He shrugged. "Won't know for sure till we check the spores and grow up a few of these ourselves, but right now I'd say that further tests will be a waste of our time."

"So we're back to the beginning."

"Almost," he agreed. He rubbed the back of one wrist against his forehead, as if to relieve a headache. "NeGruli will have presented tonight as soon as he got to the council. You can bet he'll have asked for more funding to work up whatever bacteria or fungus he brought back from his trip, then he'll call for a vote. But we've already arranged for Sommatio to stall the other elders. She should be able to buy us enough time to verify whether or not these samples are the same as the ones we saw before. If they are, then neGruli's hiding what he does from his own lab workers. If they're not the same, we'll have to start over with the duplication of his work. Either way, we have to talk to Sommatio tonight to find out how much time we have and what she wants to do."

"We? Or you or me?"

Lit grinned without humor. "You want a choice? One of us should stay here and finish these samples; one of us has to ride to the Elder Sommatio. Doesn't matter which of us goes where—"

"But," she prompted.

"But I think I could finish this up by dawn. If you're up to the ride, and Gray Vlen is still around, I'd rather you took the news in. Just keep to the east road to avoid the Durn—they'll be waiting for council members to ride home—surrounded three of them last month and held them there for an hour to get their point across."

She nodded. "Vlen's not far—hunting starrats in the next commons, I think."

Lit gave her a sharp look. "You can't tell?"

She shrugged. "The bond isn't strong enough yet to be in place all the time. I know he's close, just not exactly where."

"So no digging in the memories yet?"

"You mean, ask him if the wolves know of a patch of fungi like what we're looking for? Not a chance. I can't even reach his own memories, let alone those of the pack."

"But?" He caught the hesitant tone in her voice.

She gave him a thoughtful look. "The bond changed tonight," she said slowly.

The harsh light cast Lit's gray eyes into deep shadows, but she could see the steely glint that gave him his shortened nickname. "What happened?"

"I got scared."

"How scared?"

"Enough to bring Vlen out like a shot from where he had been waiting. What came back with him was . . . was like a rush of wolves in my head."

"More than Vlen . . ."

She nodded. "I think Vlen projected my fear onto the pack. I could hear their voices behind his—like an echo, or like a distant din that swelled up over his own voice."

Lit rubbed his temples again. "If you can hear the rest of the wolves already, you should be able to ask them about where neGruli's traveled."

"NeGruli," she agreed. "Or Father." She sighed at his expression. "Ah, hell, Lit. You know I won't."

He did not lose his stern look. "Father took off because he had something private he needed to do."

"And he was upset with Vlen."

"With you bonding with a wolf," Lit corrected. "If Father's having trouble accepting your bond to the Gray Ones, think how he would feel if you and Vlen followed him—spied on him."

She gave him a sidewise look. "But neGruli—?"

"That's different." His grin held no humor, and Rezs was suddenly reminded of a wolf just before it tears the flanks from a deer. "There's been more gold poured into his business in the last twelve years than to half our social programs in twenty. He's created new jobs with that capital, but he's taken six other workshops down."

"At least he's never made a move against us."

"Not in the last two years," he agreed.

"Come on, Lit. NeGruli's practically avoided us like the plague ever since Cal's mate was lost."

"Doesn't mean a thing. Two years ago the other labs were more vulnerable, and neGruli was not as powerful as he is today. He has no competition now but us and Hanronti. You can bet by all nine moons that his next project will be one of us." He stared down at the glass containers. "The elders won't support that kind of business much longer if he doesn't come up with something pretty damn impressive to compensate for the loss of competition."

"He's lost eighteen people on his research trips—and somehow it's never his fault. And that host of new products that no one can copy? We've made advances in the last fifty years, but not that kind of progress."

"Without the Ancients' libraries, without their equipment, without the metal reserves we'd need . . . At the rate we've been going," Lit said thoughtfully, "re-creating the sciences—especially the mathematics—should take another two hundred years."

She nodded. "Yet neGruli has somehow bypassed all that to create things we shouldn't be seeing for at least fifty years. By the fires of the seventh hell, Lit—his work is like the answer to the wish list of the Ancients. We need a more efficient bacteria to decompose our wastes? NeGruli strips funds from the reconstructions and comes up with one in six months. A faster accelerator to harden the rootroads? NeGruli has one in a year. Better lighting on our roads in the night? Lo and behold, neGruli takes his little trip out. And a month after he returns, he's bred a new fungi that increases the rootroad bioluminescence by more than a factor of four. We can't grow these things; we can't breed them. But he's got them all. Every improvement the Ancients had planned—we're making those changes now. Or rather, neGruli's making them for us. He's getting rich while people lose their homes, their jobs, and their lives. I just can't see how he could do these things without using the biotechnology of the Ancients."

"You and Cal both," returned Lit. "But the Ancients' domes were looted down to their door frames by the time we'd been here two centuries. After more than eight hundred and fifty years there's nothing left to take but the stones the domes were built with and the plague that still clings to their walls. There's just no way to explain what neGruli does—his progress or his products."

"There were always rumors, Lit, of caches of technology. And who really knows what's left in the domes? With death by plague a certainty, how many people go there to search the buildings? If neGruli's found something in one of the domes, it would explain everything."

Lit gave her a sober look. "The work of the Ancients always leaves its mark—usually in the form of a gravestone. The thing to remember here is that it's neGruli, not the Ancients, we're after." His eyes glinted coldly. "He might have taken something from the Ancients; he might have something he's stolen from someone else in one of the other counties. All I know is that he's dirty—like a dnu in a summer dust pool. We just have to prove it."

She followed his gaze to the vials. "And if we can't?"

He shut off the light for the scope and leaned back against the counter. For a moment his gray eyes looked black. His voice, when he spoke, was soft and cold as ice. "Then we better keep watch for more bodies."

IV

Under the moon-and-cloud-crowded sky, the rootroads glowed. Few insects clouded the thoroughfare beneath that rootroad arbor. Two years earlier, the faint luminescence of the street would have attracted masses of gnats, but a new bacteria had been introduced into the roots of the trees. Now one of the excretions of the bacterial colonies was a gas that drove the gnats away. NeGruli's labs had developed that bacteria just two years after he created the luminescent fungi that inhabited the rootroads. Before she had bonded with Vlen, Rezsia had not noticed the scent of the gas, but her nose now sorted out that odor like a cook sorting tubers by smell.

Rezs's dnu moved smoothly on those hardened roots, its hooves beating out the dull rhythm of its scurrying lope. Tired, but unwilling to be left behind, Gray Vlen was a dark shadow cast by the two-o'clock moons before her. The yearling's dogged determination to stay with Rezs filled her own mind with will. She had to remember not to push the dnu to get the ride over with more quickly. At ten months, Vlen did not yet have the stamina to run the distances that the adults of his pack took for granted.

The outskirts of her own city hub were well lit in spite of the clouds, and with four of the nine moons now hanging in the sky, the sharp, black shadows between the airsponge buildings were sharply delineated from the faintly glowing streets. Gray Vlen remained on the shadow side of the road, the darkness veiling his yellow eyes from the light. Deliberately, Rezs chose to ride in the moonlight.

It was quiet. The wagon traffic that moved between the two

city hubs was sparse, and visible long before it was close enough to hear. The first half hour of riding went quickly, but as she neared the midpoint between two more city areas, she found her shoulders stiffening, and her hand straying to the sword she had belted on before she left home.

She could have ridden out the other road. It was nearly two-thirty, and Isak and Biran should be on their way back from the council meeting by now. She could have met her brothers and convinced them to ride back with her along the other road, to Sommatio's home. But the elder's house was west of the council meeting by another ten kilometers, and it would have taken her another half hour to traverse the extra distance. This way was shorter, flatter, and faster. It had only one drawback: the Durns.

Close to the midpoint, she rounded a corner to see two more wagons in the distance. The drivers, dressed in layers of worn clothes, did not smile or lift a hand to greet her as she neared. Their faces were dark and almost hostile; and Rezs found herself stiffening as she felt the intensity of their gazes. Not until Gray Vlen circled out of the tree shadows to growl softly did the drivers straighten in their seats. They glanced from the cub to Rezs, then deliberately half lifted their hands in greeting. Rezs did not smile as she raised her hand in return. It was enough to pass without words.

But half a kay later, when she could see the lights from the camps of the homeless, the wolf cub stiffened and snarled. *Wolfwalker!*

Rezs was already alert. "Vlen—what is it?"

The hunger in the shadows . . . His young mind projected danger, wariness. Already in the treeline, he faded instinctively into the dark hollows between the roots so that his shadow did not cross the faint glow of the road.

Rezs kept her voice soft. "It's just the Durns, Vlen, and I'm not a speaker or an elder. They shouldn't harm us."

But Vlen sensed something else. His lupine mind grew chaotic, and Rezs found her shoulders hunching as if her own hair would bristle down her spine. She slowed her dnu, but did not stop it. Better to keep moving, she told herself deliberately.

Vlen growled in her mind. He did not want to move forward farther, and he no longer spoke to her in word images; his mental sense was clouded with the menace he felt ahead.

"Stay with me, Gray One," Rezs breathed.

But he whined and paced behind her, unable to come closer. He stopped short of the stretch of road Rezs now rode, and even with the growing distance, his growl tightened her throat so that she found it hard to whisper. Unbidden, her hands clenched the reins. Her dnu skittered a step, and automatically, she calmed it. Easy, she thought at it, as though the beast could hear her mental voice.

At first, she could see nothing on the road but shadows. The moons were too bright, and the contrast between light and dark too sharp to distinguish anything in the black areas. Then two moons shifted behind a cloud, and her eyes began to adjust. She stiffened.

They were silent, like the trees. Durn. Thirty of them. Lining the street like breathing, watching statues that had grown between the trees on the edge of the road. They stared at her, and their eyes caught the moonlight like tiny mirrors. The line seemed to lengthen from out of nowhere. Not thirty, she realized with a tighter grip on the reins. Fifty. They were growing like the poverty that had begun to line the county. Rezs did not trust herself to speak, but she turned her head slightly and looked at each one as she passed, acknowledging their presence.

They weren't dirty or ragged, but even in the shadows, their clothes showed long use, and some of their faces were haggard. She had seen this in the light of day, but their eyes seemed more sunken at night, and the overuse of their clothes more pronounced. She was suddenly, acutely aware of her own attire: her cloak of brushed fibers, warm and waterproof; her boots almost new and clean of mud. Even her bridle ornaments glinted dully, showing off her family's cast-silver swirls.

It was that thought finally that caught her breath: Rezs had the ornaments handed down from her father's side, but her brothers used the same pattern on their tack. If the Durn knew that Isak was speaking in council . . . Deliberately, Rezs kept moving.

The night breeze seemed to whisper through the trees, but Rezs knew the sound was not the wind. Low frustration, resentment, envy—the sounds made her back stiffen up and her muscles tense. But it was the hopelessness of the murmur that made her ears cringe and laid out the shiver across her skin.

The fifty became eighty—the line two deep—and the tree-line thickened. Silently to her ears, Gray Vlen howled in her head. From a distance, yellow eyes gleamed, and a second gray voice echoed. The pack, she thought—responding to Vlen's fear. She tried to calm her thoughts, but the tension in her body was as palpable to the cub as if she shouted.

"—Randonnen—"

It was the tone of the whispered word from the right that touched her own fear. "I am no threat to you," she said softly.

Something shifted in the line of watchers, and she looked ahead to see a single figure in the street.

Rezs's hand shifted toward her sword before she could stop it. Keep moving, she told herself harshly. The man did not budge. His face was in shadow; hers was in the moonlight, and her eyes cringed from the brightness that took her sight. Closer, she urged her dnu. The riding beast was skittish, as if he could sense the threat in the man or the fear in Rezs's body, and the howl in Rezs's head grew louder. Rezs slowed her dnu to a walk, then halted as the man remained in the road.

"Sir, I bring no harm to you," she forced herself to say.

The man was silent for a moment. "No harm," he repeated quietly. His voice was so low that at first she wasn't sure she heard him. "You call me 'sir' as if you held me in respect, but what respect is there in you that keeps me here in this camp? Look at me, Randonnen." He gestured sharply at the treeline. "Look at us. We're poor. We'd work if you'd let us. We're skilled enough for any job you have, but there's no work with no one hiring."

The man did not step forward, but he somehow seemed closer and taller, and his thin shoulders gained the weight of menace. "No harm," he said again. His voice sharpened like a chill that enters a soft wind, and he half raised his fist. "We can't afford the sponge stock or hardeners to build new homes. We can't afford the food and clothes we need for our children. But you don't help us with homes or food or clothes. When our young ones are with us, they are sheltered, and they have enough to eat—we make sure of that. It is we who go without. But you don't see that. Instead, you ignore what we tell you and take our children away as if to punish *them* for being poor. As if to punish us for losing our homes to the flooding and sponge worms that not even the Ancients could have prevented."

"—Randonnen. Randonnen—" The whisper was a breath of hopelessness and anger that seemed to sink into Rezs's head with every spoken word.

"The promise of jobs and work—they'll never materialize, will they? The gold that used to go to jobs in the county—it now fills pockets more than paychecks."

"—Randonnen—"

"You tell us you're growing homes as fast as you can, but"—his voice grew tight with anger—"only twelve for us this year? There are three hundred families here." His fist raised a little higher, and Rezs saw that it was clenched around something. She could not help the call she opened through her link to Vlen. "Three hundred families in every city in Randonnen and Ariye."

Rezs stared at the man. In her head, she could feel Gray Vlen come closer. Not all at once. Not directly. But in the shrubs that lined the gaps between the buildings, she could feel his shadow slink. "Sir, I—"

He cut her off. "You tell us there are no extra jobs. That there's not an hour of work for a craftsman who doesn't own his own equipment. Yet you find work that has more danger than pay for those who are willing to risk it." He stared at her, and she could now see the rock in his hand. "We work a little faster, a little less safely. We tell ourselves that it's worth it to try to get out of this hole of poverty. Or we work for less, because you claim you use the rest of what you'd have paid us to take care of our children—the children you took from our families. Do you know what it's like to give the care of your four-year-old daughter to someone you don't even know? Just to make sure she has enough to eat and the warmth she needs through winter?" The man's voice was soft. "Do you have children, Randonnen, that you love enough to give up?"

Rezs's mouth felt dry. "No," she said finally. "I have no children of my own."

"No," he agreed. His voice was suddenly drained, as if he was exhausted. "You have ours instead." He raised his fist in a single, swift motion, and the rock flew to her face.

Like a hatchet, the stone smashed into her chin. Rezs's head snapped back, and for a moment the slash of pain stunned her more effectively than any fear she had felt. Her mind blasted with a howl of gray.

Wolfwalker! Gray Vlen's legs seemed to stretch with violence and fear. Beneath Rezs, the dnu danced sideways, half bucking as it felt the instinctive clench of her thighs, and she threw up her arms, waiting for the rest of the rocks.

It was the silence that made the dnu settle down, and Rezs slowly look up.

The man still stood in the middle of the street; the watchers were silent and motionless. They didn't even move when Gray Vlen burst out of the trees with a vicious snarl, landing between Rezs and the man. The man held his ground. His hands were empty now, he made no move to fill them with stones; and though his eyes flickered at the sight of the wolf, he did not bow to the Gray One.

Instead, his voice was steady as he said, "You aren't being attacked, Wolfwalker."

Gray Vlen's snarling was a constant, in both her ears and her mind.

Gingerly, she reached up to her chin. Blood dripped onto her hand before she touched the split, swelling flesh, and only pride let her probe the tenderness without crying out. An inch higher, and it would have broken teeth and pulped her lips apart. An inch lower, and it would have smashed through her trachea. If there were bone chips in the gash, she couldn't tell, but the pain that radiated along her jaw and up to her ears was sharp and throbbing, and the blood was dripping and staining her saddle.

"What pur—" Her voice broke off as the movement of her mouth pulled along the gash and released a new spurt of pain. Deliberately, she dropped her hand. She was amazed at how cold and steady her voice sounded. "What purpose, sir, did this then serve?"

"It is a gift," he said softly. "A reminder that wounds come in all forms, and the ones that are visible are not necessarily the worst." He nodded slightly at the blood on her hands. "You have a wound that you can see, obscured only by the darkness of this night; our wounds are obscured by the darkness of your regulations and your so-called interim charity."

"Those regulations," she said sharply, "are needed—"

"Needed," he cut her off, "to keep this county livable. To keep the forest from being stripped; the fish and game from being hunted out; the meadows and commons from being overgrazed, and their topsoils from being destroyed." His voice grew harsh. "For eight hundred years we managed to live with the land, not just on it. Eight hundred years—since the Ancients came down from the stars—and we found work for every willing body. The oldEarthers would let food rot before they would give it to the needy; they'd let buildings crumble before they'd allow their use as shelters. It was politics and religion—plain greed and bigotry—that put the poor on the streets of oldEarth. But we left those politics and religions on oldEarth when we came to this world." He took a step forward, ignoring the rise in Gray Vlen's snarl. "Or did we, Wolfwalker? Every year fifty families lose their homes to worms or wind or age. But suddenly there are funds to regrow only half their houses. As a county, we're not overpopulated; as workers, we're not underskilled. So what keeps us from jobs that would give us back our lives?"

A name rose unbidden in Rezs's mind: neGruli.

"Our children are growing up with poverty as their guide to life. There is no silver to pay for our schools; no money for teachers or books or labs. What do you expect these young ones to grow into? Businessmen? Craftsmen? Leaders? Or raiders and robbers and thieves?" The man took another step forward, and Gray Vlen trembled as his snarl shook his young frame.

Vlen— Rezs sent. The yearling didn't lunge forward, but neither did he subside.

"You spend your money to develop your businesses rather than help us become independent again. You claim that the businesses will create jobs for us—so we can feed our own families. You tell us we have to stay here, in these camps, while the councils reassign monies and lands, equipment and tools to cover our added burden." His voice was almost brittle with emotion. "Yet no such resources are reassigned. No tools become available; no growing plants open to us. And we believe in the laws of the Ancients—we trusted our leaders as we have done since the Ancients first landed—so we stayed here, obeying the laws, living on your charity, while little by little, like the blood on your chin, our self-esteem leaks away."

For a moment they stared at each other. A sigh seemed to sweep through the ranks of the watchers, and Rezs felt the wind cool the hot pain of her chin. "I hear you," she said finally. Her hand twitched, but she did not touch her chin. "Others will hear your words as well."

The man did not move for a moment. "Wolfwalker," he acknowledged softly.

Another heavy cloud mass eclipsed the moons, and the light patches dimmed to a dark gray black. Gray Vlen snarled. The man was gone. Rezs blinked. She felt the reins cutting into her hand and realized that the tension she felt was all her own. She did not turn her head, but she eyed the treeline carefully. No more Durn lined the street; Gray Vlen and she were alone in the night.

Slowly, Rezs urged her dnu forward until it stood on the spot where the man had stood, then halted her dnu. Slowly, she turned her head. "I will speak for you to the elders," she said softly to the night, "but I would suggest"—she touched her chin—"that you don't give your gift to any others on this night."

There was no answer; she did not expect one. But there was a sigh in the wind, and the sense of the gleaming eyes that followed Vlen did not abate as she rode away.

V

The elder's house was on the south end of the commons, where moonlight caught on the roofs and left the homes themselves in shadow. With Vlen beside her, Rezs led her dnu to the shared stable. Quietly, she settled it in an unlit stall by the door. Leaving the stable dark as a closet, she took a lice rag and comb from the cleaning rack by the door and began to work over the beast by touch. Wild dnu never got lice, but city dnu did; and even an hour's ride could end up with a dnu being infected. That was one more thing on her family's list for the future: figuring out the components of the wild dnu's diet so that it could be incorporated into standard feed or bred into cultivated plants.

Rezs's jaw still throbbed, and although the cut had clotted, every shift of her head made her intimately aware of the growing bruise on her chin. There was still tension in her hands, too, and she rubbed the dnu harder to work the fear from her muscles. There was something comforting in the routine of such a mundane task—as if the structure of life continued, no matter what violence was done to it.

Vlen growled low in her mind, and there was a tint of shame to his voice. *Wolfwalker,* he sent.

"You honor me, Gray One," she returned softly.

I should have stayed with you. I should ... have torn ... His voice lost its focus as his agitation grew, and the images he sent were hot with blood and raw muscle and bone.

Rezs tensed and clenched her fists, and the dnu shifted with sudden fear. Abruptly, she closed down sharply on the link. "Vlen—"

His snarl was audible now. Rezs ducked out of the stall and grabbed him by his scruff, pulling his head around so that he was forced to look into her eyes. There was an instant of resistance, as if the challenge of staring at each other was more than their bond could work through. Then their worlds combined. Rezs breathed through Vlen's lungs; Vlen saw through her eyes. His snarl became hers, and her thoughts swept through his mind with a calm as smooth as a lake of glass.

Wolfwalker . . . Vlen butted his head between her arms so that his hot breath puffed on her elbow.

Rezs buried her face in his scruff. *Gray One—*

The night calls.

"I feel it," she whispered. "Soon, I'll run with you. On the heights, by the river . . . Wherever you want."

He lifted his head, and his yellow eyes gleamed.

Rezs gripped his scruff, then rose and turned back to the dnu. Vlen watched her for a moment, then explored the barn, sniffing at the stalls and standing up against the railings on his hind legs to peer into the birthing bins. None of the dnu were nervous at his nearness. Either he was not projecting hunger, or these dnu were used to visits from Gray Ones. Rezs had once heard that, when the oldEarthers first landed on this world, the wolves hunted with impunity. The predator sense that they projected to their prey was not the sense that the creatures of this world were used to. It had taken years for the wildlife to understand that the wolves were like worlags—pack hunters who separated, then brought down their prey on the run.

As if he could hear her thoughts, Vlen's cloudy images seeped into her mind. *Wolfwalker,* he sent, *the pack is with us.*

She worked her way back to the dnu's hindquarters, running the comb through the lice rag with each stroke. "I felt them through you," she agreed in a low voice.

His yellow eyes followed her movements. *They're calling us to follow. They run for the high hills tonight.*

She could feel the eagerness in his limbs and the tiny pangs of hunger that had begun to curl around his belly. She stretched her toes inside her boots so that she could feel the pads of his feet more clearly through their bond. "Your feet are sore, Vlen. Do you really want to run that far tonight? If not, I'll get some jerky from my saddlebags, and you can have that for now."

He hesitated again, and deep in her mind, Rezs could hear the mental howl of the pack. It was like a spider thread, floating in a wind. Thin and far away—almost nonexistent in its tenuous image. She reached down and gripped his scruff, shaking him gently, then scratching around his neck and head. "Go if you want to, Vlen. I'm as safe here as if I were at home."

He took a few steps, turned back, and whined. *Wolfwalker*— "I can't go, Vlen."

He seemed to sigh in her mind. Then he made his way to a pile of straw in the corner, trenched it out, sneezed at the dust that clouded up, and lay down with his head on his paws.

Rezs felt her way to the stable laundry pile and stuffed the warm rags underneath the others where they would not be quickly noticed. Deep in her mind, far beyond the link to Vlen, she could still hear an echo of that thin thread. She paused, her hands on the wooden rails of the laundry bin, and concentrated so that the gray fog sang with the mental howls of the pack. Yes, they were running—she could not feel their feet or smell the scents through their nostrils, but she could feel Vlen's awareness of them clearly. Their hearts were pounding steadily; their feet loping with smooth rhythm across the ground. Yellow eyes that hung just within that fog seemed to watch her movements with Vlen, and Rezs shook herself, closing her imagination from that vision.

There were wolfwalkers who could read the memories of the wolves as clearly as if they read a book. Old Roy could do that—and there were others. Rezs slipped out the stable opening and made her way to the shadows cast by the back porch of Sommatio's home. The howling that rose kays away to the east—it carried on the moist air and echoed off the buildings. Her eyes turned to follow the sound. Like a tide that rose in her mind, the Gray Ones called her to run to them, away from the city; away from the roads. She could almost feel her own throat tighten with their song. It washed through her mind and left her cold and sharp. "Someday," she whispered, she would run with the pack. She would swim in their minds like a dolphin, cutting through that fog until she knew every thread that made up its currents.

The lights were on in the lower rooms, and someone moved about inside. Rezs eased her way onto the porch, then knocked so softly the sound could not have been heard four meters away. There was an abrupt cessation of movement inside. She waited a moment, then repeated the knock, and added in a soft voice, "Rezsia."

She heard footsteps; a door shut, cutting the light to near darkness. Footsteps again, and the back door cracked open. The scents of bread, day-old stew, soap, and the older woman's perfume were immediately in Rezs's nose. Quickly, Rezs stepped in and closed the door quietly behind her. The elder crossed again to the inner door and opened it, so that the light from the other room spilled again into the back room and turned the black shadows gray. The old woman's voice was low and almost wispy with age. "I was expecting Litten, not you, Wolfwalker."

"Lit was still working on the samples. He asked me to ride in instead."

Sommatio nodded. "And?" she asked without preamble.

"The samples I got tonight seem to be the same as the others. We'll run some more tests, but we can't see how that fungi could be what neGruli's using now."

The old woman watched her for a moment, then moved slowly to the table. "So. Another new species with no precursors."

Rezs rubbed her chin gingerly. "He's not breeding them out of his lab stock, if that's what you mean."

The elder followed her gesture. "By the moons," the woman said involuntarily. "Your chin—what happened?"

Rezs's voice was dry as she dropped into the chair Sommatio indicated. "Let's just say that I had my lesson in charity tonight."

The elder's old, pale, gray eyes narrowed. "The Durn?"

"Their message was a good one, Elder."

"Good enough to be worth that?"

The old woman's hands trembled as she gestured at Rezs's chin, and it took Rezs a moment to realize that Sommatio was angry, not afraid.

"Did you really expect them to remain quiescent in poverty while the rest of us prosper?" Rezs returned sharply. "Some of the Durn have been stuck for years in an old warehouse and a set of leaky tents."

The old woman's voice was vehement. "Stuck or not, they must not turn to violence. It will cripple the empathy that many of us have for them now."

"Perhaps it's just that—a change in our attitudes—which they most want." Rezs's voice was just as sharp. "Violence— verbal or physical, political or social—has been used by everyone from cowards to kings to change the minds of oppressors. From all the legends, the homeless Ancients on old-Earth were no different from the Durn today. Their violences are the same."

"Their violences, perhaps, but the Ancients had enough science and power to flee their world and create new ones throughout the stars. We have barely enough science to understand what we've lost. We certainly can't just leave our world like riding out on a Journey, choosing the problems we'd take with us like baggage for the ride."

"The domes could still hold secrets—"

"The Domes of the Ancients are pockets of death." The woman's voice was flat and uncompromising. "No one has survived their walls for eight hundred years. We will never be able to rely on that science to save us from the violence we create here."

Rezs fingered the pocket that had held the glass sample vials. "Our sciences," she said slowly, "have nearly doubled in knowledge in the last twenty years. NeGruli alone, dirty as he might be, has brought our biologies forward in veritable leaps."

The elder's voice sharpened. "Those leaps don't matter if they can't be repeated. Science isn't something you can just pull out of your pocket—it's discipline and method and risks and an absolute determination not to quit till you find some sort of solution. Ah, moons, why am I lecturing you? Any one of your family members could teach an entire county about discipline and determination—" She broke off abruptly.

"You make it sound like a curse," Rezs said mildly.

Sommatio sighed. "You're so young, Wolfwalker. So eager to make a difference."

"Is that so bad?"

"Not for me. But then, I have a use for your skills."

Rezsia hesitated, and a memory of the gray music floated into her head. "Elder, who is Grayheart?"

Sommatio looked at her sharply. "Why?"

"I . . . met someone—a while back—and the name popped into my head when we touched."

"He intrigued you."

"He . . ." Rezs shrugged uncomfortably. "He surprised me," she said finally.

"Ah." The elder did not smile, but she paused, as if to gather her thoughts. "Grayheart is more a story than a name. Before he got his wolf-name, he was a young violinist with great talent. He was training under Gaana—one of the finest teachers in the county."

"I've heard of Gaana. He lives in Latten, at the southern end of Randonnen."

"He moved there because his student, Grayheart, was too young to leave his family at the start of his lessons."

"Somehow," Rezs said dryly, " 'violinist' wasn't the word that popped into my head when I met him."

Sommatio shrugged. "The boy—Grayheart— was talented in many things: swordwork, archery, running, riding, woodwork. He would have made a fine ring-carver; any weapons master would have been proud to call him a student."

"Usually people don't have that many talents."

"That's true," the elder agreed. "There are many people who are good at a lot of things, who never achieve true greatness. And there are many people who are good at one or two things, who never seem able to manage the rest of their lives. Grayheart was a rare child—one of those talented in many things, but who also had a special expression in everything that he did. He could have been a master swordsman or a great researcher, but he loved the music most. And his father, Ronin, who had lost an arm in a chemical accident, encouraged it more than anything else."

"Because he loved music, too, but couldn't play without two arms?"

"Because he was a bitter man," the elder said heavily. "Ronin could not acknowledge the loss of his arm. So he convinced himself that there was no need to relearn to use a sword with his left hand. No need to push Grayheart or any of his children to the discipline required to learn the sword or any other weapon. The music, he told Grayheart, would be enough for him.

"The day Grayheart's family was killed, Gaana had, as usual then, taken the young man up in the hills to train him to translate what he saw into what he felt on his violin. Grayheart was young, brilliant. But he did not have the life experience to give his music depth, and Gaana wanted to give him new eyes and ears for his music.

"They had started back when the raiders came. But it was dusk, when it's difficult to see, and they stopped to let their music fade into the night with the sunlight. And while they played, the raiders destroyed their village—killed or took away everyone who did not escape into the hills. Ronin, one-armed, tried to defend his wife and three other children. He failed. The raiders beat him, then crushed his left hand and hamstrung him, leaving him alive. They could have killed him, but they told him that they knew it would be better torture to leave him living than to give him the quick, guilty death for which he begged.

"Grayheart felt their deaths through the wolves—even then, the wolves knew he would be one of theirs. Grayheart raced back, but he was too late. The flames had consumed over half of the barns. A third of the fields were charred, and the only thing still standing was the amphitheater with the speaker's stone—even the raiders couldn't pull that down. The bodies of his family and neighbors were lying in the mud like lumps. Moons know how long it took Ronin to prop that sword against the charred beam of his house. But when Grayheart found him, his father had the sword in his crushed hand. 'It doesn't matter,' Ronin told his son, 'how cultured you are. It doesn't matter how many histories of the Ancients you know; how many strings you play; how well you carve your message rings. The bottom line is simple: when you forget how to survive, you die.' And then he shoved himself onto his sword."

"By the moons," Rezsia whispered.

The elder nodded. "The man died in his son's arms. Grayheart went to the village center and laid his violin on the speaker's stone in the amphitheater. And he walked away. Gaana, his violin teacher, didn't know where he went. For days, Gaana remained in the village. Grayheart was his finest pupil—he refused to believe that the young man would give up his music forever. The days turned into ninans. The ninans into months. Gaana has never left, and Grayheart has never returned. But each year, on the anniversary of the death of the village, Gaana goes to the amphitheater and places the violin in the center. And he waits."

"For Grayheart."

"He was Gaana's life."

"There are other students," Rezs said flatly.

"And other talents. But sometimes you find a student who has the potential to combine his talent and his life into an expression. Music, ring-carving, healing—it doesn't matter. In Grayheart's case, he could combine the threads of life to weave his music through any pair of ears and bring out the emotions of any man's heart." The old woman smiled faintly. "I've heard Gaana play eight times. The first time, I was barely more than a girl. He was visiting his eldest sister near our village. He hadn't planned a performance, but he stood in at the harvest festival for one of the other violinists. I can still remember the beauty of what he played. If Grayheart had the talent that Gaana claimed he had, the boy would have grown beyond Gaana's abilities within a decade. That kind of talent is worth waiting for. If the man that youth became ever gained the wisdom Gaana hoped he would, he could be one of the greatest violinists since the days of the Ancients."

"But no one's heard him play since he was a boy."

"No."

"Too bad. If music could ever change the heart, perhaps it could change neGruli."

"Not likely." The other woman rubbed her temples. "Those hungry for power rarely allow themselves to see anything but opportunities, and rarely mourn anything but the loss of that same power."

"The moons know that neGruli has been finding enough opportunities here."

"And the fallout of his takeovers is obvious," Sommatio said sharply, dropping her hands from her head. "It's not that we don't recognize the problem, Wolfwalker. We just haven't found a solution. If the man is deliberately trying to acquire power at our expense, he's had believable enough excuses so far. On top of that, he runs or owns a piece of one third of the businesses here. He carries more weight on the council than half the elders combined. Without proof of his crimes to undermine his powerbase, he can simply counter any law we try to pass."

Rezs studied the elder's face. "You want him taken down, don't you?"

"What I want . . ." Sommatio looked up, and her gray eyes

seemed to gleam like Vlen's in the dark. "I want a look in neGruli's mind. I want to see what his goals are. Maybe he's just accumulating power, but maybe he has something more focused in mind." She rapped her fingers on the table with absent irritation. "Year by year, for the past decade, he's been gathering power, taking it from everyone else. We reap the benefits of his power—in the form of rootroad lighting and housing hardeners—but the price for that power is the Durn."

"Surely some of you saw that that would happen?"

"Short-term? The trade-off seemed worthwhile. But once the process started, it became hard to stop. Now it seems impossible, and the price for that process of concentrating power is growing steeper with each passing month. At this point, we'd have to tax ourselves out of our own homes to properly support the number of Durn we've suddenly acquired in exchange for our new molds and fungi and glues."

"We've acquired nothing," Rezs returned, the anger growing in her voice. "Those people might not have lived right next to you or me, but they lived in this county somewhere. They were just as much our neighbors before they lost their homes."

The old woman gave her a hard look. "It's not your place to lecture me, Rezsia Monet-Marin maDeiami. I've lived through more poverty and pain than you will ever imagine. I am not the one who lacks compassion."

Vlen snarled deep in Rezs's mind, and she realized that her anger had grown until it twisted into the gray line that stretched between her and the cub. She took a breath. "Forgive me," she said in a low voice. "As my own frustration grows, I forget the wisdom of those around me."

The other woman smoothed a wisp of gray-white hair and sighed. "Ah, Wolfwalker, your frustration is not a crime. And I suppose it speaks well of your family that you can still become angry with the abuse of others." But her voice took on an edge. "Just don't misdirect your anger."

Rezs hesitated. "Elder, I don't presume to know what's best for the county, but I have to ask: Why don't you confront neGruli in council? If you had enough suspicions to hire us to investigate him in the first place, surely there is some kind of evidence somewhere."

The elder didn't answer for a moment. When she did, her voice was heavy. "If there is, we haven't found it. We have no proof that he killed his people on those trips rather than that they died through accident. No proof that that fire last year was set on purpose to hide a lab mistake. No proof that the disease which grew out of last year's fungi experiment was not an aberration. No real proof that he's developing things too fast to be doing it on his own."

"But no one in this county can duplicate his work," Rezs said. "Lit's rechecking what I brought out of neGruli's lab a few hours ago, but neither of us holds out any faith that we can tell you differently next ninan or next month. That in itself must be some kind of proof."

"Proof of what? His lab is bigger than any other; he has more money to spend on processes; more people to hire to work longer hours. How can you say for sure that your failure is not tied to time or gold?"

Rezs felt her face tighten at the word "failure."

Sommatio nodded at her expression. "Just because you can't duplicate his process doesn't mean it can't be done. It means that you've failed. And once you bring that out in council, you'll undermine your own family's position. Your father's words will carry less weight, and neGruli will win again. There's just too much power in his hands already for me to sanction that."

"That kind of power—it's like carbon, I think," Rezs said slowly.

The elder raised her eyebrows. "I don't follow you."

"Power—like carbon. When it's unconcentrated, it's like diffuse carbon—like a pile of soot. It's easy to move ashes around, separate them into different areas, pile them where you need them or shape them with other things—like clay—into something useful. But concentrated power is like quartz or diamond. Even if you could break it, you'd still be left with those hard, kernel pieces—the elements of greed or intolerance or whatever the center of that power was. Not until it's powdered or melted and reformed from its atoms up will you get away from those evils and back to a malleable substance."

The older woman absently rubbed her sternum. "I'm not sure I can agree with that. I don't think the kernels of greed are something that can ever really be reshaped. You can only mix them in such small quantities that they can't do massive harm.

Once you allow the greed to consolidate, you begin to see men like neGruli."

Rezs studied the woman for a long moment. The edge that had grown in the elder's voice was something Rezs had heard in her own brother's words—a bitterness for something that had no solution: Tegre's mother, gone or dead for two years now, and no way to find out what happened . . . This elder had that same tone in her voice, as if nothing Sommatio did could make the difference, and so every act was a sacrifice that held no lasting value.

Gray Vlen intruded suddenly on Rezs's thoughts, and her eyesight blurred. The gray thread tightened between them. Faintly, she heard the hoofbeats of another dnu. The cub rose quickly to his feet, and Rezs didn't even have to urge him to the entrance of the barn to see who rode into the courtyard.

Wolfwalker. Gray Vlen's voice was eager, and his yellow eyes seemed to gleam in her head. He was already moving, sliding into the shadows like a kayak into the sea. From the barn entrance, the cub clung to the darkness and turned his eyes toward the house. What he saw was so blurred in Rezs's vision that she could make nothing out, but the smell of what he sent was more clear: a human, the odor of the forest, mud and dnu grime . . . There was a new dnu stamping its feet near the railing by the corral, and the riding beast radiated warmth and musty sweat.

"Elder," Rezs interrupted sharply.

Sommatio froze.

Silently and swiftly, Rezs was already moving into a shadow by the cupboards. Her hand half pulled her sword from her scabbard before she realized it would clunk against the cupboards. *Gray One.*

From near the barn, Vlen eyed the dnu, then let his yellow gaze follow the figure that moved silently to the porch. No glints of metal flashed in Vlen's lupine eyes from a bared weapon, and once the figure reached the porch, it became so still that Vlen almost lost its position. The thin figure was as much a part of the night as the darkened barn. Thin, and definitely narrow in the shoulders, Rezs realized as she peered through Vlen's sight.

She let her blade drop back into her scabbard. No one built like that would be neGruli's man. Vlen, feeling her tension dissipate, snarled low in her mind. He refused to retreat into the barn. Instead, his yellow eyes gleamed as the man hesitated before knocking softly. Through Vlen's blurred sight, Rezs saw the thin man turn, and slowly—ever so slowly—study the yard behind him. Then he twisted back and rapped softly on the door, speaking his name with a whisper: "Bany."

Quickly, Sommatio opened the door partway, and the man slipped inside. From her place in the shadows, Rezs studied him, her nostrils flared to verify the scents that Vlen had pushed into her mind. Even in the dim light, it was clear that the wisps of hair that stuck out from under his warcap were as grayish white as the elder's. He was tall, but his frame, thin with the age of a hundred and thirty years, was wiry with nearly as many decades of trail work.

He gripped arms with the elder woman. "Where's the wolfwalker?"

Rezs stepped forward. "Here." She looked at him steadily. "How did you know I was here? You didn't enter the barn, and you weren't close by when I rode up."

The old man offered his arm in greeting, and automatically, Rezs gripped it. "Saw the wolf. Nice gash," he said, gesturing with his own chin at hers. "Fist?"

For a moment he sounded like Lit, and Rezs's lips twitched. "Rock," she corrected, adding obliquely, "Gray Vlen was in shadow."

"Eyes reflected the moonlight," he answered. "Gotta watch that if you're going to try keeping him hid. Thrown or held?" he asked.

Sommatio looked blankly at Bany, but Rezs shrugged. Lit had always talked on more than one subject at a time. She was used to that kind of banter. "Thrown," she answered. "Though I thought, for a moment, that it had knocked me out of the saddle."

"Lucky you weren't knocked out completely."

She grinned without humor, wincing abruptly as it stretched the scab across the wound. "I inherited a lot of things from my grandma, but her glass jaw wasn't one of them."

"You use your sword on them?"

"Uh-uh—"

"Why not?"

She cocked her head and gave him an odd look. "I guess I didn't think of it," she said slowly.

The older man dropped into a seat, stretching his long legs out under the table. "So we're riding guard, not just scout?"

"Guard?" She looked from Bany to the elder. Then she realized what the old man had said. Her cheeks heated slowly, but her voice was flat. "I can use blade or bow if the need arises. I've ten years' experience in the fighting rings."

He nodded, but she had the feeling he had no confidence in her statement. The thought of it rankled, but there was nothing to say; she *had* cowered, she admitted to herself, not stood up to the Durn when he threw that stone at her face.

"Guard for what?" she asked again.

Sommatio gestured for her to sit down. "I guessed that the samples you got tonight would be no different than the ones I'd given you before. So I asked Bany to come by. I was hoping it would be Litten or Callion who rode in tonight . . ." She gave Rezs a tired smile. "But you're as involved as they. And this will be your decision, more than theirs, to make."

It was not the implicit request that startled her; it was the tightening of her stomach in eagerness, rather than the fear she would have expected. Her skin prickled. She was a wolf-walker now, she reminded herself. Any elder could ask for the use of her skills. In her mind, Gray Vlen seemed to howl. *Soon,* she sent back restlessly.

"The elder's wanting us to ride out after neGruli," Bany explained. "Find his trail. Figure out where he's been going and where his research really comes from."

Rezs chewed her lip. "Lit thought you'd want to do that, but Olarun isn't back yet."

"It's not your father who would be riding out." Bany watched her carefully.

His scrutiny made her uneasy, and she shifted in the chair. "Won't it be better to wait for drier weather—even if you left tonight, the rain would have washed away his tracks already."

"Not necessarily," Bany answered, "And anyway, I'll be looking for campsites, not tracks." He gave Sommatio a meaningful glance. "Someone else will be finding his actual trail."

"Why campsites? I thought tracking had to do with moving around, not sitting in one place."

"Sometimes," he agreed. "But people don't go bushwhacking in this kind of weather. Between the mud, the nightspiders, the worlags, and the badgerbears, it's too dangerous for most. And staying with existing roads and trails means there will be only certain places that afford enough shelter for comfortable camping."

"You know he likes comfort?" Rezs couldn't help asking. "You've tracked him before?"

Bany shrugged. He glanced at the elder. "I've got four scouts lined up. Where and when do you want us to meet?"

Sommatio answered. "You'll have to meet outside of town—probably to the north—and it will have to be soon."

"Tonight?

"Not tonight," Rezs cut in. "I can't be ready that quickly. We have test samples to prepare, biogels to pack, gear to get together . . ."

"Tomorrow, then?"

"If I ride straight through town," she agreed, "I can probably make it to the north crossroad by the following dawn."

But the elder was already shaking her head. "I don't want you both riding out the same route—that would be broadcasting our movements, and no one has ever accused neGruli of being unaware of his competition—especially the movements of your family, Rezs. I'd rather you ride out to the west, then circle around town to meet up with Bany in Greenston."

"We'd be better off leaving after the wolfwalker, then," said Bany. "It will take us three days to reach Greenston; it will take the wolfwalker two or three more to get there going around the settled area."

Rezs frowned. "I'm not very familiar with trail riding. I'd rather not ride quite so far by myself."

Bany's old, blue eyes took in her expression, and Rezs was glad there were shadows to hide her flush. "All right," he said. "You know of the Water Wall, just north of this settled area?"

She nodded.

"The trail up is muddy," he explained, "but clearly marked. Climb it. At the top, you'll see the hollows for the signal-fire pits. One of them points the firelight north along the top of the wall. Light a blaze in that one. We'll be there within a few hours."

She nodded again, then hesitated. She wondered if this was the time to tell him that she had never built a fire outside of a fireplace. "What if it's raining?" she asked.

"Don't worry. We'll still see the fire."

"No, I mean, what if I can't start a fire?"

Bany frowned at her. The elder cleared her throat. "I think Rezs is saying that she's not familiar with the wild firewoods."

Bany's gaze seemed to pierce her thoughts. "Use randerwood," he said finally. "Or pocketwood. Wet or dry, either one will burn well. Just don't use jaurwood or petsel—the first one smokes like a stopped-up chimney, and the second one releases a scent that—even in the rain—will attract every poolah in the county."

Rezs nodded, and the old woman continued, "From Greenston, you'll be going north and west. Toward Ariye and Kiren."

Rezs felt her stomach tighten again. The Kiren domes were on the border between Ramaj Ariye and Kiren.

The older woman continued. "Once you pick up some of the memories of the Gray Ones, you'll know for sure which way to go."

Rezs raised her eyebrows. "You expect me to find the trail?"

Bany studied her for a long moment. "You ever done any tracking?"

She almost laughed. "No."

"Ever run trail with that wolf of yours?"

"Uh-uh."

"Been on your own in the forest?" he pressed.

"For more than thirty minutes? No."

Bany's voice was mild, but Rezs had the feeling that he was probing her abilities as carefully as if they faced off with swords. "I had understood you to have made the bond with your Gray One a month and a half ago. Six ninans isn't much time to learn the minds of the wolves."

She shrugged. "If it's got to be done, then I'll learn how to do it."

"Just like that?"

"You think I should wait?"

He chuckled. "Wait half a year till you know your bond with your wolf as well as you know your own voice? I don't think the elder will go for that plan." Bany glanced at Sommatio, but the old woman shook her head sharply. The tall man nodded. "So my job is . . . ?"

"Watch out for worlags," the elder returned. "And lepa— there have been signs of them flocking already—poolah, badgerbear, and everything else. Teach Rezs the trails as you know them, and find whatever sign of neGruli you can. Oh, and—" Sommatio smiled faintly "—most importantly, keep the wolfwalker alive."

Bany nodded and got to his feet. His touch was firm as he gripped arms with Rezs again, and the expression in his old, blue eyes was almost challenging.

Slowly, Rezs grinned. She could feel her lips curling with the sense of Vlen's mental snarl, but she didn't care. "Don't worry," she said softly. "I've never yet failed to meet one of my goals. You might have to teach me to survive on your trails, but if there is a trace of neGruli in the minds of the Gray Ones, I'll learn to read it. In the end it won't be me who slows you down."

Bany smiled. His teeth were not straight, and the light from the other room gleamed on them faintly. "Then I'll see you at the Water Wall."

She nodded and moved to the door. She was not aware, as she slipped outside, that she already moved with quieter feet than she had a ninan before. She did not realize how many scents her nose took in and ignored as Gray Vlen tasted them for himself and discarded those without interest.

Inside the elder's house, Bany listened carefully, but Rezs left no footsteps in his ears. "She learns quickly," he agreed softly to the elder. "She might survive after all."

"If survival was all I needed, you could train her here, near the city." The older woman put her hand on his arm. "I need more, Bany. There are only two labs left in the city that can do the work I need. And of those who work in the labs, three of the four people I would have sent are not available now. Rezs is inexperienced, but at least she's a wolfwalker. She'll have a better chance than Yhani with his clumsiness or Cal with his healing leg. Just keep her alive till she finds what I need. She'll know what to do by then."

Bany strained his ears, but he couldn't hear Rezs even after she reached the barn. He imagined Gray Vlen's yellow eyes, gleaming at him in the dark. He glanced down at his hands. There were dark smudges on his skin where the dried blood from Rezs's hand had rubbed off on his fingers. Deliberately, he rubbed his own together. That gash on her chin had not disguised the determined set of her jaw. "Till she finds what you need," he agreed softly. "That, at least, I can do."

VI

Tegre was waiting for Rezs at dawn. The girl's skinny legs kicked back and forth, swinging in and out of the light that shone across the railing. She didn't smile as Rezs came out of the house, rubbing tired eyes. Instead, she gave Rezs a serious look at odds with the piquant style of her two, long, black braids. Tegre had the voice of a child, but there was a matter-of-factness to her words that always startled Rezs, and this morning was no different. "You're leaving, aren't you?"

Rezs leaned on the banister beside the girl. "Uh-huh." She didn't look at Tegre, but searched the commons with her gaze for the shadow of the cub.

"Yesterday, you said you'd be staying for at least a month."

"I did," Rezs agreed. "But later last night—long after you went to bed—your uncle Lit and I found out about something that had to be done, and the elder said it must be me who does it."

"You didn't tell me that when you came up to tuck me in."

"That's because," Rezs said dryly, "you were supposed to be asleep."

"You knew I wasn't."

Rezs gave her a sidewise look. "Now, how did you know that I knew?"

The girl shrugged, and one of the braids slid over her skinny shoulder. "When you think I'm asleep, you stand in the doorway so you won't wake me up." She tossed the braid back as if irritated with its behavior. "When you think I'm awake, you come in and talk to me in a soft voice."

58

Rezs glanced at her thoughtfully. "Are you always awake when I look in on you?"

Tegre shrugged in a gesture far too adult for her skinny frame. "My mama used to look in on me at night."

Rezs didn't know what to say. "Honey . . ." Her voice trailed off.

"I wish . . ."

"What, Tegre?" Rezs asked gently.

The girl's voice was small when she said, "I wish you would talk to me every night."

Rezs looked at her for a moment. "I will," she said finally, simply.

"You're not here every night."

"Then I'll give you something to keep you company on those nights that I cannot be here. What about a peltstone? I'll look for one on this trip and bring it back for you. Promise," she added.

The girl looked up, and her green eyes seemed to stare through Rezs's violet gaze as she slid stiffly off the railing. There was a strange, almost painful wisdom in her voice. "Don't make promises you can't keep." Then, before Rezs could speak, the girl dropped from the porch to the courtyard and walked out onto the commons.

Rezs looked after her, rubbing her hands on her arms as if to remind herself that the sun had risen warmly and there was no reason for this chill. How many careless promises were made to children like Tegre and never kept by their parents? How many times was hope used as a weapon to gouge power from someone else? Rezs touched her chin and felt the soreness of the bruise that surrounded the hardened scab. Invisible wounds, she thought slowly. Deeper than any flesh could hold . . .

When Gray Vlen jogged around the corner of the lab, Rezs did not greet him. Instead—deliberately—she kept herself separate from the link he opened toward her. Be objective, she told herself as she watched him move through the courtyard. Was he really ready to run the trails without the rest of his pack?

Compared with the older wolves she had seen, he was skinny across his chest. The breadth that would come with age would not be his for most of another year, and the cunning he should develop—that would not come without help from the pack. In the short time since they had bonded, he'd killed with the pack and hunted his meals alone. He ran back and forth to the forest every other night—and sometimes every night when he was with her in the city. Though he did not yet have the endurance of the older wolves, he had the speed of youth, and he was quickly building the distance strength into his muscles.

With Rezs cut off from the bond, Vlen, his ears laid back, hesitated halfway across the courtyard. He stared at the porch. For a moment he did nothing, but then a snarl began to grow in his throat. *Wolfwalker?*

Rezs opened her mind. *It's all right, Vlen. I was just thinking.*

He crossed the rest of the courtyard. As his yellow eyes met hers she felt the abrupt tightening of the thin cord that stretched between them. It was not quite a fear that he sent to her. More like an anxiety that his pack—his wolfwalker—had left him behind or thrown him out of their group. *You shut yourself off*, he said unhappily.

"I needed to look at you," she said softly.

We are bonded. Why do you need to separate us to see me?

She smiled and reached for his scruff. There was a ring of blood and dirt around his snout, and his fur was not yet washed. A mat of dirt and rotted leaves was caught in his fur like a nest of clumping mites. She tugged at the mat and pulled it free, along with a shag of loose hair. "Because I made a decision for us last night, and I want to make sure it's the right one."

Wolfwalker, he sent. *We are right together. We can sing the packsong in any road or forest.* He sat back, licking his muzzle to clean it. *You should run with me through the ferns. The hares are fleet, but fangs are faster, and you have never yet hunted with the pack.*

He shot her a shaft of pleasure, and Rezs almost writhed in response. His emotions were intensely pure, and they swamped her senses with images she didn't understand. She wanted to comb her hands through his fur, to scratch his ears and stroke his pelt to show him how pleased she was. She wanted hands to rub her own flesh—roughly and firmly so that the force of it extended deeply into her muscles. It was an effort to smooth her expression when she heard the hoofbeats of Cal's dnu on the road.

Her brother waved as he rode in from his early-morning work. He looked tired, she thought. He merely grunted when she mentioned it as he joined her and Vlen on the porch. He didn't wait to pull off his boots sitting down. Instead, he dropped them on the porch as he made his way to the door, shrugging out of his work jacket in the doorway.

The faint cloud of wood dust that shook out of his clothes made Vlen snort so that Rezs choked on a breath. The skin around Cal's eyes crinkled. He could always tell when Rezs and Vlen were linked. He tossed his jacket on a hook next to Biran's coat and kicked his boots to the side of the door. Vlen stretched his nose to sniff them, and Cal paused, scowling heavily at the cub. "Don't even think about it," he told Vlen. "I see one tooth mark in that leather, and I'll make my next pair of boots out of your hide." He shook his finger at Rezs, stopping her comment midword. "He stole my work boots last ninan and had them shredded within three hours. He'll do it again if he's got the chance." He gave Vlen a hard look before going through the door.

Rezs looked down at Vlen. "You'd better find some other place to clean your face. I think he means it this time, and I don't want these"—she touched the boots with her toes—"to be too much temptation."

Vlen's eyes gleamed. But he jumped from the porch and trotted back into the courtyard. He looked over his shoulder once, eyeing the boots, but Rezs was firm.

Cal was waiting for her in the living room. "You and Lit figure out what we're going to do?" he asked as she crossed the large, open space.

"Pretty much," she answered. The distorted rectangles of yellow sunlight from the windows skewed a massive checker pattern across floors and furniture, and the work dust in Cal's dark hair made it look almost gray in the sunlight.

"Where is everyone? In the back?" he asked.

"Dining room." She pointed. "Watching Isak finish his breakfast."

The oval table in the dining area felt crowded with four brothers and her mother. Lit, the tallest, was sipping his breakfast drink and seemingly lost in thought. Next to him, Biran, the only one with brown hair and darker skin—took after their mother's side, their father had always said—nodded at Rezs and Cal. Biran had put on weight this year, so that he was thicker now in the chest than even Cal; Biran's skin, usually windburned to a dark mahogany shade, had remained a light reddened brown like their mother's, even through the winter. From the window behind him, Biran's shadow cast itself across the table, darkening, but not hiding his tension as he kneaded his fingers constantly.

The youngest, Isak, sat on the other side of Biran and mopped up the last of his meal with a biscuit. Isak, like Cal, looked like a smaller copy of Lit—or younger copies of their father. All three brothers had the same black hair and high cheekbones; the same glint in their gray eyes when they were thinking sharply. This morning, the glint in Isak's eyes was almost cold, as if his thoughts were icy even after the hot meal of gravy over biscuits. Rezs, meeting his gaze briefly, felt a tiny chill, as if some piece of last night had gotten caught in Isak's eyes and cut through his image of her. She knew Lit had told Isak everything, but she didn't know what her younger brother had decided—to support Rezs and Lit, or go along with Cal in continuing to wait.

Beside Isak was their mother, Monet, a slim woman with dark brown hair, an oval face, and straight, almost sharp nose. The older woman gestured for Cal to join them, while Rezs leaned against the kitchen counter and watched from the edge of the room. Cal's eyes met hers sardonically as he sat, and Rezs, still standing, shrugged almost imperceptibly. Ever since she had bonded with Vlen, she found it harder and harder to sit for breakfast in the crowded room with her family. She hadn't thought that Cal or the others had noticed. She hadn't really noticed it herself, she realized, till Cal spoke to her last night. She wrinkled her lips back, and the gesture caught Isak's attention. Carefully, she smoothed her expression.

Isak didn't take his gaze from hers. Rezs shifted uncomfortably. His slender shoulders and long-fingered hands looked relaxed, but his voice had a note of sharpness when he asked Cal, "Done for the morning?"

Cal nodded. "What's the word?"

"The fungi are junk," he said flatly. "Whatever Rezs

brought back, it's not what we're after." The fine lines of tension around the edges of his eyes made him look even more like Lit.

Lit added, "The elder doesn't want to wait any longer for Father to come back to start tracking neGruli's source. She wants to send Rezs and Vlen to start looking for it now."

"What's the rush?" Cal looked from Lit to Isak. "NeGruli's left us alone for over two years, ever since—" His voice broke off. Ever since Kairyn died. He didn't say it, but the words hung over the table. He shrugged deliberately and glanced at Rezs. "It's not as if you and Lit have suddenly run out of time to follow neGruli's work."

"It's not our time the elder's concerned with," Lit reminded him sharply.

Cal gave him a hard look right back. "It might not be our time, but it sure as hell is our lives she's playing with. Has she been considering the risks we take for her? Moonworms, Rezs isn't even trained to the forest like Father was."

"Is," Lit corrected. "Father hasn't lost it just because he's lived here in the city for a while."

"Thirty-eight years of city living isn't a while, Lit, it's a lifetime. And Rezs—" Cal broke off at Rezs's guilty expression. "But you've already decided, haven't you?"

She shrugged uncomfortably. "Lit and Momma and I talked it out last night."

Lit leaned forward. "We've known for years that neGruli had his eye on our business. He's taken down one lab after another until there's only two of us left—and he could have ground us into dust two years ago if he'd kept up the pressure. I can't see him leaving us alone forever. He'll eventually try for us again. We have time now to act. If we wait, we'll be too weak as a business to spare Rezsia or anyone else to investigate his actions. Now or six months from now—the difference in timing is in our strength, neGruli's pocketbook, and the number of Durn he puts on the streets."

Cal took a breath. "All right," he conceded. He looked at Rezs. "When do you want me ready to ride?"

Rezs and Isak looked at each other. Lit's voice was uncompromising as he said, "You're not going, Cal—none of us are. Only Rezs. The elder has already hired some scouts to keep her safe. All Rezs has to do is help Vlen find the trail, either through his nose or the memories of the wolves. The guards will keep the badgerbears and worlags off her back."

Cal rubbed his thigh where the ache of the knitting bone was still with him. "You're not expecting much, are you?" He gave Rezs a sidewise look. "You know she couldn't follow a trail if it dragged her along."

Rezs's violet eyes sparked with the warning. "If I promise not to get lost," she said sarcastically, "can I go, big brother?"

He didn't smile. "Promise on the pelt of your Gray One."

They locked gazes stubbornly. Slowly, Rezs grinned. There was something feral about the expression, and Biran rubbed his hands nervously together. "Cal, we've all been trying to look out for each other, but, like last night, this task is for Rezs, not us."

Their mother gave Cal a steady look. "And much as you'd like to think otherwise, your leg needs another ninan before you can do much long riding—let alone forest work—Cal."

Cal didn't take his eyes from Rezs. "Monet could go with you. She's one of the best riders in Randonnen."

But Monet was already shaking her head. "If you can't go, well, neither can Lit or I—it would be obvious that this is a working trip, not just a new wolfwalker learning her Gray One's terrain. As for Biran, too many Durn rely on the reconstructions to take him off the building sites. And while your father is gone, Isak is our representative to the council, and we need everyone we have to speak out against neGruli." She spread her hands. "There are other wolfwalkers in or near this city. But Evans has been lame ever since that fire the winter before last. Old Roy is a hundred and fifty-six, and even though—ten years ago—he used to ghost it on the trails as well as any scout, he's still weak from that cough he caught this winter. Sulani is four months' pregnant, and Bunairre is committed to another project."

"Well," he admitted, "Rezs is young and strong and unhampered by anything but ignorance."

Rezs gave him a sour look. "Before Bunairre left for Ariye, I spent half a ninan with him learning to work with the wolves. When I bonded with Vlen I became a wolfwalker, Cal, not automatically an idiot."

"And not automatically a scout, either," he countered. "You're twenty-eight, and you've spent your entire life in a city. All you know is chemistry and labs and something about riding dnu. Even with what Bunairre told you, what you know about trail running would fill a thimble and leave room for the thumb."

Rezs hid her unease with a shrug. "I'm going to have to learn the forest sometime. Where better to learn about running trail than from someone who's done it for a hundred years? Bany—the lead scout—will be a good teacher for both Gray Vlen and me. It'll make the journey do double duty."

"You really think you can learn enough fast enough from this Bany to keep yourself from getting killed?"

"*He's* supposed to keep me alive, Cal. All I have to do is find the trail."

He snorted. "How are you going to get into the minds of Gray Ones other than Vlen? Old Roy told me that it was damned hard to read their racial memories. If your Gray One hasn't smelled for himself what you're looking for, taking in a secondhand memory is like trying to see something clearly at the bottom of a murky bay when the waves at the surface are fast and choppy, and the wind blows the salt in your face."

Lit gave him a sidewise look. "Did you make that one up yourself?"

"Those are Old Roy's words, not mine," Cal returned dryly. "I've never seen a bay."

Isak chuckled, and Biran rubbed his hands again absently. "Think of it this way, Cal. As long as neGruli thinks Rezs is out learning to be a wolfwalker, neGruli will be our worry— not hers. We keep him here in town, and she can treat the whole trip like a vacation. And being a wolfwalker, Rezs has an advantage in learning the wilderness that none of us has, since Father never trained us to tracking or any other forest skill."

Lit gave his older brother a sharp look. "You can't still blame him for that. Take a look someday at those scars on his chest and shoulders. He doesn't carry those for pleasure."

"Your father's not afraid of the forest," Monet said sharply.

Lit gave their mother a measuring look. "Someday, you'll tell us how he got those scars, Momma, and we'll understand it then."

For a moment the older woman looked down at her hands. Her long, slender fingers were as weathered as Biran's face, and her nails rough from her work. "It was a long time ago," she said softly. She looked out the window, as if the distant sun would close the gap between cold, graveyard memories and the warming dawn of spring. "Your father was nine." Her voice was quiet. "His brother, Danton, was eight. Their mother, Dion, was teaching them to identify different plants while the wolves were hunting deer in a nearby valley. The trees were thick, and the forest beneath the canopy as dark as always, which is why none of them noticed the lepa flocking on the horizon. Had they remained on the ridges, they would have seen the flock gather. But they stayed in the lowlands, and by the time they moved out into Still Meadow, the lepa were as thick in the skies as flies on a badgerbear's carcass."

"The wolves didn't notice?" Biran asked.

"Lepa can create a flock in less than two minutes, and these came out of the western cliffs, from behind Tenantler Ridge. The wolves were in Moshok Valley to the east and saw and heard nothing before the lepa dove like a rain of arrows on your grandmother and her sons. Dion and the boys ran for the caves on the east side. Your father was in the lead, but when he saw the lepa dive, he froze. His mother grabbed him and threw him bodily into an opening, but by then the flock had descended. His brother didn't make it. Dion grabbed Danton's leg as the lepa snatched the boy up. They were tearing at the boy already—the lepa were—and Danton's screams . . ." The distant look in Monet's eyes gave Rezs a shiver. "Your grandma was finally dropped out of the flock. She fell near a hole in the ground, and it was steep and dark enough that when she crawled inside, the lepa who followed her down couldn't reach her."

Isak cleared his throat. "And Father?"

Monet looked at him. "Your father's cave had a larger opening, and the lepa had seen Dion throw him in. He burned the blackgrasses to keep the lepa off until he could make a torch and fight them with the fire. Those slashes across his upper arm, shoulder, and left chest—those are from the lepa that got inside." She looked at each one of them in turn. "Your father watched his brother torn apart alive. He watched his mother fall into the rocks and thought she had left him alone to face the lepa. And the wolves who had always protected your grandma and her family before—they were nowhere to be seen. He didn't know—as a child, he couldn't know—that his mother had kept the wolves away on purpose."

"Gray Ones have no defense against a lepa," Rezs said slowly.

Monet nodded. "They would have been torn to shreds like Danton. They could never have helped your father against the birdbeasts."

"But Father thinks they should have."

Her mother shrugged. "He knows deep down that what he feels is not fair to his family, but somewhere back inside, in that place where childhood memories remain black-and-white and stronger than rationality, he still believes that the forest—and the Gray Ones—took his brother, betrayed his mother, and left him to face the lepa alone."

"He's carried those scars a long time," Lit said flatly. "After all this time I can't believe he's not grown at least a little bit past them."

Monet sighed. "His guilt is a deeper wound than those on his skin. If he hadn't hesitated, Danton would still be alive."

"He can't know that," Rezs said simply.

Her mother shrugged. "No, but the guilt that built that wall within him—it's helped him reject his mother for most of his life, as if he could lay blame for Danton's death on her healer's hands, not his hesitation. Every story of her work as a healer strikes him like a tiny knife: she saves others, but not his brother. She fights for others, but not for him." Monet shrugged. "Remember, your father was little more than a child when all this happened. And he was terrified. All his life, he's seen his mother heal his neighbors and friends, take time to treat the injuries of others. To his child's eyes, she had time for everyone else but him. Now he's lost family and countless friends to the forest. He'll be damned if he'll give it our children, too."

It was Rezs's quiet voice that broke the silence. "Moons," she said softly, "how he must hate my bond with Vlen."

Monet rubbed her temples. "I don't think any of us can deny that he resents what the Gray Ones symbolize. He resents what they've taken from him. And now . . ."

Lit's voice was flat. "Now Rezs has a bond with a Gray One."

Monet nodded at Rezs. "Even more than he did before,

your father sees his own mother in you. And it hurts him like betrayal."

Rezs couldn't even identify the emotion she swallowed. She cleared her throat. "If I go out on the trail, I'm leaving without even saying good-bye. If he thinks his own mother abandoned him for the forest, how will he take my absence now?"

"He'll understand." The older woman shook her head at their doubtful expressions. "No, he will. He's always acknowledged his obligations and duties. He would expect nothing less from any child of his."

Cal hesitated. "Momma—after what you've just told us— of all people, Father would not agree to sending Rezs and Vlen out alone."

Isak interjected. "She'll have that scout, Bany, and at least three or four others. And from what Rezs said, Bany's been running trail longer than the four of us put together have been alive. He probably knows every rock between here and the Kiren domes. If we sent her out with all of us, she would be no safer than with him."

"As soon as I meet up with him," Rezs agreed, "I'll be riding out on the west road, then circling around to the Water Wall. I'll be outside the barrier bushes for two or three days on my own."

"Three or four," Biran corrected. "Since you don't know the trails."

"Four," Cal said flatly. "You'll have to carry the test samples with you. Pack'll be heavy for the dnu."

They fell silent.

Lit studied his sister's face. "Rezs—are you okay with this?"

She hesitated. She felt the eagerness in Gray Vlen's mind— smelled the odor of the morning through his nose. She could feel the quickness of his heart beating as if it touched her own ribs, and it gave a twist of anticipation to her stomach. What Old Roy had said was true: Vlen was beginning to draw her— out of her home, out of her city, toward the place where the Gray Ones ran. To the packsong that filled the back of her head more strongly every day. "I'd be lying," she said slowly, "if I said I wasn't scared, but—"

Cal met her violet eyes steadily. "Then don't do it."

She looked at him, then at Lit and Biran and Isak.

Cal's voice was harsh. "If you don't think you can do it, don't go."

His words stung. Rezs straightened. "I've been given a chance to make a difference in this county, and because I admit to being nervous, you think I should turn it down? Which of you would do that? I almost got killed last night, Cal. We've spent months planning this, and almost half a year just waiting for the right time to act. And when it was time to act last night, I risked my life—and Vlen's—for those fungi samples. I stole—me, Rezsia Monet maDeiami—stole from another businessman." Her eyes glinted with a flash of lupine yellow. "We're hiding our work in the night like raiders, and wandering around like zombies in the day, and it's still not enough to counter neGruli's greed. But you want me to sit back as if I've done my share and don't need to do any more."

Cal's voice was quiet. "The more you do for the elders, the more they'll expect from you, Rezs. Grandma cursed herself near to death with her obligations to Ariye, trying to do everything they asked of her." He leaned across and touched her arm. "Be careful, Rezs, that you don't do the same."

"I just want to do what's right, Cal. That's all."

Lit looked straight at Rezs, and his voice was hard. "Then find the heart of neGruli's source, Rezs. Ride straight to that heart."

VII

At first there was an exciting tension to the ride. Gray Vlen loped ahead of her on the trail, and the canopy of trees was tall enough that she felt as if she rode within an airy cave of greenery. The black tree trunks were like pillars supporting a roof of sun-speckled leaves; the lower growth—still unfurling with constant rustling sounds and spreading with the warmth of spring—was a mosaic of new growth that left her eyes bewildered. Anything could happen, she told herself, reveling in the tiny thrill that twisted up in her stomach. An encounter with a hungry poolah; a glimpse of a band of worlags . . . She imagined a raider behind that boulder; a dark raptor up on that branch . . .

She could feel Gray Vlen whenever she stretched her mind to meet his. Even when she didn't, she could feel the faint yellow eyes of the pack gleaming at her in her mind. She felt protected, as if the wolves knew where she was and walked the trail with her.

But by the end of the first day she grew so sore from the saddle, she couldn't sleep except on her stomach. Not that she slept—the small noises of insects and the calls of the night birds that discovered her camp kept her eyes from shutting soundly, while the twigs that snapped from clumsy or uncaring hooves brought her heartbeat to a quicker pace each time she started awake. The first dawn, she opened her eyes to a mouthful of fangs and hot, panting breath that froze her heart and brought a near scream to her lips.

Wolfwalker, sent Vlen. *It is day!*

Rezs caught her breath with a gasp. "By all nine moons above, Vlen," she snapped. "Don't do that to me."

He snorted lightly in her face. *Do what?*

She shoved him away. "Moonworms." She dropped her head back on her arms.

The young wolf nudged her, then pawed at her side.

"Vlen!" she snarled.

The yearling jumped back playfully. *Get up? Hunt?*

"Oh, gods of the Ancients," she muttered, shifting slightly in the bag and groaning as her body ached. "What have I done to myself?"

Gingerly, with alternating winces and moans, she eased out of her sleeping bag. It took more than a moment to push herself all the way to her feet, and when she did, her thighs nearly buckled as they tightened the first time to take her weight. It took so long to hobble to the nearest peetree that when she finally made it, she thought she would actually cry.

Her second day of riding was spent half standing in the stirrups to keep her weight off her rump, and she took every chance she could to walk instead of ride. She explored two shallow caves, one of which was tall, clean, and light, with no signs of denning. The other cave opening was raw from a recent rock slide, and its floor was littered with the skeletons of varied creatures.

Rezs ducked into that one gingerly while Vlen investigated a patch of woolweed nearby. Most of the bones weren't scattered, and there were as many rat and scavenger shapes as those of larger animals. It wasn't until she saw the pockmarks on the ceiling of the cave that she understood what had killed the creatures. The distinctive spiral pattern of those round pockmarks was the mark of roofbleeders. She must have projected something to Vlen because the wolf was suddenly at the entrance, and his low snarl caught her ears.

"It's all right, Vlen," she told him absently. "I'll just be a minute."

Curiously, she ran her fingers along one of the depressions. Its spiral edges were smooth, not sharp, as she would have expected; but when she stepped up on a boulder to examine it more closely in the dim light, Vlen whined. Reluctantly, he picked his way between two skeletons to get closer to Rezs. One of the bone piles shifted, and Vlen jumped awkwardly away, tangling in a set of skeletal jaws. He panicked, unsettling Rezs, thrashed his way clear, and leaped for the entrance.

"Moons, Vlen—be careful."

He shot her a shaft of fear mingled with embarrassment. His image of the sunlit trail was unmistakable.

Rezs sighed. "I'm coming." Carefully, she jumped down from the rock. "But this is the first time I've ever seen a place where roofbleeders actually lived. It takes decades, you know, for a roofbleeder to etch such a perfect pattern. The parasites in this cave must have been huge."

Vlen's expression of disgust was clear, even without the bond. *Caves don't make good dens,* he sent. *You'd be better off digging your night place out of the soil than looking in here for a bed.*

Rezs chuckled. "It's barely noon, Vlen; it's not a place to sleep I'm looking for." She picked her way to the cave entrance. "Lit and I finally got those ganacids developed, and I want to test them out—if I can stand to be around the roofbleeders long enough to set out the dishes and watch the worms' reactions, anyway. If those acids keep the roofbleeders away, the miners and cavers will jump at the acids, and the money from them alone will keep our business out of neGruli's clutches for at least another year." She looked up again, studying the pockmarks. "I was looking for something more than a dried nubbin of a worm, but there's nothing left here but husks."

The flavor of disgust in Vlen's mind made Rezs grin as she ducked carefully through the entrance—it wasn't low, but it was jagged, and she had already bruised her shoulder on the rock. She straightened with a groan, and stretched her arms over her head. "Don't worry. That cave is too well lit now that the opening's been enlarged. No roofbleeder could survive in there for more than an hour. We'll have to find a deeper cave if I'm going to try out the acids."

Vlen snorted again, then turned and trotted back toward the trail and the place where she had tethered her dnu. He paused to look over his shoulder at her. *Better to hunt a meal that will fill your body, not a worm that will suck it dry.*

Rezs grinned as he faded into the brush. She didn't bother trying to follow him quietly. Her legs were so sore that walking softly was not an option, and the noise of her sword catching on and breaking the brush made it impossible to hide her passage.

By the third day the peace of the forest was beginning to pall. She'd seen no other riders. She'd encountered no night-spiders with their insidiously numbing bite; no worlags with their snapping, beetlelike jaws; no mudsuckers in the two ponds she circled; and no lepa in the muggy sky. And aside from a light rain in the afternoon and the diminishing ache of her body, there was not even real discomfort to keep her company on the ride.

"Bored." That's what she was, she told herself as the forest began to darken to night. She tried to find Vlen with her eyes, but it wasn't until she opened herself to their bond that she sensed him at all.

When Vlcn felt her in his mind, he sent her a flash of image—of forest cats and field mice. The distance between them was short in his mind, and Rezs relaxed.

Rezs nodded. "I read it, Vlen. You're getting stronger."

Wolfwalker, you should run the trail with me. You should smell this in your own nose, not just through mine.

Rezs snorted. "If you think I'm getting out of this saddle just when I've gotten used to its feel, you're crazy." She clicked her tongue against the roof of her mouth to tell her dnu to pick up its pace. "Not much farther," she told it, "and we'll bed down for the night."

The riding beast flicked its small, flat ears as if acknowledging her command, and Rezs rubbed its neck absently. The ground here was rocky and rough, and the trail wound around the jutting rocks so much that she was beginning to think she had ridden sideways more than forward. It didn't seem to bother Vlen, but Rezs was getting impatient. She kept getting glimpses of the Water Wall from the top of nearly each rise, but somehow never got closer to it.

"I wish you could tell me how long this is going to take," she told the wolf. "I feel as if I've been riding in circles."

We are circling, he returned. *The pack trail follows the way of the deer who move from meadow to meadow. We can go all the way around this ridge.*

She sighed as she reached another rise in the trail and saw, over one more wind-etched ridge, another gray-black facet of the distant Water Wall. "At least I know I'm not lost," she muttered. She glanced up at the sky. The mugginess of the afternoon was turning into cool evening air, and the wind that had lifted the leaves through the forest earlier was dying down. She peered through the now ragged canopy to see if she could find a place to camp. She'd be lucky to find a spot free of both roots and rocks, she told herself sourly.

Wolfwalker, Vlen sent.

His voice was more distant now, and she didn't know if he had gone on ahead or if she was just too tired to maintain the link between them. Slowly, she halted the dnu and peered through the leaves until her head began to ache. She couldn't see Vlen through the tall, black trunks and airy leaves; and the slightly blurred view from his yellow eyes made her tense up her whole face as she frowned. "Where are you, Vlen?" she asked shortly.

She couldn't understand what he sent: the jumble of scents made her head spin with unfamiliar odors, and the only thing she recognized was the gray fog that, with Vlen's voice, filtered into the back of her head, and the yellow eyes that seemed to watch her from inside her mind.

When she finally caught up with him, he was sitting on the side of the trail as if he'd been waiting for her all day. Rezs didn't even spare him a look of disgust. She just reined into a sandy clearing at the base of one of the short cliffs, checked the overhang for signs of animals, and dropped tiredly from the saddle. She spent the last ten minutes of light tethering the dnu near the grass, setting up her gear, and rolling out her sleeping bag. She was still chewing the last of her jerky when she crawled inside the bag and wedged her hips more comfortably into the sand. This time she had no trouble falling asleep. The yellow gleaming eyes that watched her settle down were echoed in her head by a haunting strain of melody that played in time to the howling of the Gray Ones on the heights.

Her fourth dawn out was blue and gray. There was no color to line the horizon or mark the clouds with gold. Just eight of the moons, propped up by the clouds that bore the weight of spring rain. From her sleeping bag, Rezs watched the patches of sky through the branches overhead. The warmth of Vlen's body was stretched against her side, and his yellow eyes watched her, alert the moment she became awake. Her stomach growled.

Wolfwalker, he sent. *Your hunger feeds mine like a den mother feeds her pup. Is it time yet for the hunt?*

"You go on, Gray One," she murmured. "I'm going to eat my own bland, human food and enjoy it far more than your raw meat and tough tendons."

Vlen yawned, and his white teeth gleamed. *You've never hunted with the pack, Wolfwalker.*

She burrowed more deeply into the sleeping bag. "I'm not likely to hunt with you today, either. Go, Gray One. Go and eat and come back when you're done. It'll take me a while to pack up."

Vlen rose to his feet, and the chill left behind where his warmth retreated from her side made her tuck the bag more closely around her. Her inner thighs were still sore, and her buttocks had worn themselves into the shape of her saddle. She groaned as she rolled over and stared at the ground. She hadn't realized how hard a leather seat could be, and neither Biran nor Lit—her only brothers who had traveled the distances between the counties—had warned her to carry saddle salve. The cloth she had tossed over her saddle had kept her thighs from being rubbed raw, but the ache in her muscles cried out for liniment.

She stuck out her hand and felt the thin drops that preceded the rains, then rolled over again and deliberately stared at the sky. The clouds were heavy this morning, and it looked as though she would be riding through showers, not just another muggy day. For a moment she envied Vlen. Then she opened her link to him and felt his own hot discomfort. His spring coat was shedding in ragged clumps, and the mats that resulted from the old hair that had not yet let go clung like shaggy hands to his pelt.

Peltstones, she remembered. She had promised her niece a peltstone, and there must be some lava caves nearby that would harbor the crystals she sought. She rolled stiffly from her bed and glanced up at the short, rock cliffs before which she had camped. If she could find one of the hairlike crystals before she reached the Water Wall, she could store it at the signal fires—Bany could show her a good place to leave it— then pick it up when she returned from this trip.

She shook out her sleeping bag, rolled it, and set it below her pack and bow. She'd tied the pack into a tree to keep the ground spiders out of it—that was one thing Lit had repeatedly warned her about—and hung her bow off its side. She didn't care if the spiders crawled over her scabbard, but there were mud beetles that ate bowstrings like candy, and leaving a bow on the ground was a guarantee that it would be useless within hours. She pulled her toiletry case from her pack, then paused before pulling her tiny travel grill out. If she wanted hot tea for breakfast, she would have to build her fire soon—there were dark, heavy clouds to the east, and that meant it was already raining in the county. Other than the few drops that kept spotting her gear, there was no sign yet of the rain increasing, but Rezs still hesitated over the idea of a fire. Finally she sighed.

"Discipline," she muttered. "Duty and discipline forever."

Quickly, she repacked her gear and changed into clean shorts. She'd already discovered that they were much more comfortable on the trail, and if it started raining, she had no desire to climb through the brush with water-soaked leggings. She glanced around the clearing, but there were only two kinds of fallen wood: complete trees that left their root masses sticking up in the air, and branch masses so tangled in deep piles of grass and new growth that without a saw, she didn't see how she would get it free. "Time for another foraging trip," she told herself.

There were several thick deadfalls within sight, but like the brush piles around her camp, they seemed to be complete entities. Some of them were made by trillo trees that had fallen, tearing thin roots out of the ground. The trees had regrown, and fallen again, repeating the cycle until the root mass and deadwood above and below the ground were heavy enough to hold the weight of the thin trunks that tried to shoot up. She had trouble yanking anything clear of the one mass she began attacking. Finally, she half climbed onto the mass of tangled wood and jerked so hard to break off the pieces that she flung herself forward onto the pile.

"Worlag piss—" she cursed. A thick knot had scraped her left thigh, leaving a long, angry, red mark, and a dozen branch ends were poking her arms and legs. She lay there for a moment, staring at the ground through the tangle. "What were the Ancients thinking? Peetrees to take care of the wastes, and extractor plants to reduce the toxins in our food—even flatwood trees for shelves and skis. But firewood trees?" She tried to pull one of her arms from the tangle and dug her left side in more deeply. "I can't believe it never crossed their mind. Of course, all I'd have to do is bring it up before the council, and neGruli would design one within six months."

She raised her eyes. Ahead, up slightly from the forest floor, was another set of dark holes in the ridge. She eyed them enviously, then began struggling free. She finally escaped the deadfall by rolling until she could get her feet onto the strongest of the green, bending branches. Then she spent the next ten minutes yanking twigs out of her hair, breaking up the few branches she dragged clear, and studying the caves. By the time she was done, she had a disgustingly small stack of firewood and a handful of hair that she had simply torn out of her scalp. She stared at her dirty hands, stained by bark juices, sap, and the loose hairs she had not yet untangled, and muttered a bland curse.

"If it's going to be one of those days," she told herself sourly, "I might as well get on with it."

She loaded up her firewood, then glanced again at the caves. There were four large openings in view: one circular; two massive, vertical cracks in the cliff; and one that looked like a mouth stretching perhaps eight or nine meters along the midpoint of the cliff. Rezs hesitated, but she was halfway to the cliff already, and it would take only a few moments to find out if they were worth exploring more fully. She put the firewood down.

"Vlen," she called. She concentrated on a picture of the cliffs. *Look—*

The yearling blasted back into her mind with a bloody joy that made her stagger. As he pounced on a rodent in a small field, Rezs's legs tightened and her throat swallowed convulsively while he gulped down the rat. The sense of his hunting almost made her feel as if she were prey herself. "Moonworms, Vlen," she gasped. "A little lighter on the impressions."

Instantly, he projected such a deep apology that Rezs had to shake it off to project her words in return: *Meet me at the cliff?*

Vlen shot his agreement back. He dug out one more rat, gulped it down, and stretched his lanky legs in a lope that brought him to the cliff in moments.

The round cave entrance was easiest to reach, and the least interesting. It was more of an overhang than anything else,

Rezs realized as she stood at the entrance and peered around its irregular inner shape. To the left, the first vertical crack narrowed so swiftly that, from the entrance, Rezs could touch the back of the cave with a stick. She hit something soft and drew back the stick quickly, only to find it covered with a pasty gray substance. She examined it closely, spread some of it on a rock to see it in a thinner layer, then wiped the rest of the slime mold off on the grass. Vlen, watching her movements, sniffed what was left of the mold, then sneezed, coughed, sputtered, and began to wipe his nose across the ground.

Rezs chuckled. "Serves you right, Gray One, for not asking first what it was."

Vlen gave her a baleful look.

It was a scramble to reach the second vertical crack. The jumble of boulders at the base of the cliff afforded little flat footing for either hands or boots. Finally, Rezs jumped, then hauled herself up to get within reach of the entrance. Gray Vlen, left down below, whined and stood up on his hind legs. When Rezs moved out of sight toward the cave, Vlen actually barked.

"It's all right, Gray One," she reassured. "I just want a peek."

Wolfwalker, his mental voice was anxious. *This smells of dry death.*

Rezs looked over her shoulder. "You mean carcasses—like a roofbleeder would leave?"

His impressions were clumsy, as if overshadowed by his anxiety, and Rezs shook her head. "I can't understand you, Vlen." Gingerly, she bent down and leaned forward to see through a wide spot in the dark opening. Instantly, three leggy shapes dropped before her eyes. She jerked back. Behind her, Vlen howled. Rezs fell back on her behind and, with her heart pounding, scrambled off the boulder. Vlen leaped away. The two of them were meters away against the trees before Rezs stopped and turned back to look again at the entrance.

Rezs shook her head and wiped at her hair and face. "Nightspiders—"

The cub snarled at the cave, his hackles bristling along his back. *You felt no fangs?*

"No." She shuddered. "But it's still disgusting to think of them crawling across my face." She eyed the cave. "I think we'll skip that one for now. I'd thought at first that neGruli would hide his work in a cave system, but even though this area isn't well traveled, I just don't see the man and his workers crawling through these rocks." She pointed along the cliff as the rain began to fall faster. "But I'd still like to find a roofbleeder. Let's go that way. There was some kind of opening down low—just behind those stones."

Vlen's yellow eyes followed her gesture, and he turned back to trot beside her as she pushed her way through the brush. *You're noisy as a pair of chitters,* he admonished.

Rezs gave him a sour look. "The day I have four feet made of soft pads instead of hard boot soles, I'll walk quietly. Until then, Vlen, you'll have to take me as I am. Besides"—she rubbed his scruff vigorously—"your nose is supposed to warn me of anything that approaches."

The yearling snorted. The sense of cave smells and rain-wet dirt suddenly filled Rezs's throat with his breath so that she choked.

"I get your point," she managed, sucking in her own breath. There were times when the acuity of his senses was more than she wanted to feel for herself. Gingerly, she closed down on the bond until only a thin thread wound between their minds. She could still feel him—especially when they were so close together. But she no longer seemed to breathe through his mouth or listen through his ears.

Vlen reached the area of the cliff sooner than she did; she had gotten tangled on a patch of brambles, and spent the better part of five minutes getting her blouse uncaught. By the time she joined him at the base of the cliff, the rain had increased to a shower and showed every sign of getting worse. It was noisy, not just cold, and Rezs scowled at the thought of the small stack of firewood she had left back at the deadfall. No matter what Bany said, there was no way she'd get a blaze going if the wood was soaking wet. "Ah, moonworms," she muttered. "Might as well get used to cold mornings."

The boulders formed a ring around the cave entrance, blocking it so that she could not walk up to it, but would have to crawl over them to get in. She wiped her eyebrows before hefting herself up on her elbows so she could see into the depression that led to the hole in the cliff. This entrance, she realized, was much larger than it had appeared from the vantage point of the other cave. "It's another entrance," she affirmed to Vlen. "Want to check it out?" But the yearling didn't answer, and Rezs looked down. "What is it, Vlen?"

Yellow eyes gleamed in her mind. Vlen's mind was jumbled, as if he could no longer think in word pictures. Only the sense of a danger getting stronger projected itself to her consciousness.

"What is it?" she repeated. "Roofbleeders?"

Reluctantly, Vlen projected his sense of smell, and Rezs did not mistake the dry-death odor he had breathed in before.

"Ah." Her hands grew wetter with the continuing rain, and she started to lose her grip. Clumsily, she hauled herself the rest of the way up. "Don't worry. I know what I'm doing. I may not be ready to sit under the worms to test the ganacids, but I really do want to see some live ones." She looked down. "Can you make it up? Or do you want to wait there?"

Vlen dropped back to all fours, then gathered himself and leaped up, but his claws gained no purchase on the stone. He scrabbled on the boulder, then fell with a twisting thud to the ground. He tried again with no better luck.

"Wait, Vlen," she said. She slid down, bent her knee against the rock, and let Vlen use her thigh as a step. This time, he made it up easily, gouging her thigh with his hard, black claws as he did so. Rezs winced, but hauled herself up after him.

There was a gap between the cave entrance and the boulders—plenty large enough for her to jump down into. She hesitated before looking into the cave entrance. Never stick your face in some other creature's doorway—her father's voice floated to her through the lupine fog in the back of her mind, and she gave Gray Vlen a sharp look.

The entrance was low—as if it led down rather than back into the cliff. And it was big. Inside, near the entrance, Rezs could already see a dried carcass—its skin was stretched over its rounded ribs as if it had starved to death, not been sucked dry by the roofbleeders. Vlen nosed forward, but he didn't want to jump down to join her, and he was not willing to go in.

"Stay there, then, Vlen. I'll just be a minute."

As before, she used a stick to knock the spiders from the edges of the rock. Then she waited till her eyes adjusted before ducking inside. Once past the opening, where the roof was low and barely a meter overhead, the cave opened into an area that stretched into black shadows and glistening rock far beyond the range of her sight. The noisy patter of outside rain was almost completely cut off as soon as she stepped inside—it didn't take much stone to deaden sound—and the new sound of running water confused her. Not until her eyes adjusted further did she realize that the stream she heard was actually within the cave.

Something brushed against her hair, and instinctively, Rezs swiped at it as she jerked back. She stumbled, caught her foot in a rough spot on the floor, and fell heavily on her hip and ribs. "Dammit," she cursed. "By the hell of the seventh moon—"

Wolfwalker— Vlen appeared instantly at the entrance, and his shape blocked some of the light.

Rezs wrenched her foot free. "I'm all right, Vlen, but you'd better get back. There's a roofbleeder hanging right over your head."

The wolfling backed out hurriedly, his teeth bared and snarling, and Rezs sat up, rubbing her side. The leather of her jerkin was gouged from the rough stone, but it had padded her fall well enough that all she would bear would be bruises. "Hell," she muttered again.

A gray tendril uncoiled overhead and stretched toward her shoulders, and Rezs gave it a warning look. "Don't try it," she told the roofbleeder. "I'm no sleeping body into which to sink your ring of teeth."

It dropped lower, its eellike mouth seeking the warmth of her body, and Rezs scrambled deeper into the cave. As the ceiling rose in height the roofbleeders became more scarce, until they disappeared completely even back where the floor of the cave rose. Rezs stepped up on the rocks and turned to see their silhouettes writhing against the entrance to the cave like sheathed worms. They never dropped into the light, she noted. Had she stayed on the lower part of the floor, she would not have seen them in the faint light from the opening. And had she—like the late owners of the desiccated carcasses and skeletons that cluttered the floor—used this cave for shelter or sleep, she would have felt nothing of their anesthetized bite. She would have woken—if at all—too weak to move from their clutch, and spent the last of her life watching the worms suck her dry. She shivered.

From outside, Vlen whined, and the echo of gray voices in Rezs's head was like the flow of water in the back of the cave—unseen, but clear and sharp. The danger that he projected filled Rezs with unease, so that she stared around the cave as though her gaze could pierce that blackness. "I think," she said softly, "I've had enough of caves and worms and darkness for the day."

Vlen's response was so short and decisive that Rezs almost smiled. The yellow eyes that gleamed faintly in the back of her head seemed intent, and her shoulders shivered again, as if there was something other than wolves that watched her. She moved more quickly to the entrance.

Carefully, she ducked beneath the worms and batted their soft, flaccid forms aside when they tried to follow her movement. She didn't realize until she stood again in the rain that her heartbeat was pounding double time, and her breathing was far too quick.

She turned her face to the rain and let it wash the innate sense of disgust from her expression. "I had no idea how depressing a cave could be," she told the yearling. "I'm more relieved than I can tell you to be back out here in the daylight."

Vlen nudged her, and she nodded. She gave him her knee to use to jump back up on the rock, then she scrambled up beside him. But Vlen's yellow eyes gleamed, and his teeth were suddenly bared, and Rezs, crouched in sudden stillness, stared at him uncomprehendingly. She tried to reach his mind, but it was chaotic and jumbled with aggression. There were no images she could understand; no feelings she could interpret. But her blood seemed to heat and her own teeth bare in violent response. And then she understood the unease that Vlen had been feeling, for from the trees, she heard a sound that made her blood freeze like ice even as her muscles tensed rock-hard. Infinitely slowly, her gaze shifted forward to stare at the edge of the forest.

VIII

There was something big against the trees. Something tall and thick with fur. Nine meters away, the red-brown agemark look-alike eyes turned toward her, motionless with their own hunger. Bestial lips shifted with the minute tremors of each silent, hunting breath. An eager tremble bared the fangs of the badgerbear that waited—lusted—for her movement. A breath, a shiver—anything would trigger the lunge that poised in its muscles.

She didn't move. She didn't blink; she didn't even shiver. Vlen snarled, and she couldn't breathe, and the rain kept falling coldly. Moment by moment it beaded on her bare skin, formed its rounded drops on her thighs and knees, then ran in chill and crooked streams across the skin of her legs. Each pulse of her heart was like an infinitely slow sound that hung in her veins like the rain that clung to her legs. Each breath was like a bubble that she caught in her mouth, afraid to break—afraid to breathe for fear it would make a sound as it passed between her lips.

She'd been bored, some small voice taunted. Bored with the riding, bored with the quiet. She'd decided there was no danger here and had left her sword behind. And now the only things between her and that badgerbear were the gap of nine meters, the snarl of the cub, and the knife still locked onto her belt.

Rezs's stubborn chin refused to tremble; her violet eyes refused to blink. Water seeped inside her jerkin and chilled her skin. She didn't notice how her crouched knees began to ache or how the bruise was darkening on her hip where she had fallen in the cave. She didn't notice how Vlen's snarl deafened her.

Details of fear filled her mind. Beside her, the flat, scooped-out stones held shallow pools that watched the sky like eyes. Like marbles on glass, their rain bubbles floated and skittered on their surfaces, then raced away toward the edges, where the tiny, air-filled balls disappeared at the rim.

And still she didn't move.

Wolfwalker! Vlen's snarl seemed to go on for years.

Her mind seemed to scream into the bond while her throat remained frozen and her eyes unblinking. She could hear the wolf—see him, like the pools, from the corner of her eyes—but the thing that filled her vision was not the cub shape of the Gray One, but the ring of brown-white teeth that slowly opened wider.

She could see the beast clearly now: thick, coarse fur with a mottled, red-black texture on the tip of every hair; red-brown eyes that looked like mud beneath the hissing rain; a flattened body that spread itself before her like a bat about to fly . . . Colors of the winter fabrics; textures of the clay and sand . . . Her teeth were locked together, but she could feel the scream that grew in her guts.

Black claws extended slowly on the ends of the massive limbs. The maw began to gape in the middle of the beast, and the nostrils on that flattened head flared with such imperceptible movement that only her mind link to the wolf told her that they opened. She could see the ring of teeth that would bite down into her thighs. She could already feel the claws that would tear across her belly like talons through mud. Deep in her ears, like the breathing of the beast, the wolves began to howl, and the snarling of Gray Vlen behind her smothered the thoughts in her skull. In her throat, her scream grew swollen like a balloon.

She sucked in a breath with infinite slowness, easing the air around the scream. Beside her, the yearling's snarl grew louder, and his scruff doubled and bristled in violent threat. The motion seemed to lock time in place. The badgerbear held its haunches taut before it spread and sprang. The cub caught its growl in a breath that had no end. And then Rezsia's scream burst through her throat and tore the ice from the moment.

Fangs seemed to leap across the distance. Mottled, red-brown fur twisted in the air. Lethal, flattened, red-black limbs spread like wings to engulf her. Gray Vlen was somehow down, over the rocks, between her and the beast. The scream that hung in the air was like the heart, ripped from the body, pumping out its futile life. And a sound—a challenge—broke across her ears as a mental command reached inside her head through the graysong and sliced off her scream like a garrote.
—*SILENCE!*

"Aiyu-chuh-chuh . . ."

The low-pitched sound came from the right, and the badger-bear halted its midair leap with a fantastic twist of body. It dropped to the ground, its ears flared widely, and its gaping maw narrowed to a deadly, silent snarl. Its sightless head swung once to the left; its ring of teeth seemed to grow. Rezs whimpered once, unable to keep the sound from crawling out between her teeth.

"Aiyu-chuh-chuh . . ."

The low, hostile, piercing sound came again from her right. Rezs dared not move her head to see. Before her, the badger-bear needed no eyes to understand that sound. It swelled up, doubling in size, then flattened again to a spreading layer of fur. She watched, frozen, a body length from the beast, as its fur rippled across its sightless head. It whistle-snarled back, "Aiyu-chuuh-chuhh—"

The tones of the badgerbear's challenge were deeper—stronger—than the sounds that came from the right. It crept toward its challenger, almost flowing in its movements. Swelled, then flattened; spread out, then thinned—like a macabre dance in which the ring of teeth grew and the out-stretched claws lengthened in a promise of shearing strength.

"Aiyu-chuh-chuh . . ." Again, that sound.

The badgerbear's eardrums exposed themselves between two rifts of fur, and Rezs could see them pulse with the sound of the challenge. But there was something in Vlen's mind that made her think that the sound came from a mouth that was not ringed with fangs. Human song—human sound. She breathed in with the realization. Bany? Some hunter who had followed the creature here? The wolfsong in her head was louder, fuller than before. Close—the Gray Ones were gathering in the woods—gathering to protect her. And that human challenge from the right—

The beast swung its head back toward Rezs, then leaped toward the noise in the woods. A howl broke through the rain, and Rezs heard it in her ears, not her mind. The cub leaped after the beast. She screamed, "Vlen!"

Vlen halted, caught for a moment by her voice. And as he hesitated a warbolt skewered the badgerbear through its open ring of teeth. A shriek pierced Rezs's ears. The beast plunged toward the gray-haired figure who slid arrows from quiver to bow as smoothly as water on glass. Another arrow plunged into the creature—this one from the side. Vlen broke free from the thin control of Rezs's mind and closed his narrow jaws on the badgerbear's leg. The beast swiped back. Tangled limbs flailed. An arrow passed completely through the badgerbear's body, flashing over Vlen and shattering its bloodied length against the rock at Rezs's feet.

Rezs scrambled to get higher up, her nails digging into crumbled stone and breaking on the boulders. Claws seemed to reach up to her legs, and she screamed again and again. The howling in her ears filled her mind. Yellow eyes looked out from hers; the Gray Ones swept into the clearing.

"No—NO! Get back—"

Someone was shouting. Five wolves lunged, snapping at the beast on the ground. Gleaming fangs tore at the badgerbeast. Mottled fur ripped away, and claws raked a Gray One's flank. The howl cut across Rezs's mind. Her teeth bared themselves to the rain. Her knife was somehow in her hand. There was fur in her teeth—she could taste it; there was blood on her paws—she could feel it. Her legs tensed to leap—

Back! someone snapped in her mind.

She caught herself on the edge of her balance, her violet eyes staring below. In a heartbeat, the badgerbeast flung the yearling back against the rocks like a broken sack of flour. Vlen yelped, and Rezs was rocked by the blow that seemed to strike her side with the stones that hit his. A vicious paw caught another Gray One on its ribs, and the older wolf shrieked in Rezs's mind. She screamed with them both, caught by the pain they shot into her skull.

"Gray Ones—back!" Snarled the voice above their yelping. "All of you, get away!"

The badgerbear lunged after a Gray One, and a warbolt pierced the larger creature's mottled limb. It twisted with a roar, and another shaft cut across its shoulder. Another cut through its neck. And then, as the wolves pulled back, the arrows homed more thickly in on its body. The badgerbear spun, clawing at the bolts. It shrieked, and its cry made Rezsia cringe. Kicking, tearing at the earth, it clawed the mud until it lay in a wallow of its own blood.

Rezsia could not move. She stood, her back to the rocks, staring at the carcass on the sodden ground. The maw that had so nearly torn her from the rocks—it gaped to the rain, and the runnels of blood that soaked those lips now matted the fur instead.

". . . all right?"

Rezs looked dumbly down at her arm. The partially gloved hand that gripped her was older, but it was certainly not old enough to be Bany's. She raised her gaze to the face of the woman. Vlen's vision still blurred hers, and she had trouble seeing. She had only an impression of old wisps of hair, once solid black, which now crept from under a warcap so old itself that it was more metal mesh and mending than material.

"All right now?" The gray-black wisps clung to the woman's face where sweat and rain mixed on that weathered skin. Beneath her worn jerkin, the woman's chest still rose and fell, as if she had been running, while behind her, a tall, broad-shouldered man bent over the badgerbear carcass and began to cut out the arrows. Dressed like a scout, but not Bany either, Rezs slowly realized, as if her brain was not yet working. Her mind seemed filled with the snarling of the three wolves who tore at the badgerbear and ignored the man except to snap at him when he pushed them aside to reach a warbolt. Behind them all, one of the Gray Ones limped to the edge of the forest. Another, an older, graying wolf, pressed against the older woman's thigh and snarled at Rezs a silent challenge.

Rezsia shivered. "Okay," she managed a belated answer. "Vlen—"

"He's fine. Bruised. That's all."

"Are you—" Her voice was too hoarse. She cleared her throat and found that, amazingly enough, it still worked. "Are you with Bany?"

"No."

Rezs pushed herself away from the rock and climbed down. She held out her hand to the cub, stretching to feel him through her mind. But Gray Vlen, stiff-legged over the muscle he had torn from the carcass, merely bared his teeth and snarled low in his throat. His mouth was full of flesh, and Rezs, caught for a moment in that snarl, licked her lips as he did.

The older woman's eyes followed Rezs's gaze, then turned back to study Rezs's face. Rezs knew what the woman saw, and she had to force herself to stand that examination. Her face would be pale, she knew—her lips still tight with the fear she had screamed with, and the pulse in her throat would be visible as a moth on a window. Her hair was pulled back in a braid like the older woman's, but she wore no warcap, and the black strands were matted and dripping with rain. Except for the rock scrapes along one side of her jerkin, and the marks of cave dust and mold, her jerkin was barely worn, and her blouse, although soaked, was made from a fine, tightly woven cloth. The tight forearm of her left sleeve had a sewn-in pad for an archer's armguard, and the right sleeve had a built-in dart pouch—empty of darts or knives. Her shorts had left her legs bare to both the rocks and rain, and the scrapes on her skin were soft with rainwashed scabs. Slowly, the older woman's eyebrows raised. Even Rezs's boots were new. The other wolfwalker could smell the leather herself beneath the mold scent of the cave and the mud scent of the ground.

Rezs could almost feel the disapproval in the other woman's eyes. But as she instinctively stretched to feel the woman's emotions through the bond between herself and Vlen, she heard the echo of another wolf. Automatically, she looked down from the scout to the aging wolf at the other woman's side. But when she met this Gray One's eyes, she gasped. Her eyesight yellowed with the vision of herself from other eyes, and as though her sleep had become confused with her consciousness, dreams flooded Rezs's mind—night images of yellow eyes that watched her from the commons and gleamed in the moonlight at her window. Old dreams, filtered by the years into shallow pictures, and soft sounds of barely remembered fears . . . It was as if Rezs recognized this wolf— as though those yellow eyes represented all the times she had felt the Gray Ones near her. "Wolfwalker?" she whispered.

The woman pulled the hood of her cloak back over her head

and eyed Rezs without answering. Finally, she stooped and picked up Rezs's knife. She glanced at it, turned it over in her hands, then handed it to Rezs. Then the woman turned away to kneel by the wolf whose side was matted with mud and fur and blood.

For a moment Rezs felt faint. Blindly, she groped for the rocks behind her. Her heartbeat was still too fast, she thought. And her hands . . . She stared down at them. They trembled as they touched the steel of the knife in her grip. She had not even realized she had dropped the blade till the other woman gave it back. Slowly she tucked it in her belt.

Unable to trust her legs to walk with her weight on them, she studied the two scouts. They both wore two knives apiece in their belts, carried swords either at their sides or across their backs, and managed to sport both bows and quivers without being tangled in either. The small, thin packs on their backs didn't seem to hamper their movements at all, and Rezs found herself comparing the lightness of their packs to the bulky size of her own gear back at her camp. The man even had a thin coil of rope tied onto the base of his pack, yet didn't once hang up on the low branches around which he moved. Both scouts worked like satin—smoothly, without wasted movement or extra motion. Their fingers were sure and steady. Rezsia couldn't help touching her own knife hilt, and she swallowed at the fear that still choked her throat—the tremble in her flesh as the steel vibrated against her hand. She took a step toward the two, but Vlen sank his teeth into the badgerbear's fur at that moment, and Rezs's words of thanks were garbled.

The woman scout glanced over her shoulder. The massive wolf by which she had knelt limped away to the carcass of the badgerbeast, where he pushed his way in and tore his own meal from the meat. For an instant the middle-aged woman's expression softened as she watched the Gray Ones feeding. Then she looked at Rezs again. Like a sheet, a reserve seemed to come down over her eyes and flatten her gaze.

"Caving, unarmed"—she said the words softly, but her voice seemed to cut like the chill of the rain that shivered against Rezs's skin—"with an untrained cub, the cavebleeders thick in the rocks, and the badgerbears out hunting for food? Where are your weapons? Did you lose your sword or leave it behind?"

Rezs kept her voice steady."I left it at my camp. I didn't need it for the cavebleeders, and I didn't know the badgerbears were hunting."

"It's spring," the woman returned sharply. The older, graying wolf looked at the woman and moved silently to her side.

Rezs met the woman's gaze with stubborn determination. She could almost see the other woman reach mentally toward the massive female wolf. Could almost smell in her own nose how the older woman took in Rezs's scent and judged Rezs by the cave dust on her new shorts and boots. "I know it's spring," she said quietly, "but what difference should that make? I've seen no predators for days. Even if the lepa flocked, they couldn't see me through this canopy."

The other woman studied her for a moment. "In spring," she said finally, "a badgerbear is a walking mouth. It doesn't have the energy reserves to dig its traps and wait for food. It hunts actively and will take the trail of any mammal or bird. A cub and a human? That's a meal to follow for days." Her voice took on an edge. "If you remember nothing else from the forest, remember that."

Rezs did not drop her eyes at the other woman's tone. "I'm not used to the forest. Gray Vlen—"

"Is a cub, and not aware of all the dangers yet. Don't rely on him to warn you or protect you."

Rezs's gaze flicked to the carcass of the badgerbear. The rain beat its blood into the soil, and the red-tipped hair was mottled now with mud, not camouflage. Vlen whined softly, and she looked back down at the yearling. She could feel the soreness in his ribs and hip where he had struck the rock. Unconsciously, she rubbed her hand against her own bruised bones as she watched the Gray Ones drag their ragged chunks of meat across the rain-spattered ground. "Wolves have racial memories. Young as he is, shouldn't Vlen know what is a danger or threat?"

"That's just the kind of assumption," the woman returned sharply, "that can get the both of you killed. Wolf cubs are like young children. They don't know how to use every part of their mind. And Gray Vlen is six months too young to look beneath the images of now to the dimmer memories of other wolves. That's something he'll have to learn as he grows. And you"—the woman pointed—"must learn that with him, if you are to run with his pack."

Rezs didn't drop her eyes. "That's why I'm here," she returned quietly. "To learn the forest with Vlen."

"By yourself." The woman's disapproval was obvious. She pulled some leaves from the sleeve of her worn tunic. "That badgerbear has been tracking you for an hour. It was just sitting here, waiting for you to exit that cave."

"I've tried to be careful . . ." Rezsia's voice trailed off at the expression on the other wolfwalker's face.

Trying and dying are the same thing; the thought echoed in Rezs's skull as clearly as if the woman had projected it through Vlen. Rezs looked down at her hands. They weren't soft hands, but neither were they the hands of a woodsman. She had muscle but not callus, and her knuckles, untoughened by rock or stone, were now skinned and scraped from both cave and boulders. The scout was right, and she had been lucky. She owed her life to these two.

She looked back up at the older woman. "We're not too far from my camp," she offered quietly. "Maybe a kay or two. Would you join me for some hot cannas? I'd be honored with your company."

The other wolfwalker hesitated.

"I'm Rezsia Monet maDeiami," she added. "Rezs, for short."

The woman seemed to stare through her eyes, deep into her brain, and Rezs shivered with a chill that had nothing to do with the rain. As if the woman's gaze was a challenge, Gray Vlen was somehow back at Rezs's side, his scruff bristling like a thistle. An instant of tension tugged at Rezs's thoughts. Then Vlen subsided. The older wolf who ran with the woman moved close to sniff at the cub. Not until the older creature finished did the woman finally speak.

"There is no camp in that direction. We came around the cliffs that way and looked."

Rezs shook her head. "I'm in a slight depression near the cliffs. You might have missed my site."

The other woman began to unstring her bow. "If you set your tent where one of the cave rivers exits, your gear is likely underwater. The runoff from the highlands can gather like a flash flood . . ."

The woman's voice trailed off for an instant, and she swayed. Rezs stepped forward and grabbed her arm. But the woman's legs began to collapse, and Rezs hauled awkwardly on her weight to keep the woman standing. "Oh moons, you're hurt—"

"Not . . . hurt." The wolfwalker sagged in her arms. "Just . . . tired."

The tall man was suddenly there at Rezs's side, taking the woman's weight and pushing them both toward the rocks. "Coale, sit here—"

"Just give me a . . . few minutes. I'm really quite . . . fine."

"You're fine, and I'm a wolf in the seventh moon," he retorted. "I'm Elgon, to you, Rezs," he added absently to her. His tall figure dwarfed the middle-aged woman, and Rezs took a step back as she realized how broad Elgon's shoulders really were. The older gray wolf pressed anxiously against the woman's calves, and the gloved hands buried themselves in the Gray One's fur. Rezs felt her own bond with Vlen tighten into an almost physical cord.

"She just swayed," she said worriedly to Elgon. "As if she was going to faint."

He barely spared her a glance. "It'll pass."

"How far did she run to get here?"

"Far enough." He unstrung one of his belt pouches, and Rezs smelled the food through Vlen's nose before the man unwrapped it.

She hovered, warned off by a snarl from the woman's wolf partner. "What's wrong with her? Is it . . . Is it her heart?" The expression that twisted Coale's lips with the words made Rezs frown. "I'm sorry. I didn't mean to presume—"

The other woman tried to straighten, but Elgon put a single hand on her shoulder and held her down without effort. With his other hand, he shook the pack dust from the meat-roll wrapper.

"There's nothing really wrong with me—" Coale started to say sharply.

"—but her attitude," cut in Elgon to Rezs. "Unfortunately, even the best healer hasn't been able to fix that." He gave Coale a stern look as he handed her the food.

But Coale's hands trembled when she took it, and Rezs's expression was worried. Coale followed her gaze. "I'm just getting old," she said, indicating the other scout. "These legs don't run as fast as his anymore."

Rezs glanced at the gray that had begun to streak the woman's once-black hair. "You're barely seventy. You've got at least a hundred years left in you. A hundred and fifty if the moons smile on you as they've done on me today."

Coale smiled faintly, and the expression lightened her face so that it seemed she dropped two decades with the humor. "Flattery, child. I'm eighty-six. But I thank you." She took a bite of the meat roll and made a face at the man. "I'll try to thank you, Elgon, when I forget that the bread in this roll is almost nine days old."

"What's a ninan?" he retorted with a wink at Rezs. "You ate a roll twice that old the time you were lost in those caves on the coast."

"Lost? Me? It never happened." She shoved him away impatiently, though there was no strength in the motion.

Elgon wiped the rain from his forehead as he looked down. "Rest, Coale." He wiped his hand against his thigh. "If you don't, I'll have Rezs here sit on you to make you stay. And I'll ask Gray Shona to guard you so that you don't get up till I'm done."

"Grandchildren," Coale snorted as she watched him move away. "Think they own the world."

Rezs hid her smile. For all the sharpness in the woman's tone, the other wolfwalker had more than a little affection for the man. Rezs hesitated, then moved after Elgon to hunker down beside him at the carcass of the beast. She picked up one of the arrows. "What were you doing out here?" she asked quietly. "I didn't hear anyone else in the packsong."

"That's not surprising." He didn't look up. "You didn't bond so long ago, did you?"

"A little over a month. But the bond between us"—her expression softened as she glanced toward Vlen—"has grown stronger every day."

This time the man gave her a dry look, and she realized his irises were not simply brown, but flecked with an almost tawny gold. Yet there was no warmth in the colors that reflected the light. The scout's eyes were cold and dark as a winter cave, and his voice was only polite. She thought of the blader who had held her in the night, and wondered what color eyes a grayheart would have.

Elgon yanked out another arrow. "Wait till you've been with them for a year," he answered. "You'll start howling at night and forget how to speak like a woman."

When she realized he was teasing, she relaxed, and she could almost feel the color begin to return to her cheeks. The more natural shade heightened the violet hue of her irises, and Elgon's gaze focused on her more closely. But instead of admiration, there was a sharp judgment in his gaze. Uneasily, Rezs shifted. She wasn't used to people looking at her that way. She half turned away. "I was lucky you were out here," she said. "If you hadn't been hunting . . ." Her voice trailed off, and she shrugged eloquently.

Elgon twisted a third warbolt from the carcass. "It's always an honor to help the Gray Ones," he returned formally, "and those with whom they run."

For a moment Rezs regarded him from beneath her lashes. His voice was deep and smooth, not like silk at all, but like a thick cotton shirt that had been worn into comfort with use. His skin was as weathered as Coale's, but darker, and where Coale's was lined with decades of wolves and woods, Elgon's skin was smooth, broken only by twin scars that crossed his chin and appeared again on his neck. His shoulders were stocky and thick with muscle, but he was so tall that he looked almost lean—Rezs came barely to his shoulders. As she watched he pushed gently past two wolves. One shifted to make room, but the other snapped at his wrist, and the tall man let the Gray One close its teeth on his arm without flinching. When the wolf finally let go, Elgon continued his motion deliberately to the shaft that stuck out of the meat the Gray One was tearing. This time the wolf let him take it, and Rezs wondered at his calm demeanor. For all his gentleness with the wolves, he was hard as a rock to her.

She glanced at Vlen, then tried to stretch her mind to him through the thinness of their bond. What did this cold scout feel like to Vlen? There was an echo of wolfsong deep in her mind as the Gray One snarled in his throat, and Rezs wondered if it was Coale who had told the Gray One to give the bolt up to the man. She could feel an echo of the older woman in Vlen's mind—a sense of rigid will attached to a shadow that flashed along the trails. It was mixed with an ancient howl that seemed to hang forever between her ears. It was not a happy sound, she realized. It was the sound of grief, distilled by time and memory.

Still uncomfortable, she studied his hands. Lined with white scar spots, his knuckles looked as if they had been gouged with countless, tiny rocks, and his fingers seemed almost twisted. She watched him cut another arrow free. "You don't have the hands of a swordsman," she said abruptly.

He shrugged and began to clean another arrow. "I'm better with the bow. Coale's the one who dances steel on the shadows."

Rezs glanced at the middle-aged woman. "I didn't know you could hunt anything with a sword."

He sat back on his heels, fingering the arrow in his hands. "What Coale hunts is a piece of her past, not a beast to make her supper."

Rezs watched him for a moment. "You travel with her to guard her?"

"Guard her?" Elgon frowned at her. "Ah—you thought it was I who pulled the badgerbear from your throat. And I who called the Gray Ones out of its way? My arrow that hit it first?" He leaned forward and wrenched another bolt from the carcass, ignoring the entrails that clung to its metal. He pointed at the other end where the fletching was torn and dangling. "See this spiraling? And the speckles in the feather? Only Coale and some of the other Ari—people from the southeast—use this type of feather. This is Coale's, not mine. I was still sprinting in her wake when she was whistling at the beast."

Rezs could not help the glance she shot at the older woman. "That skinny, scarred-up woman made that violent challenge sound?"

He wiped the guts from the shaft. "If she didn't, I don't know who did." He rinsed the arrow in a puddle and examined it for damage. "You judged her by her looks and limp and thought she was too old to run the woods with the pack?"

Slowly, Rezs flushed. "I'm sorry. I'm not usually so . . . rude or stupid. I was just surprised. It's not the kind of sound I'm used to a woman making."

Elgon gave her a steady look. "You'll have to learn that call yourself, you know—if you want to run with the wolves."

"I don't plan to be a scout, Elgon. I've no need to learn that kind of call."

"You might not plan to be a scout, but you surely are a wolfwalker. You can't ignore the calls that will help keep you alive. It's just another aspect of learning to run trail. And Rezs, you're going to be spending a lot more time than you think running trail."

"You've not much to base that assumption on: You don't know me from a worlag."

"Maybe not. But I do know wolfwalkers and as sure as the wolfsong rises with the moons, you'll be running the trail more often than not."

"I don't think so," she retorted.

He didn't answer except to shrug, and Rezs gave him a sharp look. "Elgon, you don't understand. My mother's family has worked for almost three hundred years to recover the chemistry knowledge of the Ancients. I'm not going to abandon that work just because I've now got a bond with Vlen."

"You think you'll have a choice?"

She raised her eyebrows. "Why not? Choices are part of setting priorities, and my work is as important as my link to the wolves. I breed new symbionts for the bacteria that etch out window glass. I make enhancers to help grow new houses faster, and I make solvents to break the old houses down when they start to lose their structural integrity. The Ancients had their work and their wolves. Why can't I?"

"Why did you come here, Rezs?" His voice was quiet, but there was something in it that made her jaw tighten.

She hesitated. She didn't know why she didn't want to tell this man the truth, but there was something in the song of the wolves that rang of wariness and shadow. She heard herself say calmly, as if it were the only reason, "To learn the forest."

"You were drawn here," he corrected flatly. "And you'll be drawn to the woods again. You won't be able to resist the Gray Ones who've entered your mind with that bond to Vlen. I know. I've been around wolfwalkers all my life." Automatically, he made room for the Gray One that pushed its way in between him and the younger wolf. "I tell you this," he added. "You either learn to live here, or you give up your bond. The Gray Ones won't have it any other way." He wrenched at another arrow. "No mere scout can teach you what any wolfwalker can. No books will prepare you; no studying in a city garden will give you the skills you need. You stay with Vlen, and what you learned here, from Coale—you'll use that learning or you'll lose your life. Maybe for the oldEarthers it was enough to live in cities and keep their wolf bonds separate from their work in their labs and gardens. But you're not on oldEarth. You're here, on a world beneath a different sun, and you can't hide behind old ideas. The wolves have had almost nine centuries to develop the gifts the Ancients gave them. That's changed them. And it's changed the way we relate to them through the wolfwalker bonds. Hell, Rezs, we might not even be the same anymore as the Ancients. But no matter what we used to be, here, now, you're a wolfwalker, and your life has changed forever. You must learn Vlen's trails to stay with him at all." He sat back and gave her a hard look. "Think about him, Rezs. As he grows—as your bond grows—he'll draw you out here more and more. And he'll try to protect you when you're here. He'll give his life for yours. You have a responsibility, Rezs—to him, not just to yourself. Learning one animal call is hardly a step toward that burden, but at least it is a start."

She stared at him. There had been no softness in his tone—his voice was harsh and cutting.

He finished cleaning the last arrowhead and slid the bolt in his quiver. "We'll see you back to your . . . campsite or on to the next city, whichever you want. And, as we go, watch Coale," he said flatly. "Study the way she moves. The things she notices. The sounds to which she listens. Don't touch anything before you ask her or me about it. Don't peer in any holes; don't sniff any flowers; don't test the pools with your toes. You're city-bred and city-raised, and if you last a month out here, it won't be because you're lucky. It'll be because someone saves you for your own old age." He noted her expression. "I have every right," he said softly, answering her unspoken thought. "The safety of a wolfwalker is the responsibility of everyone who runs the woods. And I take my responsibilities seriously."

"Do you speak this way to Coale?"

Deliberately, he looked at the carcass in the mud, then back at Rezs. He scraped blood from his hands onto the fur of the beast. "For the most part, Coale can take care of herself. Can you say the same?"

Unconsciously, Rezs's hand tightened on the hilt of her knife. Across from her, the wolf cub looked up and snarled at the man.

Elgon noted both movements and smiled without humor. "You have a lot to learn, Rezs," he said softly. "Don't let pride or ego stand in the way of staying alive. Take advantage of every teacher you can find, but take nothing at face value. Not out here in the forest. The things you think you know today could betray you badly tomorrow."

Her own voice was quiet. "Are you speaking of yourself, of Coale, or of both of you?"

Slowly, Elgon got to his feet, until, at full height, Rezs had to blink through the thinning rain to see his face. His voice was so quiet that his words slid like a chill into her ears. "I speak, not of me or of Coale, but of your judgment, Rezsia maDeiami."

For a moment her lips tightened. "You're right," she said softly. "I have no experience to form good judgment. I thought . . . Gray Vlen would be enough of one for me"—she had to bite her lip to keep from saying Bany's name—"but I was obviously wrong."

"Gray Vlen has to learn from his pack. And you—get yourself hooked up with a wolfwalker, Rezs. It's a heck of a lot easier to learn about your bond with Vlen from someone who understands it. Any scout can teach you about survival, but being a wolfwalker is more than just learning to read sign or pack the right gear for a hike."

Rezs stared at the carcass, at Elgon's bloody hands, then at Coale, still resting against the rocks. "You think I should go back home, don't you?"

He gave her a sober look. "I think you're an accident waiting to happen. Have that accident inside the barrier bushes, and there's people around to help you without worries from worlags and beasts. Have that accident out here, and everyone who gets involved will bear the risks of that rescue."

Rezs was silent for a moment. She looked from Elgon to Coale. Then, slowly, she took her knife from her belt, reversed it, and held it out, hilt first, to Elgon. "I thank you for my life," she said formally. "And for that of Gray Vlen. From this day forward my home and family shall be as yours. Consider me as your daughter, so that I may serve you as you have served me." She glanced at Coale. "I ask this of you: that you take up for me the burden of my safety, which you carried so willingly before. I ask that you teach me to survive."

Elgon's gaze flickered with something akin to startlement. He didn't move to take the knife. Rezs forced herself to be silent as she realized that he was waiting for the older woman to give the answer for him. But the other woman's face was tight, as if she felt a pain deep in her body.

"Elgon—" Rezs said in a low voice, worried.

He didn't look at her, and his voice was so low that it was more for her ears than Coale's. "It's all right," he said. "It's just her heart."

Something seemed to shatter in Coale's eyes, and for an instant Rezs felt a wave of emotion so tight it made her blanch. Gray Shona bared her teeth at Vlen; the cub laid back his ears. Vlen's voice became a snarl, while Shona's grew until it was as loud as his. In the cub's scruff, Rezs's fist tightened so far that the cub twisted with a snap.

Abruptly, Rezs clamped down on her link to the cub. Shona's voice dimmed like night, and Coale seemed almost to stagger. Rezs couldn't seem to focus. Her mind seemed to echo with voices that had just filled its space, and she realized that it was the sense of the other wolf and wolfwalker that had been so strong. Old Roy had not had half the power in his bond to the wolves that this middle-aged woman did. She struggled to clear her vision. She could hear Elgon shifting near her; she could feel the cub at her side—but it was moments before she could break away from those yellow, gleaming eyes. Finally, she managed to swallow. By the moons, she realized, if Coale was willing to teach her, she could learn more in a ninan than in a year with Old Roy back home.

Across from her, Coale pursed her lips. Her voice was wary as she asked, "You want us to teach you about Vlen or the forest?"

"Both," Rezsia managed.

"You don't know us."

She glanced down at the carcass, then back at the other woman. "I know enough," she said flatly.

The woman's brows drew together, and she pushed herself away from the rock. She took a few steps as she began to pace, then stopped. "What if our"—she indicated herself and Elgon—"plans take us away from this county?"

"I can travel. In fact, I'm meeting friends and moving north and west for the next few ninans anyway." She frowned at the way the woman favored one leg. That trembling in the woman's hands, and the way Coale had been exhausted . . . Of course, she had no idea how far the two had run, but Elgon hovered far too protectively over his grandmother to allow Rezs to believe that the woman should be on her own. "I don't wish to give you a burden you cannot bear," she began slowly. "But please, Coale, consider my request. I'm ignorant, not incompetent; and unsure, not weak. I learn quickly, and I learn well. I wouldn't disappoint you as a student."

The woman's dark eyes seemed to stare right through her, and Rezs shifted uncomfortably. Rezs could almost feel the other woman listen to the way Rezs said the words as much as to the words themselves. Coale's voice was quiet when she finally said, "Teaching a wolfwalker about the pack is not a task for just a few days' or ninans' journey."

Rezs shrugged. "How much time do you have?"

"How much time will you commit?" the other woman countered.

"As long as it takes. As far as it takes."

That brought a faint smile to Coale's lips. "Wolves will range a thousand kays in a year. Travel isn't something a wolfwalker can easily avoid."

"Will you go with me? Now—to the north?"

"Do you have to travel north?"

Rezs smiled faintly. "Right now, west actually, to get the firewood I dropped back there on the trail; but after that, yes, I travel north."

Elgon studied her face. "You said you were meeting someone. Is this a working trip?"

She hesitated, then made a decision. "I wanted to learn about Vlen. But I'm not going to waste the trip while I'm out here. There are fibers in the forests that the Ancients never got to discover before they lost their lives to the plague. Hundreds of plants they seeded into the soil and planned to breed for products. Mineral sites they mapped but never actually saw . . ." She began to gesture as she talked. "There are supposed to be eleven cadmium deposits in this area alone, but in all the years that the mining worms have been searching, only four small sites have ever been found. Moons know we need the metals—" She broke off. "You're staring at me," she said mildly.

Elgon shook himself. "Sorry. You just . . . sounded a lot like someone I know. Threw me for a moment."

Coale stepped forward abruptly. There was a strange note in the wolfsong that rang deep inside Rezs's skull. Then Coale took the knife from Rezs's hands and tucked it in her belt. The older woman's hands were steady as she handed Rezs her own blade. "You are welcome in our midst," the woman said formally. "You are welcome as a daughter. Ride and eat and fight with us, and your children shall be as my own."

Gray Shona threw back her head and howled. Vlen joined in. Within moments the hissing of the rain faded into the breathing of the Gray Ones, and there was nothing in Rezs's sight but yellow, gleaming eyes, and the gray-tipped fur of the wolves.

IX

The rain lightened in the forest as they slipped along the trail. Ahead and to the side, Gray Vlen loped almost silently. Rezs stared after his shadow. She didn't understand how he made his body move so quietly through the forest. She could swear by all nine moons that every twig under her feet snapped as if the wood was brittle and dry. Every wet leaf seemed intent on slapping her face. Even after the rain stopped, each branch she ducked under dropped a bead of water down her collar or inside her boots, so that she was continually chilled. And it was her, no one else, she thought with something akin to resentment. Elgon, with her firewood on his shoulder, seemed to avoid every bough. And Coale, who walked with a limp, still moved with a gracefulness Rezs could only envy, not imitate. When Rezs glanced back, the older woman seemed to fade out of the shrubs and stones like a breath of wind. She had to focus hard to see the other woman. And as for seeing the wolves—she knew Gray Shona was nearby, but she couldn't even catch a glimpse of the Gray One near the trail. The only gray-black fur she saw belonged to Vlen, and she located him by his sight, not her own.

She stretched her senses to feel the heat of the wolf cub's coat, and her chilled skin flared with a sweaty warmth. The bond was not as clear at this distance as when she looked into his eyes, but it was stronger with Coale there than it had been before, when she was alone. Yet it still wasn't a focused sense at all—not like Old Roy had described it. It was more like a soft sort of breathing that had a double-time rhythm to hers. A second beat to her heart. There was a noise in the back of her mind that sounded like the howling of the Gray Ones as heard through a handful of batting.

Vlen—She sent the mental call through her mind, to touch the thoughts of the wolf. Instantly, her sense of smell seemed to sharpen. The taste of the moist air was heavy on her tongue, and she licked the inside of her teeth, as if she could rub it off and experience it again.

Gray Vlen's head turned as he ghosted through the trees. Yellow eyes gleamed, and his teeth bared. *Run with me, Wolfwalker.*

The energy in his young voice reverberated in her skull. "You honor me, Gray One."

For a moment the bond between them tautened. Vlen's energy surged, so that it swamped her with his lupine senses, and she had to pull back to see out of her own eyes. She stumbled, caught herself, and took another whipping branch on her hip, where the slap made her hiss at her new bruise.

"When you've been together longer, you'll learn to see through his eyes more clearly."

Coale's voice was quiet, but Rezs heard it as if it had slid inside her head with the pulse of the wolf. She twisted to look at the other woman. "How did you know?" She slipped as her feet hit the trail sideways, and it took her a second to straighten out. "Can you hear me through the wolfsong?" she asked over her shoulder.

Coale shrugged. "Sometimes." She hesitated, then added almost reluctantly, "When I listen for your voice, I can feel it in Vlen's part of the packsong."

Rezs studied Coale covertly. She could tell that the woman was herself listening to the Gray Ones—Coale's eyes were almost unfocused as she looked forward at Rezs. "How long have you been"—Rezs's voice cut off with a sharp grunt as she slipped in another puddle—"been bonded to the wolves?"

"Sixty years. Give or take a few."

"Gray Ones don't live that long."

"No, but they have pups, and their pups have pups." Coale's voice was dry. "It's a rather natural progression."

"So Gray Shona is a cub of the wolf you originally ran with?"

"Grand-cub."

"Were you there when she was born?"

"Shona was fourteen when we met. She's twenty-six now."

The memory of those yellow eyes floated in Rezs's head. "From around here?" she pressed.

The other woman shrugged. "Females don't travel as much as males, but territories change, and game migrates. A single wolf can easily cover ten thousand kays in a lifetime. Sometimes, I think Shona has seen more of the nine counties than I have."

"But you've traveled with her across Randonnen."

"Randonnen, Ariye, Kiren, Bilocctar . . ."

"And before her?"

"I spent some years away from the pack."

"Completely unbonded?"

The woman nodded.

"That must have been difficult if you'd been bonded before."

"Even with distance, I could hear the pack. They haunt you, you know. Once bonded to a human, they never let go. Who you are is locked into their memories like everything else they experience—your voice, your scent, the way you run and fight and sing. You can't escape the wolves once they've chosen you. They'll chase you through your dreams."

Rezs shivered. "What about before Shona and that break? How many wolves did you run with?"

Coale didn't answer at once, and Rezs had a sudden image of older eyes—one whitened with the cataracts of age, and the other sharp and yellow as gold. It triggered something. She blinked as the night eyes from her memories shifted shape and color. When she reached automatically out to Vlen, his own yellow eyes bleared her memory.

"Only one," the woman said finally.

There was something in Coale's response that made Rezs pause—just in time to have her response slapped back in her throat with the branch that whapped across her cheeks. This time she stopped abruptly and clutched her face, cursing under her breath. When she looked back at Coale, the older woman's lips were twitching. "All right, Coale," she said sharply. "You've not been touched once by a branch or twig, and I'm getting beaten to death with every meter we run. What am I doing wrong?"

Coale called ahead to Elgon, and the man halted, turned,

and walked back to meet them. "Stop there," she told him when he had come halfway back. Then she turned to Rezs. "How far away is he from you?"

Rezs eyed the distance. "Eight and a half meters."

Coale raised her eyebrows. "Good eye."

Rezs shrugged. "I could tell you to the centimeter, if you wanted. Distance is one of the things I'm good at."

The other woman nodded. "New scouts always have a tendency to run too close to the man ahead—as if it's a race to keep the pace. You don't pay attention, and soon you're a meter closer, then another meter, until you're right behind him. Don't be caught up by that." She motioned at the red welt on Rezsia's cheek. "You do, and the branches slap back from the man ahead of you, and you catch the force of the swing like a whip."

"That, I had noticed," Rezs said sourly.

"That's why I prefer running farther back."

Absently, Rezs rubbed the welt. "What about the mud? Why don't you slip half as much as I do?"

"You watch the forest; I watch my footing. That, and I don't put my whole weight down until I feel what's beneath me."

Rezs gave her an even more sour look. "I was trying to be aware of what went on around me. You listen to the forest through Gray Shona; I was trying to do the same with Vlen."

The scout shook her head. "Your bond with Vlen is not yet strong enough to hold the looseness—not tightness—of constant communication. Shona and I have a loose bond—a link that's always open between us. It allows us both to keep in contact while we concentrate on other things."

"What about dangers like the badgerbears? Don't you lose reaction time by not keeping your attention completely on Shona?"

"We've run enough trails together that she knows the sounds and scents that I consider a danger." Coale gave her an odd look. "Just how much do you know about the wolves, Rezs?"

"I spent four days with one wolfwalker. There's another one who told me some other things, but his throat was crushed a long time ago, and it's difficult for him to talk."

"Old Roy? I've met him."

"I know more about wolves from observation, not study with the other wolfwalkers," Rezs admitted. "The Gray Ones always seemed to be around when I was out gathering materials." Coale raised her eyebrows, and Rezs shrugged uncomfortably. "I could hear them howling when no one else heard anything. And I'd swear that they came into our commons at night."

"You saw them there?"

"No, but I found prints more than once. The few times I saw them, they were outside the city. One time it was when I was swimming, and three Gray Ones came down to the water. They just sat and watched me for an hour."

"You were afraid?"

Rezs thought back. "Of all the things I remember about feeling watched by the Gray Ones, fear was not a part of it. I used to think . . ." Her voice trailed off.

"Yes?" Coale prompted.

She shrugged. "It's nothing."

"What?"

Rezs shot Coale a sidewise look.

"Tell me." The woman's voice was quiet and steady, and Rezs felt almost compelled to speak.

"I used to think they looked after me," she finally answered. "Guardians."

Rezs nodded. "Exactly like that. Once, when I was riding between one village and the next, a couple of strange riders started following me. I got nervous, and next thing I know, there's a pack of wolves on the road, keeping pace with my dnu. They stayed with me all the way to the next village. Those other riders—they stopped short of the village and rode back into the woods. I don't know if they were raiders or robbers or what, but I tell you, I was never more glad that the Gray Ones were nearby."

A gust of wind slapped water across their shoulders, and Coale wrapped her cloak more tightly around her lanky body. "We should hurry," she said as she glanced at the sky. "The rains are thinning out, but the streams will continue to swell as long as the rain continues to fall to the north. If you did camp right next to the cliffs, your gear has probably been washed all the way down the Missing River."

Rezs glanced ahead at Elgon, but the tall man was still

keeping his distance, waiting to return to the trail. She nodded at Coale, then moved to follow Elgon. This time she ran farther back, and the branches, which before had whipped her flesh, now merely waved at her passing.

Sloppy footsteps and drying skies filled Rezs's ears and eyes. Where the trees thinned out, the gray overhead did also, breaking into spots of blue, so that the air had an even heavier, muggy feel. As they got closer to Rezs's camp, small streams began to cut across the trail in roiling ribbons of muddy brown. She splashed through the first one easily; the second was deeper, and its waters reached halfway up her calves. Vlen sniffed that one with misgivings, then followed Gray Shona as the older wolf found a more narrow crossing farther up.

When Rezs got to the other side, Elgon offered her a hand up onto the crumbling bank. A moment later he offered a grip to Coale. The older woman took the grip gratefully. Coale's face was pale, Rezs realized, not flushed as was her own. She watched the older woman from under her lashes. Blurred as her eyesight was from Vlen, there were still details to see: Elgon's features really looked nothing like Coale's. Their noses were both straight, but Elgon's was heavier. His chin was more square, and the shape of his eyes was not as almond. If Coale hadn't claimed him as a grandson, Rezs wouldn't have thought them related at all. Elgon murmured something to Coale, then turned to Rezs. "Ready to go on?"

She pointed. "I can't see a trail anymore, but I'm sure my camp is that way. Shall I lead?"

"No," said Elgon flatly. "Best if I do."

Rezs didn't argue. There was something inherently comforting in seeing his tall body ahead of hers in the woods; something solid and protective in the way Gray Shona and Vlen paced to the side. She hadn't realized how lonely the forest had seemed before. The few times she had been out, she'd almost always ridden with Cal or Biran or some of her girlfriends. This time, by herself, there had been a silence in the forest—in her ears—that remained untouched by the wolfsong that rang in her head.

Fifty meters, and they came abruptly to a halt. Rezs could see a glimpse of rock to the right and the cliffs that rose behind the trees, but suddenly there was simply no more ground. The area was awash with water. A rushing, roiling brown-gray river had spouted from the cliff in the distance. The trees through which the water swept looked like pilings in a tidal bore. The tangled deadfalls were islands of brush that caught in the current and built themselves taller with each branch they caught.

Vlen, who had trotted to the edge of the water, wrinkled his nose in distaste, and Rezs almost choked with the thick smell that invaded her lungs. Instinctively, she covered her mouth and nose with her hand. The noise was not so loud that it filled her head, but with the smell Vlen sent came the sensitivity of his ears, and she found herself stumbling back.

Coale caught her arm. "Steady . . ."

Rezs stared at the wash.

"It's Vlen you're sensing," the older woman said sharply. "Tighten up your mind. Control your link."

Rezsia's eyesight blurred, and colors seemed to shift. She seemed to be too close to the ground.

"Cut off the cub. Now," Coale snapped.

"I don't know how—"

Vlen turned his head, and his yellow eyes met her violet ones. *Wolfwalker* . . . His young voice echoed in her skull, crowding out her thoughts.

She felt herself drawn back into her own mind until she seemed to crouch beside the rush of water. Her nostrils flared, and her shoulders hunched with the feeling. "You honor me," she whispered. And then Coale's voice snapped across the song of the wolves, and Vlen abruptly pulled back. The silence that echoed in Rezsia's mind was almost a physical pain. "What have you done?" she cried out.

Coale gripped her arms tightly and stared into her eyes as if she could pick out Rezsia's thoughts. For a moment Rezs struggled, but the older woman's grip was like iron, and those aged fingers seemed to press right through her flesh. Rezs forgot about the stream; forgot about the song of Vlen's voice in her mind. She stared with blind eyes at the shadowed face until her panic subsided and the other woman released her.

Rezs stumbled back, staring at Coale and rubbing her arms. "Why did you do that?" She didn't control her voice, and it rose sharply. "Have you broken our bond? Broken my link with Gray Vlen—"

Coale put her hand up as if to halt her, and Rezs closed her mouth with a snap. "Listen," Coale said. "Look back in your mind. Do you hear it—the song of the wolves?"

Rezs forced the tension to seep from her muscles. There, like a distant breeze—barely heard, but constant—the song of the wolves still rang. One voice was stronger than the others, and as she concentrated, Vlen's howl came to the fore. Slowly, she nodded.

"Vlen never left. I only pushed him back so you could think for yourself."

Vlen whined softly at her from the bank, and the hurt tone in his mental voice made her cringe. She moved to his side. Softly, she stroked his head, ignoring the wet hairs that stuck to her hand.

"But why?" she asked Coale, looking up at the other woman. "You said that seeing through Vlen's eyes was what I was supposed to do—"

"When your bond is stronger," Coale corrected sharply, "and when your will is more dominant over his—then you should practice seeing through his eyes. Until then, look through your own. A wolf will try to assert dominance over anything that is or seems weaker than itself."

Reluctantly, Rezs nodded again.

Elgon, warily giving the two wolfwalkers plenty of berth, walked slowly down along the stream, eyeing its length and breadth. He waited till the tension seemed to dissipate between Coale and Rezs, then returned and motioned toward a stand of monkeyroot trees. "Best to cross there. There will be pits where the water catches in the holes between the roots, but at least we'll have something to hang on to."

Coale nodded. Then both glanced at Rezs and waited.

Rezs raised her eyebrows. "You want my agreement?"

Elgon shrugged. "When we travel together, we make our decisions together. If you've ideas or misgivings about this crossing, now is the time to state them."

"No. I've none." She looked again at the stream. "I'm not afraid of water."

Coale gave her a sharp look. "Dark water hides its denizens like a forest does its raiders."

A drop of rain fell down Rezs's collar, and she felt a shiver crawl after it. "What kind of danger is here?" she asked slowly.

Coale's expression didn't change, but she seemed somehow pleased. "You're direct," she said flatly. "That's good." She gestured at the water. "Even shallow streams can drown you," she said. "Swift water can pull you under; a rolling log can break your legs or crush you; a dip or hole can steal your footing—" She looked suddenly upstream, to where the two wolves eyed the water. "Wait here."

As Coale moved toward her own Gray One, Rezs glanced at Elgon. "She's rather like one of those old-school fighting-ring teachers, isn't she? Waits for you to ask a question before she decides what kind of information to give out."

He shrugged again, but his brown eyes twinkled.

"So that," Rezs guessed, "was some sort of lesson, wasn't it?"

Elgon grinned faintly. "Probably, but don't ask me."

"Meaning?"

He squinted at the stream. "Meaning that I've been around Coale all my life—I've studied with her since I was fifteen— and I certainly don't always know what she means or why she does things. As for Coale herself, she's been running trail since she was born, and even she still doesn't know the depth of the wolves or the extent of the forest. Being around her is more than just a lesson in survival. It's a lesson in life."

"So what do you study with her?"

"Botany. She knows one heck of a lot about plants."

"But she's not a healer?"

"Anyone who runs trail knows some kind of crude healing skills—enough to get yourself back to town when your leg is broken, anyway," he added wryly.

"That happen to you?"

"More than once. Look, Rezs, no matter what you learn, you must remember that everything here is a lesson, and every encounter a test."

Rezs studied him carefully, listening to his voice, watching the way he moved his hands. "How do I know if I've passed the tests?"

He glanced significantly at the knife she now wore in her belt. Automatically, her hand touched its hilt. "I think," he said softly, "you know the answer to that one."

Absently, she shifted Coale's blade until it stopped poking into her ribs. The memory of the woman's hands, trembling with exhaustion and fear after the attack, was all too real. El-gon didn't have to say the words. She could almost hear his voice in her mind: You've passed if you stay alive.

He looked toward Coale and caught her signal, hefted Rezs's firewood back onto his shoulder, and gestured. "This way."

Silently, Rezs followed him downstream to a bend in the growing creek. Coale fell in behind her, and Vlen and Shona, remaining upstream, watched their progress with yellow, gleaming eyes, then trotted out of sight in search of their own crossing.

Elgon ducked under a monkeyroot branch and, gripping it tightly, eased out into the water until he could reach a tall, arching root. The dark-haired man moved smoothly across the stream, and with the water only halfway up her own calves, Rezs followed confidently, leaving only a tiny vee behind her in the water. A submerged branch hit her calf, but it swept past before it caught on her boots. She made a small sound, but Coale caught it. Rezs shrugged. "Just a branch," she told the older woman. "I'm fine."

Then she slipped off a root, into a knee-deep hole. Startled, she cried out. In her head, Vlen howled as cold water coursed over the tops of her boots. Instantly, she tightened her grip on the branch.

Wolfwalker—

Vlen— She didn't notice the edge of panic in her voice.

"Don't call the cub." Coale's voice cut in sharply over the noise of the stream. "And stay still."

Wide-eyed, Rezs looked up. "My feet are jammed together. I can't seem to unstep one for the other."

Elgon looked back, but Coale waved him on and patiently made her way over to Rezsia, who calmed her breathing as she waited. Neither Coale nor Elgon seemed to think there was danger. She just wasn't used to water except in structured swimming holes.

"Hole between the roots?" Coale asked as she reached Rezs.

Rezs nodded.

"Hold tightly on to the branch."

Rezs cast her a wry look. "Did you think I wouldn't?"

Coale chuckled. The woman's weathered hand took a grip

beside Rezs's on the branch, and a moment later Rezs felt the older woman grip her belt and lift.

"Wait a minute, Coale—you can't pull me out by yoursel—"

"Not now, Rezs," the woman said sharply. "Just get your feet free."

Quickly, with her weight lessened, Rezs wriggled one foot free. "I'm out," she asserted. Instantly, Coale released her. Rezs pulled her other foot out and felt around under the water for a better step.

"Try not to step on the roots as much as you do around them," the woman advised. "Better to step deep and solid than shallow and slick where you can be washed off in a blink."

"I'll remember."

The other wolfwalker seemed unexerted by the strain of holding Rezs up, but Rezs examined her face carefully. With the other woman's face still shaded by her cloak, it was difficult to see her expression, but Rezs didn't have the feeling that Coale was tired any longer.

Coale raised her eyebrows at Rezs's scrutiny. "You might be taller than me, Rezs, but I'm hardly so old that I can't help out where I'm needed."

"I didn't mean—"

"Yes, you did." Coale motioned for her to continue. "I'm old enough to be pleased, not insulted by your concern—although, there are scouts in Ariye who are a hundred and ninety. There's even one in Randonnen who's two hundred and twelve. As you reminded me earlier, I've got at least a hundred years to go before I become too feeble to take to the trail with the Gray Ones."

Rezs made her way under another arch of roots. "Are you from Randonnen?"

Coale shrugged noncommittally.

Rezs decided that was as close to a yes as Coale would give her. "So you know this county well?"

"As well as anyone, I suppose."

"Do you know most of the other wolfwalkers?"

Coale ducked under the arch, and her answer was lost in the rush of water.

"What?" Rezs called back.

Coale emerged from the root bed as Rezs hauled herself up

onto a meter-wide island at the base of another tree. Elgon was already across, and Rezs watched him wade out and check his belt and boots for the weapons he carried there. A moment later Coale joined Rezs on the island. At the tip of the small stand of earth, a thick branch struck and tore off a chunk of mud, which swirled away and sank. Coale gestured for them to continue.

Rezs grasped the next branch and waded back in. She was gaining confidence, and it felt good—she wondered what it would be like to do this with her brothers. "So you know the wolfwalkers in Randonnen?" she asked casually. "Tevyan, Abbrou, Soklovic, Damir, and"—she hesitated almost imperceptibly—"Dion?"

The other woman shrugged again.

Rezs kept her expression carefully neutral. "Will I meet them through the wolves?"

"When your bond with Vlen is stronger, you'll hear their voices in the packsong."

Rezs gave the other woman a speculative look. Either she was asking the wrong questions, or Coale didn't like giving out answers. She wondered what the woman would say if she asked Coale to help her find neGruli's trail. Her gaze shuttered suddenly. Who better to watch a wolfwalker than one who could hear the packsong? Set a thief to catch a thief . . . A wash of rolling pebbles struck her boots beneath the water, and she hurriedly grabbed the next arching root. Carefully, she closed down on her link to Vlen and kept her thoughts from projecting. She didn't speak again until they reached the other side.

The ground was drier here, and there was less mud on the trail. Rezs slipped only twice where seeps had begun to form. Overhead, where the trees thinned out again, she could see the wind tearing away at the clouds. As fast as the gray-white sky formed, it was shredded into blue. As fast as the branches whipped they threw off their rain in secondary showers. Rezs blinked as another spray of drops hit her face. For some reason, it seemed to take twice as long to get back to her camp as it had to leave it. It didn't seem to bother Vlen; the young Gray One was already teasing the older wolf mercilessly, romping around her grayed hindquarters and throwing himself on his back in the mud when Gray Shona nipped him smartly. Rezs caught herself grinning at his antics, even at that distance.

But she lost her grin when they reached her campsite—or what was left of it. Brown water rushed through the trees that had surrounded her sleeping spot, and the roiling expanse spread out from the cliffs and across the ground like a river. Stupidly, Rezs stared at her clearing. No longer was there sandy soil. The torrent sprang from the rocks like water from a spigot and covered the ground as if it had always been there. There was no sign of her dnu, her firepit, her pack, or her bedding—everything was gone except the river that now raced in its place.

Abruptly, she pushed past Elgon, but he grabbed her arm. "Watch your step," he said sharply. "This stream is deeper than the last, and there's more debris in the water."

"My dnu— My gear—"

"We told you it was gone."

She shook him off. "My dnu was tethered here. He could be tangled in the water or brush—"

"Dnu don't mind rain, but they certainly don't like water." Elgon gestured sharply at the water. "He'd have pulled his line and run off the moment the water started running past his hooves."

"But my gear— It can't all be washed away—"

"Look at the water, Rezs. The standing waves are tall; the troughs are deep and wide. It takes a massive volume of water to create those shapes. Your gear was probably washed away hours ago while you were out exploring."

She searched the stream with her eyes. "Maybe some of it is caught in the roots. Maybe it's right here—just submerged."

"And maybe it's spread out for kilometers downstream. You want to go swimming in this to find out?"

She forced herself to take a breath. "No," she said finally. "But there's got to be something left." She stared at Elgon. "By the second moon, you're laughing at me, aren't you? It took me a year to collect that gear, and you find it funny that it's washed away."

Elgon tried to keep a straight face. "Well, you have to admit that on a rainy night, setting up camp in a dry streambed is just a bit shortsighted."

"Moonwormed bones of a swaybacked dnu," she muttered.

"I've never been out here before. How was I to know it was a river waiting to happen?"

Coale joined them on the bank, and Rezs glanced at her. "I suppose this is funny to you, too."

The older woman shrugged; Rezs had the impression that beneath the hood of her cloak, her dark eyes twinkled.

"Did you look at that cave before you parked yourself in front of it?" Elgon asked. "Or examine the ground? Didn't you notice how clean it was? How . . . scoured?"

Rezs sighed in disgust. "Yes, yes. But that's partly why I chose it. There weren't any spider nests or centipede holes; there weren't any cavebleeders up in the rocks . . ." Her voice trailed off at their expressions. "I understand now," she said irritably. "It was scoured clean because it's a water conduit. But that doesn't help me regain my gear now."

The other woman glanced at the sky. "It's stopped raining here, but it will still be falling to the north, and the water from the highlands will continue to vent through these cliffs for days."

Elgon tried unsuccessfully to swallow his grin. "You'd better figure on replacing your gear at the next town. Unless you want to wait for the water level to drop, I don't see how you'll recover anything here for a ninan."

"A *ninan*?"

He nodded. "Next time, when you find a nice, flat spot for a camp, lust after it all you want, but put your pack on high ground."

"I haven't time to wait for the river to run itself out." She stepped close to the edge of the water. "Look where those trees have washed together. Can you see it? The blue tip just barely sticking out above the water? I think that's my bow."

"I see it." He studied the flood. "But there's a town barely a day and a half away. Between Coale and me, we can keep you comfortable enough to reach it, and you can then replace your things there."

"It's not my comfort I'm worried about," she returned sharply. "It's my work."

Coale gave her a thoughtful look, and Elgon raised his eyebrows.

"Look, I don't mind replacing my gear in town," she explained. "But I can't replace my work samples—it takes too much time to prepare the gels and papers, and it's already taken me four days to get this far. Going back, having more samples prepared, and coming all the way back here would take me more than a ninan."

Elgon studied her. "If time is so important, why didn't you just cut through the last town instead of going around?"

Rezs kept her expression calm. "Because I wanted to spend some time alone with Vlen. But I'm supposed to meet Bany and the others today. I don't have time to run back and forth again—" She halted. "How did you know," she asked slowly, "that I went around the last town instead of through it?"

Coale shrugged lightly. "Vlen and Shona have been singing the packsong together for several nights now. It was hard to mistake Vlen's path."

Rezs nodded slowly, but she had the feeling that the woman was weighing her words carefully and listening with more than her ears to the way Rezs responded. Suddenly uneasy, Rezs shifted away. She tried to read the truth of Coale's words through her bond from Vlen to Gray Shona, but all she felt of the other wolf was a pair of yellow eyes that gleamed faintly in her mind.

"My sword and other gear might have washed away," she said finally, turning back to the stream. "But my pack and bow were tied up on two trees to keep them off the ground. I can see the tip of my bow over there, so the pack has to be nearby."

Elgon eyed the flood. "Even if it was, your samples would be ruined by the water and mud."

"They were sealed in waterproof glass. The pack has to be here," she insisted. "I tied it securely to that tree."

"You remember which one?"

"That one. Right over . . . there . . ." Her voice trailed off. There was no tree where she pointed.

Elgon followed her gesture. "Where the water is thickest?"

"The tree probably fell," said Coale. "Look at the brush downstream—the branches all point the same way, and that root mass over there doesn't have enough weathering to have been there long." She shrugged at Rezs's expression of disgust. "The topsoil here is thin, and many of the trees—the chanwas and the trillo trees—have shallow roots. Wind or water can tear them up."

"Well, we've certainly got the water." Rezs's voice was sour.

"Give up?" Elgon suggested.

"I've never quit anything in my life," Rezs said shortly. "I'll be damned if I quit this either without at least trying to get back that gear."

"That's a lot of hope to pin on a fallen tree."

"It's barely fifteen meters of water. I'll wade or swim or crawl out to those samples if I have to. But I'm not leaving without them."

Elgon glanced at Coale, and the older woman sighed.

"Give in?" Rezs couldn't resist teasing.

"All right," Elgon conceded. "We'll try it."

"Me. Not we—" Rezs began.

But Coale put her hand on Rezs's arm. "You and I will stay here. Elgon will go and look for a way to cross to the bow."

Rezs glanced down at the other woman's hand. In her head, Vlen began to growl. Another gray voice seemed to respond, clipping across that of the cub.

"Don't," Coale said softly.

Rezs stared at her. For a moment there was a sense of tension in her head—as if the bond between her and Vlen was being pulled in both directions. Then she felt Gray Vlen beside her, and her hand dropped to his scruff.

Coale's voice was still soft. "This is not a question of control, Rezs, but one of practicality. You haven't the weight or the strength to stay upright in this flood."

Rezs could see the woman's lips moving, but she heard that soft voice more in her head than through her ears. "It's my gear. I'll get it," she heard her own voice answer.

Coale didn't drop her hand from Rezs's arm, and the pressure of the other woman's fingers began to make Rezs's skin tingle all the way up to her skull. In her head, Vlen's snarl became a song. She felt her neck tense as he howled along the faint thread of music.

"There's a balance to strength, Rezs. Too much independence, and you grow so far away from others that you're no use in any team. You can destroy yourself with pride. Too much dependence, and you'll never be more than someone else's toy. The wolfpack, Rezs, is the balance. Each one strong; all working together. This is Elgon's turn, not yours, to lead."

Rezs felt a pull in her mind—as if she tried to turn inside her skull. The wolfsong in her head was still loud, and the power of Coale's grip was almost hypnotizing. She forced her lips to move. "Can any wolfwalker do that?"

Coale looked blankly at Rezs for a moment. "Cross a stream?"

Rezsia looked deliberately down at the woman's grip on her arm. "The power. I can feel it in your grip."

As abruptly as if dark cut across the sky, the tingling ceased. Rezs almost staggered with the absence of it. The hand that gripped her arm then was solid, but there was no sense of anything else, and Rezs stared up at Coale.

The other woman didn't seem to notice. She steadied Rezs as if it were perfectly normal for a young woman to nearly faint, and then gestured for Rezs to follow her to a sitting log. For a moment Rezs resisted, then gave in. "I still think I should do it," she said tightly.

Elgon gave her a hard glance. She swallowed her words, but couldn't help the tightening of her lips. He did not miss it. "Since we've been here," he said coldly, "the water has risen two more fingers' width on the trees. You lose your footing in that, and you'll be swept away like a straw and bashed against every root and rock underwater. Don't kid yourself, Rezs. You don't even know how to walk in the woods, let alone wade through a water run like this."

She glanced down at her boots, still new-shiny between the cave scuffs. "You've made your point," she said softly.

"Good." He turned back to the water and began to uncoil his rope. "Now, where was the tree you marked with your bow?"

Silently, she pointed. The tiny blue point of the tip of her bow bobbed in the tangle of deadwood. Dark vees of water trailed downstream from each trunk, and as she watched, the branches shifted and trembled with the force of the water.

Her work, she thought. Gone with a single rain. And she needed those samples to test whatever fungi she found at neGruli's source. If Bany thought that they had only a decent chance of finding neGruli's trail by leaving now, what chance would they have if she lost those samples and took a ninan to replace them? Slim? None? If they had to wait another six months for neGruli to take a trip out before they could track him again, there would be thirty more families on the streets, and neGruli would be well settled in council. It would take a plague to touch him then. Everything they had fought for— everything they had planned . . . She clenched her fists. Gray Vlen whined softly in his throat. Her nails cut into her palm, and she stared down at the wolf. Vlen's yellow eyes met hers, and her vision blurred. She saw herself from his eyes; watched her lips move as she spoke. "I cannot lose those samples . . ."

Wolfwalker, Vlen sent. His muscles tensed as she gripped his fur. He gathered his weight on his haunches and sprang from under her grip, out into the water.

X

"Vlen, no!"

Like a flash, Coale twisted at Rezs's voice and, almost before the woman looked, leaped after the cub. Coale's hands closed on air. Vlen's splash was drowned by the sound of the stream, but his sudden panic was like a shout in Rezsia's mind as he tumbled instantly beneath the waves. Rezs screamed out—half in her mind, half out loud—as water seemed to choke her nose and the silent terror of the cub filled her mind as no wolf howl had done before.

Elgon lunged after his grandmother. From the side, he caught the edge of Coale's jerkin and, without hesitating, followed her momentum to sling her about and around like a sack of tubers. For a moment the older woman hung out over the roiling water. Then Coale hit back on the bank with a solid smack, almost knocking Rezsia over.

Coale snapped, scrambling to her feet, "Elgon, the rope!" She grabbed Rezs by her arm and dragged her downstream, sprinting and slipping in the mud as she fought to keep the cub in sight. "Hurry!"

Rezs jerked as Vlen was slammed into a root mass. His limbs were pinned by the stream. Stones pelted him like rain as the water forced itself past his body. His small lungs sucked for air. "Vlen!" Rezs screamed.

Coale shoved her against a tree and placed Rezs's hands on the bark as if that contact would keep Rezs safe from the stream. Elgon threw the bulk of the rope at Coale and hurriedly knotted one end around his middle. "Where is he?" he snapped at Rezs.

"There— There, just at the surface—"

"At the streaktree?" He threw off his bow and quiver and thrust them into the crotch of a low tree.

"No— The base of the root mass. He's in the roots—"

"I see him." He thrust his sword into a joint in the tree. "Get back from the edge."

"Coale—" She turned in a panic.

"Get back here," the woman snapped. "I need your help with the rope."

Rezs could almost feel the woman stretch out to the Gray Ones, and she hesitated, reaching out to Vlen. She didn't know that she almost lunged toward the edge of the stream. She snarled as she was thrown suddenly back. It wasn't Coale—it was Gray Shona beside her, shoving, almost herding, her back to the other woman. Rezs hissed at the creature and lunged around those massive, graying shoulders, but the old wolf shouldered her brutally, turning her back to Coale by slamming into her thighs.

Elgon poised on the bank, staring at the stream as if he memorized its waves. "Set?" he snapped at Coale. The older woman braced one foot against the base of a tree and took the line in one hand. Rezs could feel the wolfwalker's voice like steel in the graysong that howled in her head. The woman sat back on the rope to snap the line taut between them. "Set," she snapped in return.

The moment Elgon stepped into the stream, he was beaten to his knees. Pebbles rained through the water, tumbling and slamming against his shins, then his thighs. He barely got a handhold on a root before he went completely under.

"Rezs," Coale said sharply. "Look at me."

She shook her head, her eyes locked on the stream.

"Rezs," the woman urged, "you must control the cub. When Elgon reaches him, Vlen will panic. The cub will try to kick free, and he's got to stay with Elgon or he'll be swept downstream and beaten to death on the rocks." The woman eased out a meter of line as Elgon regained his feet. "Rezs," she said harshly, "look at me!"

Rezs tore her gaze from the stream. She didn't realize her hands were clenched together. "How?" she returned. She did not recognize her voice. "How do I control him?"

"Think what you want him to do. I can reach him only

through Shona. You can reach him directly. Think to him. Tell
him to stay calm. Tell him you're coming."

"But it's Elgon who's wading out—"

"It doesn't matter who's doing it," Coale snapped. "Just
think it." She jerked up against the tree as Elgon slipped again.
Using her body as a pulley, she let out another meter of line.
"Do it," she snarled. "Keep him calm. And lay out that line behind me."

Hanging between the stream and the woman, Rezs hesitated. Shona bared her teeth until her black nose creased with
the snarl of her threat. Rezs let out a half-strangled howl, then
grabbed the mass of rope at Coale's feet.

Gray One, she sent in her head. *Vlen—don't panic. I'm
coming.*

Wolfwalker—

His mental voice was cold and sharp with fear. Water
surged into his face, so that he swallowed and choked on it.
She could taste it herself on her tongue. She could feel her
muscles strain and jerk with every stone that slammed him.
She could feel her back bruise as his body pressed into the
roots. A surge in the flood loosened the hold of the roiling
stream, and Rezs screamed at him to stay where he was. More
than one pair of yellow eyes seemed to burn through her brain.

Elgon reached the root mass and struggled to get in front of
it. The current stripped his footing away again, driving him
back to his knees. Water surged and blinded him. He threw
back his head to get a breath, and with one hand on a branch
and the other groping in the water, he forced his way forward.
Half a meter, then another. His hands plunged into the water.
He grasped thick fur.

"That's him!" Rezs screamed. "You've got him." She
dropped the rope. "Pull him up—"

"Rezs, no! Stay here—"

She didn't hear Coale as she flung herself at the edge of the
flood. It was Shona who caught her on the bank and closed
sharp teeth in Rezsia's jerkin. She was brought up short, slipping to her knees in the mud. Twisting, jerking against the
wolf, they tangled for a moment, until suddenly Shona's yellow eyes met hers. There was an instant of shock, and then
Coale's voice seemed to slam into her mind.

Hold her, the woman sent urgently to the wolf.

I have her fur in my teeth, Shona sent back.

Rezs froze, one hand on the rope, as if she thought she could haul the cub and the man in by herself. In her head, the gray voice was deep and resonant, and the wolfsong suddenly a thick tension. Threads of voices hung like urgent music, and eyes—gray human and yellow lupine—pierced her mind. Her sight was locked on the gaze of the wolf. The bond between Coale and the Gray One was like some kind of cable, twisted of emotions and memories she didn't understand. Strong as love and loose as trust, Shona's bond swamped her link with Vlen until both she and the cub were pulled in through that contact. The graysong swelled. Strength seemed to flow from Shona to Vlen. Then Shona's eyes flicked toward the stream, and the contact was broken.

Rezs's head rang with emptiness. *Vlen,* she sent in sudden panic.

The cub howled in her head. Her link with him was thin, even through his fear, and she hauled on that as if to bind him to her so that not even the flood could tear him away. In the river, the tall man had twisted, so that his legs were braced against the roots where Vlen was pinned. Then he dug his hands into thick fur and heaved. Like a sodden towel, the cub came free, heavy and awkward in the water. For a moment Elgon bowed with his weight, then he lifted the struggling cub and braced the wolf's body between himself and the trees. A tumbling log smashed into the roots beside them, then swept past. Elgon didn't seem to notice.

Wolfwalker—

Vlen's voice was full of fear, and Rezs's legs jerked as the cub scrabbled for footing against Elgon's thighs and she hauled herself abruptly to her feet. *I'm here,* she sent. *Don't struggle.* Her fingers curled into fists. She tried to steady her thoughts. *Vlen, trust the man. Don't fight him. Elgon will bring you back—*

The tall man heaved the cub up so that Vlen's forelegs hung over his shoulder. A moment later he twisted, so that the water struck his hip.

"Rezs," Coale shouted harshly, "get back here and help me bring them in."

Blindly, Rezs turned at the other woman's voice. Her eyes were unfocused, and her hands clenched into her own jerkin so that she crumpled the leather like cotton. Mud scent, stream scent—the smell of sweat in her nose . . . And then Gray Shona's fangs came out of the shadows like a worlag.

Back, snapped the Gray One in her mind. Her gleaming fangs closed on Rezs's arm, shocking her. Stiff-legged and snarling, the massive wolf stood between stream and Rezs with her scruff bristling like a brush as if to challenge Rezsia's will. *Back—*

Rezs jerked free and stared at the yellow eyes.

Take the rope in your paws. Shona's voice was firm as it rang in Rezsia's skull.

Blindly, she touched the rope. It was slick and coarse, like fresh burlap, and it burned her fingers when Coale hauled in. Stumbling, she followed it back to the other woman, then moved to the other end of the rope and grabbed it.

Coale glanced at her face. "Brace yourself as I do. If I lose my grip, you'll have to hold them."

Rezs nodded and copied the woman's movements. She moved to the opposite side of the tree and set her feet against the trunk. Like Coale, she then sat back on the rope until she felt it cut into her behind. Then, as Coale pushed herself away from the tree to take up half a meter, Rezs braced for the weight of the line.

"Got it?"

"Yes."

"Then hold it there. The current will swing them to shore."

"They'll be half-drowned—"

"They're that now," Coale returned dryly.

Out in the water, Elgon looked over his shoulder, waited for another twisted branch to wash past, then shoved off from the root mass. Instantly, his footing was swept away. Rezs cried out as Vlen submerged again.

"Stay calm," Coale snapped. "They're fine."

"You can feel him?"

"As well as you. Watch. They're already halfway here. Just hold on."

Vlen's head, then Elgon's, broke the surface as they fetched up against another tree. Both women jerked as the rope bent around a trunk and the man and wolf fetched up short.

"They're tangling—"

"Elgon knows how to stay clear."

"That's easy for you to say," Rezs snapped. "That's my wolf out there."

"And my grandson."

Coale's own voice was harsh, and Rezs swallowed her retort. The tall man fought to the front of the tree and let himself be whipped around with the current that washed past it. The rope jerked again as the stream picked him up and tumbled him and his cargo.

Coale kept her eyes on the pair struggling through the water. "You're caught up in the bond," she said shortly. "In time, you'll learn which emotions are yours and which are his, and how to keep yourself separate."

Elgon reached a shallow spot and rested for a moment before plunging back into the thigh-deep flood. A few moments later he thrust the cub on the bank and hauled himself out. Rezs dropped the line and sprinted to Vlen, but Coale did not let go until Elgon had crawled a meter from the edge.

"Vlen," Rezs whispered, throwing her arms around him. The yearling stank of muddy water, but she didn't care. The tremble in his limbs mirrored hers, and his panting breaths were no faster than her own. When he twisted his head to lick her ear, she almost cried. She held out her hand to Elgon. "Thank you."

On his hands and knees, he looked up. "You . . . honor me, Wolfwalker."

Some part of her mind noticed that his leather jerkin and trousers were dark and dripping with water, and that both hung from his hard body like overstretched skin. Some other part noted the texture of his voice as he spoke. But what caught and held her gaze was not the determination he still radiated, nor the strength in his long limbs, but the tawny flecks in his brown eyes, which caught the light from the sky. And the expression he wore was a wary reserve at odds with the speed of his rescue. For a moment Rezs could not respond. Then, slowly, she nodded.

Gray Vlen licked her again, and she sucked in a breath so full of his scent that she nearly choked on the smell. "I almost lost you," she told the cub. Her hands stroked and checked him, seeking out his new bruises. Ribs, hips, legs—everything had been struck by stones or branches.

Coale worked her way toward the shore as she coiled the

rope that lay across the mud. By the time the woman greeted her grandson, the man had unknotted the line from his waist and gotten to his feet.

"All right?" Coale's voice was soft.

"Bit of bruising," he admitted. "The debris is pretty heavy. Should be a little better upstream."

Coale handed him the rope, then squatted beside Rezs and Vlen.

The cub looked up and began to growl, low in his throat. The older woman ignored him. Rezs's lips tightened at the expression in Coale's eyes, while behind Coale, the torrent rushed past like rage.

For a moment the wolfwalker didn't speak. Slowly, Vlen subsided, so that his growl was almost inaudible. Coale stretched out her fist to the cub and let him sniff it. Then she said, "Do you understand, Rezs, why Gray Vlen jumped in the water?"

Rezs stretched to feel Vlen, but he was already in her mind, his voice soft as a hundred-year quilt. He was reading her, she realized. Somehow, in his fear, he had drawn them closer together. The thread of their bond was gaining strength.

"He jumped in the stream," she said slowly, "because I wanted my work samples."

"You drove him to seek them out."

"I didn't know—"

Coale's voice was flat. "You projected your emotions so strongly that, through your link to him, they became his emotions—his needs."

"I didn't know he would react that way."

The anger in Coale's voice was beginning to seep through. "A bond with a Gray One is not some kind of conversation, Rezs. Wolves don't understand the words you think, but the images you project. To project the kind of need—desire—you sent to him upstream is to make him nothing more than an extension of yourself. It's one thing when you need his help. But never, *never*"—she emphasized—"when there is risk only to him." Her gesture included the cub and Elgon. "You must learn to control yourself before you use the bond between you and Vlen for anything but communication. If you can't learn that control, then go back to the city where you can't hurt him till you gain better discipline."

"No," Rezs said sharply. "I must go north—" She broke off. "I'm sorry. I will learn here—I *am* learning here. Look, Coale, I understand your anger at me—"

Coale looked startled. "I'm not angry with you—" she began.

"I can feel it as clearly as if you slapped me," Rezs returned. "I nearly lost Vlen through my own stupidity, and all I can say is that I am learning as much about this bond with Vlen as I am about the forest—and you know how ignorant I am about that."

For a moment Coale was silent. "I'm not angry with you, Rezs," the woman repeated finally. "I'm angry with myself for assuming that you knew how your emotions would affect your Gray One. Had you lost Vlen—"

"It wouldn't have been your fault, but mine." Rezsia looked at Coale steadily. "I asked you to teach me, Coale. I didn't make you responsible for me. Something I noticed a long time ago is that when you want to learn something, people treat you as if you're young—as if you're some kind of schoolchild. I'm not a child, Coale. I'm an adult, with an adult-sized brain. I don't need you to protect me. I only need you to teach me." She glanced at Vlen. "And perhaps, to soften the blow of my ignorance so that Vlen and I survive this trip together."

Coale regarded her thoughtfully. Finally she said, "You turn emotions well, Rezsia Monet maDeiami."

The way Coale said her name brought a sharpness to the gray fog that still cluttered her brain, and Rezs stared at the other woman. Yet even though she sensed that Elgon barely respected her, she had a feeling that Coale again approved.

The older woman nodded slowly. "You've turned my anger at myself into acceptance of your desire to learn. You're sensitive to emotions. Have you never thought of becoming a healer?"

"No." Her voice had been curt, and Coale studied her for a moment. Rezs looked down at her hands, covered in mud and wet hair. "Healers have obligations I don't wish to take on," she said finally.

"Your grandmother, Ember Dione, is a healer."

"She is." Rezs halted and gave Coale an odd look. "How do you know that—that Dione is my grandmother?"

"Your mother's family name—Monet Deiami. Monet is

mated with Olarun Aranur neBentar. Olarun is the second son of Aranur Bentar neDannon, weapons master of the Ramaj Ariye." The woman shrugged. "Aranur's mate is the healer, Dione. So if you are Monet's daughter, you are the granddaughter of the Healer Dione."

Rezs didn't say anything for a moment. "I am," she admitted finally.

"You could ask her if the obligations are worth it."

"I don't know her."

Absently, Coale watched Elgon retrieve his bow and quiver from the trees. "But you want to meet her."

"Maybe. But if I do, it will be some other time. Right now I'm meeting some friends and searching for new materials."

"And something else?"

Coale's voice was soft, but Rezs gave the woman a sharp look. She could almost feel the probing in the woman's words. "Doesn't everyone search for something else—something more than themselves?"

Coale got to her feet. "Perhaps." She looked down at Rezs. "But perhaps it is yourself you look for, not what you think is beyond it." She motioned to Elgon to move back upstream toward the cliffs.

Rezs stared after her in silence.

XI

Three of the nine moons hid behind the thinning thunder-heads, while the seventh moon hung on the edge of a cloud pack. Rezsia stared at the sky as it cleared further. She could see Elgon from the corner of her eye as he uncoiled the rope and laid it out carefully on the ground. When she let herself float in the graysong that filled the back of her mind, she could feel Gray Shona through Vlen as the older wolf sniffed through the forest with Coale.

Before her, the stream water was deeper by another handspan, just as Elgon had predicted. The trees that held her gear looked like a tangled stand of thin timber, while the water that streaked past the trunks shoved the branches more closely together with each half hour that passed. The tip of her bow, still caught on one of the branches, poked out of the rushing water, caught in a glistening shadow.

Beside her, Gray Vlen whined and pressed against her thigh, but after she had been shoved around by the strength of Shona, his young weight felt thin and unsubstantial. Gently, she stroked his head. She could still smell the stream through his nose; still catch a glimpse of the water through his eyes. His fear had tightened the bond between them, so that the taste of him lingered in her mind. He whined again, softly, and she knelt to meet his yellow eyes. "Gray One," she whispered. "You touch my mind like a fog—you creep in until I am sur-rounded by your senses."

Elgon pulled a collapsed grappling hook from his pack, snapped it together, tied the line onto its end, and gave it a practice twirl. "You sure about this?" he asked Rezs one more time.

She nodded. "I need that gear. If there's any chance that I can get it back . . ." She shrugged.

The tall man nodded. He hefted the hook, glanced at the line to make sure it would come smoothly out of the coil, then began whirling the hook overhead. Just before it tangled in the trees behind him, he let it fly. Like an air snake, it spun out. Then it crashed down into the brush and tangled a few meters from her bow. Elgon tugged on it gently, then with more force. He scowled.

"It is set?"

He shrugged. "Pretty flimsy hold. I'll let it sit there a bit. Either the force and debris of stream will set it harder, or it will help to knock it free."

Rezs couldn't help the hunger in her gaze, and Vlen's lips curled back. She could hear the mental snarl that entered his voice. *Your need,* he sent, *is like a gnawing in my belly.*

"It's my need, not yours," she told him flatly. "The hunger is in your mind."

He panted, watching her with those yellow gleaming eyes, and for a moment she felt herself in two places at once.

"Gray One," she told him softly. "I don't know how to keep my emotions separate from you. Don't let me push you back into the water."

But the scent images he sent her were of old wet wood, mud, and the sweet, apple scent of shrub grasses. He pulled away, his ears flicking toward the forest. *You are needed.*

Rezs eyed Elgon, then the forest, warily. "So Coale called us through you? Why didn't she just give a shout?"

Yellow eyes gleamed. *It's the way of the pack, Wolfwalker. We don't howl through the throat on the hunt.* And with that, he faded into the trees, so that only a moving shadow marked his passage.

"Moonwormed mutt," she muttered. She glanced at Elgon. "Coale seems to be calling me," she told him.

He nodded, and Rezs hesitated again. Then she shrugged and went after Vlen. The cub's path took him over logs and around the shallow puddles that Rezsia had to climb or splash through. When she finally caught up with the cub, it was a moment before she saw Coale. The woman's worn clothing faded so perfectly into the forest that only her movement showed her position.

"Here," Coale called softly.

Vlen was already gone, moving away with Shona. There was an odd sense of subtle snarling in her mind, and she pressed her hands to her temples before she realized that the two wolves were singing their packsong together.

She shook her head to rid her sight of the yellow tinges from Vlen, and moved clumsily toward the older woman. "What is it?" she asked as she squatted beside the wolfwalker.

Coale pointed. "Delion—one of the extractor plants. You're familiar with it?"

"In its cultivated form."

"The wild plant is more potent, but also more bitter. What I meant was to ask if you know how to cook with it—how to use it to remove the toxins from the indigenous plants."

Rezsia nodded. "I prefer the lesopa extractor, but I've used both the powdered and grain form of delion—it was one of the few things my father taught me about the forest."

Her voice was not bitter, merely matter-of-fact, but Coale shot her a sharp look. "Your father didn't enjoy the forest?"

She shrugged.

"But you are a wolfwalker."

Rezs hid her disgust as Coale shook the curled-up parasite slugs from the rootball of the plant. "It was hard for him to accept. The day I told him I'd bonded with Vlen, he could hardly speak to me. Then he packed up and disappeared. We haven't heard from him since."

"But you aren't angry."

"I was, at first," she admitted. "But not now. I think he's afraid that, like they did to the Healer Dione, the Gray Ones will destroy the ties I have to my family."

The woman sat back on her heels. Her face was expressionless. "He thinks the Gray Ones took his mother from him? He still hates her for that?"

Rezs shrugged.

"And you? Do you hate her also?"

Rezs sat for a moment on her heels. "Hate is a strong word, Coale. I don't know my grandmother. I can't know why she did what she did then or does now what she does." She glanced at the other woman. "You're a wolfwalker, and Elgon said you've traveled all over the nine counties. Have you met her—the Healer Dione?"

"Dione knows almost all the wolfwalkers." Coale handed her the rootball. "You'll need another seven or eight plants."

Rezs took the extractor with distaste. For all that she worked with plants like these, she preferred them already gardened. She hated having to pick the parasites off. "Why so many? I can replenish my extractors at the next town—when I replace the rest of my gear."

"Always carry a full pack of extractors," Coale said flatly. "As long as you move off the rootroads, you can expect to have to eat indigenous food, and that means you need these plants to remove the toxins during cooking. Never," she emphasized, "expect to reach your destination on time. No one patrols the forests except the Gray Ones, and there are dangers other than badgerbears to waylay you on the trail."

Rezs ripped another plant from the ground and shook off its rootball. "You talk an awful lot about dangers, Coale."

For a moment the other woman said nothing. Then: "This planet didn't evolve with human life in mind. Don't expect it to grant you any favors in survival. Like the Ancients who first landed on this world, you haven't lived with the wilderness enough to understand what constitutes a threat. Your partner could brush against a fruga bush and bring a host of eye mites back to you, blinding you within a year. Your wolf could contract an ibakka fungi and spread it to you when he licks your hand. The trail you think is perfectly clear could hide a poolah just waiting for you to step close. Everything and everyone out here is a threat. And the more innocuous it seems, the more warily you should treat it."

Rezs studied the way Coale favored her right side. "Is that why you travel with Elgon?"

The older woman's expression softened. "Elgon travels with me because he doesn't believe my aging bones can take care of themselves." She motioned at the sodden forest. "Get the roots you need, then join us on the bank. Elgon should have the line ready by then."

Rezs watched her move away in silence. There was something wolflike about the woman, something in the way she moved—like the wind itself, slipping between the trees without ever seeming to touch the branches, leaving the grass barely bent. Curious, Rezs stood and followed her path. Instinctively, her nostrils flared as she bent to study the ground where Coale had strode, but Vlen was far away, and the scents that filled her nose were not of the mud before her, but of rabbit, wet and warm in the rain.

Looking down again, she realized that the other wolfwalker had stepped either on stone, or where the mud was hardest. There were no deep prints in the mud other than Rezs's clumsy steps; the broken twigs on one side of the path were from her own slip on her way in to this tiny clearing. "At least I can't get lost," she muttered sourly. "I just follow my own prints back to the stream. They're deep enough to swim in."

By the time she was working on uprooting the last plant, her digging stick had broken until it was too short to do more than score the mud, and the bough she tried to replace it with was too green to snap off. She didn't use her knife—if Coale or Elgon had caught her stabbing the blade into the ground, there'd have been no end of tirade, of that she was sure. She'd been around weapon masters before: They were fanatical about their steel. She rubbed her bruised ribs uncomfortably, then dug her hands into the sodden soil with an expression of disgust. She got the plant out with a glop of mud, then absently slapped at a gnat on her neck. Mud splattered across her collar.

"Aw, hell . . ." She drew her hand back and stared at what was left of the broken tendril roots of the plant. "You never said it would be like this," she said sourly to the two moons overhead. "You said nothing about mud and slugs and rootballs. Didn't mention flash floods or blisters or rain." She wiped her hands on her shorts. "And I could swear by all nine of you that you never, *never* said anything about badgerbears and spring. And don't laugh at me," she snapped. "It's only clean up there in your sky because you just rained yourselves out. I'm the one stuck in your mud. Moonwormed backbiters," she cursed as she waved her arm at the growing cloud of biters. "And you"—she shook her fist at the sky—"keep your rain to yourself."

"You really think they'll listen?"

Rezs scrambled to her feet, slipped, and straightened in a flash.

Elgon's lips twitched. Coale had said it would take Rezs a

few ninans to get used to the forest, but the old wolfwalker had no idea. There were smears across Rezs's forehead and under her nose where she had wiped her face without thinking. Her bare legs were as brown as the leather of her footgear. Her new clothes, so clean before, were now almost black with filth.

Rezs glanced down at herself, then looked cross-eyed at her own nose. She could see a blotch of brown across the tip of her nose, while her boots were so clumped up with mud, they looked twice their normal size. "Get your laughs in now," she told the tall man shortly. "In a month it won't be me who's looking like this anymore."

He pulled a small cloth from his pocket. "Don't think a month will teach you to keep out of the mud." He tossed her the cloth. "Never met a wolfwalker yet who could stay clean when his Gray One called."

Rezs wiped her cheeks and nose with the cloth, making a face as she ground the grit into her lips with the motion. She pointed at the small pile of rootballs. "I'm done, but I don't have anything to carry them in."

"Just bundle them with some linegrass. They have to be exposed anyway until they dry. You can carry them over your shoulder."

She glanced around the forest, then back to Elgon. "Where do I find linegrass?"

He pointed at her feet. "You're standing on it."

"Oh." She moved quickly to the side. "This?"

He nodded. "I thought you were a biologist."

"Sort of. A biochemist, actually. I rarely see whole plants."

He showed her how to twist the grasses together and bind the rootballs so that they formed a figure eight. "Put them over your shoulder," he advised. "If you're going to carry something around here, let it be a weapon."

"I got the lecture already from Coale." She gave him a lopsided smile.

He didn't return it. "Where is it—your knife?"

She followed his gaze to her empty belt. "Just over there." She pointed vaguely. "I'll get it in a second."

But he took a step forward. Abruptly, he gripped her arms so hard she cried out. "If I were a badgerbear, what would you do?"

She didn't think to struggle. Instead, she stared at him. "Probably scream," she snapped.

"That's right. Because you wouldn't have a knife. No sword, no bow, no blade at all. Just your wimpy little fingernails against my hide." He released her, almost shoving her toward the dropped blade. "Don't ever—*ever*—set your blade out of reach again. If you have a sword, you wear it, Rezs. If you have a bow, you don't leave it behind. If you walk out of your camp, your weapons go with you. When you sleep, they're beside you. When you run, they're in your hands. Never think the forest is safe, Rezs. You're just another meal for its fangs."

For a moment Rezs stared at him. His square jaw was tight, and behind the coldness of his voice was anger and something else. It wasn't disgust for her stupidity. It wasn't a sense of pity for her ignorance. It was . . . fear. Like Cal, when he heard about the blader, this man felt the anger-fear combination of family. She wondered what she meant to him—what person she represented.

Slowly, she turned and retrieved the knife from the log on which it rested. Thoughtfully, she tucked it back in her belt. She didn't speak as she followed him soberly back to the stream. She studied him covertly, but could no longer see the emotion in his eyes when he turned to caution her. He had closed himself off and, except for a muttered explanation when they skirted a deepening mudpool, said nothing at all on the way. Her eyes sharpened suddenly, and absently she touched her neck. It struck her that the thread of music she had heard in her mind the night she kissed the blader—that thread had shut itself off the same way as Elgon did now. If someone had followed her to neGruli's warehouse, why not, as the elder had said, also out of town? She chewed her lip thoughtfully, but said nothing, and Elgon didn't seem to notice.

Coale was waiting at the flood bank, and the woman nodded as they approached. "The line shifted twice, but it's still set," she said to Elgon, pointing with her chin at the rope that stretched between her and the flooded stand of trees.

He squinted at the trees, then moved to the line and tugged on it twice. "It won't take my weight. I'd break half that mass free and send the whole thing downstream."

Rezs tossed her extractor roots onto a log. "Will it take mine?"

Coale looked at the stubborn set of her face. The woman sighed. "It's my weight or hers," she said to her grandson.

Elgon scowled back. "You weigh less," he said to Coale.

"Not by much," Rezs cut in flatly. "And it's my gear. If I want it, I should be the one to get it. Just tell me what I have to do."

Elgon and Coale exchanged glances. The man tugged again on the line. He looked at the water, then back at Rezs. Finally, he said, "First, understand that the grappling hook could be caught on just about anything, so if it's holding to the fallen trees, your weight will shift the mass unpredictably. We can't haul the hook in and reset it, because even if we could drag the whole mass to the bank to get the hook, we'd probably lose the things we were trying to reach as they broke free and were swept downstream." He studied her build. "We'll rig a harness for you," he said. "And we'll clip you to the line. If you lose your grip, don't worry. The harness will hold you to the rope. Just feel for the connection and follow it back to the rope. When you get to the tree mass, try not to get between the trunks. If they shift, they can trap you between them. Got it?" He waited for her nod. "If you can get the hook free of the brush once you get there, take it once around a solid trunk, haul in the line until you have enough extra rope to throw the hook back to the bank, and toss us back your end so we'll have a double line across the stream. We'll secure both ends here. That will give you a way back that isn't quite as brutal as the one I used downstream, and we'll be able to clothesline the rope back in so that we don't have to come back and retrieve it when the water level drops."

Coale laid out a set of straps on the bank and helped her step into the leg holes. "One more thing," the woman added. "You're already tense, and Vlen can feel that. You must control your thoughts so that you don't call him into the water again with you. If you're scared, no matter how much you're frightened, you must not project that." Shadowed eyes met Rezs's violet gaze. "Do you understand?"

Rezs nodded soberly. The only rope they had was between the shore and the grappling hook. There would be nothing with which they could rescue Vlen if he went in the water again.

"Then"—Coale tugged at the harness to pull and connect the leg loops to the carabiner at her waist—"you're set." She clipped the carabiner onto a short length of rope that Elgon attached to the taut line.

Rezs stepped to the edge of the bank, then scrambled back as that section of mud broke off and swirled away in the water. She glanced back. She didn't know that her eyes were wide as she looked at Coale, then Elgon.

"Remember," Coale repeated. "Do not call the Gray One. Keep him here, on the bank."

Rezs nodded. Then, with both hands tight on the line, she turned to the flood and stepped into the shock of cold water.

XII

Instantly, she lost her footing. The water sucked at her length, and she cried out, her mouth clogged with grit and silt. For an instant fear froze her as she was, hanging off the line, and her body lay out in the water like a rag, whipping in the current. She couldn't see for the water rushing in her face.

Wolfwalker! Vlen's voice was full of the memory of his terror. His shadow seemed to surge through the forest.

Gray One, she snapped. *Stay calm. I'm not hurt.*

She forced her head up against the water until she could see the line to which she still clung. Slowly, she dragged herself back to the line and hooked one arm completely over it. She turned her head to look at the bank. Elgon was gripping Coale's arm as if to stop the older woman from jumping in after Rezs, and his own face was sharp.

Rezs forced herself to grin. "Just practicing," she called.

Elgon's face relaxed, but Coale still looked grim.

This time, as she continued, Rezs did not attempt to regain her feet. As Elgon had said, she didn't have the weight to hold herself to the uneven bottom in the force of this flood. Instead, she let her body drag from the line as she pulled herself along, one handspan by another.

Pebbles hit her torso, and small rocks were tiny fists that bruised her body. A sharp branch scratched along her thigh, then her calf, like a thin claw. She could feel Vlen's concern as if it was her own. *Gray One*, she managed, *I'm fine.*

Wolfwalker, don't leave me . . .

Stay with Shona. Do not try to reach me— She caught her

138

breath as a small stone struck her hip right on the bone. *I'll be back on the bank in a few minutes.*

Your paws are not strong enough to hold you against the water.

The panic in his voice was clear. Rezs tried to strengthen the bond between them so that she could reassure the cub, but in the wake of that widening, her mind was flooded. Flashback images of water churning in Vlen's—her—face. Loosened branches striking his abdomen. His back crushed into a tangle of roots . . .

Stop it! She snarled. *There is no danger here. I am tied to the line. This is a human thing, and it is secure, not weak.*

From above the rush of the water, she could hear the urgency in his howl—could almost feel it ring off the inside of her skull. She started to let go of the rope to clutch her temples. *Stop it!* she shrieked through her mind. *Control yourself. You must not make this harder for me than it is now.* She felt her lips curl back in a vicious snarl as the older woman grabbed the cub by his scruff.

Vlen struggled against the other wolfwalker until Coale snapped at him through Shona. The yearling's eyes never left his own wolfwalker, and he subsided with a snarl, but his mental whine became a single note in Rezs's head, distracting her from the stones that slammed into her legs. She started to cut him off, but the surge of panic he projected forced her to tighten her own hold on the gray thread that stretched between them. Safety, reassurance, calm acceptance—she sent those back along the gray thread.

One chill hand's length, then another. She crossed the flood with curses muttered at each stone that hit her ribs. Twice, her knees rattled against the rocks that made up the streambed, bruising and scraping themselves raw. When she finally reached the mass of downed trees, it took all her strength to pull herself in front of one of the standing trees so that the current held her body against the trunk for her. She hardly realized that she was shaking as much from the cold as the effort.

She could see the tip of her bow, but it was meters out of reach, caught on a branch that stuck out at a shallow angle. The tree that had held her pack now rested across the crotch of a streaktree, and there was a tangle of scrawny branches in the downed canopy.

She leaned in to grab another tree trunk, then pulled herself carefully closer to her bow. Reached and gripped another arching root. Stretched up to get a hand on that segmented, overhanging branch . . .

And screamed.

The branch shifted, jerking out of her reach. Skeletal feet unfolded and clawed at her hand. Another skeletal foot snapped out from the trunk and shoved against her head, using it as a ladder to climb higher, but its nails caught in her hair, jerking her head against the one solid tree as the stickbeast tried frantically to escape.

"Aaahh . . ." She thrust her arms against the branches and beasts. Her sleeve tore in the nails of another scrabbling foot. All around her, the trees were moving, crawling, stretching out their branchlike arms and sprouting claws. Flattened jaws clacked together as another stickbeast unfolded from the trunk ahead of her and scrambled farther up the tree. Something clawed her back, then dug into her shoulders.

"Vlen!" she screamed.

Wolfwalker—

"Gray One!" she screamed again. Yellow, urgent gaze burned into her skull. Gray Shona snarled behind him. Then violet eyes, blurred and somehow larger and different than she remembered, seemed to stare into her face as if she looked at herself through Shona's eyes.

Coale's voice, frigid as a blade of ice, cut across her mind and shocked her into silence. *Stop it! Be calm— They are stickbeasts. There is no danger. They are afraid of you. Let them go. Do not hurt them.*

Rezs's hands were tangled in slick wood. One foot was caught in a root mass. She tried to hold her breath, and it came out in a half sob as the bony creature caught in her hair tore itself free and hauled itself up the trunk. A shiver struck her like a block of wood, and she realized that she was cold as the voice of the other wolfwalker.

"Stickbeasts," she gasped. She trembled against the trunk. Slowly, she lifted her head and looked up in the tangle. The mass of beasts was still shifting, securing themselves to each other and to the few real branches among them.

Wolfwalker, Vlen sent urgently. He tried to tear free of

Coale's hands again, but the older woman had a grip on him like a steel clamp.

Vlen, I'm here, she told him, letting her words sweep to him through her mind. *I'm okay. Stay calm. Stay with Coale.*

Your heart beats like mine. I can taste your fear.

I'm afraid, she admitted. She closed her eyes for a moment, and Gray Vlen's senses were suddenly sharper. The smell of mud and Coale and newly dug roots overwhelmed the odor of water that she breathed in through her own nose. The feel of his paws in the soft bank made her spread her fingers instead of gripping the trees around her.

She took a deep breath and opened her eyes. *Stop fighting with Coale,* she told him firmly. *She was right. I'm not hurt. I'm in no danger.* She looked toward the bank. Even at that distance she could see the muscles in the woman's arms relax as the older woman loosed the cub. Vlen sprang free, but Gray Shona darted after him so that he could not leap into the water.

"Stay!" Rezs shouted from across the stream. "Stay there."

Wolfwalker . . .

"Stay," she repeated, more calmly. Vlen whined in her head, but she was firm, and after a moment his mental howl blended into the tune that haunted the back of her mind. Grayheart, she thought. Gray eyes and yellow eyes and the heartsong of the pack . . .

She looked up at the fallen canopy, but she could barely see the stickbeasts now. Only a minute movement here or there spoke of their still-settling shapes.

She leaned out again and reached for the tip of the weapon. This time she got her hands on it and began to pull it up from the water. She had to jerk and work it free, and each time she did so, the stickbeasts overhead scrambled for better holds. One last yank ripped it free of the boughs.

By hooking the tip of the bow around one of the more slender trunks, she took her weight off the line to shore and hauled herself toward the tree in which she had tied her pack. Even though the water was gray-brown with flood murk, there was a dark shadow beneath the surface, and it was thick and round.

Anxiously, she waded closer until she could grab the trunk. The pack was not deeply submerged, and it took more strength than reach to get it free of the water. She slung it on her shoulder. "Got it!" she shouted across the stream.

"Wait there." Elgon gestured.

"What?" she shouted back.

"Wait there. We want to put another line across."

"I can come back just fine on the one I crossed with."

"Not for you," he called. "For the stickbeasts." He nodded at her frown. "Stickbeasts can't cross running water. They're too fragile. They'd be washed away and broken like twigs. They won't be able to cross on a single line, but they could on a double rope."

She glanced up. Even now, knowing where they perched, she could barely tell where they were. "Why can't they stay here till the stream dries up again?"

"Could be days," he returned. "They could starve, or the whole tree mass could break free and wash away with them on it. If you can't get the grappling hook free, I'll shoot you the other end of the line. Then you can toss it over a higher branch, and knot it to your end so that it makes a clothesline loop."

"Moonworms," Rezs muttered. She signaled that she understood, then waded back to the hook. She gave it several tries, but she didn't have the strength to untangle it from the mass of branches into which it had set. "No can do," she shouted back to the tall man.

But Elgon had already strung his bow, and now he poised on the bank, eyeing the mass of trees. Coale glanced at him, then called across to Rezs. "With the rope on the bolt, this shot won't be accurate."

For an instant she hesitated—among the trees, the stickbeasts, and herself, she was the only thing big enough to shoot at—and she couldn't help the wariness she projected to Vlen. The cub snarled in return. A moment later both were soothed by the deep voice of Gray Shona. Rezs shook off her misgivings and nodded back across the stream.

A second later Elgon's bolt flew raggedly into the tree mass. The tip of the arrow thunked against a trunk. Within seconds the line floated down and landed in the water. Rezs lunged to grab the shaft before the tip pulled free and was dragged down into the stream. The line attached to the arrow went suddenly slack. She lost her footing and went to her knees, submerging in the water.

"Moonwormed, dik-dropped stickbeasts," she sputtered as she hauled herself up by a sagging branch. For an instant she merely hung over the bough like a stuffed toy. The water dragged at her legs and feet, and the glistening waves roiled past as if they hadn't even noticed her lapse. But they were waiting, she thought. Waiting for her to weaken—just like Elgon and Coale. Rezs could almost feel the tall man's scrutiny through the yellow eyes of Vlen. And she could sense the older wolfwalker studying her through the cub, feeling for her emotions, listening to her mental voice. A spark of anger grew in her guts. "I'll be damned if I give in this easily," she swore under her breath. "I wanted to do this, and do it I will."

By the time she forced the grappling hook free and had both ends of the line in her hands, she was thoroughly chilled. It took her almost a dozen attempts to get the arrow over a sturdy enough branch, and her hands were shivering as she finally signaled Elgon to tauten the rope. Cautiously, the tall man drew back on the line. It pulled free of the surface of the stream, hung up for an instant in the crest of a wave, then snapped out and almost leaped into position in the air. Trees creaked and wood began to bend as he wrenched it tight. Coale added her weight to his, and the two of them leaned at a crazy angle as they braced and pulled to increase the tension. The eyes of the stickbeasts flared open. Their perch began to bend beneath them, and they chittered as they reassembled themselves among the thin branches. Finally, Elgon tied off the rope and twanged on the line to check its tautness.

"Now what?" Rezs called from her own perch above the water.

"Just come on back." He backed off a few meters and studied the bridge. "They'll follow once they see you cross."

"Are you sure?"

"If they don't follow you, Coale can recross—while you warm up here—and herd the beasts toward the bridge."

Rezs eyed his expression for a moment. Then she looked up, unhooked her safety line, and hauled herself up onto a thick branch.

"Rezs—" Elgon shouted. He cursed under his breath. "Rezs, clip back on the line—"

Rezs glanced across the stream, then resolutely back up at the stickbeasts. "If Coale can do this," she muttered to herself, "so can I." She balanced on the branch and reached up higher. A bony creature overhead seemed to spring from its perch and scramble away. Ignoring the bark fragments that shook out from its feet, she deliberately shook the tree.

Stickbeasts seemed to explode among the boughs. Scrawny arms struck out; skeletal legs sought new holds; brown claws spiked into thin branches, twigs, leaves, air—anything that was nearby. One of the stickbeasts fell from the tree. For an instant the creature hung over the water. Then it caught itself by a hand on an angled trunk and one foot clawed over the top line of the crossing. Another stickbeast scrabbled for a hold where its hand was clinging to the trunk, and the first creature jackknifed down again toward the stream. This time it caught one arm and one hand on the top line, while one of its bonelike legs caught a hold on the lower line.

"Yes—" Rezs remained motionless. They had it now.

The stickbeast swung for a moment on the ropes until the lines steadied out. It started to crawl back to the trees, then it stopped.

Rezs held her breath. "That's it."

The creature seemed to peer toward the other bank. Rezs followed its gaze. For an instant fear chilled her more than the water. Gray Vlen—he was gone. Elgon and Coale and Shona—they had disappeared from the bank as if they had never been there. She felt suddenly naked and exposed. "Vlen?" she whispered urgently.

Wolfwalker!

The joy in his voice was clear, and Rezs felt relief sweep her fear away like a tide. He was close. The shadows and shrubs might hide his gray shape, but they could not hide his mind from hers. Her lips tightened for a moment. She had not realized how much she already relied on the others' company. Without Gray Vlen . . .

Wolfwalker, I am here.

Gray One, she sent as the stickbeast shifted again. *You honor me.*

Before her, the creature seemed to make a decision. Within seconds it moved warily out onto the rope bridge. Above it, another stickbeast moved down toward the water and tested the rope with its skeletal hand. Beneath it, the water rushed past with brown glints and roiling, standing waves.

"Go," Rezs whispered as she watched the first creature. It eased out over the water, then halted and eyed the opposite bank, then the stream. From where Rezs waited, the stickbeast looked like a bundle of half-meter sticks that had somehow caught on a line—like a broken kite without its cloth. The skin around her eyes crinkled at the image, then she sobered and held her breath as the second stickbeast dropped onto the rope.

Suddenly the entire canopy seemed to detach itself from the trees and migrate toward the rope bridge. "Like a forest crawling," she breathed. "There must be twenty of them crossing."

As the first one reached the bank it dropped off, straightened, and turned to watch the others crawl across. Even with their weight, the top line barely sagged to the lower line, and the lower line remained half a meter above the water. As the second creature gained the bank the first one stalked back into the forest. One by one, they crawled across the ropes and stalked across the muddy bank. In less than ten minutes they were gone, leaving only faint scratch marks where their feet had disturbed the mud.

On the bank, Gray Shona, then Vlen were the first out of the shadows. A moment later Elgon and Coale faded out of the trees and motioned for Rezs to make her way back across. She slid clumsily down from her perch, then clipped back onto the lower line and waded back into the tangle of roots and water. A few moments later she was being hauled out of the stream by Elgon.

He didn't speak as he handed her to Coale. Her teeth were beginning to chatter, and she clenched her jaw to keep from biting her tongue. Coale's warm hands pulled her away from the bank, unstrapped her pack, and stripped her jerkin from her unresisting shoulders in one smooth movement.

"Are th-they gone?" she stammered.

The woman nodded. She unfastened Rezs's shirt, helped her out of it, wrung it out, and toweled her dry with Rezs's own damp clothes. A few seconds later Rezs was huddled into Coale's warm jerkin while Coale nodded to her to sit on a nearby log.

"Boots," directed the woman.

Rezs nodded and, still shivering, tried to toe them off, but Coale pushed her back and knelt to pull her footgear from her clammy calves. Abruptly, Rezs put her hand on Coale's shoulder to brace herself. She did not expect the rough, scarred ridges of muscle she felt beneath her hand, especially compared with the slenderness of Coale's shoulder. She found herself staring at the top of the other woman's warcap. Her eyesight was blurred again, from the sense of Vlen too close, but even at that, she could see that, mended a dozen times, the warcap seemed held together more by the secondary seams than by its original fabric. Where the slight ring circled its shape, the leather and metal were almost translucent. Bany's warcap had shown such use, she remembered. In fact, almost every scout she had ever seen had clothes so worn they seemed more like Durn than Randonnens.

The thought of the Durn made her lips tighten. Coale and Elgon weren't Durn, but did she know where they came from—who they really were? If she thought about it, she had to admit that she knew nothing of the two people who had rescued her from the badgerbear. Vlen had heightened her fear and deepened her need—and Coale and Elgon had fed those needs, so that now, she had taken a training bond with them, and Bany would have to accept them. Rezs, trying not to react to the feel of Coale's hands on her ankles, reached back in her mind. She let her thoughts curl around the gray thread that bound her to Vlen. The music that seemed to come to her thoughts with that thread . . . The yellow eyes that watched in her mind . . . The sense of reassurance she received was not from her own instincts, but something that crept in with the bond. Something that maybe came from Shona. And why would a wolf reassure her? If it was from Coale, not herself, that she felt this, then Coale was not what she seemed.

Coale must have felt her slight recoil, because she stopped with the left boot halfway off. "Okay?" she asked.

"Will we st-stay here to dry my clothes?"

Coale shook her head. "The streams around here will only continue to deepen, making this area hard to hike later. We'll just dump out the water, then get on up to higher ground. We'll build a fire up on the heights."

"The Water Wall," Rezs managed. "Signal fire in the pit facing north."

"All right." Coale studied Rezs's face. "Good job," she said quietly.

Rezs looked up. The approval that flowed from the woman brought warmth to her touch. For a moment Coale's expression softened. Then something sharp cut across her shuttered eyes, and she turned away to shake out Rezs's boots.

Rezs stared after her. Her hand clenched as it remembered the scarred shoulder it had gripped before. Visible marks; invisible wounds . . . She barely noticed when Vlen shoved his nose under her hand, and the sound she made at his demand for attention was almost a mournful howl of her own.

XIII

The night was full of moons and motion. Rezsia sat close to the fire, so that its heat scalded her skin, while its yellow-white light flickered in her eyes. Beneath the one log that was left, the bed of coals glowed like a thousand tiny suns, which, trapped and crushed together on the ground, turned and spat their light at the sky.

Bany sat across from the fire, shaving a stick into the coals, while Elgon rummaged in his pack, and two of the other scouts pored over a map of the northern terrain. The last two scouts worked at pitching their bedrolls and bivvy sacks in the shadowline of the trees. Coale had left Elgon and Rezs to light the signal fire, and Rezs hadn't seen the other woman since. If she was hunting Rezs's dnu, she'd been gone a long time; but Elgon said not to worry. He'd know, he said, if Coale was in trouble.

Bany had brought four scouts with him: Welker, Touvinde, Ukiah, and Gradjek. Welker was a tall, spare woman, with broad shoulders, a narrow waist, wide hips, and a ready smile. Like Coale, she was somewhere in her eighties, but her brown hair showed no gray as yet. Graceful and smooth when she was moving around, Welker somehow lost all that when she was motionless. Where she sat next to Bany, the woman looked as awkward and gangly as a day-old dnu. And with her size, every time she opened her mouth, Rezs expected to hear a booming laugh, but the scout's voice was soft as winter drizzle.

Touvinde was barely taller than Rezs, and had the same narrow shoulders, black hair, and high cheekbones. But there, any resemblance ceased. Touvinde's face was blocky and

148

harsh, with a square jaw that almost jutted from his neck. His stringy, black mustache accentuated the planes of his face. He looked cold and hard, as if he wouldn't even begin to know how to smile. Yet his sense of humor was as sharp as his knife, and his acid tongue had caught Rezs off guard more than once—the first time, when he joked about missing the ends of two fingers, the second time when he teased Vlen directly. She liked him, she thought. He was not at all what she expected.

Ukiah, however, seemed to be a classic scout. He was lean and taller than Rezs by almost a head, but his shoulders were square enough to make his jerkin hang loosely when he moved. His skin was as weathered as Elgon's, and his hair brown; his eyes, brown-black in shade. But where Elgon's jaw was blocky, Ukiah's was classically shaped. Where Elgon's cheekbones were heavy, Ukiah's were just well-defined. It was as if Ukiah were a softer, handsome version of the other scout. Even his fingers, scarred and scabbed, were long and slender instead of merely thick with strength. She studied them surreptitiously, and the tune that had been haunting her thoughts for the last half a ninan popped into her head. She had to bite back the comment, as she gripped arms with him in greeting, that he should have been a musician, not a swordsman, with those hands. Confident, competent, and he didn't once smile with his eyes, she thought as she watched him from beneath her lashes.

Gradjek was the oddest of Bany's group. Had Rezs looked only at his darkly weathered skin, she would have thought him ninety, but he was only fifty-two. The facade of age that littered his face with lines was created by such deep weathering that the moons may as well have simply carved out his face. There were crow's-feet around his eyes; deep gashes of line around his mouth; wrinkles across the bridge of his nose; and canyons in his forehead. His skin was spattered not only with freckles, but liver spots, and it was dry enough that it seemed to be perpetually peeling. He was spry—there was no other way to describe him, thought Rezs as she watched Gradjek spread out his sleeping bag with short, jerky movements. Barrel-chested, with skinny arms and stick legs, the man moved quickly and abruptly. Bany and Elgon, Ukiah and Coale—they all moved like wolves or ghosts; Gradjek moved like an irritated bird.

Thoughtfully, Rezs watched Gradjek fold up the maps. He made some comment to Ukiah that sent the other man's gaze toward Rezs, and she met his distant look with one of her own. For a moment the thin trail of smoke obscured his face. Then the breeze caught again, and the sparse branches parted to let the curl twist up like a seeking snake.

Rezs dropped her gaze, but somehow remained aware that Ukiah kept his eyes on her. There was something about the man that bothered her. It struck her that of all four scouts that Bany had brought with him, Ukiah was the only one built like one of neGruli's men.

She didn't know her body had tensed until Elgon said, "Relax. It's just the whippins."

She looked up sharply. "Whippins?"

"The hooting." He pointed. "There's a pair of them over there."

She followed his gesture, but saw nothing but two moons that floated overhead. Their shine created grotesque streaks of light back in the forest where the firelight could not reach, and her eyes, blinded by the fire, could see only light and dark. Behind her, Gray Vlen had lain down in the shadow of a root, and she couldn't see even the glint of his yellow eyes when she glanced over her shoulder.

But as if he had been listening to her thoughts, Vlen raised his head, and his yellow eyes gleamed suddenly. *Wolfwalker. You are ready to hunt?*

Unconsciously, she licked her lips. Her eyes tracked Ukiah as the tall man turned back toward Gradjek. *I think I am hunting, Vlen,* she agreed softly. *I just don't know what I'm looking for.*

Slowly, Vlen's teeth bared until they shone whitely in the night. *The hare is close to the fang, Wolfwalker. I can taste his scent in your nose.*

Rezs felt her gaze sharpen as Ukiah raised his head. Her eyes were blinded by sparks, and her head full of images and tactile feelings that crowded out her thoughts. Abruptly, she got to her feet and strode away from the fire. Ukiah made to move after her, but the wolf cub had already risen and trotted after her, and Elgon gestured for the other man to remain at the fire. It was Elgon, not Ukiah who followed Rezs.

She knew the man followed her. Silent as he was, she could

hear him clearly through Vlen's ears, and feel him on her trail. As he caught up with her Vlen's hackles rose, and Rezs had to soothe the cub mentally as she turned to face the man.

"All right?" Elgon asked softly.

"Fine," she returned shortly.

Elgon glanced from Rezs back toward the camp. "You're not comfortable with Bany's people, are you?"

"Not uncomfortable," she returned firmly. "Just . . . wary."

"I thought you said these people were your friends."

"I thought you said to trust nothing and no one," she retorted sharply, though her voice was low.

In the dark, Elgon studied her closely. "You want to talk about it?" he said finally.

"No." Then, a moment later: "I'm sorry, Elgon. I'm just . . . edgy."

Elgon's voice was soft. "Bany and his men—they're not really friends, are they?"

There was something in his voice that reminded her of Vlen, and it was difficult to keep her voice casual. "We work together," she answered at last.

"But you don't like them."

"Does it matter?" she asked quietly. "You don't like me, yet you're still here with Coale. What do you have to gain by hanging around with an incompetent like me? Does it make you feel good to point out how stupidly I act out here?"

For a moment Elgon stared at her.

She nodded shortly. "It's as plain as the chin on your face, Elgon."

"Perhaps it is," he agreed mildly, surprising her. "But perhaps you have a decade's worth of learning to do in a couple days, and if I were any less hard on you, you'd be dead twice over."

"By the moons, Elgon, everything you say ends up with 'if this or not that, then you'd be dead.' It gets tiring after a while. I understand that the trail can be dangerous. You've hammered it so deeply in my head that it's like a song in the back of my mind: danger danger danger. Can't you relax every now and then? Smile, perhaps—and mean it?"

"When Coale accepted responsibility for you, I did no less. You don't have to like me to learn from me, Rezs."

"No," she agreed in turn. "But it would make this a hell of a lot easier."

"It's not supposed to be easy," Elgon snapped.

His voice was so sharp that Vlen snarled. Rezs caught the cub by his scruff. "It's all right, Vlen," she said quickly. She studied the tall man for a long moment. "Instinctive, but not easy?" she said softly.

Surprise flickered in his eyes.

Her own voice sharpened. "I'm ignorant, not stupid, Elgon. What is instinct to you is novel to me."

For a moment they stared at each other. The tall man nodded. "I'll remember," he promised softly.

He turned without another word and made his way back to the fire. Rezs watched him move, then knelt beside the cub. "He doesn't like me, Vlen. He docsn't trust mc. And he certainly doesn't respect me. I wonder . . ."

Wolfwalker?

Absently, she scratched his ears. "What I wonder, Vlen, is if he has bound himself to Coale so thoroughly that his word to me means nothing."

The cub nudged her hand. *That one doesn't hunt you; you hunt him. What does it matter what he says?*

She chuckled. "Gray One," she said softly. "What a man says is often exactly what he doesn't mean—if he is even aware himself of what he feels or means. If Elgon doesn't mean what he says, then I have to listen to what he doesn't say to figure out why he's here. But if he means what he says—gods, this almost makes sense—then he's hiding something else. I can feel it, Vlen, in my very bones."

You want to hunt him? Smell the fear on his breath?

Rezs smiled faintly, but there was no humor in the expression. "Somehow," she said softly, "it's not fear I think I'll be seeing."

When Rezs returned to the fire, Vlen settled back down in his roots and became invisible; and Rezs deliberately moved to a spot between Elgon and Touvinde. Elgon glanced at her, nodded, and went back to braiding the line he was working on.

She held out her hands, toasting her skin on the blaze. "It's been hours, but I still feel cold from the stream."

Touvinde adjusted a skinny log in the fire. A cloud of sparks flew up and circled his head before disappearing into the sky, leaving his face harsh with shadows. "Might as well hit the sack then, Wolfwalker. Be warmer in a few minutes there than here."

Rezs studied him surreptitiously for a moment. She could hear the faint music of the wolves in her head, threaded with that haunting tune. As she watched the scout handle the firewood, the memory of those iron hands that had gripped her arms at that warehouse flashed back in her mind. Fear expanded all one's senses—what if Grayheart was not as tall or broad as she had thought in her panic? What if, as the stories said, he was a bitter, age-hardened man? It might be more romantic to think of Grayheart as tall as Elgon or as handsome as Ukiah, but the reality was that she had never seen the man. That sharpness in his voice when he had spoken to her at the warehouse had been like Touvinde's in its acidity. That jawline—square and harsh with stubble—could have been Touvinde's jaw.

The fire was bright, and she didn't want to move back from its heat, but she nodded and began to unstrap Coale's blankets from the older woman's pack. Touvinde stopped her with a gesture. "Not here," he said. "Better to move back where Vlen is."

She glanced at him sharply. Her voice was thoughtful when she asked, "You can see him?"

"Of course. You can't?"

She looked over her shoulder, searching for a glint of those yellow, lupine eyes, then shook her head.

"You've been staring at the fire," Touvinde said. "Wolf or no wolf, you won't have any night sight like that."

She kicked a coal back into the firepit. "Why build a fire if you can't enjoy it at least a little?" Elgon opened his mouth, but Rezs sighed. "I know. Safety—always safety—first." She gathered up Coale's blankets and looked away from the fire, but the shadows were an inky black, and she still could not see Vlen. She found her eyes drawn back to the tiny flames. "Elgon—" She watched his expression carefully. "About Coale's heart . . ."

Elgon glanced meaningfully at Touvinde, and with a shrug, the other man got to his feet and moved away toward Welker. "Coale isn't unwell," Elgon said softly when Touvinde moved out of earshot. "There is no sickness in her."

Rezs's voice was equally quiet. "That's not what I mean, Elgon, and you know it."

Absently, he put down the line and took up Touvinde's fire stick, turning over one of the logs. For a moment fire flared around the log, then subsided into a glow of yellow-white heat. The tiny flames that were left danced on the coals until the edges of the embers turned red, then red-black as they cooled. "Have you ever really looked into a fire, Rezs?" he asked softly. "Not stared," he added. "Not daydreamed. Really looked into its heart—when the wood is gone and all that's left are the coals? The light is almost as hot in your eyes as the fire itself on your skin." He stirred the coals so that they flared, then cooled and reddened again on the edges. "What you see in the coals is what's left when everything else is gone. That's the heart of a fire, Rezs. That's the essence of whatever life was burned away by time and heat. What Coale seeks—it's not just that heart. It's the life she let slip away." He let the tip of the stick catch fire, and the golden flame licked up the whitened wood. "She'll never find it," he said, more to himself than to her. "What's burned is gone, and what's gone so long is now less than a memory of heat in the rain. There's no wood left in this life to burn. Coale . . ." He shook his head almost imperceptibly. "She can only sift the embers to feed a newer flame."

When Elgon moved back from the fire to unroll his bedding, Rezs remained where she was. She tried to feel Elgon through Vlen's sleepy senses, but the cub's dreams were of running, and she got little more than a leg twitch from his mind. Absently, she watched the other scouts around the fire. Welker and Touvinde were getting ready for sleep; Gradjek was out of sight; and Ukiah was talking softly to Bany. The old man, still whittling his stick, gestured sharply, and Ukiah glanced up to meet Rezs's gaze, but she didn't look away. He raised an eyebrow.

From across the fire, Rezs had a sudden vision of yellow eyes narrowed and focused. Her stomach tightened. Abruptly, she grinned.

Ukiah's eyes flickered. Then he grinned back, and his teeth gleamed in the firelight. Touvinde murmured something to Welker, and a tune—deep and haunting like a midnight pool—tied the gray voices together in her head, so that, for an instant, Ukiah's face was superimposed on that of a wolf. The man rose to his full height. Rezs's stomach tightened instantly, but the tall man merely moved to join her.

"Still staring at the fire, Wolfwalker?" he asked softly. "Or are you studying us through the Gray One's eyes?"

"I see in black-and-white, Ukiah. Vlen sees in shades of gray. I'm just comparing the two visions."

He dropped to sit on the log. "Coale's not back yet. Is she coming back at all this evening?"

Rezs shrugged. "She didn't say. She tires easily, though, and we're sharing bedding tonight, so I expect her back by my watch."

Ukiah nodded. Absently, Rezs noted that nothing glinted in the man's clothing; no sheen of steel or brass flickered in the firelight. Only his eyes glistened and reflected the fire. "You know her well?"

Rezs's gaze sharpened. There was an undercurrent to his voice that made the hair along the back of her neck prickle. "Not well," she said carefully. "Do you?"

"Never met her before. I'm usually farther north and east; she's usually farther west."

"How did you hook up with Bany, then?"

He shrugged. "Scouts go where they're needed, and I never turn down a chance to see new country."

"You don't like to stay in one place, you mean." Ukiah gave her a sharp look, and Rezs could almost feel him withdraw. She didn't know what pushed her to do it, but deliberately, she added, "You're running from your roots."

"Are you always this abrupt with people you've barely met?"

For an instant Rezs heard another voice in her head. "Only when I'm curious," she retorted, focusing on the tall man. She couldn't help the glance she cast at Touvinde, and she kept her voice low as she asked, "Did Bany tell you where we're going?"

"North and west. Get some sleep. You and Bany have the two A.M. watch."

The sleeping bag was cool, but it took only a few moments for her to warm up enough to start dozing. Rezs didn't know how long it was before she felt Gray Shona through Vlen's mind, but the stars had shifted, and the second moon was almost down behind the treeline. "Coale?" she whispered.

"It is I," the woman murmured. The wolfwalker shifted out of the shadows.

From across the faint bed of coals, Ukiah, still on watch, didn't seem surprised, but Bany's eyes opened sharply. Rezs didn't sit up. "How long have you been there?"

The older woman seemed to shrug. She had already wrapped the hilt of Rezs's knife so that the metal of the handle was no longer bare, and only her eyes, like those of Vlen, gleamed in the firelight.

Gray voices snarled softly in her head, and carefully, trying to be quiet, Rezs rolled out of the bag. "Did you find him—my dnu?"

"I did."

Rezs tried to read the other woman's expression in the dark. "But?" she pressed.

"A poolah got to him first. Your riding beast was already gutted by the time I reached the site."

"It was my fault, wasn't it?"

Coale's voice was tired. "The tether line had caught and tangled the dnu in the trees. The poolah walked up and killed him where he stood."

Rezs didn't speak for a moment. Then she abruptly smoothed out the sleeping bag. "It's time for my watch," she said shortly. "You might as well take your bedding back now."

Coale didn't speak, but she pressed something into Rezs's hand.

Rezs looked down. The small, ornamental plates glinted in the moonlight. "My bridle ornaments . . ." She stared back up at the other woman. "I thought poolah didn't leave their kill."

The other woman shrugged. "You'd lost so much else. I thought you would have wanted them back."

"I did—I do. They belonged to my father." She tucked them in her belt pouch. "Coale, thank you."

The other woman had already sunk to the bedding. Now she merely nodded again, lay back, and closed her eyes.

Rezs eyed her for a moment, then joined Bany and Ukiah on the other side of the firepit.

As soon as she moved away from the bedding, Gray Vlen

joined her from out of the shadows. Rezs was glad for his company. Even with the others to camp with, and five moons overhead, the night still seemed filled with darkness.

"Took Coale a long time to find that dnu," Ukiah commented as she drew back from the faint firelight to sit beside him. "What did she give you, anyway?"

"My bridle ornaments." She dug them from her belt pouch and held them out for him to see. "Said a poolah got my dnu. She probably had to wait until it left before she could cut these off."

"This the dnu you lost this morning?"

She nodded.

He turned the pieces of metal over in his hands. "Poolah don't leave their kill until it's down to the bones. That takes a few days with something as large as a dnu."

"She got the ornaments somehow."

"Could have killed the poolah," Ukiah mused.

Bany reached over and took the ornaments from the other scout. "Had to have wanted those things awfully badly to do that. Poolah might look cute and furry and slow moving, but they're dangerous as moonwarriors—even when you can see them coming."

"The ornaments are a family thing," she said to the two men. "They'd not be worth that kind of risk to her."

"Maybe it wasn't the ornaments she wanted." Bany's voice was flat.

Rezs's gaze sharpened. "You think she was searching for something else?"

"You have a better idea why she'd challenge a poolah for a piece of ornamental metal?" He tossed the metal pieces back.

Rezs fingered them for a moment before tucking them back in her belt pouch, but her jaw had tightened, and beside her, Vlen's scruff began to bristle.

Bany glanced toward the shadow where Coale now slept. "Did she try to get into your gear while you were together?"

"No—" But Rezs halted. "She did suggest I leave it behind. And she insisted on going alone to find the dnu while Elgon waited with me for you to show up."

Ukiah followed Bany's gaze toward Coale and her grandson. "You tell them what you were doing out here?"

She shook her head. "Just that I was gathering work samples—and meeting you. Nothing else."

"Good." Bany's voice was almost sharp. "Let's keep it that way."

Rezs nodded slowly. Ukiah rose and, for a moment, rested his hand on her shoulder. His touch was warm and firm, and she started, but Vlen ignored her movement. "Stay alert, Rezs," the tall man said softly. "But don't get jumpy. Learn to relax and listen. Your ears are worth more than your eyes any night."

She nodded again and watched him bed down.

XIV

Two days later they purchased another dnu for Rezs in a village to the north. Gray Vlen had chosen the dnu himself by making the other one so nervous that she couldn't consider taking it. Along with the dnu, she replaced her gear, bought an extra pair of boots, and traded some herbs Coale had helped her gather for some saddle salve. She knew she would need the salve: the only saddle she could buy had been worn in by a larger rider than she. By the time she was done with her purchases, she felt as if she was outfitted for a year's journey. But like Elgon, Bany had insisted on a full setup of gear.

"We'll only be gone three more ninans," she said to Bany as, ahead of them, Elgon led the dnu away from the corral.

"Maybe," the old man agreed. "But you never know how long it will take once you ride outside the barrier bushes."

"Moons, Bany, you sound like Coale."

He lifted his warcap and scratched his head, leaving one gray lock hanging out over his ear when he replaced the cap. "Is that a compliment or a complaint?"

"Does it matter?" She hefted the sword she had chosen. "You won't stop giving me advice for all that I've heard it before."

He didn't smile. "There's a reason for that, Wolfwalker. I made a promise to that elder, which I intend to keep."

Ukiah joined them with her saddlebags, and Bany took advantage of Rezs's silence to take the sword from her hand and heft it. "It's light," he commented.

"Better to choose one that's too light than one that is too heavy." Her voice was dry as she repeated his earlier advice

159

back to him. Ukiah gave her a sharp look, and abruptly, the graysong tightened in her head. Vlen snarled softly, singing his voice into the tune that rose with the tide of gray. Coale was changing her, she thought. She no longer listened with only her ears, but through Vlen as well, and when the young wolf touched her mind, she felt more than just gray voices in her head. Ukiah—he was distant, locked off, like the blader who had frightened her with his knife on her neck. Bany was solid and steady and tough. Elgon's voice was a hidden, subtle disapproval that felt like the rasp of a metal file behind the wisdom-edged strength of Coale. Touvinde, whose tongue was so sharp, was barely a ghost in her mind; Gradjek startled her—as if she could not get used to his presence. And Welker, who felt as open as a meadow, had a hard knot, like a rock, in her center.

As if the woman had heard Rezs's thought, Welker raised her eyebrow. "You ready to ride out of here now?"

There was no impatience in her tone, only amusement, and Rezs glanced at the saddlebags Ukiah had over his shoulder. "Soon as I saddle up," she returned. "Give me ten minutes."

"You mean, soon as I saddle up for you." Gradjek jerked the saddle he carried up onto the tether bar and automatically brushed his dry skin from the leather.

"Do you mind?" Rezs teased the smaller scout.

Gradjek's liver spots seemed pale compared with the dark look he gave her. Bany chuckled.

Ukiah slung the travel bags over a post, then shook out his hands. "You're going to have to watch the weight, Rezs," he commented soberly. "These pack bags are heavy, and that saddle is a work saddle, not a journey saddle. If you don't ride carefully, you'll tire your dnu before we've gone ten kays."

She nodded. She caught Elgon's gaze for a moment. There was a look in the man's eyes that reflected disapproval so clearly that Rezs almost stumbled. Vlen growled as Bany caught her arm with his free hand. "Careful—"

She shook him off. "I'm all right." She nodded to Vlen. *Go on, Gray One. Go find Coale and tell her we're ready to leave.*

But Vlen didn't trot away. *Coale and Shona ran without me this morning.*

Without you—

Bany cut in, "You're going to have to learn to stay out of the minds of the Gray Ones when you walk in a town, Rezs.

It's all right to see your surroundings through wolf eyes when you're scouting, but it's better to stick to human eyes in human places. You'll be a danger to yourself and everyone else if you react like a wolf in town. I thought Coale was teaching you that."

Elgon halted the dnu at the tack post. "She is," the man returned sharply.

"By all nine moons," Rezs retorted. "How can you tell when I'm thinking through Vlen anyway?"

"It's your eyes," Ukiah explained. "They become unfocused." He gave Elgon an expressionless look.

Rezs pushed Vlen away and took her sword back from Bany. "I'll watch it," she said deliberately to both of them.

Bany's lips twitched. "Where's Touvinde?" he asked Welker.

The tall woman glanced at Elgon. "Still talking with his cousins."

Still asking about neGruli's passage, Rezs translated. She watched Elgon carefully. That flicker in his eyes—he had to know that they were talking around him, not *to* him, about what Touvinde and the rest of the scouts were doing. And Bany—that sharp tone when he mentioned Coale suggested that he was beginning to wonder if the other wolfwalker was teaching Rezs what she needed to know. She could almost see the old man's thoughts: If Rezs couldn't even learn to control her sight through Vlen's eyes, how would she ever gain the precision required to read the memories of the wolves? But Coale was teaching Rezs that and more. In two days Rezs had begun to feel as if Coale defined her mornings. It was almost as if she listened to the forest more through Coale's link with Shona than through her own ears.

She saddled and bridled her dnu by rote, searching through Vlen for Coale's voice. At first she couldn't find the other woman—only Shona, a soft, solid wave of gray that blanketed weariness. Then she felt a sharp stab of awareness in her mind. Her hands clenched on the reins; the dnu shifted irritably, and Gradjek jerked away from its hooves.

"Moonworms," he cursed. "What are you trying to do? Trample me?"

Vlen snarled at the man, and the small scout moved hurriedly back farther.

"Sorry, Gradjek." Rezs soothed the riding beast automatically.

Elgon looked at Bany and the other scouts. He didn't say it, but by now, Rezs knew what words he was thinking. "We're in town, Elgon," she said to the man, her voice low and sharp. "Surely I don't have to be as alert to worlags—and other dangers—here. And I know Bany asked me to stay out of Vlen's mind, but I'm practically standing still—what harm could I do here?"

He gave her an expressionless look. "I'll go find Coale," he said shortly.

Bany watched the dark-eyed man go, then motioned for Gradjek and Welker to join him in finding Touvinde. "We'll be back in a few minutes," Bany told her.

Ukiah nodded, but he was still watching Elgon's back with a hunter's focus. "You don't like him either," she said softly.

The tall man looked down at her. "Actually, I do."

"You do," she repeated. "Why?"

"I understand him."

"I notice you didn't say you trusted him."

He grinned, but the expression didn't lighten his brown-black eyes. He settled her bags behind the saddle, and his long fingers lingered for a moment on the bulges of the bags.

"And Coale?" she asked. "Do you like or dislike her?"

"Hard to say. Have you ever seen what she really looks like?"

Rezs didn't answer for a moment. Even though, by her side, Vlen didn't snarl, she could feel the sharpening of the cub's attention. "What kind of question is that?" she returned. "I've been working with Coale for two days solid—of course I know what she looks like. She's slender, not quite my height, has a weak leg, dark eyes. . . ."

He shrugged. "She doesn't hang around with us much. Dawn and dusk—it's all we ever see of her—except at a distance. Bany's beginning to wonder about her."

She watched the scout's face carefully, and this time Vlen snarled low in his throat. It was not a threat; the wolfling seemed to be reflecting not only Rezs's feelings but Ukiah's. "Touvinde said she had a reputation for being a . . . lone wolf."

"Could be," he returned noncommittally. "A lot of wolf-walkers run trail alone."

She adjusted the bridle and cast him a shrewd look from the side. "But you think there's more to it than that."

He shrugged again.

"There's a lot of grief in her, but I don't think she's dangerous—not to me, anyway."

"Hard to say."

His voice was still noncommittal, and Rezs's eyes narrowed thoughtfully. "I should feel any threat from her through her Gray One."

From down the street, Bany waved, and Ukiah gestured for Rezs to bring her new riding beast with him as he went to meet the old man. "Can you feel Coale right now?" he asked softly.

Rezs hesitated, looked toward Bany, then shrugged to herself. She concentrated on Vlen and let his thin gray voice fill the back of her mind. From the fence line, his yellow eyes gleamed, and his mental howl spun out into the packsong. Shona's voice, strong and clear, swept across Vlen's voice like a tide and made the cub's voice thin as a crosscurrent line in that sea of howling gray. Coale had to be there—she knew it. She could hear the echoes of human voices all around the wolves—familiar tones that made her think of home, gray swirls that seemed to sing with distance, and a shaft of power that was the lupine sense of Coale. As if by locating it, she had latched onto it, that energy began to distinguish itself like the beat of a pulse in her head. It was insidious. Hypnotic. She felt pulled into it like a dancer. She didn't notice that she dropped the reins or that Gray Vlen had begun to snarl.

Ukiah grabbed her arm. "What is it?" he asked sharply. "What do you feel?"

"Energy," she whispered. "The beat of a drum . . ." She looked up into his eyes and saw, not brown-black irises, but two wells of gray. Vlen bared his teeth. The link between Rezs and the cub thickened like storm clouds, and the gray fog swirled like a vortex. Yellow eyes swam out of the fog. The din of the wolves swelled. Deep in the packsong, Grayheart, she thought.

"Rezs—" Ukiah shook her.

Rough hands, strong fingers . . . right where that blader had grabbed her before. Rezs cried out in her mind, and abruptly, the bond to the wolf pack was cut. The silence in her mind amputated the pulse. Disoriented, she clung to the scout.

"What do you feel?"

His voice was taut—almost urgent—and Rezs stared at him. Not: Was she okay? she thought in some back part of her brain. But: What did she feel? "I felt Vlen," she managed. "And Shona and Coale. And a dozen other voices. I felt . . . like I was in a whirlpool made of snarls and growls and yellow eyes."

He searched her face. "Better now?"

She nodded, and he loosed his grip. She fumbled for the reins of the dnu. "Moons," she muttered. "I must be getting more sensitive."

"To the Gray Ones."

It was a question more than a statement, and she nodded again. "I've been hearing this . . . fog of voices in my head ever since I bonded with Vlen, but it's been getting stronger. And yesterday, it started to swirl—like now—and I felt almost dizzy."

"When yesterday?"

"Afternoon."

"It's afternoon now."

She shrugged. "Twice isn't a pattern, if that's what you're trying to imply."

"Maybe you just need to eat more often. I've known wolfwalkers who have had to eat more than usual when they're bonded, and you don't eat much at noon."

"Maybe." She was dubious. "Maybe it's Coale's influence. I didn't feel this way before I met her. I could never feel Old Roy like this. But now—I feel as if I can find Coale and read her like a message ring."

Ukiah studied her face. "If you can feel her by now," he said slowly, "how well do you think she can read you?"

Rezs hesitated. "She links to me through Vlen. How deep a link like that goes . . ." She met his eyes soberly. "If you're asking if I can tell when we're linked, yes. If you're asking me if I can tell if she's reading my intentions—the reason we're out here, and what we're looking for—I can't answer that."

Slowly, Ukiah nodded. Neither one spoke again as they walked the rest of the way to meet Bany.

* * *

For five days they continued north, along the border between Ramaj Randonnen and Ramaj Kiren. It rained off and on every other day until a storm front arrived. The deluge it brought with it was so heavy that they simply stopped for four hours to wait it out in the lean-to shelters they built. Every stream they crossed was swollen against or over its banks, and the rootroads were mushy with water. Even for Rezs, it was easy to tell when a road had been recently used; beneath the puddles, the center line was hardened up, while the sides remained treacherously slick and spongelike.

Once, they saw worlags, but the pack was small, and half of the beetle creatures were young. They followed Rezsia's group for a while, then left for better game. Twice, the scouts saw lepa in the sky, but the bird creatures weren't yet flocking, and the scouts stayed beneath the trees. Both times the lepa struck east, in meadows where herds of the brown-spotted springers grazed.

One dawn Rezs woke to a feeling of danger. It was sudden—like a shaft of warning from Vlen—and it left her frozen in her sleeping bag, motionless except for her eyes. The yearling snarled, low in his throat, and Rezs felt Coale, awake and just as still as she. She could feel Ukiah's awareness, but she could not see the scout. Gradjek, on watch, did not move, and Rezs stared at him. The fear emanating from his body was like a cloud that clung to his shoulders. But his fear was not focused outside of the fire, but on himself, and as Rezs shifted her head infinitely slowly to see, she realized that there was something dark attached to his leg, just behind his knee. Vlen's snarl grew, and Shona's joined him briefly. Gradjek's eyes flicked across the fire and met Rezs's eyes.

Coale's voice snapped out across the gray fog. *Keep quiet— Don't move.*

What is it? Rezs questioned sharply. *What's happening?*

Nightspider. Don't wake the others. Sounds and movements will make it bite him.

Moonworms. Coale—what should I do?

Keep still. I've got a good angle; I'll try to take care of it from here.

Ukiah's awake—

He knows to keep still, the woman cut in. *He's out of position to shoot.*

Rezs paused. *How does he know not to move?*

The other woman's voice was curt. *Shona told him.*

How?

He can see her eyes.

Rezs fell silent, but her bond with Vlen left her mind boiling with the chaos that the young cub projected. The danger sense was overwhelming, and the wolf kept his snarl low, but didn't stop.

Meters away, the middle-aged woman shifted slightly, one inch at a time, until she slid her grip around her bow. Gradjek's eyes were locked onto the infinitely-slow shifting of Coale's body. When the woman got her left hand onto her quiver, one of the bolt tips scraped gently against another one, and the blue-black creature on Gradjek's leg stiffened and half rose into its biting position. The scout didn't gasp, but his eye seemed to drown in the certainty that he was going to die. And then Coale notched her arrow and drew the bow back. Slowly—oh, so slowly that it seemed as if the woman's older, slender arms could not hold the strain so long—she drew back the string until her bow fingers touched her lips. She held it there for eternity. Finally, the spider rose to its full biting position, and Coale let the arrow fly. The string snapped. With a *thwack*, the bolt skewered the black spider, pinning it against a log behind the scout.

Elgon and Welker snapped awake and rolled in single motions out of their sleeping bags, grabbing their swords like lightning. Bany and Touvinde were barely a second behind. Gradjek was still frozen, waiting for the numbing bite.

"What is it?" Welker hissed.

Coale got out of her sleeping bag. "Nightspider," she returned softly, as if there was still a need for silence. "I think I hit it."

Slowly, Gradjek looked down at the back of his knee. There was a small black stain on his trousers where fluid had splattered, and a single spider leg clung in a macabre grip from his pants, but the spider itself was gone. He glanced behind him, along the trajectory of the shot, and saw the body split and dripping around the shaft of the warbolt.

"Moons, Coale," he said unsteadily.

She shrugged, unrolled, and shook out her moccasins, then pulled them on and made her way around the camp to the log, where she worked the bolt free. The other scouts slowly relaxed, but Bany gave the older wolfwalker, then Gradjek, a thoughtful look. He said nothing, but began to build up the fire for breakfast as the gray dawn lightened the woods. Only Ukiah and Touvinde went back to sleep. The others stayed up for the dawn. It was a striking sky, with reds and purples that faded into yellow-golds, and as if those bold colors set the tone for the day, Bany spiced their gruel even more than usual. They hit the trail two hours early that morning.

The next evening Touvinde shot a branch from beneath a forest cat that had perched over Elgon's bed. The cat fell, unable to coordinate its leap, and Elgon yanked the sleeping bag over his head while the cat landed in a panicked tangle, then raced away. Elgon poked his head out of his sack cautiously as a mole. Had Touvinde wounded the cat, Elgon would have been shredded in the death throes of the beast. As it was, only his sleeping bag was torn. He examined the tears in his blanket roll while Touvinde, watching him, twisted the ends of his stringy mustache.

"At least the claw marks match the design of the cloth," Touvinde offered dryly.

Elgon stared at the rips, then actually grinned. "I consider them an aesthetic addition." He nodded to the other man, then crawled back in and went to sleep as if nothing had happened at all.

The fourth night out, Vlen and Shona were far away, and Ukiah and Welker were switching watches, when the forest erupted around them. Yellow fangs and pink, slitted eyes flashed across the fire. Thick bodies hurtled out of the darkness. Ukiah shoved Welker out of the way, and the woman snapped out her sword as she fell, skewering one of the bihwadi just as it leaped for her throat. Three of the other dog beasts took Ukiah down, tearing at his neck and body. His arms went up to cover his throat. Then Bany was on them, yanking the bihwadi off and splitting them in half midair with his sword. Ukiah ended up on the ground, puddled in gore from the fanged creatures, rubbing at his torn chin and arms. He stared at a carcass, still draped across his legs, then up at the old man. "I owe you my life," he said finally.

The old man shrugged as he dragged a bihwadi body away from the fire, where the flames were burning the fur. "Doesn't matter," the old scout returned. "You'd have done the same for me."

"Would have, before," Ukiah agreed. "But now it's different."

Bany met his eyes and nodded shortly. Rezs, who had been frozen, looked from one to the other. Her heart was still pounding, her throat still closed with fear, and Ukiah and Bany were trading casual comments as if an attack was a common occurrence. She finally scrambled out of her sleeping bag and went over to Welker. The lanky woman had rolled against a tree and used the carcass of one bihwadi as a shield against the others. Welker sported three sets of teeth marks along her arm, but shrugged them off with a smile at Rezs. "Better than my late mate," she said dryly as Rezs offered her a bandage. "Now, there was a beast with a temper."

"By the moons," Rezs muttered. "Is it always so dangerous out here?"

Welker looked up. Her voice was as soft as ever, and Rezs was hard-pressed to hear any leftover fear in its tones. "It's a challenge, Wolfwalker—to stay alive."

"And you like it."

The woman pressed an antitoxin powder into one set of teeth marks, then wrapped the bandage around that wound. "It helps you value what you love."

"That's a pail of worlag piss, Welker." The sharpness of her own voice startled her. "There's more to feeling challenged or valuing your family than always being in a life-or-death situation."

"True, but life-and-death situations give you a sense of mortality. When you lose that, you begin to be less considerate of others. You start to think, it won't really hurt that person to cheat him a few silvers on this deal. It won't really matter if you take a little more for yourself, or feed your neighbor's dnu a little less. We become a little more selfish; a little more greedy. And then we start developing bullies because it's easier for them to find a niche in a society where people are willing to let a tiny social crime go without punishment in order to be more comfortable themselves."

Rezs stared at her. "You fight off a dog-beast, then spout philosophy like an Ancient? What do tiny social crimes have to do with survival?"

Welker looked up, then back at her arm as she worked. "Comfort and image and those little social crimes become a cycle, Wolfwalker. A cycle in which the challenge that teaches you the value of life becomes lost in the challenge of looking better than your neighbor." The woman gestured at Bany, who, with Touvinde, was strapping the bihwadi carcasses to one of the dnu to get rid of them away from camp. "Out here, it's hard to look better or worse than anyone else. Doesn't matter if you're reacting to a bihwadi attack or running from a lepa flock or trying to cross a swollen stream. You can't hide what you are out here. The challenges, the need to rely on others, the teamwork required to stay alive, and the knowledge that life is precious—that it can be lost because of that slightly less well-fed dnu, or lost because the poorer steel was all a man could afford after he was cheated of that silver—we hold on to the sense of those things on this world."

"I don't think location determines your values."

The woman shook her head. "Look at oldEarth. Humans there lost all consideration for each other—all value for any kind of life. Their societies were based on hoarding power, not on promoting teamwork or valuing our differences. They paved paths in the canyons, and turned the forests into matchstick farms. If they had any respect for their world or for each other, it became nothing more than blasé dismissal because there was no reality to the concept of wilderness or what it took to survive." The woman knotted the wrap on her arm. "Here—" She gestured with her chin at the bandage as she tied it off. "We work together or we die. You can't be inconsiderate of your neighbor when you need that man to protect your back—his well-being is your protection. If you cheat your partner, you simply cheat yourself." She glanced meaningfully at Bany and Ukiah. "If Ukiah and Bany were working against each other, Ukiah would now be dead, and it would be his carcass, not those of the bihwadi, that the old man was hauling away."

"Not everyone wants to live in the wilderness."

"Now that's an odd thought—coming from a wolfwalker."

"I'll not deny that I've always wanted to run with the wolves, but I never thought I'd enjoy doing it in the rain or mud."

"And now you do?"

Rezs shrugged. "I didn't at first. But the longer I'm with Vlen, the less I seem to notice it. Now, yes," she admitted, "I think I almost enjoy it."

"You won't even blink at the rain in a year."

Rezs gave her an odd look. "I suppose you think that everyone—merchant or not—should spend some time out here."

"Half a year—on the venges, on a scouting post, on a road-growing crew—should be enough for anyone to appreciate the value of life." Welker's eyes flicked toward Coale. "But experienced or not, you have to respect this world, Wolfwalker. You have to live with it, not control it till there's nothing to it but a sterile garden of steel and stone and dead wood." She indicated the older wolfwalker, and Rezs followed her gesture. Coale was picking her herbs out of the dirt where they had been thrown off their small drying tray. "Every handful of plants is important. Ever watched that wolfwalker harvest her herbs? She never takes the propagating stock, only the extra growth, and she cuts that in a way that thins the base stock out so the plants that are left have more room to grow."

Rezs had never heard Welker speak so much in all the days they'd been riding together. "You don't run trail with Coale," she said slowly. "How can you tell the way she harvests plants?"

The woman shrugged. "I see the herbs she dries near the fire at night. The golden engrel—the stems are thin, and I know she's taken the new growth that won't hurt the base plant from which all new growth comes. The variegated vames—she cuts the older, thicker roots, leaving the new, growing roots to continue spreading the plants." Welker started working on the second set of teeth marks. "Everything we do reflects on our world, Wolfwalker. When we lose respect for our world, we show only our lack of respect for ourselves. The oldEarthers taught us a valuable lesson. They controlled oldEarth to its death, and the one thing it showed was their need to control each other. There are other, better ways to live."

Rezs looked deeply into the other woman's eyes, and what she saw made her pause: There was a bitter acceptance of the control of which Welker spoke—a resignation that, in spite of the woman's words, stripped all expectation from her. Welker might see the need of the challenge for others, but Rezs wondered if she really felt the joy in it herself. Thoughtfully, Rezs handed the now silent woman the last bandage. With everything that Welker had said, the woman had no real connection to anyone else, she realized. On the surface, the lanky woman was the perfect scout—protective and competent, strong and supportive . . . But the wall she had made between herself and her emotions served only to keep her from those with whom she rode. The teeth marks on Welker's arm were the most realistic contact she had had with any creature. And Rezs, staring at the awkward woman, realized that that was the way Welker wanted it.

Abruptly, Rezs stepped back. Welker did not seem to notice. After a few moments, Rezs went back to her bag and crawled in. She did not offer to help with the carcasses; Bany and Gradjek had loaded them on a dnu. All she could do was lie back in the dark and dream about pink, slitted eyes.

For hours each day Coale had her run trail with Vlen. Rezs grew so used to ducking and crawling through the sudden arches and brush tunnels in the game trails that she began to feel like a four-legged creature herself. Hoof divits, scratched trees, nibbled leaves, yanked weeds—she fingered and examined them. Urine streaks and dung piles filled her nose with both sweet and bitter odors that Vlen separated sharply in her mind. But it was Coale's voice, firm and clear in the gray fog, that colored her very thoughts.

When they were together, the other woman became something more than a teacher. There was a sense of freedom contained—or an almost restrained joy about the woman. Each morning, when Coale exchanged her riding boots for running moccasins, the woman changed the way she moved. She ran more lightly, with less limp. She sang her voice into the packsong, so that Rezs was eager to find Coale's tone as if in that daily search was some kind of hide-and-seek game.

Twice, Rezs felt as if she looked through the eyes of other wolves, and the shades of gray she felt were suddenly filled with her father's and Cal's voices. She had to fight the tightness that gripped her throat when she heard them. It could have been imagination that brought their voices to her ears; it could have been the wolves, but either way, she could not escape the fact that, had her father returned, as Cal had promised, she had not been there to greet him. She'd not been there to show him how good Vlen was to be with, nor how strong their bond was growing, nor what she had learned of neGruli through the link with the cub. If her father had been so angry that he'd left without even meeting Vlen, how would he feel when he found she had left to run trail with the cub instead of waiting for him at home? She gripped Vlen's scruff absently, then stroked his back with a bittersweet sense of closeness. No matter when she returned home or what she brought with her, the yearling now stood between them like the distance. And the voices that haunted her mind—like the music that had been with her since that blader's knife on her throat—Cal's steady murmur and her father's sharp tones— they were as addictive as dator.

She couldn't help stretching along the distant bonds to listen to the voices. At night, when she let herself relax, her mind was filled with the song of the wolves and the voices of her family always hidden in that fog. Gray fogs, gray howls . . . She would find herself rubbing absently at her neck—where the steel had touched her flesh—and would hear again that haunting music. Piercing eyes would float behind the gleaming yellow gazes, and she would think of a man whose center was as gray as the wolfpack . . .

"Is Grayheart a wolfwalker?" she asked Coale one time.

They were jogging along a trail, and the other woman looked back, then halted. "Grayheart? No. Why?"

Rezs took off her warcap and shook out her hair. "When I think of him, I think of music and hear the wolves at the same time."

Coale shrugged. "Some people will always remind you of the wolfpack."

"He was very young when he left his teacher."

"Sixteen."

"You'd think he'd have gotten over it by now—accepted the music back into his life."

Something flickered in Coale's eyes, and she looked away from Rezs's gaze. "Youth is unforgiving," she returned softly. "Shock a youth with a loss like that, and he'll bear the grief forever."

"And reject anything that reminds him of that grief? Even a child has to let go of it sometime. You can't let it define who you are."

Coale smiled faintly. "You're either very wise yourself, or very inexperienced."

Rezs put her warcap back on slowly. There was something in Coale's tone that made Rezs stretch her bond to Vlen. The cub's ears perked, and for a moment the gray fog tightened with its own unhappiness. "You disagree?" she asked.

Coale shrugged. "I think you accumulate grief as you go through life, and it can make you bitter, empty, cold, or wise."

"That's very pessimistic."

"Unless you believe that most people will eventually end up wise."

"But Grayheart isn't one of those people?"

The woman looked down at Gray Shona and absently scratched the wolf's ears. "Grayheart will never get past the emptiness that sucks at his soul until he opens himself up again. To a lover, to his music, to the wolves—it doesn't matter to whom or what."

"To the wolves?"

"He would have become a wolfwalker," she explained softly. "But after the killing of his family, he closed himself off—not just from his feelings, but from the packsong itself. The wolves think of him as one of their own, but he will not acknowledge them. So he runs with them and without them. His heart is gray as the song of the wolves, but his mind is walled off from that heart."

"So why can't the wolves make a bond with him anyway—reach into his mind the way they do mine?"

"You can't walk into a closed room, Rezs, without first opening a door. You can't fill a sealed box. Grayheart will never have anything inside himself but emptiness until he lets someone in his heart. Can you force someone to love you? No. You can remain near him, giving him a chance to see you, but one-sided hope is obsession, not love." Coale sighed. "The wolves watch him—they're aware of him as you are aware of me through Vlen. But they do not intrude in his life. A bond with a wolf is like a link to family—it is an attachment that grows through time. Someday, perhaps, he will let a Gray One near him. Until then, he will run alone."

"A lone wolf . . ."

"Yes."

"Like you?"

Coale raised her eyebrows, then actually laughed. The expression lifted the woman's face, and for a moment Rezs thought those dark eyes looked violet.

"I never thought of myself as a lone wolf," the older woman returned. "I travel quite a bit—we all do. Elgon and I—well, when you don't know how long you'll be gone, it is easier to travel with only one or two others, who don't care when they return, than make plans to fit with some group. Travelers usually expect wolfwalkers to act as scouts. Once you commit to running trail with them, you cannot just leave them in the middle of a wilderness to go off on your own with your wolf. You and Bany—your group is made up of scouts. It doesn't hurt you to have me leave for the afternoons on my own."

Rezs glanced at the sky. The sun had shifted so that the shadows were nearly vertical. "Like now," she said.

The other woman nodded. "We'll have to hurry to rejoin the others before they stop for lunch." She motioned for them to continue.

When Coale was done with Rezs for the day, and Rezs returned to the rest of the scouts, Bany or Gradjek grilled her on her lessons. Afterward Ukiah made remarks or asked questions, but they centered more around how Rezs felt or interacted with Coale than about the subtle differences between animal tracks.

Rezs eyed the tall scout more than once. The handsome men she had met at home generally talked more of themselves than anything else. This scout seemed almost as distant from his recognition of his own good looks as he was from the rest of the group. Vlen seemed to trot beside Touvinde's dnu more than anywhere else, but the cub tolerated Ukiah better than any of the others, and the packsong that rode the back of Rezs's mind was more distinct when she was near him. Curious, she tried to get Ukiah to talk, but he was as close-mouthed as a clam at low tide. Finally, she deliberately tried to provoke him.

The first time, they were riding just ahead of Bany, and Ukiah had just come back from gathering tribeetle eggs for the group. Rezs looked down at the globules in her hand, then up at Ukiah. "You really eat these," she said flatly.

He popped a couple in his mouth. "Suck on them first. You get the sweet taste from the shell that way."

"I thought we couldn't eat anything without combining it with extractors."

"For the most part," he agreed. "It's too difficult to teach children and most people the subtle identifications of what they can and can't eat, so the general rule is, no food without extractors. For fruits, roots, and most animals, it's very true—they're all toxic. But there are eleven insects you can eat, three different moss bulbs, one seaweed, two types of Yucky leaves—"

"Yucky leaves?" she interrupted.

He nodded. "They grow only in the alpine areas, but they're a good source of vitamins. In a pinch, they'll sustain you better than most other foods."

"How did you learn all this?"

He shrugged. "I've been running trail nearly thirty years."

She studied his remote expression. "How many times has someone saved your skin?"

"Three times. Bany makes it four."

"You say it as if you owe him a debt."

He gave her a sharp look. "I do."

"But how can you repay a life?"

"That's what loyalty is for."

"As in, you'd do anything for him now?"

He shrugged. "As the Celilo folks would say, Bany now owns my soul."

Rezs watched him crunch down on the beetle eggs.

"I wonder," she said softly, "how many souls he owns now."

Something flickered in Ukiah's eyes. "Too many," he answered shortly.

Gingerly, she put an egg in her mouth. "Sometimes I wonder how a person gets to be the way he is," she said around the egg, careful not to bite down yet.

"Same way as the rest of us—we take our child selves and make them older."

"I have a hard time imagining Touvinde as a boy."

Ukiah looked away as he answered. "He didn't have much of a childhood."

"You knew him when he was younger?"

"We were neighbors." He seemed suddenly withdrawn.

"So you played together?"

"We trained together in weaponry."

"As children?" she pressed.

Ukiah gave her an expressionless look. "Touvinde's father didn't see the boy as a child, but as a newer version of himself—as if he could rework his own life through his son. He pushed Touvinde in everything. Got him special teachers. Directed his training in every area of study. Pressed him to be the best, no matter how young he was compared to everyone else. When his family died, Touvinde just seemed to . . . burn out. He rode away, and hasn't looked back since."

The gray thread of music clung to Ukiah's words, and Rezs looked down at her hands. Touvinde . . . Grayheart? Without thinking, she sucked on the egg, then raised her eyebrows in surprise—it was sweet.

"What about Gradjek?"

"Big family. Has relatives just about everywhere."

"So those really were his cousins back at that town?"

Ukiah glanced back along the line. "Gradjek has so many brothers and sisters, cousins and aunts and uncles that he could fill an entire village with his family alone. He runs into them in every county."

"Even among the raiders?"

"Even there," Ukiah agreed. "But those branches aren't as keen on reunions."

"And what about you? What kind of boy were you?"

He shrugged.

"What did you dream of being?" she persisted. "A glass-blower or mathematician or musician or miner?" She caught his hesitation. "You've gotten me curious now, and I should warn you that you can let me go on questioning you all day, or you can just tell me what you did. I'm not going to give up."

"I could just ride on ahead."

"I'd follow you. And then I'd get in some kind of trouble, and you'd have to save my life, and I'd be the one in debt." She teased gently, "Do you really want to own a soul like this?"

"No." But his voice wasn't joking, and his expression seemed suddenly even more remote.

"Tell me." Then, lower, "Please."

For a long moment, he didn't answer. Then, in a voice so casual that he could have been reciting directions, he said, "I trained with Touvinde, but not as seriously as he, so I never learned what I needed to know to keep my own family safe. Then, when I should have been fighting for their lives, instead I watched them die."

Rezs felt suddenly intrusive. She bit down on the egg, and as the sudden bitterness hit her tongue, she swallowed with a choke.

Ukiah raised his eyebrows. "Shock you?"

"Just tasted something bitter," she returned.

"I know the feeling."

"So there isn't anything else in your life—no family, no friends. Not even an interest outside of trail running?"

"Nothing that has value. Does that disappoint you?"

She didn't answer for a moment. She glanced at Vlen, and the cub's sense of the man permeated her mind, so that she felt the untruth of his words even as he said them. Whatever scars he carried inside made Vlen's scruff bristle slightly and his yellow eyes eager to seek out his prey. Rezs eyed the way Ukiah's jerkin hung from his broad shoulders; the way his strong hands and long fingers held the reins almost negligently. She could almost see them holding a sword as casually to the throat of a raider; setting an arrow to sinew almost as carelessly as he drew bow on a deer. "No," she said finally. "I'm not disappointed at all."

Slowly, Ukiah grinned, but there was no humor in it, and for a moment, as the light hit his face, his eyes seemed to gleam yellow. Rezs studied him for a moment, then looked down at the two eggs in her hand. She held them up. "Show me where to find these?"

He raised his eyebrows.

She popped both eggs in her mouth. Deliberately, she chewed so that their bitter juices burst over her tongue. "I think I like them."

Ukiah eyed her without speaking, and she wondered briefly how many other pairs of eyes watched their exchange. The packsong that lifted through Vlen's mind made Rezs think that what she saw with her eyes was only a shadow of the man who hid in that fog of thick, gray voices. Then Ukiah nodded, a short, single motion, and they rode along in silence.

XV

As the altitude increased, the rootroads gave way to stretches of rarely used worm-carved stone, cracked by weathering and subtle shifts of the earth. They had passed the last homesteads—restorations of ancient buildings—the day before, and since then had had nothing but wilderness and ruins for company. In two days they startled few creatures: a poolah feeding on an old dnu carcass; a pair of water cats spitting and hissing over a fish; and a herd of small, half-striped deer.

From dawn till late into the mornings, Rezs ran trail with Coale. Sometimes it was by dnu, sometimes on foot, but always with the wolfpack. The older woman didn't mind Rezs collecting samples—in fact, once she understood what Rezs was looking for, she seemed to encourage it by pointing out species Rezs might not have seen before. There was a mold that grew only on the tips of piletree nuts, and one that draped like moss on trees infected with white spitting worms. There was a lichen that inhabited the cracks between rocks and turned bright red when the sun hit it. Once, when they stopped and examined the pits between tree roots, they found a bed of moss that held three different lichen: one spotted with purple and green in which the nightspiders hid; one stringy and tough and toxic, which the spider ate to intensify its own venom; and one succulent and spongy, sweet and aromatic, which attracted the rodents and rabbits and bugs on which the spider fed. There were puffy black balls that grew out from the blacktree bark, which burst when she touched them. There were flat, blue circles on towering wolinda trees that were not fungus at all, according to Coale. Those were the excrement rings of the tiny beetles that parasitized the wood.

They went only twice into caves. Coale didn't seem to like the dark places, and Rezs wasn't sure if their off-trail exploring just happened to lead them away from caverns, or if the other woman was deliberately avoiding them. But Coale was patience itself when they were working with plants. Rezs learned quickly—she knew that pleased her teacher. But it was more than that. In every other way, the woman was alert to every sight and sound in the forest. Coale smelled things; she listened through Gray Shona's ears. Every few minutes she cautioned Rezs about this plant or that creature. Between cautions, she identified species and gave Rezs some silly anecdote or story of lifesaving properties. But every now and then the two women would stop and Coale would be quiet and still. Sometimes they would be harvesting herbs, sometimes just watching a tumbling creek. Sometimes they would stand on the edge of a meadow and listen to the field mice graze. Those were the times that Coale seemed at peace. Rezs couldn't quite see it, but she could feel it through Vlen. At other times the mental lupine fog seemed to roil with sounds, as if the din of the wolfpack was made up of separate currents that twisted around each other. But when they simply stood and listened, the gray fog became calm. It was at those times that the sense of other people was strongest in Rezsia's mind. The voice of the blader seemed to be in her thoughts, and the feel of his iron hands on her arms. When she concentrated, her father's voice seemed to float through the fog, and her brother's voice to reverberate like a subsonic hum.

The scout Touvinde ran with them once. Coale wasn't pleased with it, but she allowed it. Rezs knew why: Bany wanted to know if the older wolfwalker was really teaching Rezs her skills. Oddly enough, Touvinde, for all his acidic comments, was as calm and adept as Coale, and both Vlen and Shona seemed eager to trot by his side. By noon, the three of them moved together almost without having to speak. Whatever Touvinde said to Bany seemed to allay the old man's wariness, because although Ukiah and Bany continued to watch the woman closely, they all left Coale alone.

When Rezs rode with the other scouts, she took her afternoon break by preparing samples for testing. She shook out spores on special papers, cut samples into tiny flat dishes, and put careful droplets on tiny tendrils to see what colors they'd turn. Touvinde, who was so good with Coale in the forest, was incompetent when it came to chemicals. It was Gradjek who helped Rezs with her work. The only drawback to that was the freckled man's impatience. Four times, he ruined the test papers she had set up, because he pulled them out too early. Once, he mixed a set of drops too quickly, and they began to foam and steam. Gradjek had been leaning closely over them as he watched for the color change, and when he breathed in, he began to cough and spit, his eyes running with tears. Rezs had to throw water on the whole thing to stop the reaction and dissipate the gas.

"Moonworms, Gradjek." Ukiah had laughed. "Would it have killed you to hold off for the ten minutes she told you to wait?"

The other scout, sputtering and wiping at his nose and eyes, emptied his bota bag over his eyes. "She didn't say it would react like this," he retorted. He grabbed another bota bag and sighed as the water began to reduce the sting.

Rezs looked up from mopping up the mess. "I didn't tell you on purpose," she said dryly. "I got tired of telling you to wait for things to finish before you messed with them, so this time I let you find out for yourself what could happen."

Ukiah's eyes glinted, and Rezs had a sudden urge to touch her neck. The back of that knife, to teach her a lesson . . . How much weight would she have given all Elgon's warnings if that blader had not scared her first? Gray Vlen, upwind, fairly bristled as the shiver of fear touched her back, and she had to shake it off before she could reassure the cub.

Gradjek gave Rezsia a sour expression. His collar was dripping, and his eyes were red from the gas. With his peeling skin, he looked like a spotted, sunburned rat with a hangover. "Next time," he told her in disgust, "remind me to ask for the cautions that come with the instructions."

"Just tell him it should take twice as long as you think it should," Touvinde put in. "That way, he'll take it out exactly when you want."

Gradjek snorted again in disgust, and Elgon studied his face. "You want Coale to look at that when she comes back? She learned a few things from a healer a couple years ago."

The other scout shook his head. "Doesn't even sting now. Unless"—he looked at Rezs—"there's something I should know about it that you haven't told me yet?"

Rezs shook her head in turn. "It will fade completely in the next half hour." She rinsed the dirty petri and tossed the leftover fragments of fungus and paper into the firepit. "At least the work wasn't important."

Gradjek looked blearily at the flare of fire that curled around the fungus. "All that," he said sourly, "for a lesson."

She felt Ukiah's gaze still on her, and deliberately, she looked up and met it. "If you learned, it was worth it."

The graysong tightened, and Ukiah's lips seemed to stretch in his own lupine smile. For an instant she felt the steel on her throat. Then the image was gone, Ukiah looked away, and only the chill in her thoughts was enough to leave the fire seeming cold on her flesh.

Early into the second ninan, Coale and Rezs were a kilometer away from the rest of the group, moving swiftly, jogging behind Shona and Vlen. Rezs was trying to separate Vlen's senses from her own as she ran, while Coale, her voice patient and steady, tested her on her plant identification. After a while, Coale's voice became faint, as if they ran at a distance from each other.

Rezs, panting slightly, looked at Vlen, then back at Coale. Her vision was still slightly blurred, and her nose and ears sharp; she could almost see—through Vlen and Shona—an image of the woman she ran with. That wolfwalker did not look the same as she did in person: She was taller in Rezs's mind, and shrouded in foggy shades of blue and gray. There was a longing in her mental voice that reminded Rezs of the way she missed her mother, and a tone of bitterness that made her think of her father. Then, as if those thoughts called her family to mind, an image of her father and one of her brothers seemed to ride out of the packsong and swing close to her on the trail. She caught her breath.

Coale touched her arm quickly. "What is it?"

"My father . . . Cal—" She tried to focus, but her sight was still yellowed and her vision blurred from the sense of the cub. Yellow eyes gleamed in her mind. She pulled back from Vlen to concentrate, and abruptly, the images faded.

"Moonworms— Here—on the trail," she said sharply to Coale. "I saw them as close to me as you are now."

Shona growled softly, and the other woman stepped back. The connection between them and Rezs disappeared, and Gray Vlen's mind seemed suddenly loud in her echoing head. "That is not uncommon," said Coale.

Rezs felt the cool air begin to chill her skin, and absently, she began to rub her arms. "Did I touch him through Vlen?"

The other woman shrugged out of her pack and worked her cloak free of the bottom straps. "Perhaps. It is easier to hear the ones you love rather than strangers through the packsong."

"But the distance—we're more than a ninan from my home. I thought you couldn't communicate when you were so far away. And they're not wolfwalkers. How could I reach them?"

"They must be near the Gray Ones, and you must love them a great deal."

But had Coale hesitated before she answered? Rezs's gaze sharpened as she watched the woman wrap herself back in her cloak. "How long were you in my mind?" she asked softly.

The woman looked up, and for a moment Rezs could swear she saw a flash of yellow in the woman's eyes. "I wasn't in your mind. You heard me through the packsong, just as you heard . . . your father."

This time Rezs was sure the woman had hesitated. "There is something about that which bothers you," she stated flatly.

"No," the woman said steadily. "I'm just . . . surprised that you have a strong enough link to hear him through Gray Vlen."

Rezs studied the other woman. *Vlen,* she sent subtly, *that image of father and Cal—was it mine or hers?*

Vlen looked up at her, so that, when their eyes met, his voice became thick in her mind. *It was in the packsong,* he returned. He stretched to let the howling music fill his mind, but Rezs couldn't find the figures anymore.

Coale didn't seem to have noticed. Instead, the woman motioned for them to continue. "Your choice," she said. "We can run all the way back to catch up with the group, or we can climb the shoulder of that hill and meet them ahead on the trail."

"You don't really think I'm going to take the first option, do you?"

Coale smiled and Rezs almost stared. The woman's expression had lifted her face from shadow, leaving it almost radiant. Rezs realized that like Ukiah, Coale had never smiled with her eyes before this. Why now? she wondered. What had changed? The images that she had seen—of her father and brother, Cal—had Coale seen some of her own? The heart of the fire, Elgon had said. The essence of whatever life was burned away by time and heat. What Coale sought . . .

But the woman had already turned away to the game trail, automatically pointing out the stinging grass by its side. Rezs stepped over it carefully and, with a thoughtful glance at Gray Shona, followed the woman again.

It didn't take long to reach the hill, but the climb was steep. They stopped more than once to catch their breath and scramble over jutting boulders. Partway up, they passed two caves that Rezs eyed wistfully, but neither one was deep enough to house roofbleeders, and both were clean enough that the fungi source she sought from neGruli could not have been within.

When they did reach the top of the shoulder, they came to a halt abruptly. The poolah had not yet noticed their presence, but the wind was blowing down from the hill, and the creature would smell them within seconds. Rezs made to back away, but Coale stopped her with a hand on her arm. "It doesn't matter," she said. "The poolah won't leave till it's done eating."

"That's a dnu, Coale."

The woman nodded.

Below, the poolah raised its sightless head and swung it across the wind. The sun shifted, and something glinted dully. Rezs squinted. "It's not a wild dnu."

The other wolfwalker nodded again. "Probably ran away from that last homestead. Their barn had more stables than dnu."

Rezs said nothing. The carcass below was bloated and carved out in death; its rib cage created a bony cavern into which the poolah had half-disappeared as it dug out its meal. Even from the hilltop, she could see that the dnu had been dead at least a ninan. And, she thought, it could have run free for a while before being caught. NeGruli had lost four men on his last trip, and the dnu he took out had not returned either. If this was one of the riding beasts from his party, she must be close to his source. He said they were attacked by worlags just after they started back.

Coale studied her face. "What is it?"

Rezs realized her jaw had tightened. "It's nothing," she returned quickly. How the woman could see her so clearly when her own eyesight was always blurred . . . She shrugged deliberately. "Can we go on?"

"Carefully, yes. As long as we don't approach the poolah, it should let us be."

Rezs watched the creature thoughtfully. "You said my bond was strong enough to reach back to my father. Is it then strong enough to begin reading the memories of the wolfpack?"

Coale hesitated.

"Or is it a question of discipline?"

"It's not that. You've developed enough discipline to keep your mind fairly well separate from the packsong . . ."

"Will you teach me, then, tonight?"

The other woman watched the poolah gnaw at the guts of the carcass. Whatever smile had touched her face before was gone completely, leaving her face once more in shadow. "Tonight," Coale agreed quietly. "We'll call the pack to us."

Camp was a sober affair that day. There had been no game in sight, and dinner was a mushy stew of beetles, roots, and jerky. For all that she had run half a day and ridden the rest, Rezs wasn't hungry. She forced down half a bowl of stew, and was about to give the rest to Vlen when Coale shook her head.

"Finish it," the woman said. "You need strength of body, not just of mind, to open yourself to the packsong."

Gradjek, on the other side of the wolfwalker, raised his eyebrows. "Why? It's just a bunch of mental howling, isn't it?"

"The . . . sound you hear might seem like that," the woman returned. "But it's energy—the combined biological energy of every wolf in the link. You tap into it every time you open yourself to your Gray One. That's why it's important to learn to keep yourself separate before you do any kind of Calling. If you can't keep your own energy distinct from that of the wolves, you can be sucked dry through your own link."

The freckled man rubbed the back of his hands, loosening another patch of peeled skin. Absently, he scraped it off and ground it under his boot into the dirt. "Sounds rather fatal," he commented.

Elgon glanced at Coale. "It can be," he answered for her. "If you go too deeply into the packsong, you can forget who you are—lose yourself. There are wolfwalkers who have almost frozen to death because they did a Calling in winter, and couldn't pull themselves out of the packsong afterward. Because the wolves were warm enough, the wolfwalker didn't know she was cold and getting colder."

As if the mention of winter sent her a chill, Coale, who was sitting farther from the fire, wrapped her cloak more closely around herself. "Wolves don't see you the way you see yourself—or any other human," she told Rezs. "The Gray Ones listen to your thoughts and emotions, not just your voice or motions. Their image of you is built more on your strength of will, dominancc, and stamina."

Rezs nodded slowly. So the image of Coale that Rezs saw through Vlen—that was Shona's view of the other wolfwalker. And the human voices in the back of her mind—those could be others here in this group, or other humans the wolves had been around.

Vlen raised his head to sniff at her bowl, and Bany, catching the intensity of the cub's look, chuckled. "You'd better do as your teacher says, Rezs. Otherwise, your Gray One will take your meal for himself."

She made a face. "I didn't mind the beetles; I rather liked the moss bulbs, and I'm becoming uscd to using wild extractors in spite of their bitterness. But the one thing I'm really getting tired of is this interminable trail stew. No matter how you spice it and you," she looked at Bany, "spice the heck out of it—you can't hide the fact that it's stew." She raised the spoon to her lips and sighed. "I dreamed last night of separate dishes: tubers in a mild sauce; grouse with rice and grasses . . . Enough time to cook each type of food with its own, separate extractors . . ."

From the other side of the fire, Welker spooned more gruel into her own bowl. "Keep talking like that, and Bany might let us make camp long enough to do some serious cooking." The tall woman nudged the old man's shoulder. "What do you say, Bany?"

"Rezs is the one who sets the timetable," he returned easily. Welker turned to Rezs. "Wolfwalker?"

She shook her head. "On the way back, maybe. But not the way out. We're behind enough as it is."

"Then, Rezs . . ." Touvinde turned the ladle over in the pot. "Have some more stew?"

Rezs shook her head hurriedly. "No, thanks." She ignored Ukiah's chuckle. "I've had enough." Quickly, she scraped the bowl clean and got to her feet. "I'm ready now, Coale."

Bany said nothing as he watched them walk away from the circle of fire, but Rezs could feel the old man's eyes on their backs. Surreptitiously, she tried to reach through Vlen to feel the old scout, but the thread of Vlen's packsong was laced with that haunting music, and all she could sense were shadow images attached to smoky people. Ukiah, her father, Bany— she couldn't tell if any of them was specifically in Vlen's mind. Only the voice of the woman she hiked behind was sharp in her bond to the cub.

The pack was already on the ridge that hung over the camp, and Coale and Rezsia climbed quickly up to greet them. There were six of them—four adults, two yearlings—aside from Vlen and Shona. The mated pair was close together, and their yellow eyes gleamed in the moonlight that was strengthening as Rezs watched. Slowly, they circled the two women, examining Rezs and Coale and voicing soft snarls that Vlen returned with his own low growling.

Wolfwalker, the Gray Ones sang in her head.

You honor me, she returned. She met their eyes and felt the link to Vlen tighten until she almost choked.

"Go easy, Rezs."

She heard Coale's warning from a distance and realized that she was already drawn past Vlen into the packsong. She forced her consciousness back, then relaxed her throat. When she could breathe more easily, she asked the other woman softly, "When did you Call them?"

"While we were eating."

"Should we kneel?"

"Not until they accept us."

"So we stand here?"

"For now." Coale seemed almost to bristle as the male of the mated pair exchanged greetings with Shona. As Rezs watched, Vlen laid back his ears and panted to show that he was not a threat; and the male, after snapping once at the cub, let Vlen be. Then the wolves arranged themselves on the edge of the cliff. One by one, their silhouettes appeared to the scouts below, until it seemed as if the sky was ringed with Gray Ones.

Wolfwalker, Vlen sent eagerly. *You will sing with me?*

Soon, Gray One, she returned. She could feel her stomach clench in that all-too-familiar sensation of anticipation. Her mind seemed drawn to the cub so tightly that her vision was more Vlen's than hers, and her view of the night became blurred.

Coale nodded to Rezs. "Now," the other woman said, "we kneel. Better to be close to the ground if you get sucked in too deeply—it's easy to fall when you don't know if you have two feet or four."

Obediently, Rezs sank to the ground. She had begun to feel as though she towered over the lupine forms.

Then the mated female threw back her head and let her howl rise into the sky. At first it was a thin howl—a single thread of music that held two tones before falling away off the third. Again, the female raised her voice. This time it was stronger, and one of the younger wolves joined her. Rezs felt her own throat loosen.

Wolfwalker! Vlen howled.

Gray One! Rezs threw back her head. The howl was thick in her ears like the fog in the back of her head. Gray, the tones blended until they swamped her thoughts and left her skull empty of all but the pack sound. She didn't feel Gray Vlen's fur against her legs; she barely noticed the ground. She didn't notice the chill from the spring wind that cut over the edge of the cliff. And she didn't see Coale's lips curled back, or notice that her own teeth were bared. She felt only the wolves—like music that flooded her ears and reduced her thoughts to sensations of sound and image. She heard only the rise and fall of a howling that became her own.

Not all the wolves sang out loud, and not all their howls were the same. The mated male never raised his voice, and one of the yearlings stayed silent. But for all their silence verbally, their presence in the mental packsong was strong.

For more than an hour, that packsong rose and fell from the edge of the cliff while faint echoes drifted back from the hill on the other side of the valley. It wasn't until the song thinned and the wolves began to curl up to sleep that Coale spoke again.

"Now your bond with Vlen is strong enough," the other woman said softly.

Rezs had to think for a moment to translate the woman's words from what Vlen sensed to human speech. "Strong enough . . ." she repeated stupidly.

"To read the memories of the wolves," Coale added.

Shona moved from the pack to sit beside Coale, and Vlen brought his hot breath to Rezsia's ear while Rezs and the older woman linked hands. Rezs was still sensitive to Vlen's mind, and Coale's hand felt rough in her fingers. She looked down. It was skin she was feeling; not the gloves the older woman wore. Ridges of toughened skin seamed the hand she gripped; divits of missing flesh deepened the pockets between the woman's knuckles. She opened her mouth to speak, but Shona's mind blended with Vlen's, and as the older wolf's voice howled softly into her skull, her vision blurred.

"Center on Vlen's voice," said Coale. "Keep a knot of yourself tightly together, and let the rest of yourself follow the thread of his voice into the packsong."

Obediently, Rezs let the cub's mental voice fill the back of her head. There was a weight of other voices there—wolfsong, human threads—and the din was like a rising fog. Obscuring her thoughts, reaching into her mind, the noise thickened. It became a mass of images. Rezs felt her mind pulled sharply, and she swayed.

"Remain calm." Coale's voice was a sharp punctuation to the mental sounds of the wolves. "Feel your way into the images. Not the ones that are sharp, but the ones that are softened with time. Look for fraying edges and weakened sounds . . ."

Falling . . . It was like falling into a pool, where one instant she saw the surface, gray and glistening with images reflected from the memories of the wolves around her, and the next she had plunged into the water. Bubbles of images burst around her consciousness. Sounds filled her skull—twigs snapping; leaves slapping against her side; bones crunching between fanged teeth . . . She couldn't breathe.

Concentrate, a voice said calmly. *Touch the images till you find the ones you want.*

Frayed edges, time-softened sounds . . . Rezs struggled and

locked onto a gray voice that was thick and strong with age. Not Vlen—the cub howled, and his voice, thin as it was, struck out and shot into her mind like a lance. She didn't know if she cried out, but the snarl that caught on her lips was reflected in her mind like a snapping jaw.

Boots in the mud; hooves slipping on a mushy, unused rootroad . . . The images, blurred in the sight of the wolves, were sharp and clear compared with the other memories. Rezs felt the passage of her own group in the minds of the Gray Ones. She spread mental fingers and sifted out the sharp sounds and sights until the din in the back of her mind came closer, and the music of the packsong began to cloud her concentration.

She didn't see that her hands were clenched around Coale's, or that her face was strained so tightly that her neck muscles stood out like stalks of bamboo. Men, feet, boots in the mud . . . Dnu scent and the sounds of clumsy feet filtered through the leaves among the warning cries of chunko birds and rodents. Packsong, threaded with music; faces, yelling; blurred and slack. And within the music, a trail that pointed north and west and led between the mountains.

There was a surge in the gray din—a wave that broke like hands of iron over her thoughts. Gray Vlen howled, and Rezsia was yanked from the packsong. She felt flesh beneath her fingers—slender bones that gripped her as strongly as she clenched them. Vlen snarled, and this time she heard him in her ears, not just her head. Slowly, her eyesight cleared, while around them the other Gray Ones faded away, leaving the two women alone on the cliff.

Rezs raised her head. "Is it always like that?" she managed.

The hollows of Coale's eyes were dark as night. "Not always. Sometimes it's like flying, and the gray voices lift you and drag you along through their history. Sometimes it is dark, like a whirlpool that sucks you in and refuses to let you go. And sometimes it is like this, where you simply sift through the images until you find the ones you seek."

"I saw dnu and riders. I saw more than one fire at night. I saw faces against the ground—but that can't have been ne-Gruli's men. They'd have been alive when they rode through here."

The older woman untangled her fingers from Rezs's.

"Sleeping, perhaps," she said. "Or dead on their way back. The party moving north was much larger than the two who returned. Remember—there is no sequential sense to the Gray Ones' memories—at least, not in the way we think of sequence. If you're trying to find a time line, you have to look at the memories of the wolves in terms of which images are more frayed, and which are more important. Importance gives a sharper edge to a memory—makes it easier to read."

"Those faces—they were of the dead." Rezs's voice was flat and certain. "There was no sense of breath in Vlen's mind. No sense of life to the memory. You didn't feel that?"

"I didn't seek that memory; I didn't feel it as strongly as you did." The woman ran a hand around her warcap. "Why do you trail these men anyway?"

"They're—" Rezs broke off. She stiffened, staring at Coale. "Dear moons, what have I done?"

Vlen, watching the two women, snarled low in his throat, and Gray Shona returned the growl. Unsteadily, Rezs scrambled to her feet. Coale rose awkwardly, her weak leg uncooperative, and Vlen's hackles began to bristle. "Stop it," the older woman said sternly.

Vlen slunk back. Rezs's jaw tightened.

"You've betrayed nothing," the other woman said quietly. "Whatever secrets you wish to keep are still yours. I'm not one to interfere with what is not my business."

There was an uncompromising flatness to the woman's tone that made Rezs's lips tighten as if she bit into a bitter root. "You read the memories with me," she returned. "You guided me to them. You must have seen what I was reading—you must know by now what I'm looking for."

Coale studied her for a moment, then deliberately adjusted her tunic and wrapped her cloak more closely around her lean shoulders. "Reading the memories of the wolves is not a simple thing, Rezs, and if I'm to help you find the trail you want, I, too, have to know what I'm looking for. What I saw through Shona and Vlen was nothing that could hurt you."

"Why are you here, Coale? Why agree to travel this far with me, just to teach me about the trail? You could have made it part of our arrangement to teach me close to a city. Are you really what you say you are—just another wolfwalker running trail with the pack? You work for yourself, no one else?"

For a moment Coale didn't speak. Her voice, when she finally spoke, was so low that Rezs had to strain to hear it. "Sometimes, I think I work for the moons—for nothing more than a hope." She seemed to shake herself. Her voice grew firm. "It's been a long time since I was able to give anything to my family. Perhaps you simply represent what I can't have for myself."

"You never say anything straight, do you, Coale? If I asked you directly if you worked for someone—like, neGruli for instance—what would you say?"

The woman didn't look away, and in the moonlight, her dark eyes seemed to burn through Rezs. "I think that until you learn to read the truth through the wolves, it wouldn't matter what I answered."

"Moonworms, Coale. A yes or no—that's all I'm looking for."

The other woman's lips stretched in a lupine grin. "And I thought you were looking for lichens and moss."

"Fungi," Rezs corrected in disgust. "Lichens are symbionts made of a combination of fungi and algae. Mosses are plants with leaves and chlorophyll. Fungi are like yeasts and molds and algae—they have no roots or stems or leaves like higher plants, but they can breed together to form new species—and *that's* what I'm looking for."

"A new species or an old combination?"

For a moment Rezs felt Coale's voice in her head, and the chill she returned through her link to Vlen made the cub bristle again and snarl.

Coale nodded, as if to herself, then turned away. For a moment Rezs couldn't move. Her hand was still clenched in Vlen's scruff, and the cub whined low in his throat. "Gray One," she whispered. "She's like Old Roy and yet not similar to him at all. And I think her words make sense until I walk away, and realize that all I have left from our conversations are questions that I can't answer."

Wolfwalker. Vlen nudged her thigh.

Rezs looked down at the cub. "I can't trust what I don't know, Vlen. And I don't know her."

Her scent is fresh in your nose, he returned. *Her voice is deep in your mind. How can you not know her?*

Rezs looked after Coale, but she couldn't see wolf or

wolfwalker in the trees and scattered moonlight. "I think she watches me, Vlen. I think I can feel her eyes in my mind."

The wolf cub snarled. *Are you the hunter or the hunted?*

Rezs tried to stretch along that bond, but only Shona's voice and the yellow gleaming eyes looked back through the packsong. "I'm not sure," she said softly. "But I'm beginning to think that her oath to teach me was something she did for herself, not me."

XVI

Two days later found Rezs and Ukiah riding along the edge of a rough cliff above a scalloped valley. The others had taken a break to hunt a deer from the herd they'd seen earlier, and with Coale gone as usual, only Rezs and Ukiah were left with the packs. The moons that floated overhead seemed too heavy to stay up in such a clear sky, and Rezs said as much to Ukiah as she shrugged out of her cloak to watch the sun on the valley.

The tall man hunkered down beside her and gazed out over the spread of green. Before them, the cliff fell away to a ragged mosaic of greens and rusty brown-black rocks. Far away, along the opposite ridge, a line of white domes huddled among the peaks like satellites at moonrise, and the truncated mountain to the southeast marked one of the places where the Ancients landed.

"That's a lot of land," said Rezs. "It will take a while to cross it."

"The lava that covers that valley floor is just a layer here," Ukiah answered. "This was an old ocean before the valley closed off a hundred thousand years ago. The limestone under that lava flow could be millions of years deep, and it's probably porous as sponge. If you're looking for caves, the karst caverns under that lava flow could run for kays beneath the surface."

"Caves, but not right here." Rezs stared across the valley. "We're close, Ukiah. I can feel it in the packsong—I can almost feel it in my blood. Two days, though . . . Maybe three, and we'll be there."

"What exactly are you looking for, anyway?"

She shrugged. "Some kind of fungi—a mold, perhaps. Maybe a combination of lichen and mold."

He raised his eyebrows. "Now tell me something that rings true, Wolfwalker."

She gave him a sharp look. "Excuse me?"

"If you're seeking a fungus, you know it's not around here. You're looking for something much more specific than that."

"It's not really your business, Ukiah. Getting me where I need to go—that's the only thing you should worry about."

"Oh, I worry about that, all right," he said. "I worry that you're getting caught up in something you don't fully understand. I worry that the people you're with aren't at all what they seem to be."

Rezs looked down at Vlen.

"I should warn you," Ukiah said softly. "You've gotten me curious now." She gave him a sharp look, and he nodded at her recognition of her own words. "You can let me go on questioning you all day, all night, all ninan, or you can just tell me what you're looking for. I'm not going to give up."

Her voice was equally quiet. "I don't want to trust you, Ukiah."

"I think you already do. If you're willing to be alone with me on the edge of this nice, steep cliff, trust is not the issue." He looked down at her steadily. "And if trust isn't the issue, Rezs, what is?"

"Loyalty," she said flatly.

He frowned. "As in, you haven't saved my life, so I can have no loyalty to you? I signed on for the job, Rezs—to keep you alive till you find what you seek. Whatever that takes, I'll do it."

"Will you give your word to me through Vlen?"

He didn't look at the wolf. "My word isn't enough?"

"I can't afford not to feel the truth in you."

"I can understand that—"

"But?"

"A man can deceive a Gray One as easily as his lover. You have my word as it stands: by itself or not at all."

She got to her feet. "Then it's a moot point."

He let her stand, then said casually, "Your family has been in competition with the other labs in your city for over fifteen years, hasn't it?"

Rezs grew still. Slowly, she turned to face him.

"I find it interesting that you're going out for samples just after one of your main competitors comes back from a gathering trip."

"And?"

"You want his trail, then you want his source."

"Do the others know?"

"Not that I'm aware of—other than Bany, who, from the way you two huddle after dark, has been in on it from the beginning."

"We don't huddle," Rezs said sharply.

Ukiah gave her a steady look.

"So now what?" she asked.

He shrugged. "Now you tell me why, when your business is doing as well as any other, it's so important to find the same raw materials as this son of a worlag neGruli."

She studied his face carefully. "You don't like neGruli?"

"I've never noticed him giving anything back to the city in products that he hadn't first stripped off the backs of poorer people."

"You sound bitter."

"I sound realistic."

"You've friends among the Durn?"

He didn't smile. "I was a Durn."

Rezs studied him thoughtfully. "There's always work for a scout—especially a good one, and ignorant as I am, even I can tell that you're good. How could you lose your home when you have that kind of security?"

He shrugged. "A few years ago I had a run-in with some raiders. They broke half the bones in my body. I lived, but I was off the trails for over a year. A friend of a friend was a healer, and I went to stay with that man's family for a while, until I learned to walk again. It was they who neGruli hurt. They'd spent their savings to put one of their girls into a metals apprenticeship program. Fine program—girl has lots of talent. Then the mother died—explosion in the glassworks—and the father was only just able to make ends meet after that. I taught a scouting class to help out, but there's only so much you can do from a bed."

"They lost their home?"

He nodded. "The rootbeetles got into their buildings. One

night, everything came down. They were lucky to get out alive. The council money for emergency repairs had gone into neGruli's project for lighting the rootroads. I think fourteen homes in that hub went down; sixteen in the next one along, while only two new workers were hired for neGruli's rootroad project. Seemed fitting, somehow, that we ended up on the very streets which the loss of our homes paid for."

Rezs said softly, "I'm sorry."

He shrugged. "Doesn't mean anything—being sorry. Caring and praying and singing group songs and all the selfish, passive things that people do to make themselves feel better while they look the other way—that doesn't take the Durn off the streets. It just keeps the Durn there while people like neGruli glean more gold off the backs of the next group of victims. He's acquired power in almost every field by buying up the businesses. He uses the council's own laws against the city, and so far the council has done nothing to change that."

"Perhaps they can't, like some of the elders say. Perhaps it's an issue of ethics for one person or ethics for all."

He gave her a hard look. "Perhaps they won't change it, because some of them are getting rich off neGruli's policies. It doesn't really matter, Rezs. Changing the laws would only force his business underground; fining him would only encourage him to better hide the truths of his work or increase the amounts of his council bribes. There's only one thing that makes a difference to a man like neGruli, and that one thing is action."

Rezs's voice was quiet. "So why are you here, then— guarding me from the worlags—when you could be spending your time going after neGruli directly?"

Ukiah met her violet gaze without speaking. For a moment the gray fog grew thick in her head, and the howling of the wolfpack drowned out her thoughts. Gray Vlen, caught up by the link, looked up at the scout intently, and his vision blurred Rezs's sight, so that she felt as if she leaned on a wall of gray and peered at a nebulous figure. She blinked. Ukiah sprang back into focus and said, "I don't have to go after him. I think you're doing it for me."

"I could be working for him, not against him."

"You could," he agreed. "And if you are, I'll find it out eventually."

"Or I'll find out about you."

He chuckled softly, but there was no humor in it.

She wrapped her arms around herself. "You know I can't trust you, Ukiah."

"So where do we go from here?"

She looked down at the cub. Vlen snarled low in his throat, and she soothed the cub automatically. "If neGruli's developing his products on his own, then I'm a worlag's daughter. I think he's stealing his work, just like he's stealing his funding from the Durn."

"And you're trying to find that source."

She scratched Vlen between the ears. "Coale's been teaching me to read the memories of the wolves, but there's no sense of sequence to anything I see. I know neGruli was here—twice—and both times close together, so I think his source is nearby." She pointed. "In that lava flow perhaps. Or just on the other side."

He squinted across the valley. "The domes of the Ancients are over there."

"They are," she agreed. "But neGruli's men died from worlag attacks, not from bouts of plague. If he'd gone inside the domes—breathed the air even once from those rooms, neGruli would be a rotting corpse by now." But she followed his gaze and felt the excitement build in her stomach at the sight of the white-topped domes. Unconsciously, she pressed her hand to her gut as if she could contain that sense and use it to propel her forward.

"Rezs—" Ukiah cast her a sharp look. "Still getting dizzy?"

"Not now, but a few times in the last couple days," she admitted.

"When?"

"Yesterday, a couple days ago, and the day after we left that last town."

He rubbed his chin, scratching at the stubble that thickened along his jawline. "Still in the afternoons only?"

She nodded. "You've never asked me the obvious question: Am I pregnant?"

"Don't need to," he returned. "I'd know."

She gave him an odd look.

"Coale hasn't been around any of those times, has she?" he asked.

Rezs eyed him warily. "That's an interesting implication, Ukiah—that she, rather than anyone else, does or doesn't have anything to do with it."

The tall scout shrugged. "You might not trust my motivations, but I think it's pretty obvious that she and her grandson are hiding something, and damned if I know what it is."

"I like her," Rezs returned. "And I respect her, but—I don't quite trust her, either."

His gaze followed her hands as she pressed them against her side. "Do you eat anything when you're out with her in the mornings? Your dizziness could be a delayed reaction."

She bit her lip thoughtfully. "We taste-test several things each day, but the woman swears that they're harmless in those amounts. She's also careful to point out things that shouldn't be tasted together. And," she added, "Coale tastes everything with me—you don't see her getting sick."

"We don't *see* her," Ukiah returned. "She leaves before dawn and comes back after dusk. When she does join us, she doesn't sit by the fire. She just beds down like a badgerbear in winter. Elgon at least we've seen and spoken with. Coale might as well be a ghost. By the seventh hell, for all we know, she could be running off every afternoon to be sick as a kid on koabi nuts."

"No—I'd feel that, Ukiah. It's almost easy now for me to pick up Gray Shona through Vlen. And the sense of Coale behind Shona is strong and almost driven—not weak or full of illness."

He nodded, but Rezs had the feeling that he didn't quite agree. His voice was carefully casual as he said, "Bany's beginning to think we're being followed."

Rezs glanced back over her shoulder. Even in its clearest part, she couldn't see a hundred meters through the forest. In some places, her vision was so limited that a pack of worlags could be dancing on the other side of a brush pile, and she wouldn't know it. She gestured. "With all this, how in the world could he tell?"

He shrugged. "Smoke trails. Movement in the distance. A feeling between your shoulders."

Rezs grinned. "I've certainly had the latter, but I think it's Elgon watching me, not some phantom on our trail."

Ukiah didn't smile in return, and Rezsia studied him, letting her bond with Vlen spin out. Like a noose, it captured the sense of them on the cliff. Scents, sights, and the threads of gray that wove themselves into a solid din of voices. There were snarls and music and howls in her head, but even though the scout sat with her, she couldn't touch his image. Her father's image was as clear as ever; her brother Cal's as strong; Coale was a driving lance of will, and the other scouts like ghosts. But Ukiah was a hard knot of gray—walled off, as if the music created by lupine minds made him withdraw into himself. A gray heart, she thought.

"Something wrong with your neck?"

The question startled her, and she looked down. She was rubbing at her throat where the blader had frightened her before. She dropped her hand. "It's nothing."

She gazed out over the valley. The floor of the valley was sparsely covered with flat-canopy trees, and she could clearly see the jumble of red-black rock that had once flowed out over the floor. The hardened river of lava stopped well short of the cliff where she sat; she could see it clearly because the shades of color that marked the lava's canopy changed from a light, dusty tone to a thick, lush shade of green where the tree roots could grip better soil. She dug her hands into Gray Vlen's scruff. "Odd, don't you think," she said, "how abruptly that lava flow stops—as if it lost all momentum and simply decided to rest."

Ukiah gave her a sideways look. "Do you always assign human emotions to rocks?"

"Rocks, moss, trees . . ." She shrugged. "How else would I describe them?"

"Black and rough. Thick and spongy." He studied her face. "You've really never been out here before, have you?"

"There was no need. I had my schooling, my family, and my work."

"And no curiosity about what surrounded your city?"

"I was curious. I just didn't go."

"Who held you back?"

She shot him a sharp look. "Who? Not what?"

He smiled slowly without humor. "Does that mean it's the wrong question or that you don't want to answer?"

"Are you prying into family secrets?" She countered, "I think that one I won't answer."

The glint in her eyes was almost yellow, and Ukiah glanced toward the shadows, but he could see nothing of the wolf. He wondered if she knew how she moved when the cub was near. As if she lost half her weight with the wolf's proximity—her feet became lighter, and her steps more careful. She was learning to ghost it through the woods, he realized. Another month and she would move like a scout.

He gestured toward the flow. "So what do you think?"

"There could be a thousand lava tubes down there—just think of all that cave mold."

He raised his eyebrows. "You know, most women don't get so excited over the prospect of a patch of mold."

She grinned. "I thought wolfwalkers were allowed to be eccentric."

Ukiah rolled his eyes. He gestured with his chin at the valley. "I suppose you want to go down there." He glanced at the gray wolf. "It will be rough on Vlen. His feet probably can't handle the rock."

She scratched Vlen's head, and the cub gazed back with sleepy eyes. "That's not a problem," she said. Her voice softened as she stroked the cub along his back. "Wolves don't like to go in caves."

"I'd heard that."

"I'm beginning to wonder if the Ancients bred that fear into them to keep them away from the roofbleeders."

"Wouldn't have been a bad idea." He got to his feet. "Caves and slow water were never a threat on oldEarth, but they're treacherous here."

Vlen's yellow eyes gleamed. *Is it time for you to run with me, Wolfwalker?*

"Yes," she murmured to his gray-furred ears. "I'm as eager as you to test my feet on those rocks." She looked up at Ukiah. "We've been traveling for a ninan now, and I've yet to see anything but trail. My lessons with Coale don't take us off the ridden path much—except to identify plants—and I'm so tired by the end of the day that all I want to do is bag out. This is the first afternoon since we started that we don't have to be on the move."

"All right. I'm game. But we'll have to wait for Bany to get back." He glanced around for her pack. "Got your samples?"

She patted the belt pouches.

"That all you need?"

"Running with Coale has taught me to travel light."

He nodded. "You know exactly where neGruli crossed this area?"

"I've gotten images from the wolves, but no pictures specific enough to tell that—I haven't the experience yet to interpret what the Gray Ones remember. I suppose," she said dubiously, "we could wait for Coale and Elgon to come back, too. Coale showed me the direction neGruli took, and said something about the scent markings that defined the trail, but I don't think I can find it by myself. All I know is that it's a couple hours that way." She pointed north.

"But you're sure neGruli walked onto this flow."

"I know he was in a cave. I know the rock itself was dark— not like limestone—and that it smelled wet and musty. And I know the feel of the cave was hollow and horizontal—like a lava tube—rather than lumpy and rounded and vertical, as it would be if it were water-carved limestone."

"But neGruli went past this area."

"We're not sure of that. We know he was among these rocks, but not whether he stopped here or turned around." She got to her feet and moved near the edge of the steep slope beside the other scout. The undercut was severe, and they stayed two meters back, but because they stood at a divit in the edge, they had a clear view to the sides. "One thing's for sure," she commented. "Between Bany and Coale, we should be able to locate neGruli's old campsites. Nothing in this area could be easily washed away."

Ukiah nodded. "I can see a couple ways to get down, but we won't be able to take the dnu with us."

"We could leave them here with Bany. When the others get back, he could bring them all down that trail Coale saw. She said it was a long trail—probably a bunch of switchbacks. We could slide down this slope and spend the next couple hours exploring, while they come around the other way."

"Or we could rappel down, explore for a few hours, and wall-walk back up."

She shrugged. "I don't really care, as long as I get a few hours in the caves. I've never seen a lava flow, let alone gotten to walk on one. I don't want to waste the chance."

"To look for mold-rotted roots," he agreed. He glanced at

Vlen. "Too bad you can't just see what you're looking for in the minds of the wolves."

"It doesn't work like that—at least for me. I can pick up the smell of their fires, the sounds of the dnu hooves, and the sense of them moving by—but not what they said or the details of what they did." She pushed Vlen away and got to her feet, slapping the dust from her trousers. "The wolves were curious enough to watch neGruli's party, but not enough to study it." Vlen's ears perked, and she heard the sounds of dnu hooves through his ears. "Bany's back."

Ukiah looked over his shoulder. He didn't see the other man for a moment. The rider and dnu were obscured by the trees. Then they loped into view. Rezs rubbed Vlen's head, pleased that the yearling had heard Bany coming, and the cub looked up, his yellow eyes gleaming.

The old man wasn't happy about Rezs wanting to explore the lava flow, but he agreed. "I know where Touvinde and the others are hunting," he said. "So I'll meet them and take them directly to that trail you saw—it will save them four or five kays of riding. But you'll have to reach Coale and Elgon yourself."

Rezs stopped rubbing Vlen's head, and the cub nudged her hand. "Reach them?" she asked, resuming her attention to Vlen's scruff.

"Through Vlen," he returned. "We can meet either at or on the trail you told us about—the one that leads off this ridge. When I went north, I caught a glimpse of it—it's a wide trail, used by many creatures. Coale and Elgon should have no trouble finding it, but they'll need to know to meet us there, not here."

Rezs nodded. She looked down at Vlen and let her consciousness sink into his yellow gaze. Her mind filled with the sights and smells of the three of them and their dnu. The soil of the forest floor was sweet and damp; the tree roots gave off a distinct bitterness. The din of distant wolfpack voices swelled and became again that haunting song. She could feel Gray Shona's voice in the distance. Behind it, faded but steady, she felt the other wolfwalker.

Coale, she called into the din. *Can you hear me?*

I hear you, Rezsia maDeiami. There was a sense of Shona

snarling between Rezs and the other woman, and Rezs had to concentrate to understand her words.

Coale had described to her the way to project images to another wolfwalker, but she didn't know how to project an image she hadn't seen. So she forced the words into the din: *We're to meet at the trail, not the resting camp.*

The trail? An image projected of a light-brown line that zigzagged along the steep ridge.

Yes, she returned. *Meet there.*

And you?

Ukiah and I are going down on the lava flow. This time she projected a view of the green canopy broken over the red-black rocks.

At first she felt a reluctance in the fog, then what seemed to be agreement. Then the sense of the other woman faded, and only Vlen and the din of the pack was left in her mind.

Bany had been watching her. "What did she say?"

Rezs's eyes were still a bit unfocused. "She'll meet you at the trail," she managed. She had trouble forming the words, and it took her a moment to realize why: her lips were curled back from her teeth. She forced them to relax.

Bany nodded. "It's getting on in the afternoon. I'll see you in a few hours. Try to make it to the trail at least an hour before dusk so we can find a good site." He gave Ukiah a deliberate look, and the other scout nodded in turn.

Rezs looked from one to the other. "I may be ignorant about safety out here, but I'm not that stupid," she told them.

The old man grinned. Then he took their dnu and packs and left them on the edge of the cliff. They walked along the cliff until they found an area where the undercut had eroded away, leaving a thin path for water to run off and down. Ukiah gestured. "Shall we?"

She stepped close to peer over the edge, felt the earth crumble away, and hurriedly moved back. "Do we just do it on our . . . behinds?"

"Uh-huh." He shifted his sword and bow so that he could hold them in front of him. "The water paths are fairly smooth, but they're not perfect, and these are damp, not wet or dry enough to make it easy to slide all the way down. Make sure you don't leave anything hanging out that can catch in a root-ball. It can flip you right off the slide." He squatted, then sat at the top of the near-vertical slope. "Wait till I'm down before you follow me. Watch where I have trouble. From the bottom, I'll be able to see if there's a better way for you to come down."

She nodded. He leaned forward, then shoved himself off. He didn't go quickly, as she expected. Instead, he half slid, half shoved himself down the cliff. Dust and small rocks crumbled away, exposing roots and following him down in a tiny avalanche. He hung up only once, where a rock jutted out, but it took only a moment to shift around it, ease himself back onto the water path, and move on. He was at the bottom in less than a minute. He waved as he shook the dirt and mud from his trousers and back. "Come on," he called. "It's fine."

She squatted at the rim. Vlen whined, and she looked at him. "What about Vlen?" she called back. "He can't do this."

"Tell him to go around."

"Go north, Vlen," she directed. "That way. The trail you saw with Shona—take that down."

But his mental voice grew anxious. *Wolfwalker—*

"You can't follow me down, Gray One, and I really want to go. You'll be fine. Shona isn't that far away."

Don't go—

"Vlen," she said more sternly. "It's all right. Just go to the trail and follow it down. By the time you get into the valley, I'll be done looking at caves, and I'll meet you with the others."

Ukiah called from down below, "What's the problem?"

Rezs turned to answer, but Vlen whined, pleading with his eyes, not just his mental voice. Rezs had to force herself to answer the other scout. "Just getting Vlen to go to the other trail."

"He won't leave until you've started down," the man returned. "He'll figure it out then."

Reluctantly, she nodded. "It's all right, Vlen," she told the wolf again. "Just come down on the trail." He whined as she dangled her legs over the edge, and she rubbed his scruff. "I'll see you in a bit."

She shoved off, and Vlen growled and nipped at her shoulder. "No—" she said sharply. Her trousers scraped on the mud and pebbles, and she was suddenly out of reach. Vlen snarled at her. "Go around," she told him over her shoulder. Then she was sliding faster along the water run. She had to ease around the same rock that stopped Ukiah, but like him, she was down in less than a minute.

Ukiah gave her a hand up. He had strong hands, she realized as he pulled her effortlessly from the rock-strewn mud. There was something about them that made her leave her hand in his a moment longer than necessary.

"All right?" the man asked.

She nodded, withdrawing from his grip. She would have answered, but Vlen snarled from the cliff top, and she turned to look back up. *Go around,* she told him firmly. *You'll be down here sooner than you can snarl.*

The cub whined, but Rezs turned her back on him and clambered up onto the edge of the flow. Ukiah jumped up easily beside her, then vaulted up another boulder. He turned and again offered her his hand.

Rezs studied him surreptitiously. There was a flatness to his handsome face—a distance that seemed ingrained not only in his eyes but in his bones. It was as if he had his own gray fog—only his stood like a wall between him and the others, whereas Rezs's lupine fog bound her to Gray Vlen. She took his hand and again he hauled her up without effort. For a moment she was balanced perfectly against him. She could feel his clothes press in against hers; she could feel the heat of his iron-hard body. She blinked. The sense of him seemed to seep through her mind, not just her skin—as if he was somehow linked to the wolves. Then the man stepped back, and the wall closed down, and he moved up to the next black boulder.

Carefully, Rezs jumped after him: up onto part of the flow; slipped on this thick patch of moss; down across that soil-filled channel where an old lava tube had collapsed . . . On the one hand, the rock was rough enough that it was easy to keep her footing; on the other hand, it was jumbled so loosely that she felt as if she was rocking rather than jumping from stone to stone.

The trees that grew between the boulders had long, straight trunks that, about twenty feet up, suddenly branched out in wide, flat canopies. Beneath them, the moss grew in patches as thick as Rezsia's forearm. Each time she took a step, she didn't know if she was resting her weight on a moss-covered stone or on an air pocket over which the moss had grown. A dozen times she knocked the moss from the edges of boulders that were undercut more than she had realized. When she looked back, she saw a trail of raw brown moss roots where her feet had torn the mats.

There was water in hundreds of rock depressions; tiny puddles in porous holes, and wide, flat pools in the irregularities of the flow. Among them, there were many black openings, but most were no deeper than her arms, and only one seemed to go back very far. That opening had a draft that rose from its tiny, irregular black hole. The next hole may have been connected to the tiny cave from which the draft rose. The one after that was just another tiny den between the jumble of ancient rock. And the dozen ones that they looked at later were either shadows or shallow pockets.

They were heading at an angle toward the trail where they would meet the other scouts when Rezs saw yet another rock well. There was a dark shadow that gave the same impression of depth that all the others had, and Rezs leaned too far to see into it. She slipped on the moss again, lost her balance, and quickly jumped to an unstable stone lower down. She balanced there, rocking for a moment before getting the nerve to return to Ukiah's path. "Moons," she muttered.

Ukiah looked back over his shoulder. "You okay?"

"I'm fine. I just feel like we're going up and down more than forward. I thought we were looking for caves." She paused. "Is it my imagination or are you climbing more than dipping?"

He jumped to the next boulder. "I want a good vantage point."

"To check behind us? Moons, Ukiah. If we were being followed by some of neGruli's men, it wouldn't be this closely."

"Maybe. Maybe not. If we're that close to the source of that fungi, they'd have to be close to stop us before we found the evidence you're looking for."

"Or," she returned, "they're just considerate riders following the same road, and they'll turn off to Ramaj Kiren or Bilocctar when we reach the ridge ahead."

"Maybe," he repeated. "There's more than one kind of predator in the woods. Even if it isn't neGruli's men, it could still be raiders."

She flashed him a grin. "If they are raiders, and they know

what's good for them, they'll keep their distance because I'm not in a good mood. We've been out here almost two hours, we've not found a single usable cave entrance, the ones we have found are too small to get inside, my hands are completely raw from the rocks, and my feet are getting tired."

Ukiah misjudged a jump and leaped back as soon as his boots hit the side of a boulder. "Now you know why Vlen couldn't come with us," he called over his shoulder.

"He'd have been fine on the moss areas," she agreed, "but his pads would have been cut to ribbons on this. All I can say is that it's a good thing we have extra boots. Mine are getting the heck scraped out of them here." She caught a glimpse of another dark hole. "Ukiah, wait. There's another opening here." She jumped down onto a wide, flat stone, then clambered back up to get closer to the edge of the depression. "It's large," she confirmed. "And the well is deep. Can you see it?"

Obediently, he began to backtrack to join her while she tested her footing on the rough rock. She could see more clearly into the depression when she climbed up on another boulder. "It's definitely a cave entrance," she called back over her shoulder. "I'd say it's a lava tube that runs out that way, and back this way right under my feet. That hole is where the top of the tube collapsed."

Ukiah swung around one of the trees and used the momentum from that swing to help him jump across a narrow rock chasm. "Is there water in the base of it?"

"Not a drop. There must be a seep that drains the runoff from this flow into a subterranean pool." She gestured vaguely over her shoulder. "There was another dry hole like this back there. Same kind of water tracks."

He crossed to the edge. He walked carefully; the rocks were loose enough to shift with every step. "Looks like a recent collapse," he said as he examined the depression. "This lava is sharp, and there's not as much dust in the pores of the stone."

She nodded and stretched her mind so that Vlen could see what she was seeing. The gray fog behind his voice roiled with mental currents. "There are rabbit droppings down there," she realized. Their sweet-dull scent was unmistakable. She looked up at Ukiah. "So it's been here long enough that the animals have begun to use the cave for shelter."

"Or food. Both rabbits and rats can eat cave mold." He

pointed. "There must have been other entrances to this cave—those are old cavebleeder knobs."

Rezs leaned carefully to see over the rounded stone edge. The rock was loose beneath her, and it clacked as she shifted her weight. The gray fog in her head was beginning to cloud her sight, and she felt a little dizzy. Abruptly, she staggered back. The rock shifted.

"Rezs!" Ukiah's voice was cold and sharp. "Get back from the edge—now!"

The dizziness hit full force. She swayed and lost her footing. Her ears seemed full of a scraping, cracking sound. Then the edge gave way completely.

XVII

"Rezsia!" Ukiah shouted. He lunged forward.

Wolfwalker . . . Vlen howled.

Her arms flailed out. Vlen's voice blinded her, so that she didn't even feel the hands that dug into her wrist and flung her up and over. The cracking, clacking sound of lava against lava filled her ears; a rushing noise drowned out the voices. And then she struck stone and lay gasping half over a boulder, one leg dangling below. Single rocks, unbalanced on the edge of the hole, skittered down into darkness.

For a moment there was nothing but the rough rock cutting through her skin. Her left knee and thigh were one shock of pain; her ribs throbbed where they had struck stone. She tried to prop herself up on her arms, but her right elbow was caught between two boulders, and her right foot kicked in the air. She struggled harder. Her sleeve ripped along her bicep, and underneath, her flesh was scraped raw. She cried out. In her head, Vlen howled. Rezsia panicked. She tore herself free from the rocks and flung herself away from the edge.

She looked around, but the only thing there, besides the trees, the moss, and the rocks, was the edge of the new, gaping maw in the earth. "Ukiah?" Then, more urgently, *"Ukiah!"*

The silence of the mossy rocks seemed to accentuate her heartbeat. The lack of wind made her breath seem loud. She could hear water, dripping, sliding into a hole, and some kind of small rocks were falling. But there was no Ukiah. She stared at the broken edge of the well. *Vlen!* she screamed in her mind.

The gray wolf shot back a howl that deafened her. She

clutched her ears. Her head still spun, and she was having trouble seeing. Her heartbeat was clumsy—as if it didn't know which rhythm to keep: fast and young or fast and frightened. She tried to suck in air normally, but the sense of the Gray One was too thick in her head. "Vlen—" she cried out.

Wolfwalker, he called back. *I come . . .*

"No. Find Bany—find Coale. Get someone here to help me."

He snarled, protesting with a flash of image that made Rezsia's heart beat harder. She shook her head to clear it. Her sight was yellowed from the link to the cub, and she had to squint to see the collapsed cave. Then, from out of the boiling din, a distant voice snapped out a command, and the tide of gray swept back. Vlen's voice was sharp and clear. His breath was the only one that filled her lungs; his pulse the drum that hit her ribs. Slowly, Rezs lifted her head. *Coale?* she sent uncertainly.

Can you hear me?

"Hurry," Rezs pleaded.

Faint, the woman's voice returned. *I'm coming.*

She heard another pebble strike, an echoing stone. *"Hurry."*

Vlen snarled and cut off Rezs's word. *Wolfwalker,* he sent. He projected an image of age and toughness that Rezs associated with Bany.

"Yes, Vlen," she whispered. "Bring him here."

She stared toward the hole in the ground. She tried to move to the edge and look in, but she couldn't. Something caught her—kept her in place. She looked down at her hands. They were clear of the cracks in the rocks; her feet were not jammed in— Again, she began to panic, and it wasn't until she realized that it wasn't Vlen's heartbeat but hers that pounded so loudly, that she understood what was holding her back.

The fear.

It had locked up her limbs like iron.

She took a breath and heard it as a sob. "Damn you," she cursed herself. "Grandma wouldn't hesitate. She'd risk a worlag if one of her partners were hurt. Even Cal wouldn't hesitate—he'd verify the edge, then climb on down like a cliffbird."

Deliberately, she lifted her hand, then shoved it forward

through the air. It was like a solid thing—the air by that rim. It took all her strength to move through it. She raised and pushed forward the other hand, and this time it was easier. She could fight this fear, she told herself.

Vlen called out to her, and his mind was pulsing with urgency. She could not tell if it was a reflection of her fear or his own anxiety to be with her, but she tried to calm it as she tried to calm herself. It was like trying to stop a whirlpool by swirling her hand in a back current. Vlen, confused, stopped dead on the trail, and was almost overrun by the rider behind him. The cub leaped sideways and snapped at the dnu; Rezs jerked on the rocks. In her mind, she could hear the cursing of a human voice.

She pressed her hands to her head. *Help me,* she sent to the cub. *Help me move forward here like you do there.*

Vlen howled and leaped forward. Instantly, her mind was flooded with heat—a glowing fire of energy that lifted her body up in a heap of urgency. She was so startled by the surge of power that she staggered and fell. One newly broken edge gashed her left palm, and the other rocks scraped her right hand. A handful of pebbles gave way on the edge. Something cracked slowly, in a long, bone-twisting sound.

Vlen! she cried out.

To her left, a rock broke away and fell. It was wide as her arm was long, and thick as her torso. Slowly at first, then with gathering speed, it slammed into the base of the lava tube, striking the side of the new hole before falling away in a fading rush of sound. *Ukiah*

Rezs was having trouble breathing. The gray voices in her head were loud again, and through them, she could hear human shouting. The combination confused her. When Vlen crowded into her head and snarled through her lips, she found herself crawling forward. Inch by inch, she eased her weight toward the edge. The black maw became a pit; the sun a lance of life that shot down into that amorphous center. Another meter-long slab scraped to her left, then broke away and fell. The gasp that shot through her mind was so sharp she thought she had sucked in that breath herself. *Ukiah—*

Vlen, she sent urgently. *Can you feel him?*

His leg—it's a fire that crawls up my bone. His chest pounds in mine.

"He's alive, then," she said harshly. "Ukiah," she shouted at the hole. "Can you hear me? I'm coming."

She forced herself to look over the edge. Did it shift? No, it was fear—not the rock—that made her tremble. She tried to focus her yellow-tinged gaze. Black-red on top, where the edges of the lava tube splintered away. Yellow-black below, where the roof of the karst had collapsed, leaving the ancient limestone bare and glistening in the sun. Across the raw lava, new water trails from broken pools began to run in trickles.

"Ukiah . . ."

She could see him now. He lay, bent over the rocks, in a broken circle of light. Half his body was in gray shadow; the other half in light. One arm dangled over the pit of the broken limestone caverns. She saw no blood, but that meant nothing; Vlen had felt the man's leg snap, and the porous, red-black rock would have soaked any bleeding up like a sponge.

Rezs forced herself to look away from his body and study the sides of the well. If she was careful, she thought, she could climb partway down, then drop from the lip of the hole near where Ukiah lay. She had climbed trees as a child with her brothers; she was not afraid of heights. She just didn't want to drop on the scout.

She backed away from the lip and made her way to the other side. She was more confident there; the lip itself seemed solid, and except for the overhang two meters below—which was left over from part of the original collapse of the lava tube—it looked like an easy climb down. She unslung her bow and quiver and jammed them in the lava flow to form a skewed cross. She tied her scarf loosely to the bow as Coale had taught her. It wasn't large, but it was red and yellow, and even without the wind, the fabric should make it easier for the scouts to find their location.

Carefully, she lowered herself along the rock, her feet kicking against the well as she sought footing. More flesh tore away as her fingers scraped across the rock. Vlen snarled deep in her mind, but she ignored the yearling. She couldn't afford to get caught up in his mental growling now. Finally, she let her weight out on the overhang. Then she got onto her belly and wriggled awkwardly, legs first, to the edge. The hilt of her sword hung up for a moment, and she freed it only with difficulty. A moment later she was dangling over the limestone pit.

Hand by hand, she worked her way along the lip until she was once again over the lava tube. She chose her spot, took a breath, let go, and dropped.

One foot landed solidly; the other with its arch on a spire of rock. She cursed, staggered sideways, and fell awkwardly to the bottom of the tube across a trickle of water. For a moment she lay still, her heart pounding and her chest heaving with the breaths she now allowed herself. Then she gingerly got to her feet.

The scout's eyes were closed, but she could see his chest rise and fall. His bow had splintered on the rocks, but his sword was beneath him, and his body lay along its length instead of bending over the rough boulders that would have broken his back. He must have twisted the blade around as he fell to protect himself from the boulders. Rezs closed her eyes in relief. Then she knelt by his side. She didn't touch his leg; the swelling had already pushed out his pant leg, so that his calf was quickly growing as large as his thigh.

"Ukiah?" She touched his shoulder. His eyes seemed to flicker. "Ukiah, can you hear me? It's Rezs. I'm here beside you." She took the hand that had been twitching and held it gently. Abruptly, he clutched her fingers.

"Thank the moons—" she breathed.

His eyes opened. Wildly, his gaze flashed from side to side. The brilliant blue of the sky was white to his eyes against the red-black of the ceiling.

"Don't move," she told him gently. "Just lie quietly. You're on the edge of a pit."

"Where . . . are we?" he croaked.

"In the lava tube."

"What happened?"

He didn't seem to notice that she was holding his hand. She stroked it absently. "I felt dizzy, started to fall. You grabbed me and threw me back from the edge. Then the lip collapsed. When it hit the bottom of the lava tube, it broke all the way through to the limestone caves underneath. You were lucky. You landed here. The rest of the rock fell down there." She gestured toward the pit.

He turned his head, gasped, and lay still. "Limestone?" he managed.

She nodded. "There must be an entire system of caverns

beneath this lava flow. Those other depressions we saw—they must be similar areas of collapse."

A ghost of a smile crossed his lips. "So I guess you could say that I fell for you."

"That's not funny," she said sharply.

He choked, gasped, and started to laugh.

She stared down at him. "I've known you two ninans, Ukiah, and in all that time, no matter what Touvinde has said, you've barely cracked a smile. If I'd known that all I had to do was break one of your bones to make you laugh, I'd have done it days ago."

"Too busy . . ." he managed. "Playing with your fungi." His eyes focused on her arms, and she realized that her sleeve hung in ragged ribbons, and the jerkin was stained with the blood from her scrapes. "How did you get here, Rezs?" His voice strengthened. "Didn't I get you clear—did you fall?"

"I'm fine. I climbed down after the rim gave way."

Ukiah's hand clenched on hers, and he raised his head from the rock. "You did what?"

Rezs didn't like the anger she heard. "I climbed down," she repeated.

"Did you use a rope?" He tried to look around without moving more than his head. "I don't see any rope."

"We didn't have a rope to use, remember? We left it with the dnu."

"Moonworms, Rezs, you never climb down into a cave without a rope."

"We were deliberately looking for lava tubes. What did you think, I'd be happy just looking at the entrances?"

"Yes, I did. If you wanted your fungi, you'd have to get it from the entrances, not deep in an unknown cavern. No one goes caving with just two people—you always have two more outside, just in case. There are gas vents, bacterial colonies, roofbleeders, widowmakers—"

"Ukiah," she interrupted. Her voice was quiet. "You have a broken leg, bruised ribs, and moons know what else battered. I needed to know if you were all right."

He gave her a disgusted look. "Moons, Rezs, you're not supposed to tell the patient how bad off he is. You're supposed to smile and tell him that everything's fine."

"And," she added sharply, "I think you have a concussion."

"Except for the headache I'm getting from this argument, the space between my ears feels great," he retorted.

She shook her head. "Either you hit your head too hard when you fell, or some moonwarrior has taken over your body. The Ukiah I know doesn't make jokes."

"Maybe you don't know your Ukiah."

"I do know he's got a broken leg and better lie still where he is."

"Dammit, Rezs, it's not your leg. You're not a healer and you haven't even touched the leg to check it. How do you know it's broken?"

"I felt it through Vlen."

For a second he stared at her. Then, abruptly, he closed off. There was no other way to describe it. One moment he was looking at her and talking; the next he had withdrawn so far inside himself that his eyes barely bothered to focus on her face. "Ukiah," she began.

He ignored her and tried to shift, then gasped and lay still again. If she had thought his face pale before, she had been color-blind. Even in the shadow, his skin was now as white as the fur of a snow cat. The freckles that had been hidden by weathering now stood out like spatters of blood.

Rezs was on her feet in an instant. "Ukiah—"

For a moment his eyes remained closed. Then he forced them open. In her head, Vlen seemed to howl. "I'm all right," the scout croaked.

Her hands hovered, but she didn't touch him. "Dear moons, I don't know what to do."

"Keep me thinking, Rezs. I'm starting to feel cold."

His words brought a chill to Rezs's shoulders, not just his. She looked toward the broken rim of rocks. The sunlight that fell into the well came from a sun well down across the valley. There was nothing in his view except deep blue sky above the pit of yellowed blackness.

Vlen, she called urgently.

The sense of brush slapping by the yearling's side made her clench her fists. He was moving fast, and the rodents screamed at him as he passed.

Coale. She projected the words as strongly as she could. *Coale, can you hear me?*

There was a distant echo, then, as if they were relayed, the words came back: *We're coming . . .*

He's cold.

Keep him warm. Keep him conscious . . .

Quickly, Rezs shrugged out of her jerkin. Carefully, she lay it across his torso. His eyes glinted. "I'm only going to strip so far," she told him. "After that, you have to close your eyes again."

"Won't need to. Sun's shifting fast. Soon we'll be in darkness."

Uneasily, Rezs looked at the sun line. Just as he'd said, his body was now almost completely in shadow. And the pit seemed somehow darker. The knobs that cast rounded shadows from the well walls—they looked almost like heads peering out from the rock. There was movement somewhere, but she couldn't tell what it was. Rodents, perhaps, creeping back to their homes after the rockfall settled out . . . She tried not to look at the roof of the cave.

"I'm afraid to move you," she told him. "And even if I did move you, I don't know where I'd move you to. I could try splinting your leg with your bow," she offered dubiously.

"Have you done that sort of thing before?"

She shook her head.

"Then better if you don't start now."

"You could tell me what to do."

"I could faint halfway through and leave us in a worse position than before. I can wait for Bany."

"Bany or Coale. They're both coming."

He nodded almost imperceptibly. "How thick is this rim I'm lying on?"

"I don't know. But several large slabs have hit it just a meter away from you, and it hasn't broken yet."

"That's not much comfort, Rezs. This tube has been here for a thousand years without breaking till we put our weight on it."

"Do you want me to move your left leg up onto the rock? It's hanging over the limestone pit."

"No," he objected quickly. "Since we're on the lip that broke," he added more calmly, "I'd be careful about adding your weight to mine. Think it's one of those things that, if I want it done, I'm going to have to do it myself."

Rezs bit her lip. "I'm not comfortable with that, Ukiah."

"And you think I am?" He forced a smile. "I'm the one with the broken leg, remember?"

The movement behind her grew, but it was a sense of something shifting—something dropping closer—rather than a sound which tightened the skin between her shoulders. She glanced at the shifting roof of the cave, stroked his hand a moment more, then eased her grip from his.

"Where are you going?" he asked sharply.

"I'm just going to set up some petris."

He leaned his head back and stared at the sky. "So I was right," he teased ungently. "You are just interested in fungi."

Her smile was tight, but her face was in darkness; he could not see the flash of yellow in her violet eyes. She sat back on her heels and fumbled with her belt pouches until she brought out what she needed. The movement behind her increased, and she looked over her shoulder more than once. She moved her vials and dishes near the scout's head, then took a loose, fist-sized stone and crushed it down on the gray, writhing tendril that had been caught by the rockfall on what was now the floor of the cave. The thing went flat, but didn't die; it just squashed out around the rock and writhed closer to the scout. There was something obscene about the way it undulated up to and past the rock that mashed it in its middle. The end of the tendril was only the length of her arm away from Ukiah, and the way the thing was pulsing, it was gaining, with each surge, a finger's width of length on the other side of the rock.

Rezs swallowed with difficulty. With her eyesight adjusting to the darkness, she could see more movements now. The cavebleeders were thick on the roof of the tube. The knobs that she had thought were rock were not stone at all, but the bulbs of gray, retracted bodies. Now that the shock of the stone fall was gone, and the lengthening shadows were darkening the pit, they were beginning to move about. It was not something Rezs could focus on directly, but when she looked away, the roof of the cave seemed to crawl. Her jaw tightened, and she took her knife from her belt.

Ukiah tilted his head. "What are you doing?"

"Just taking care of a few unwanteds."

Carefully, she pressed the point of the knife into the

wormlike roofbleeder she'd hit with the rock. Its body was as thick as two of her fingers together, and it reacted by flattening itself into a tapelike shape. A tiny drop of purple-red fluid exuded from the skin of the parasite. Rezs's lips curled back in distaste. This time she drew the blade across the roofbleeder body in a sharp movement. The worm molded itself to the rocks, but she did cut it—when she jerked her knife back, the edge of her blade was dark with the purple-red fluid. Instantly, the worm became a thin, whipping demon on the other side of the rock. It slammed itself back and forth, writhing and pulling in a pulsing motion to get its body from under the rock. Fluid oozed out on the porous rock and, like Ukiah's blood, disappeared.

Rezs shuddered. She tried to ignore its thrashing as she placed the first petri near Ukiah's head, balancing it across two crumbled rocks. The liquid from the two vials she poured into the dish mixed and turned dark brown. A tiny wisp of vapor began to form. Rezs sniffed lightly and wrinkled her nose.

In her head, Vlen breathed through her lungs, then snorted and rubbed his nose against a patch of grass. His yellow eyes gleamed, and behind his voice, far back in the fog, Shona's howling began. *Wolfwalker,* Vlen sent. *There's danger around you.*

They're roofbleeders, Vlen. I'm taking care of them now. She tried to project confidence, but Vlen's mind grew chaotic as he smelled more of the roofbleeders through her nose. He stretched his lanky limbs across the trail.

Ukiah had been watching the roof over her head. When he spoke, his voice was calm and distant. "Rezs, I want you to find a way out of this well. Stop what you're doing, and start looking for a wall you can climb before the sun puts this whole place in darkness. I'll be all right until Bany gets here."

She didn't answer the scout. The motion she had felt was becoming more distinct as she filled three more petris and placed them behind her. She had only four flat dishes with her, and they barely formed a rude semicircle of glass and vapor on the floor of the cave. By the time she was done, Ukiah's body was in nothing but shadow.

"Rezs—" His voice was sharp.

"I heard you," she returned. "But I think that concussion is affecting you again."

"That's not funny, Rezs," he said deliberately.

"Ah, the Ukiah I know is back. There's no humor in your voice."

He shivered, cursed his weakness, and glared at her. "You're right—I'm not kidding. Now get yourself up and out of this well."

She took his hand and refused to let him jerk away. Her jaw tightened, but her voice was quiet when she said, "Ukiah, your hands are like ice. Your leg is swelling like a sponge in water, and I think you're going into shock. There are roofbleeders all around us. The sun is going down. And you *want* me to leave you here alone?"

"Yes."

She nodded. She spent a few minutes gathering up her vials and repacking them in her belt pouches.

He watched her closely. "No protest?" he asked sharply. "No assertion of independence?"

"No," she returned simply. "I'm sure you're right, and I should get out of this pit well before dark. But there's just one thing." Rezs looked at the side of the well. "I dropped from the lip to get down here, Ukiah. I can't jump high enough to get back out." He stared at her, and she nodded. "I can't get back out alone."

"Spore-wormed pail of worlag piss," he cursed.

She shrugged.

"By the moons, Rezs, you never put yourself in a hole if you can't get yourself out. What in all the Ancient worlds were you thinking?"

"I was thinking that I didn't want you to be down here alone."

His voice was harsh. "It was a stupid thing, Rezs. You should have stayed on top."

Rezs heard the anger in his words, but it wasn't that which stopped her response. It was the fear that lay beneath his voice—the sense that he was far too glad she was with him—and that it was that which angered him even more. She stroked his hand lightly. This time he did not pull away.

"You'll be using Vlen to direct . . . Bany here?"

"Bany is already on his way" she told him. "And Coale and Elgon, too. I don't know about the others." At the mention of the other wolf, Rezs's mind automatically sought the other voices. She let one part of her mind sink into her bond with Vlen as she tried to keep the scout talking.

"What is that stuff you put in those dishes?" he asked.

"A solution we—my brother Lit and I—developed to repel roofbleeders."

He gave her a sharp look. "You don't sound very confident in your work."

"We never had a chance to try it out. I was to find some roofbleeders on this trip and see if it did the job at all."

"Guess we'll know pretty soon. You've got one over your shoulder."

Rezs jerked and flinched away from the dangling tendril of gray. The sheathed worm waved back and forth. It's mouth was not completely open, but it was seeking, and she could see its gumline with the slightly lighter edge where its retracted needle teeth waited. It pulsed to extend its length another few inches, paused, and seemed to test the air.

"Is it dropping lower?"

"No—" But she couldn't help shrinking back as it curled to seek her warmth.

"Is it just the one?"

She hesitated.

Ukiah's voice was dry. "I've been in caves before, Rezs."

She gathered her wits. "There are perhaps ten or twelve that I can distinguish, but my eyesight isn't too good right now."

"You'll adjust. Just don't look at the sky."

But his words slurred slightly, and Rezs turned to stare at him. "Ukiah," she said sharply. "Are you all right?"

"Cold," he managed.

With the worms overhead, she didn't want to do it, but she closed her eyes anyway. Deliberately, she forced her consciousness toward Vlen, back into the howling gray, back toward the dim voice of the other wolfwalker. *Coale!* she called. *Coale, help me.*

The woman's image floated in the fog of gray. *We're coming,* the other wolfwalker returned. *We're near the cliff.*

Shona's senses lay over Vlen's, so that Rezs felt as if she ran on two trails at once. She pressed her hands to her forehead. *He's going into shock,* she projected.

There was a flat acknowledgment, then Shona's images

stopped. Vlen raced and jumped down the switchback trail that led to the lava flow, and his motion made Rezs dizzy.

Rezsia! It was Coale, calling.

Rezs could feel the woman pause on the cliff. "I can hear you," she returned, unaware that she was whispering the words.

Listen to me, then—carefully. There is a way to use Vlen to transfer your energy to Ukiah. I will have to guide you into Vlen's mind, and control it. You will have to trust me and relax completely into your bond with Vlen.

"I don't understand."

But I do. Trust me. All wolfwalkers can use the bond in this way.

The woman sent a shaft of reassurance that soothed Vlen's snarl and made Rezsia open her eyes. "What do I do?" she asked firmly.

Go to the scout. The image Coale projected was filled with a haunting music, and Rezs recognized the tune that had filled her mind. *Place one hand so you can feel his pulse and his body heat—his neck is best. Place your other hand near or on the broken bone.*

Ukiah watched her warily. "What are you doing?" he demanded. His words were still slurred, and although, with the growing shadows, it was getting difficult to tell, his eyes seemed unfocused.

"I'm going to use my bond with Vlen to get you warmer."

Alarm flared in Ukiah's eyes. He clenched her hand, holding it away from his neck.

"Coale's helping me," she said flatly. "It's do this or let yourself go into shock, and we don't have a healer here to help us."

Slowly, he relaxed his grip, but he did not let go. Vlen's snarl brought Rezs's expression to a feral grimace, and she could not seem to smooth her lips down. She pressed her hand against his neck, then laid her other hand on the swollen part of his leg. It felt rock hard, and she hesitated as Ukiah gasped.

"Go ahead," he bit out.

"Coale, I'm ready. Now what?"

Relax. Let Vlen guide you toward me, and Shona will guide me to you. You might feel dizzy for a moment.

Rezs nodded. She let her mind spin out along Vlen's snarl.

The gray din grew, then separated into voices and images that became more and more clear. For an instant she felt her consciousness grabbed by the din, then she almost cried out. The dizziness was an abrupt spiraling that sucked her into the gray. Vlen's voice was clear now, as though it was made of chimes, and the Coale/Shona images were a single presence that created a wall. Then Ukiah's pulse was sucked into hers, and she felt her heartbeat slow. From behind the wall, power burst along that mental beat. It surged into the pulse along Vlen's link, into Rezsia's mind, and out along the gray image of the scout who lay on the rocks. That power held steady, and another wall seemed to form. From behind that wall, tiny sparks of energy lit Rezs's mind. She flinched, yet felt nothing. It was as if she was being bypassed—as if energy that spilled into her link with Vlen was separate somehow from herself. Images filled her brain: blood, bones, fluids pocketed between muscle mass . . . And the gray tide that rose against the shield wall in waves.

When the gray fog withdrew, Rezsia remained where she was. Vlen's voice was tired, and there was a twisting pain in his guts. Rezs opened her eyes and took a breath. Her own stomach cramped.

"Ukiah?" she asked.

The scout was staring at her. "What did you do?"

"Are you all right?" she asked, ignoring the question.

"I heard the wolves—they were in my head again. And I feel stronger—not as cold. My leg . . ."

He tried to shift, and Rezs put out a hand to stop him, but she was too weak. She stared down at her own hands. "What's happened to me?" she whispered.

Ukiah propped himself awkwardly on his elbows and studied his leg. Deliberately, he twitched his foot. Although his face twisted with pain, he did not cry out. He stared at the swollen limb. Then he realized Rezs had not moved. "Rezs?" he asked sharply.

She looked at him. "I'm tired, Ukiah." She rubbed at her forehead. "I'm sorry. I'm trying, but I don't . . . think I can stay awake."

He patted the rock. "Lie down here beside me."

"The cavebleeders—"

"Will stay away," he cut in. "They haven't dropped closer

than a meter since you put out that fluid. Lie down before you fall down. You can help keep me warm."

Obediently, she stretched uncomfortably beside him. He sucked in his breath once, when she bumped him, but he reassured her with a word. Then he tucked her head against his shoulder and held her close.

"Feels . . . wrong," she murmured. "I should be comforting you."

He stroked her shoulder. His narrowed eyes watched the sheathed worms dangle and pulse. "Doesn't matter. Bany will be here soon."

Or Coale, she told him. But her lips didn't move. She was already halfway asleep.

Ukiah looked at her head on his shoulder. He couldn't handle her sword at this angle, so he eased his knife from his belt and kept it in his hand. Then he shifted his right leg onto the lip of the pit. He clenched his teeth and paled, but made no sound as it pulled the muscles across the break of his left leg. What had been excruciating before—as if the bone ends ground together—was now a sharpness that stabbed, then subsided. He studied his leg, then looked up again at the roof. Once the worms learned to crawl below the fumes, he would be unable to stop them. And Rezs had collapsed like the roof of the tunnel. The energy she'd given him had helped stabilize his body, but it had sapped her too far. And now they were both parasite bait.

He watched a roofbleeder curl and pulse. His hand gripped the knife like a lifeline. The gray fog that Rezs had had in her head—he could almost hear it echo in his own, and unconsciously, he projected his fear into that packsong. Somewhere outside, a lone wolf howled. Then another added its voice. The sounds trailed weirdly across the rocks, and Ukiah shivered. One of the worms dropped lower. Like a nightspider, the worm tested the air, seeking the source of warmth it could feel, but repelled by the fumes of the fluid. Another pulsed down along the sides of the shadowed lava tube. "By all the moons that ride the sky," he whispered, "I hope to hell you hurry."

XVIII

Vlen was running, and the packsong he sent to Rezs was thick in her head like a storm. Rezs could feel the threat behind her, herding her into a canyon. The sides closed in, and steepened, and the canyon floor dropped away. Yellow rock rose like walls, darkened with shadows that crawled. And the wolves behind her dropped away as they were sucked into the shadows that became a pit. The pit became the mouth of the worm, and grew until it engulfed the canyon in leaps. Ahead was a fog that filtered in from the sun, and at its center was a heart—a gray heart, that pulsed with haunted music, but could not give it voice. It called to her, and she ran faster toward it, stumbling across the canyon. Behind her, the roof-bleeder gained on her—taking the very stone from under her feet. The white gumline of the pit mouth was now a row of needle teeth. It stretched. The gray heart pulsed. It gaped. The heart hung in its mouth and screamed. And Rezs cried out—

She opened her eyes abruptly. Ukiah was watching her closely.

She stared at him. The sky overhead was deep blue. The rocks as black as ever. And the worms dangled like writhing roots from the ceiling of the tunnel.

"All right?" Ukiah asked.

"They're still there."

He nodded.

She cleared her throat. Carefully, she disengaged herself from his side and sat up. "How are you?"

"Fine," he returned lightly. "It's not every day I get to sleep with a wolfwalker."

She gave him a sharp look. Her stomach was still cramping, but she didn't feel as exhausted, and her link to Vlen seemed somehow more set in her mind. She could feel the cub almost without consciously reaching out. Absently, she wondered if this was the looseness to the bond that Coale had described before.

"Bany?"

"Not here yet."

"How long was I asleep?"

"Not long."

She glanced at the petri dishes. The fluid level was down by half, and the fumes were beginning to thin. She tried not to look at the worms that dangled overhead, but she couldn't help seeing the gray, sheathed tendrils curl out toward the open area where the shadows from the well protected them from the light, and the heat from the two humans beckoned.

"Come on, Coale," she murmured tightly.

Vlen snarled low in her head, and she let herself see through his eyes. He was pacing at the edge of the flow, and there were shadow figures that climbed out on the rocks in his sight. Gray Shona was nearby the cub, and the older wolf snapped at the yearling when Vlen got too close to her space. Rezs found her own teeth bared as Vlen growled back. Even in the dark, Ukiah did not mistake the yellow glints that reflected in her violet eyes.

"Rezs—"

The scout's voice snapped her out of the bond, and she blinked. "They're coming," she reported. "I can see them out on the flow right now."

"Coale and Elgon?"

She nodded. He glanced at the worms, and she followed his gaze. "They'll get here in time," she said. She wasn't sure which of them she was reassuring. "The fluid will last awhile longer before the potency evaporates, and it won't take them as long to reach us as it did for us to get here—we spent a lot of time digging around in the crevices. They'll come here directly."

But the minutes stretched, and the gray worms writhed. It was more than a relief when Elgon's voice floated to them from above.

"Rezsia—can you hear me?"

"We're here," she shouted. Ukiah winced. "Sorry," she said belatedly to the scout.

"Are you all right?" Elgon yelled. "Is Ukiah conscious?"

She gave the man a sideways look. "He's conscious and irritating as a howling bird in heat. When can you get him out of here?"

"Soon. Which side of the well are you on?"

"West side."

A moment later a handful of pebbles fell away from the east edge of the hole, and Elgon's face peered over the rim. He studied them, looked around the well, narrowed his eyes as he caught sight of the roofbleeders, and said something over his shoulder to Coale. He pointed toward the same overhang from which Rezs had dropped. When the older woman began climbing down over the overhang, Rezs caught her breath, but in spite of the woman's weaker leg, the wolfwalker's hands and feet were sure on the rocks. Coale didn't drop as Rezs had done, but somehow clung to the underside of the rock with her hands and feet, easing down gradually so that she didn't risk a sprained ankle with a jump. Not even the roofbleeders that writhed around Coale's shape fazed the woman. She merely brushed them aside, then crouched beneath them and crawled over to Ukiah.

"Smart," the woman commented as she examined the man. She noted his position and the sword beneath him. "Falling on your blade like that. It probably saved your spine. May I?" she asked with bare courtesy. She was already peering at his leg.

"Go ahead," he said dryly.

Coale's eyes glinted. "How does it feel?"

He shrugged. "Not bad. Was a lot worse before Rezs linked me to the wolves."

The woman didn't glance at Rezs, and Rezs felt somehow useless. "How much of that link did you feel?" the woman asked absently as she prodded his leg gently.

"Nothing specific, but one heck of a lot of power. Crawling sensations in my leg—as if the fluid was being pushed out of the area. I couldn't move it before, but after that, I could wriggle my toes."

The woman's hands touched the swollen flesh, and Ukiah's jaw tightened. "Yell if you want to," the woman told him. She adjusted her position. "Whether it's broken or not, this is going to hurt." Then, with one, quick motion she set his leg.

Ukiah screamed. Gray Vlen howled, and it struck Rezs's ears with a shaft of gray pain that almost glowed. She staggered back, knocking over one of the petris, so that it shattered on the rocks, and fluid splashed out on a worm. The sheathed form jerked and writhed, turning brown as its rubbery flesh burned from the chemicals, and Rezs stared at Ukiah.

His voice was a harsh croak. "Is it done?"

"Almost. Close your eyes for a moment."

"I've had broken legs before." His voice was more steady, but his hands were clenched and trembling.

"I realize that. Closing your eyes is for me, not you."

Ukiah averted his face and did as she asked. The woman then beckoned to Rezs. "Here." Coale directed Rezsia's hands. *Now link with me through Vlen. I'm too tired to do this alone.*

Even though Coale was right beside her, the woman's voice was distant in the gray din. Vlen's voice was still as clear as cold water, and Rezs hesitated.

Link, Rezsia.

This time the dizziness was abrupt and uncontrolled. The gray wall that built up between them was frayed and ragged, and Rezs could feel the triad of human heartbeats that cluttered up the din. Shapes and colors sped by in her vision, and she clutched Coale's arm as she swayed. Gray Vlen growled in the distance; Shona's voice was a firm howl. And then the woman cut her off, leaving her drained and weak.

Coale studied her face. *This is not something of which we speak outside of the wolfwalker circles. Do not describe what you did to others.*

Rezs met the woman's eyes steadily. "I understand," she returned. But her tone had a warning note, and Coale nodded shortly. The woman did not mistake Rezs's questions.

"Later," Coale said obliquely. Then, to the scout: "We're done, Ukiah. I don't think it's broken. I think it's been wrenched, and most of the pain is from the swelling. But just in case—" She glanced at Rezs. "Get me the halves of that bow."

Rezsia nodded and gently worked them free from underneath the scout. Ukiah braced himself for the splinting, but

Coale's hands were gentle, and he did not cry out once. Then Elgon draped his jerkin over the edge of the lava tunnel to pad the rope and lowered the line to the three. A few moments later Rezs was being drawn up. Once at the lip, she scrambled onto the rock, loosened the rope, nodded to Elgon, and lowered the line back down to Coale. Ukiah was next, and while the scout was being hauled up by both Elgon and Rezs, the older wolfwalker gathered up the petris, poured out the extra fluid, and packed them in her belt pouch to return them to Rezsia. A few minutes later they were all up on the rim.

Ukiah was sitting on the rock, his splinted leg stretched out across a rough boulder. The sun shone steeply through the sparse trees, and the scout squinted across the lava flow. "Now what?" he asked.

Coale loosened the rope and handed it back to Elgon. "We wait."

Rezs glanced at her thoughtfully, then opened herself to Vlen. Instantly, she realized what the other woman meant: The sense of the other scouts was clear in the cub's mind. "Bany's already on the flow," she told Ukiah. "They'll be here within half an hour."

"So it's the stretcher for me."

Elgon coiled up the rope. "Unless you want to spend the next two ninans here waiting for your leg to heal enough to walk on," he agreed.

"With cavebleeders in every crevice? Not likely," he retorted. "I'd rather crawl off this river of rock than stay a night near these caves."

Rezs looked west, judging the angle of the sun. "I hope they hurry," she said in a low voice to Elgon. "This will be near impossible in the dark."

"There's time," he returned. "It didn't take us long to get out here to you; they won't be far behind us."

The tall man was right, but Rezs and the others still had time to eat before any of the scouts showed up. Without Bany's spicing, Elgon's meat rolls were as bland as bread, and hungry as Rezs was, she almost had to force herself to swallow. Now she knew why Coale had complained of Elgon's trail food when they first met.

By the time the other scouts showed up, Elgon and Coale had rigged a stretcher by weaving their rope in a fishing-net pattern between two poles cut from a fallen tree. Welker and Touvinde donated their jerkins to pad the rope, and Ukiah was then installed on it. He cursed more than once as they dropped him and dragged him and lurched over the rocks, but he was off the rock flow by the time it was dark.

They lost eight kays of riding that day and ended up back at the base of the cliff where the trail reached the valley floor. Ukiah wanted to ride on, but his face was pale and sweating by the time they reached the trail. Bany, pulling up at the first clear area they found, told Ukiah to get down off his dnu or he'd pull the younger man down. The younger scout cursed the old man roundly, but Bany just laughed. Then, with a practiced jerk, he hauled the scout off his saddle, draped the tall man across his shoulder, and set him down on the ground.

"Bany—" Rezs dismounted and hurried to Ukiah's side.

The old man straightened. "I may be old, but no bashed-up hero is going to act the fool around me. He stays down, and we camp here. Coale, you'd better check the splinting on that leg."

A half hour later the fire was built, the camp stew boiling, and Ukiah settled against a log while Welker designed for him a crutch. The lanky woman shrugged when Rezs asked her about her work; turned out that Welker had spent a good part of her youth at a woodworking shop. She didn't have the wood-specific worms to carve designs, she told Rezs as she pegged and lashed the form together, but she also wasn't being judged on aesthetics. It was amazing, Rezs thought as she watched the other woman work. Where the tall scout was awkward sitting or standing, Welker was confident and dexterous as she handled the wood. She seemed to forget who she was until she was done, but as soon as she finished fitting the crutch to Ukiah, she became self-conscious again. She moved clumsily around the fire and didn't speak again until it was time for her to take watch.

It was Bany who wrapped Ukiah's leg, but Rezs hovered as the old man did it. Gray Vlen, who was lying down with Shona, watched the old scout as closely as Rezs, and Rezs felt herself tense every time the old man took a turn with the strip of cloth. She suffered through half the procedure, then slowly stiffened.

Touvinde raised his eyebrows. "Either you've suddenly gotten an idea, or an oshparivat bug just bit you."

She shook her head. It was Vlen, she realized—but not Vlen who was giving her this anxiety. The fixation on watching Bany treat Ukiah—that was coming to the yearling through Gray Shona, and then on to Rezs, until she wanted to take the bandages from Bany's hands and do the task herself. She looked around for Coale. The older woman was already bedded down, but Rezs knew she wasn't sleeping. She could feel the eyes of the other woman through her link to Vlen.

When Bany was done, Ukiah struggled to his feet and beckoned at Rezs. "Want to help me try these out?"

"Since I'm the reason you have them," she returned, "I suppose it's only fair." She steadied him as he arranged his weight on the crutch. "How does it feel?"

"Amazingly good." He winced as he eased his leg over a root. "I think Coale's right—it's wrenched, not broken. I might have a bone bruise, but it sure doesn't feel like a break anymore. I can put most of my weight on it now."

"Coale's going to look at it later?"

He nodded. "I should be able to ride in fair comfort by morning. As for tonight, with this crutch, I'm almost as good as new. Tomorrow, Welker can turn it back into firewood."

"That seems awfully fast for a healing, Ukiah."

"The more use it gets, the stronger it'll grow," he countered.

"Isn't that the hardheaded approach to healing?" She steadied him as he stumbled. "Maybe you should ask Coale before cutting up your new crutch in some kind of idiot independence."

"And what idiot put me on this crutch to begin with?"

An image of Rezs's brother, Cal, flashed into her head. Broken legs and gray-fogged pain . . . She frowned. There was something nagging at the back of her mind, and she couldn't quite get ahold of it, but it had to do with the other wolfwalker.

Ukiah paused, glanced over his shoulder to check the distance between them and the camp, then gave her a sharp look. "Nothing to say?"

"Not right now."

"You're thinking of Coale," he said flatly.

"And you're thinking of peeing." she retorted. "If you want to do it soon, you'd better start hobbling again. With bihwadi and worlags and roofbleeders at night, I'm not going to wander out here with you for more than a few minutes."

He gave her a serious look. "She is hiding something, Rezs."

Rezs didn't smile. "So are you. I felt it, you know. When Coale and I were linked through the wolves. You were like this wall of gray, behind which there was nothing."

Ukiah turned away. "That's not something I want to talk about."

"But you want to talk about Coale."

His voice was flat. "I was hired to protect you. Who hired her, and for what? What's she hiding? She watches you like a hawk, Rezs. If she took off this morning so long before Bany did, how come she and Elgon reached us first out on the lava flow?"

Rezs had no answer for that. Coale had watched Ukiah, too—or Bany, she acknowledged as she realized she did not know which one Gray Shona had been more interested in. Coale might not trust the other scouts, but she hadn't hesitated to help Ukiah when the man fell. Yet as soon as the others had arrived, she kept her distance again and watched the others, as Ukiah said, through the eyes of her wolf.

Ukiah nodded at her expression. "I think she's more aware of what you do than you are."

"You're not a wolfwalker," Rezs said slowly. "How do you know what she sees—what she thinks?"

"I don't have to bond with a wolf to understand its song. Gray Shona sings the song of a hunter, and the one she hunts is you."

Rezs laughed, but the sound was hollow in her ears.

"Let me ask you this again, Rezs: Could you describe that woman to me?"

Rezs bit her lip, disturbed. She tried to think of a time when she had seen Coale's hair, and her memory came up with nothing. A wisp of it near the edge of Coale's warcap; but never the full head of color. She would have seen it when they bathed, except they'd shared that only once—at night. And although she had seen the scars that littered Coale's lean body, she had no idea what the woman's face was like at all.

Ukiah nodded as she closed her mouth and her eyebrows drew together. "I've never seen her eyes, Rezs. In firelight, yes, but not in the day. I've never seen her expression when it was not hidden in shadow or night. Even when she came down into that rock pit, her features were hidden by darkness. When we reached the rim, she was far enough away and in enough shadow again from the trees that I never saw her eyes. What is she afraid we'll see?"

The trees sighed, and Gray Vlen rubbed against Rezs's hand. Absently, she stroked his fur. "Her eyes are dark," she said softly. "Some medium shade—maybe brown or gray . . ."

"And you even can't be sure of that."

She gave him a sharp look. "You're saying she might not be Coale at all. But if she isn't, then who is she really? How many wolfwalkers are there who can fit her description?"

"Female wolfwalkers, between sixty and a hundred, with graying hair? Three dozen in these counties. Who can move like a ghost in the forest? Easily a dozen."

"Who have had run-ins with lepa?"

"Four that I know of: Coale, Felina, Dion, and . . . Sapha."

"Sapha's ribs were broken last month—I met her when she was traveling through my town to get to Sidisport. And Sapha's got very long fingers. I'd swear that Coale's fingers are not as long as they should be if she were Sapha instead of who she claims to be."

"And Dion's feet are larger than Coale's—I've seen Dion's tracks before—and Dion walks with a different limp than Coale. A couple decades ago Dion's right leg was chewed up pretty badly by the lepa. But Coale limps on the left. I think it's from three years ago, when her knee was wrenched out in a venge she led against the raiders to the south."

"Felina's supposed to be in Randonnen," Rezs said doubtfully. "But supposed to be doesn't mean that she is."

"But Felina has a long, bony face. From what little I have seen of this woman, I just don't see her face as having one of those long, dour structures."

"So we're back to Coale again." Rezs started back to the camp. "Bany said he met Coale only once when she was younger. She could have changed more than her face with age—and the woman he knew as a young man may not be anything like the one who runs with us now."

"You're saying her motivations might not be as pure now as they were back then? That she could be one of the reasons neGruli's men don't come back."

She shrugged. "How many times can a man be attacked by

worlags and be one of the very few to escape? NeGruli's had far too many run-ins with the beasts. A wolfwalker would know when the beasts were coming and be able to tell neGruli to get out of camp. All he'd have to do is walk away. And if he was on watch, he'd leave his men unaware until it was too late. With worlags, he'd not be taking much of a chance that any would be left alive."

Rezs stared into the trees as if she could see the beetlelike creatures crawling. She shook her head. "No," she said slowly. "I just don't buy it. NeGruli's killing his own men—that I can believe, but Coale? She's truly concerned with people. When she teaches me, she has a love for what she does—I feel as if we're as close as sisters, even though we hardly speak. And you—when you br—hurt your leg, she was right there, feeding you her energy to keep you out of shock." She gestured at his leg. "It drained her, Ukiah. I could feel it. I just can't see her as a killer."

"Maybe not," he agreed readily. "But anyone who has kept her face from being seen for eighteen days on the trail is doing so deliberately. And anyone who hides such an obvious thing so well has had a lot of practice. Coale might be Coale, but that only proves one thing: We haven't a clue what Coale really is."

They made their way slowly back to the camp, and Ukiah paused more than once to rest. By the time they returned, he was pale and sweating, and for once, grateful to be back on his bedding.

"Are you sure you're okay?" Rezs laid his crutch beside him.

"It might not feel bad," Ukiah managed, "but it sure as heck doesn't make me want to dance."

She couldn't help hovering again, and Bany finally pulled her away and pointed to the other side of the fire. "Go hang over someone else's shoulder. Sit by Gradjek or . . . go talk to Coale," the old man directed. "Ask her if she has any sense that we're being followed on this trail."

Obediently, she made her way away from the scout to sit beside Elgon. Both Vlen and Shona were back in the shadows, avoiding the heat of the fire where the flames reflected off the rocks and formed an ovenlike pocket. From across the fire, Rezs sought the gleam in Vlen's yellow eyes, and the cub yawned, showing off his teeth instead. Beside the cub, Gray Shona scratched another shedding mat of fur into the dirt, and Vlen sniffed it, then snorted, so that the gray hairs rolled like a hesitant rat. Rezs shivered and turned her eyes back to the fire, but the tiny tendrils of smoke made her think of the roofbleeders, and she couldn't help rubbing at her arms.

"Cold?" Elgon asked.

"Thinking of cave creatures," she admitted.

"Like roofbleeders and lepa?"

"Not lepa actually, although I think the fear of those beasts is ingrained so deeply in us—my brothers and myself—that I can't think of a flock without feeling that one is about to form."

"Why such ingrained fear?"

"My father was once attacked by a lepa flock."

Elgon tossed a twig into the fire. "He was a lucky man, to survive that."

"He was a boy," said Rezs.

"Then he was even luckier."

"Sometimes I think it was a curse—not a blessing—that protected him."

From the other side of Elgon, Coale made an odd sound.

Rezs glanced at the other woman. "We say sometimes that our grandma's cursed," she explained. "Dion does the right things, but somehow always ends up paying for it as if she were being punished. Yet she keeps doing those right things. It's as if she thinks the moons will someday stop taking from her and give back some joy in exchange." Slowly, she shredded the twig into the fire. "She's lost so many people . . ."

"To the lepa?" Elgon asked casually.

"To raiders and lepa and everything else in the forest. The run-in with the lepa was when my father was nine. She was out with him and one of his younger brothers when the lepa started flocking. The birdbeasts took Danton—her other son—and killed him when she threw my father into safety in a cave. You see, the moons let her keep one son, but only in exchange for the other."

Elgon peeled the bark from another twig. "I know that story," he said slowly. "It's said that Dion wouldn't let go of Danton even after the lepa grabbed him up from the ground. They say she fought the lepa midair for him, using the leverage of one beast's grip against the others. Used her knives until she was torn to shreds by their talons and dropped, near dead, to the rocks."

Rezs cocked her head. "I never heard that."

The tall man shrugged. "Your father probably never wanted to talk about it much."

Coale sat up slowly. "I know that story, too," she said to Rezs. "They say that Dion never forgave herself for losing her son to the lepa."

Elgon gave the older woman a sharp look. "They also say that her other son, safe in his cave with his torch to protect him, never forgave her either." His voice was steely, and he gave Rezs a hard look. "It's said that your father, Olarun, never really spoke to his mother after they were taken back home. It was her adopted son, Tomi, and her uncle, Gamon, who nursed her back to health. Even her own mate, Aranur, who couldn't stand to see her so wounded, and who couldn't believe that his son was dead, never blamed her for the lepa flock. Only Olarun did that."

"But he was just a child," Rezs cut in.

"And terrified for a long time afterward," Coale added. "It was not his responsibility to nurse his mother when he himself was traumatized."

"He wasn't traumatized," retorted Elgon. "He was selfish."

Rezs looked from one to the other. Elgon's voice was sharp enough that Touvinde had begun to watch them, and the older wolfwalker gave her grandson a warning look. "That's a pool of moonworms, Elgon," the woman said, lowering her voice deliberately. "He'd just seen his brother die and his mother badly wounded—"

"Badly?" The man snorted. "Try mortally. It was only the bond with the wolves that saved Dion and gave her the strength to crawl into that hole. She bled out there for hours while the flock tried to get at her. Even you have to admit that if Olarun hadn't frozen, Danton would have made it into the cave before the flock hit them. As for Dion—even though she lived, her wounds were so deep, they say that she'll bear them onto the path to the moons and beyond. Every time Olarun looked at his mother, he saw what he had done. He couldn't cope with the responsibility for that, so he put the blame on his mother."

Rezs cleared her throat. Coale and Elgon had forgotten her, and she had the feeling that they were replaying an argument that was older than she was. "Coale—" she tried to break in.

"Olarun was nine years old," the woman said sharply to her grandson, ignoring Rezsia completely. "Did you expect him to act like a seasoned fighter? He'd never seen a lepa before. He was probably as terrified as you were the first time you saw a flock in action. Or don't you remember that?"

"I remember," Elgon said grimly. "But I also know that he took the blame of Danton's death for himself, and refused to give it up. He punished his whole family for his own guilt. You can't justify rejection, Coale," he said deliberately. "Families are more than jumbles of names, linked by lineage or blood. The family is your history and your future—it's half of what makes you who you are, and it defines the person you want to be, either for good or ill. To deny your family is to cut off your legs and tell yourself that you're whole—"

"Perhaps," Rezs broke in, "it was the expectations."

Elgon and Coale halted. For a moment they looked at her blankly.

She nodded. "The expectations he felt from his parents. My grandfather was one of the weapons masters of Ramaj Ariye—not just another fighter from the hills. And his mother was a wolfwalker and master healer. They had a set of reputations that Olarun couldn't live up to. Perhaps it was that—as much as his guilt—which drove him away."

Irritably, Coale adjusted the blankets of her sleeping bag. Her voice was sharp. "It's not for children to live up to or down to a parent's reputation. Every man must grow to know his own strengths and skills and beliefs. All his parents can do is teach him how to learn those skills, how to stand up for his beliefs, and how to change those beliefs or skills when they become thin or inappropriate. Olarun—your father—learned all that, but he never learned to accept his own mistakes. And that is what crippled him as a child."

Rezs met her gaze steadily. "My father drives himself harder than anyone I've seen. He learns from every mistake. And we might have a small business, but because of him and my mother, our lab has had one of the best track records in development in our county for over fifteen years. We've been able to stay solvent even with the takeovers of other businesses in our field."

"And all of you drive yourselves as your father drives himself," Coale returned. "But tell me, Rezsia, why do you drive yourselves? Why do you, Rezsia, drive yourself? Is it insecurity? Is it guilt? Is it the need to be as good as your father thinks he should have been? Do *you* compete with your grandparents for the reputations they built?"

"I—" Rezs stared into the fire. "If I do compete," she said softly, "it's because I want to do something important."

The older woman's voice seemed suddenly tired. "Not everyone can save the world, Rezs."

"I don't want to save it. I just want to be proud of my contribution to it."

"Many people—ordinary people—simply live in the manner of which they can be proud. They tolerate each other's differences, allow each other's beliefs, and simply by their lifestyle support their neighbors as if they were more like family. That, Rezs, is enough for anyone to be proud of."

"Unless you want to do more," Rezs returned.

The woman studied her for a long moment. "You can always do more, Rezsia Monet maDeiami. The question is, what will you give up to do it?"

Rezs was silent for a moment. The fire popped once, and its sparks made Vlen's ears twitch.

Coale's voice was so soft that Rezs had to lean in to hear her. "With Olarun," the older woman said, "it's love he's given up for pride, and his family he's traded for his guilt. And now it's the weight of time, not distance, that keeps him from reaching out to his parents. He's been away too long to make part of the bridge back to them himself."

Elgon shifted to place his hand over his grandmother's, and Rezs felt somehow intrusive. She glanced across the fire and, noting Bany's scrutiny, opened her mouth to ask about the sense of being followed, but said nothing. Instead, she stood and moved back from the fire, leaving the two alone.

XIX

The dawn was quiet, and Coale slid out of the shadows with it. Rezs, standing on the edge of a boulder to watch the sky colors, shifted so that she faced the other woman. She had yet to mend her sleeve from the day before, so she had merely rolled it up, and the cool air, filled with a moist chill, covered her skin with goose bumps. She rubbed absently at her arms. "How long did it take with Shona?" she asked softly. "I mean to learn to control your thoughts like you do now? And to understand hers?"

Coale didn't answer at first. Instead, the other woman climbed up on the boulder beside her, so that they stood as tiny needles in a sea of shadow. Around them, the stillness of the lava flow seemed to hold up the silent moons. The rocks were a mass of blackness beneath the sparse green canopy, and the trunks of the trees which stuck out of the stone flow were pillars that held up the patchy roof. Above that roof, the sky was not clear, and the strips of clouds that spread across the rough horizon caught up the dawn colors in striking pinky golds. Far away, to the southeast, there was a small flock of lepa, but the group of birdbeasts disappeared moments after it formed. There was no threat in the air.

Rezs could feel Gray Vlen in the distance, hunting rats with Shona. With the looseness she had achieved in their bond, she no longer jerked each time he leaped on a racing rodent. His senses had begun to be part of her, she realized, and—just as Coale had predicted—she was beginning to be able to separate herself and still read the yearling's images. She stretched now, into that gray fog. The voices that at first had been so indistinct were now much more clear. She could almost hear her father's words as he rode beside Cal on a trail . . . She could hear music floating on the fog. She glanced at Coale and then closed her eyes, reaching into the packsong to pull out the threads that spoke of memory, not current sights and smells. And for the first time since she had started trying, she found in the packsong the scents of the dung heaps of a large party of dnu. She could actually take in the scent images of newly used peetrees. Shadow figures of men and women, moving between the boulders, edging along a trail . . . Then Gray Vlen howled his welcome, and her eyes flew open as Gray Shona's yellow eyes gleamed inside her mind. She stared at Coale.

The other woman did not take her eyes from the dawn. "I did not help you," the older wolfwalker answered softly. "You reached the packsong on your own."

Rezs pulled back from the gray fog.

"Shona was full-grown when we bonded." Coale wrapped her cloak around herself as she answered Rezs's previous question. "She had learned to control her thoughts already, and I had run with the wolves before, so I was able to feel through her within the first ninan of bonding."

Rezs rubbed her arms against the chill. Gray Shona's eyes were like the orbs that had haunted her childhood dreams, and there was something unsettling about seeing them beside Gray Vlen's inside her mind. "Vlen still doesn't understand a quarter of what I send him," she said slowly.

"You are still trying to send him information that is too complex. The ancients engineered him to bond with you, not be like you. He's a wolf, not a human, and he won't understand sentences and words. What he will understand are images."

The sky lightened, and the colorless rocks began to grow green mosses and blue-tinged fungi. As the area lightened, Rezs's gaze sharpened. For the first time since she had begun running trail with Coale, her vision was not as blurred near the other woman—the power that Coale unconsciously projected was offset by Rezs's growing strength. Startled at the realization, she gave the other woman a surreptitious look. What she saw this time was almost clear. Age—not the age of too many decades, but the age of living too many years with burdens that couldn't be lightened enough by laughter or love. She stared. The lines that creased Coale's face could no longer hide the height of the woman's cheekbones, nor the straightness of her nose—

And then, slowly, the woman stiffened. "Don't," she said softly.

As if that word broke the clarity of the lupine fog, the sense of the wolves swept back into Rezs's mind. Vlen howled, and his eagerness filled her skull, so that Rezs couldn't shake him off. But she grabbed Coale's arm as the woman tried to turn away.

"You've deliberately kept my eyesight blurred," Rezs said wonderingly. "You've used your bond with Shona to keep me from seeing your face."

The woman shrugged. "Any wolfwalker can do this."

"Like the energy transfer you did yesterday?"

"Something like that," the woman said reluctantly.

"But this is different—you're doing this all the time. What we did for Ukiah—that was focused like a beam of light. They're not the same—"

Coale gently extracted her arm from Rezs's grip. "They're not the same," she agreed. "Transferring . . . energy must be done quickly enough that you don't become drained by the process. It has to be focused so that it is directed exactly where it needs to go. It isn't something to try on your own."

"How did you learn? Old Roy never spoke of this."

"He might know how to do it; he might not. If he did know, he wouldn't have spoken of it to you until you were ready to learn the technique. Here, we had no choice. I had to do it—through you—to keep Ukiah out of shock."

"And the Gray Ones? They built a wall that seemed to shield me from that energy. I could feel it streaming by like a fast current."

Coale nodded. "They don't just build that wall—they *are* that wall. It's what protects them from what we do. You must never take energy out of the wolves, Rezsia—only from another human. No matter what you do to yourself with this, never break down that shield wall."

Rezs could feel the steel will behind those deceptively soft words. "Coale, you've been teaching me to read the minds and memories of the wolves, and you've been teaching Vlen to find the memories I need. Even I can feel Vlen and me growing more able every day. But this . . . energy thing is different. How long before I'll be strong enough to learn to do this on my own?"

The woman didn't answer for a moment. "If you've done it once," she said finally, "you can do it again on your own. But—" She cut into Rezs's immediate reply. "It saps you. You need to have a strong body to bear the drain. You need a strong mind to keep from falling into the Gray Ones' packsong when you become weakened after the transfer. You have to know exactly what you're doing with the energy, or it can harm both you and your patient. And Rezs, it's not something to speak about. Not to other wolfwalkers, not to anyone. Mention it only to those of us who already know the technique."

Rezs raised her eyebrows. "How can I talk about it only to those who know it if I can't ask anyone whether or not they know it?"

"When you know the technique, there are differences in the way your link appears to the wolves. They're not big differences—in fact, they are fairly subtle—but you'll be able to recognize them." The woman paused, seemed to make a decision, and finally spoke again. "Rezsia, you must not hint to anyone that you know this thing. It's an Ancient thing, and it has to be taught properly, or it can kill you and your student in the teaching. And even if you understand the technique, if you do it improperly—as in taking energy from, not through, the wolves—you can kill the Gray Ones who help you. You must not," she repeated, "talk about this to others. The risks are too great that you will end up responsible for someone's death."

Slowly, Rezs nodded. "And the blurring?"

"That's something else. Anyone can learn to project what he wants—not necessarily just what he really sees—through the packsong."

"But why would you need to do that?"

Deliberately, Coale ignored the hint. "Because," she answered, "there are times when you have to lie to your wolf. It's not a subterfuge for amusement," Coale said sharply at Rezs's expression. "With certain types of danger, your Gray One won't go forward. He can be confused by fire or certain smells; he can't see certain things happening—like mud slides or tidal bores."

"So I learn to project what I want him to do. I project an image of less danger where I want him to go?"

"That's it exactly. You can close your eyes and feel your way out of a burning area. A wolf can't do that by himself. But you can do it for him, by blinding him to what he sees and projecting the way to escape."

"So, how do I develop that skill?"

The woman smiled faintly. "The same way you work on sending an image to another person. Build it in your head—like a painting. Then project it to the wolf. It will be a game to Vlen—he'll help you practice." The woman jumped awkwardly down from the boulder. Her game leg almost buckled, but Coale didn't seem to notice it. "We won't run trail until after you leave the lava flow, so I'll meet you in the afternoon or evening. Practice sending your images to Vlen."

"Coale—have you been here before?"

The woman looked up. "What do you mean?"

"Have you been here—in this area? On this trail?"

The older woman hesitated.

Rezs let herself reach out to Vlen, to see if she could tell through Gray Shona what the older woman thought, but there was no connection to the older wolf. Vlen and Shona howled together, but Coale's mental voice, behind that of the other wolf, was barely even faint. "I need to know," she said flatly.

"I've been in many areas," said the woman slowly.

"Where does this road lead?"

"To the cliffs."

"Toward the dome?"

"It's not a good place to go, Rezs. Death clings to those domes like mold to a wall."

"The domes are pretty much looted, aren't they?"

"By the end of the second century," she confirmed. "Two hundred and seventy people gave their lives to lift what they could from those buildings. They died so that we—their descendants—could keep the knowledge they brought to this planet. Welker probably knows more about that than I—my studies were almost completely limited to one field, and I paid little attention to things outside of that." The woman paused, giving Rezsia a speculative look. "But if the old knowledge has been stripped from the domes, what is left in any of those buildings to attract you?"

Not what, Rezs thought, but who: neGruli. Whatever he found had not been on the lava flow, nor in the forest between here and home. It was on that opposite ridge, close enough to the domes to be part of the Ancient site itself. She felt Coale watching her, but she didn't answer, and with a sigh, the woman turned away, slid down from the boulder, and walked back in the shadows to camp. Rezs knew the woman would be gone by the time she herself returned, and she found herself wondering why.

She remained on the boulder, thinking, until the dizziness hit. It was mild this time—it barely made her sway; and was so familiar by now that she almost casually went to her knees to keep from falling down. It was Coale—she was sure of it. That energy transfer that the woman had done—the other wolfwalker was doing it now.

She reached out to Vlen and let her mind join with his, but he wasn't running with Shona as she expected. He was sitting with the other wolf, their mental eyes meeting and merging in one pair of gleaming orbs. The wall of gray that shielded them from the energy was thick and strong, and Rezs couldn't even deform it with a mental prod. But she could feel the sense of heartbeats, the feel of fluids racing, and almost see the molecules that changed and shifted from one tissue to the next.

Rezs opened her eyes and looked up at the moons. The gray sky was becoming blue, and the stars had faded into day. There was a tension to the morning; the feel of it had settled between her shoulders, and it centered around the use of the link between that woman and the wolves.

"Learn it," Rezs whispered to herself. "Add yourself to it, like you added yourself to the packsong."

She closed her eyes. Then reached out to Vlen. Deliberately, she opened herself to the fog. There was an instant of resistance, then on the other side of Shona, Coale seemed to accept her presence. The gray voices swept in; her mind spun out and down. And she was drawn into the heartbeat of Ukiah like a raft on a racing river. This time Rezs studied the way Coale moved her energy—there was a pattern to it—and a balance, she realized. Like a tug-of-war, the woman pulled, and the wolf resisted. And it was Shona, not Coale, who controlled it.

This time, Rezs wasn't even fazed when the gray wall collapsed and the link disappeared. There was a tiredness in her arms, and her stomach growled, but didn't cramp. "Vlen?" she breathed, reaching out to the yearling.

Wolfwalker, he returned.

She touched his mental voice as if she stroked his fur. "You honor me, Gray One."

He howled, and in it was the joy of youth. Gray Shona joined him, and the rest of the gray din seemed to sweep into her mind. The hunger he felt merely tied their bodies together; the howling matched their breathing. Rezs released him to hunt, and the cub raced away, leaving her motionless on the rock with the sense that she pelted forward.

She didn't move until Bany came out to join her. The old man climbed up as Coale had done, and Rezs moved over to make room for him to watch the last dawn colors fade from the sky. Bany glanced at her, offered her a salted seed, then tucked a couple in his own mouth. "Coale's looked at Ukiah's leg. Says the swelling's down."

She nodded.

"Did you ask her about being followed?"

Rezs frowned. "I forgot," she admitted. "Last night, when they were talking about my grandparents, it felt as if they were arguing about something more personal than that. It just didn't seem like the right time. And this morning, we talked about something else again."

Beside her, Bany studied her face. "Interesting," he commented softly, "that they know so much about your family."

"I thought so at first, too. But of all things you could mistrust them for, that shouldn't surprise you. Everyone knows the Aranur and Dion stories."

"Don't start liking her too much, Rezs. You haven't the luxury of trusting anyone you meet—not out here. Not where we're going."

"I know." Her voice was flat.

He sucked on the seeds, then popped the kernels. "Are you thinking of taking them with us all the way to neGruli's source?"

"I can't send them away," she said slowly. "I forced Coale to make the training bond with me. I made her responsible for me."

"Did you? Or did she encourage it by telling you that you needed her?"

Rezs's eyes narrowed. She thought back.

"I see," he said obliquely.

"They did save my life—as you did with Ukiah that night the bihwadi attacked. If I was Ukiah, and Coale was you, I wouldn't question anything she asked me to do. Loyalty for life, remember?"

"Loyalty is like anything else, Rezs. It can be used against you. If Coale is one of neGruli's scouts, taking a training bond with you would be the best way to get close to you. All she would have to do is stick with you till you find his source, then let you put yourself in danger—or direct you to danger without you knowing of it. If she's a little slow to help, her job is done for her. She can pick up the pieces and trot back to neGruli at her leisure."

"She is a wolfwalker, Bany."

"Don't be naive," he said sharply. "Just because someone runs with the wolves doesn't mean she's a paragon of virtue. Wolfwalkers are just as susceptible to greed as anyone else. Take Tiruvavar, for example. He sold out an entire wolf pack for a handful of gems. Or Kubein—that one traded his sister's sons for raider gold. By all nine moons, you offer anyone enough gold and he'll do whatever you want. Coale is no exception." He spat a seed to the side. "I could buy her with a Gray One's cub. And Elgon—the man is far too aware of you."

"I'd trust Coale before Elgon any day," she agreed.

"Don't be deceived by age." Bany's voice was sharp. "Of the two, the woman is more dangerous."

She hesitated.

"What is it?"

"It feels wrong, Bany, to distrust them so. It feels as if there is a link between us—between Coale and me. As if the wolves have bound us together in a kind of shadow family."

"That's typical among wolfwalkers. Don't give it more weight than it deserves." He let his gaze roam the forest, noting the way the shadows resolved in the growing light. "Besides," he added, "from what I can see, Elgon is all the family she needs. He's damn protective of that woman."

"He's probably protecting her from me," Rezs returned sourly. "Elgon doesn't respect me much."

The old man chuckled and popped another handful of seeds in his mouth. "That much is obvious."

"It's not that funny," she retorted. "It's uncomfortable as hell to be around someone who's always watching for your mistakes."

Bany's smile lost its humor. "I'd thank your moons, Rezs. That could be a warning sign that ends up saving your life. When we get closer to neGruli's source, watch Elgon closely. He's easy to read, that one."

"And Coale?"

"I'd still rather you sent her away. We're too close now to our goal. I don't want her in the way."

Rezs rubbed her arms. "If I send them away now, they can just follow us through the wolves. There's no way to lose them with both of us linked."

Bany frowned. "You're right, of course."

"Could your sense of being followed have to do with a wolf pack?"

"It's riders, Rezs. I'd stake my life on it."

"NeGruli's men?"

"Or raiders. Or maybe just some early traders or miners looking for another mineral deposit—the geology out here is interesting enough that there are plenty of small, individual sites that could be located." He glanced over his shoulder as if he could see through the forest to another dawn camp. "We'll know for sure if they don't turn off at the ridge. There are only three routes through those mountains: one to the west, to Ramaj Bilocctar by way of the desert, then the Ariyen Slot; one to the east, to the old, flooded county of Ramaj Kiren; and one straight in, to the domes." He turned back to study her face. "If they follow us, they'll be watching us. We'll have to be careful on the trail—not just if we're being followed," he warned. "But also because of Coale."

"What should I do when we get to the source?"

"Do what you have to, Rezs, and leave the woman to me."

Rezs felt a chill. "You won't kill her—"

He was shaking his head before she finished speaking. "Of course not. But I will put her and her grandson out long enough that you can get what you need from wherever that source is. I've a vial of sleepers that I brought just in case—use it on darts for rabbits. I'll just put it in their food. Don't look at me like that, girl. It's something your own grandma did with the raiders one time—saved her skin and one of your great-great-uncles." He clambered off the boulder, then turned and offered her his hand. His leathery skin was dry and his bones hard; fragile as she knew age to make a man, Bany seemed to be nothing but wiry strength.

"How long would something like that last?"

"Depends on how much she eats before taking it in; how tired she is. Even with all that, I'd say it would give us a good eight hours. Is that not enough time?"

Rezs chewed her lip. "I don't know. But then, I don't really need to prepare huge amounts of samples either. I just need to verify the source and gather enough proof to take back to the elders."

He nodded. "What about the wolves?"

"Coale shouldn't know where we've been unless she asks Gray Vlen directly, and as long as she thinks she was sleeping normally, she shouldn't think to do that."

"That's not a guarantee."

She shook her head.

"It might be best," he said slowly, "when it comes time, to send Gray Vlen away. What he doesn't know, he can't tell another wolfwalker."

Rezs frowned. "That, I'm not comfortable with."

"It's not a matter of staying comfortable, Rezs. It's a matter of staying alive."

She bit her lip. Finally, she nodded.

"You won't be alone," he reassured softly. "We'll be there with you. We'd be poor guards if we couldn't handle one gimpy woman and a wolf."

Rezs said nothing, but in her mind, the tide of gray that seemed to rise made her think of a wave cresting far out to sea. A wave that gathered speed as she moved closer to the shore. There was strength in that wave, and an inexorable power, as if too many things were rushing together. She couldn't help thinking, as she followed Bany back to camp, that there was something she was missing.

The trail that wound through the lava flow was interminable. Its only saving grace was that it had originally been a road, worm-carved by the Ancients, so that there were long stretches where they could lope instead of walk their dnu.

Even so, the half day that it took to cross the valley seemed like two days by itself. Rezs wasn't sure if it was because it was so much of the same—just red-black rock and flattened trees—or because it was the first morning in two ninans that she hadn't run trail with Vlen. The yearling, trotting ahead of the party, looked back often to see her, but with all the noise of the riders, she felt crowded on the trail. That, and the only difference between the morning and afternoon on the lava flow was the rise in altitude they covered and the number of times her ears popped to compensate for the differences in pressure.

It was afternoon before the trail climbed out of the lava flow. Bany found two meadows where other riders had camped in the last month—the cropped circles from the dnu had regrown, but the twigs that had been chewed back by teeth clearly delineated the tether circles of the beasts, and with a little careful spreading of roots and grasses, Bany even found the holes where the tether stakes had been pounded.

By late afternoon, they were well up on the ridge, and the temperature had dropped ten degrees. A new pack of wolves had begun to pace them, and Gray Vlen howled in Rezs's mind as he left the riders to link up with the pack. Rezs caught only a momentary glimpse of his gray shadow shape in the trees; then he was out of sight. She was glad when they stopped to build a fire and take a break. She wanted the heat of the flames to counter the chill that his howling, offset by the haunted grayheart music, had brought to her mind.

Bany squatted beside her as she stacked the twigs into the firepit that the previous riders had used. "Did you send the cub away yet?" he asked.

"Not yet. We're close, but I need him to be more certain just where I should be looking before I send him away." She glanced at Vlen, and sent him a shaft of reassurance as his yellow eyes flicked to watch Bany.

"So Coale is still helping you?"

"Yes. My bond with Vlen is not strong enough yet to make a solid connection to the pack on my own."

"You sound disappointed."

She shrugged. "I probably am." She broke some twigs, making a face at the pitch left on her hands.

Bany raised his eyebrows. "Don't compare yourself to Coale, Wolfwalker. It took that one decades to develop the kind of strength in her bond that she uses now. You're a wolfwalker of barely six ninans—you can't expect to do what she does simply by concentrating for a couple days."

She looked at her hands and rubbed absently at the pitch. "I know you're right, Bany, but it's hard to be around that kind of strength and not want it for myself. The last couple days have been like a year in the amount of focus I've gained, but I still don't understand what I need to know. I can't interpret all the memories; I can't comprehend the images. I need more time, but that's the one thing I don't have, and if I don't learn how to interpret those images by the time we reach the top of this ridge, I'll have to ask her to help me find the source itself. Ah, moonworms," she muttered, drawing her cloak close around her before setting the thicker branches on the pile. "The one thing I can understand now is how my father felt, trying to be like his parents."

"You're not just comparing—you're competing with Coale," he said flatly.

Or her grandmother, Dion, she admitted to herself. She looked at the old man. "Maybe I am competing," she agreed. "But at some point you can't help but become aware of just how much there is to learn, and the goal then seems so far away that it becomes nigh onto impossible. Being around Coale is like being a beginning painter when your teacher is one of the masters, like Lokoza. The interpretation is everything, and I don't have the eyes yet to see what the Gray Ones are trying to show me."

The old man sat back on his heels. "When I met you, you were still learning to be quiet with the way you placed your feet. You weren't aware of the way the metals on your clothing glinted, and you couldn't tell a redroot from a beetle's egg bulb. Now you walk like a scout, you can run trail for kays at a time, and you ride like you were born to the saddle. You keep your bowstring loose and your sword oiled, and you can actually point out the differences between the calls of the bihwadi and the cries of a night-beating bird. If you asked me, I'd say you were doing fine."

She looked at her hands, then gave him a slight smile. "Thanks."

"But?"

She shrugged, struck a match, lit the shavings, and watched

them flash in a brilliant flame that leaped up to the twigs, curled around them, and turned their edges red.

"Wolfwalker," said Bany firmly, "the only thing you need to do is your job. Not my job, not Touvinde's job, not your father's job, not Coale's—whatever that ends up being," he added. "Right now there are only two things you have to do to get your own job done: read the memories of the wolves—and you're doing that well enough to have gotten us this far—and read our backtrail through your link with the Gray One to find out who's behind us. Nothing else should be important to you, because nothing else is anything you can control. So . . ." He indicated Gradjek and Welker with his chin. "Now, go on up the ridge with them and find out who's on our trail. Don't compare yourself to them as you hike. Don't worry about Ukiah's leg. Don't compete with Coale in how well you can look into the minds of the wolves. Just do what you have to do: Look out over the lava flow and ask Gray Vlen if he feels hunted."

"He does."

"So we are being followed."

She nodded shortly. "Last night, when Coale and I tried to read the packsong, I felt the riders behind us. Their night fire was in the minds of the wolves."

"Could you identify them? See what they looked like?"

She shook her head. "It doesn't work like that. The wolves don't seem to see people as we do, but as representations of how much threat or challenge the person has—how much more like predator or prey. I can look at you and see a slender man of a hundred and thirty, with gray-white hair and sharp eyes, but Vlen sees you as a tough old male with gray-white hair and a hunter gaze."

Bany gave her a thoughtful look. "How does he see Elgon?"

She hesitated. "Big, tall, wary. Not trusting. Not one to challenge. Solid."

"And Coale?"

"A hunter," she returned without thinking. "Like you. Half-wolf, half-human. But that's not really it," she corrected herself. "More as if they think of her as a wolf sometimes, and as a human other times. They respect her as a wolfwalker, but it's as if she's so much a part of them that they hardly notice the things she does that are human. I see her limp with every step she takes, but they notice it as a weakness—the side on which to attack—if they could ever do that to her. I guess the way to describe it is that I see her body, but they see her heart."

He took off his warcap and absently scratched his hair. "So how can you tell if it really was neGruli who came this way—and not some other party? You can recognize him through Gray Vlen's mind?"

She hesitated. "If Vlen has met a human when I'm there and I connect his vision to what I see in his head, then, yes, I can recognize someone through the link. But if he hasn't met the human in person, I have to interpret the images as best I can based on how I know the person myself."

"So neGruli, leading his 'pack,' would be interpreted by the wolves as the lead male of the human group."

"Maybe. Human groups are confusing to the wolves. The one that is most dangerous is not necessarily the leader. So although I know that neGruli is leading that party, I can't tell if he is the wolves' idea of the alpha leader. Instead, I look at the group rather like the way you check his old campsites. You look for similarities in the way a camp is set up. I do the same with the wolves' memories. I look for the way a voice hit a Gray One's ears; a posture or a certain smell. The overall picture of the group that rode through here four ninans ago—that I'm sure is of neGruli's men."

He nodded thoughtfully. "And you can do this now without Coale—tap into those pack memories?"

"Two days ago, no," she admitted. "But now—yes, I think I can. Not clearly, but I can do it. If there's been a wolfpack anywhere near those riders today, I should be able to tell."

"Good." He nodded slowly. He stood and squinted to the west. "The sun will be in your eyes, but if you can read the Gray Ones' memories, it shouldn't matter." He gestured at Gradjek, and the small, wiry man joined Welker near the trail. "Don't take too long," Bany added. "I want to put a few more kays between us and the lava flow. I just don't want to go up that exposed ridge before I know where those riders are."

The trail was steep—more like running stairs than hiking along a path. More than once, they had to stop to catch their breath. By the time they cleared the trees on the ridge, their ears had popped several times, and their calves, for all that they had been toughened up by constant riding and running, were burning. The slanted afternoon sun added a muggy heat to their sweat, and its brightness made them squint as they moved between tree shadows.

Rezs could feel the weight of wolves nearby and wasn't surprised when Vlen disappeared up the trail. A few minutes later the yearling made his way back down the path and blocked Gradjek from moving on.

The older man looked at the yearling, then back at Rezs. "Wolfwalker?"

She was already moving up past him. "Vlen? What is it?"

His yellow eyes gleamed, but there was a snarl deep in his mind, and Rezs felt her neck tense and her teeth bare themselves to the wind. *Wolfwalker,* he sent, *the pack is on the trail. They do not want to come near the others, and they cannot get down from the ridge.*

She stretched and felt the other voices. They were thick and swirled like a knot in her head. It was a family group, she realized, and their voices blended into a single song because they were so close. She turned to the others. "We have to get off the trail," she told them quickly. "There's a pack that has to pass us."

Gradjek scratched at his skin. "Here? How?"

Rezs looked around. The scout was right—the trail was narrow, and far too steep to step off without risking a long landslide. The boulders that lined the other side of the path were large, but even if they climbed up on the rocks, they'd still be close to the path. The trail had been the same for a kay, so there was hardly a better place to which to go back. She looked at Vlen. "This will have to do, Gray One."

The yearling growled, but acknowledged her, and Rezs motioned for the other two humans to get up on the rocks. Welker jumped up easily, then offered her hand to Gradjek. Carefully, they clambered up another meter till they could go no farther. Rezs made her way up after them. A few moments later the first gray wolf materialized on the trail. One moment the trail was clear; the next the massive male seemed to fade out of the rocks. One ear was scarred and split at the top, his teeth slightly bared, and his baleful eyes gleamed. His back was dark—nearly black in shade—but the shedding fur that clung to his whiter haunches and belly was gray. Rezs didn't have to stretch out to link to the male; when their eyes met, the gray fog in her head seemed to split as if blasted apart, and his voice rang out in her skull. This was different from reading the memories of the wolves—when she had called the pack with Coale, the wolves who came had been curious and willing; this was a partial challenge.

Wolfwalker, the massive male snarled low. His eyes flickered toward Vlen.

She clenched her fists. *Gray One,* she sent steadily. *You honor me.*

This is our trail.

She could feel the sense of the females and yearlings behind him. "We do not dispute your territory," she told him quietly. "We're on this trail only to look out over the valley; then, tomorrow, we will pass through. We offer no challenge to you; no danger to your yearlings."

He watched her warily, and she could feel the strength in the swirling fog that contained the voices of his pack. Vlen's hackles were raised, but he held still while the male moved to sniff him. The male growled, low in his throat, and submissively, Vlen lay down at his feet. The male did not speak again to Rezs, but remained in the trail, standing over Vlen and watching the scouts with an almost predator sense. For two minutes neither side moved. Then, as if he sent them a signal of safety, his mate moved onto the trail. Cautiously, the female padded past the male until she stood slightly downtrail. She was lighter in color than her mate, but although, like the male, her pelt hung with clumps of shedding fur, the ragged coat could not hide her swollen breasts. She had cubs back at her den. The she-wolf gave Rezs as wary a look as the male, then positioned herself where the trail turned, and waited for the second female. This one's scruff was torn across one shoulder, and her gray markings created patches all along her back. Two yearlings, a young male with a limp, another female, and one last yearling moved past the scouts. When the pack was past, the mated male met Rezs's eyes once more.

Wolfwalker, he sent. Then he turned and trotted away.

Immediately, Vlen rose to his feet and took a few steps after the other male. Rezs snapped at him in her mind. Behind her, Welker started to climb down, but Rezs motioned for her to wait also. Only after several minutes passed, and she felt the distance between them, did she gesture for them to return to the trail.

Gradjek jumped down from his boulder. He didn't say anything, but he gripped Rezs's shoulder, and his wrinkled, peeling face grinned. Welker scrambled down after him. Rezs disentangled her arm from the smaller scout and gestured for them to move on.

But Gradjek didn't budge. He searched her face, then looked down at Vlen. "Thank you," he said in a low voice. "I've never been that close before. The wild ones are different, you know?"

Slowly, Rezs nodded. She knew what he meant. There was a look in the eyes of the Gray Ones who had not bonded with the humans—a predator sense that was more focused than Vlen's or Shona's.

Welker turned. She touched Rezs on the arm, and merely said, "Wolfwalker."

Then they moved up the trail.

XX

The ridge became a wide shelf around the next bend, then branched off to sweep back into higher-altitude valleys and peaks, and the trail offered a clear view of the lava flow. As soon as they stopped, Welker leaned against the boulders that lined one side of the trail and began to unlace one of her boots. Gradjek rubbed absently at his face as he squinted across the valley. "You see anything, Wolfwalker?"

She shook her head. The mugginess of the spring afternoon left a haze down in the valley, and the sun was already low enough in the sky that it blunted her vision with brightness. When she reached through her link to Vlen to try to read the packsong, she could hear one of her brothers' voices, but she could not find the riders. Instead, threads of music wove through the gray that clouded her sight, and her father seemed suddenly closer than the scouts beside her. Yellow eyes gleamed like small suns. Abruptly, the shadow riders came into focus. There were still just the two of them, but in the eyes of the wolves, they were wary, and there was something about the way they rode that made Rezs frown. She could hear her father's voice overlaid on the shadow riders, and in the distance another group of wolves merged their packsong with the gray fog, so that their howling made Rezs's neck prickle, and she lost the link to the pack. Vlen looked at her and snarled, and she reached down to grip his scruff.

Wolfwalker, he sent urgently. *The pack is hunting. The deer is driven into the shrubs—*

I feel it, Vlen, she returned. She tried to sort out the voices

255

again, but the gray fog was jumbled, and she was tired. She squatted and rubbed at her temples.

"What is it?" Welker asked softly as she shook the rocks out of her other boot and put her footgear back on.

Rezs did not look up. "It's . . . nothing."

Gradjek glanced down at her. "The wolves are too far away to read their memories?"

"It's not that. Every time I try to link up to Vlen," she explained slowly, "I hear my father's voice. I had heard a lot about wolfwalkers before I became one, but I never thought my family would begin to haunt my mind."

"They say that the wolves keep track of their own. Now that you run with the pack, they're probably watching your family."

"I wish they'd do it a little more quietly, then. They're giving me a headache."

"I'd rather they gave you a vision," Gradjek returned.

"Not today," she said sourly. "I know they're down there, but I don't know where. For all I can tell, they could be on the ridge by now."

Welker glanced at Gradjek. "Bany won't like that," she said softly.

The other man nodded and rubbed absently at his cheeks. "Maybe one of us should stay behind tonight."

The woman nodded. "I'll mention it to Bany." The lanky scout offered Rezs her arm to rise, then, with a last look at the valley, motioned for them to return down the trail.

It seemed to take mere minutes to go down where it had taken them half an hour to hike up. Even so, by the time they reached the other scouts, the shadows were long and the ridge getting dark beneath the trees. Coale and Elgon had not yet caught up to the group, but Bany didn't want to wait any longer.

"Ukiah." He took the other scout aside. "How's the leg?"

Rezs didn't look up from checking the saddle on her dnu, but she heard the old man clearly through Gray Vlen's ears. The yearling had lain down behind some shrubs to wait for a sickle beetle to come back out of its den, and Bany and Ukiah were near him.

"Good," Ukiah answered the old man. "I barely feel a twinge in it now."

"Then I'd like you to stay behind and find out about those riders."

Rezs looked surreptitiously over at the two. She saw the tall man nod, but his expression gave her a chill. His eyes were distant as he looked down the trail. "Find out about them or discourage them from following us?"

"Just make sure they turn off to one of the other counties. If they don't . . ." Bany's voice trailed off, but he glanced meaningfully at the bow that hung from the tall man's shoulders.

"Any justification?"

The old man's voice was quiet. "Do I need any?"

Ukiah smiled without humor. "I guess you don't."

The lean scout nodded. "It is important, Ukiah. There's a chance that some of our riders aren't who they say they are. And, there's a chance that we're looking for something we shouldn't be finding. Either way, it will come to a head on this ridge, and I think those riders are part of it."

"What about Coale and Elgon?"

"If they're a threat to the wolfwalker, I'll take care of them."

The younger man nodded. Rezs stretched through Gray Vlen to feel for the scout, but he had walled himself off so completely that even the Gray One could barely feel the man's energy. She turned hurriedly back to her dnu, adjusting her bridle ornaments as if they had come loose, while Bany walked back to the dnu. The old man motioned for the others to mount. As they rode away Rezs couldn't help looking back. Ukiah was watching her, and his brown-black eyes followed her like a hunter as he checked the tension on his bowstring. She had no doubt, she thought with a chill, that he would be competent in the kill. It wasn't the cooling air that brought the goose bumps to her skin. It was the realization that if Ukiah owed Bany his own life, she owed Ukiah hers—and what would she be asked to do, when the time came to pay that debt? Her hand strayed to the hilt of her sword. She'd never drawn it yet. But if Bany was right, that steel might have to taste the blood of one of the riders here.

"Goddammit," she muttered, "I like them all."

The moons didn't answer. She looked up and caught the second moon as it rose past the ridge into a sky half-filled with clouds. Ahead of her, Welker glanced back and nodded at her;

behind her, Touvinde called a joke up to Gradjek. Rezs gripped the hilt of the weapon hard and felt her jawline tighten. "Goddammit," she whispered again.

The trail, which had seemed steep but smooth by foot, was rough and awkward by dnu. The six-legged creatures humped and lurched up the steepening ridge, so that it began to feel more like a wagon ride over boulders than a saddle trip up a trail. They weren't making any better time than she had made earlier by foot, and Rezs was tempted to dismount and lead her beast by the reins.

When they finally reached the top of the first ridge, Bany rode close to Rezs and gestured almost imperceptibly with his chin at the peaks that were bright from the late-afternoon sun. "Are we close?" he asked in a low voice.

"Very," she returned. "I can't tell exactly where yet, but I've twice gotten a glimpse of a rough rectangle of light in a black-dark place. It's got to be a cave."

"There are canyons that are filled with caves about two hours from here."

She leaned forward, her excitement suddenly focused. "Then we could get into them tonight."

"No," he said sharply. "Not tonight. We'll go at dawn tomorrow."

She didn't answer for a moment. The tension in her stomach became a rock that crushed itself until it crumbled, and she felt suddenly relieved, as if knowing that it would be over soon took that pressure from her chest. Dawn . . . She stretched herself to reach Vlen, and felt her eyesight blur as she caught his vision of a pack of rock badgers.

He lifted his head and halted as he felt their bond tighten. *Wolfwalker,* he sent. *Run with me!*

Not this time, Vlen. Take Gray Shona with you instead— and stretch your legs as long as you want. I'll see you tomorrow.

The yearling projected a wary confusion and Rezs tried to reassure him. She wanted him gone, but she wasn't abandoning him or chasing him away. It took several minutes to project the right images to make the cub take off willingly. When he finally raced away, Rezs clenched her fists. Not until she felt Gray Shona's howl in his young ears did she relax her hands on the reins.

Bany had been watching her eyes, and now he asked obliquely, "The cub?"

"He's gone," she answered shortly. She didn't like the tension that had crawled back into her stomach. Sending Vlen away right now just didn't seem quite right. The hunter sense that Vlen projected was making her shoulders tight.

"Gray Shona?"

"She's with him."

He didn't say anything else, and Rezs was glad. There was a sharpness to his questions that betrayed his own tension, and it made her wary—as if he sensed a hunter that she had yet to catch a glimpse of. For the second time her hand strayed to the hilt of her sword.

The farther they rode into the mountains, the heavier became the gray fog in her head. It was as if, with every kay Vlen ran, the presence of the fog grew thicker. But it wasn't Vlen, she realized after a while. It was the weight of other wolves—and not just those in the ridges around them. Old Roy had told her once, long ago, that the sense of the wolves was always most disturbing near the Ancient places—that the strength of the Gray Ones' memories was multiplied by the number of packs in which they first landed and explored this world. Now, riding close to one of the nine Ancient domes, Rezs could well believe it. She had to rub her eyes to keep her vision clear. When she stretched to feel Vlen, she had to close down on their link to keep the other images from ringing off the inside of her skull. It was as if the ghosts of ancient wolves ran beside the ones in her time, and the combination was like a heady wine.

By the time the old scout passed up the first valley that opened back into the mountains, Rezs was ready to get off the dnu and find a glacier stream to shock her thoughts clear again. But Bany motioned them on past, and Rezs raised her eyebrows at him. He murmured, "We want to be close, but not too close."

She nodded reluctantly. She couldn't help the glance she shot at the spray-fogged stream she could see in the distance. She didn't even realize that it was a shadow image, projected from the packsong.

They ended up in the second valley, where the meadow pockets linked themselves by game trails, and the trees provided enough cover from the sky to keep any lepa from seeing them. Gradjek and Touvinde staked out the dnu while Bany and Rezs started cooking. Rezs's hands were clumsy, and the old man finally ordered her away. "Get more done by myself," he muttered, taking the pot from her hands.

"So what do you want me to do?" she asked in a low voice.

He gave her a warning look. His voice was so low that even she barely heard it. "When this is ready, take your bowl and join me, but don't eat."

She understood. She went to her pack and rummaged in it restlessly. Since she had not collected any samples that day, there was no real work to do. She joined Welker for a few moments, but the woman was carving on a stick, and Rezs had shown neither talent nor patience for such a hobby. The best she could do was shave twigs into the fire.

When dusk finally arrived, the shadows grayed so quickly that it seemed as if the light was sucked into the ground within the space of ten breaths. Coale and Elgon barely caught up with them by the time the shadows had changed to darkness, but they brought a small deer with them, and Bany, for all that he watched the two as carefully as ever, joked casually with the tall man as he spiced the venison as he had the stew, and skewered the meat out for the fire. Rezs wondered if the deer was part of the kill of the wolfpack she had heard, but Coale seemed preoccupied, Elgon seemed distant when he wasn't with Bany, and Rezs was too jumpy to ask.

Dinner was almost a silent affair. Coale, who rarely spoke in the group, sat near Welker, who said nothing, but merely worked on her wooden figurine. Gradjek was on cleanup duty; and it was Elgon and Touvinde's turn to repair the gear, so Elgon spent the next hour setting up the bacterial colonies to scrub the deer skin clean, while Touvinde, dexterous as if he wasn't missing the ends of two fingers, spliced the frayed rope they had used for Ukiah's stretcher.

"How long will it take?" Rezs asked Bany in a low voice.

"Hours," he returned. His gaze roamed the woods as he searched for a pile of winter detritus in which to bury their food.

"Why so long?" she asked sharply.

"If they didn't fall asleep normally, they'd know they were

being drugged. They'd react, and we'd have a fight on our hands."

"I thought we were only going to drug Coale and Elgon. I don't like this putting them all down."

"You think Coale and Elgon wouldn't have noticed if none of us but them were eating? Or if I spiced only their food to cover the flavor of the drug? Gradjek has been closer to Coale since the wolfwalker shot that nightspider off his leg; Touvinde and Elgon are almost getting to be friends. Drugging all of them means arguing with none of them. And this way, there is nothing in Touvinde or Gradjek or Welker to betray the fact that they're all going down."

"For the night."

He nodded. "For the night." He gestured for her to walk with him, and they moved out of sight of the camp for a few minutes while Bany quickly dug a hole, and they buried their dinners in it.

The mixed food looked as unappetizing as bile, and Rezs made a face. "I'm almost hungry enough to wish I'd eaten that anyway."

He handed her a meat roll and chewed on one himself. "It's all I've got, but better hungry than drugged. And Rezs—no snacking. I put the drugs in everything."

She nodded reluctantly. They made their way back to camp, rinsed their plates, and packed their things away. Without Ukiah there, the camp seemed somehow subdued. None of the scouts seemed inclined to talk. Rezs found herself killing time by letting the gray fog cloud her mind.

In the din that rolled out of the Gray Ones' memories, she saw the white, stone domes of the Ancients, floating on top of the mountain ridge, between the peaks and the moons. Shadow shapes moved along flat shadow roads, and tiny ships crossed the sky above them. If she heard a voice call out to a wolf, she heard a hundred voices. If she saw a Gray One race its human from the domes, she saw four hundred races. Twice, in the back of the memories, she caught a glimpse of a weight—a pressure—of something new and alien. She tried to follow the wary thread, but the sense of it was one of power, not shape, and the only impression she could define was of yellow-streaked eyes with slotted pupils and hard, beaklike alien lips.

Rezs felt a chill when she realized what the gray fog was holding: The birdmen who lived on this world first were the bringers of the plague that stripped the domes of life. They had been here—in this low range of mountains—long enough to impress the graysong so deeply that the wolves carried the sense of them for nearly nine centuries without losing the memory of the threat. She didn't know that she clenched her fingers around the stick she held as she caught again the sense of that threat. The birdmen . . . The plague . . . The packsong shivering in fear as something caught their humans in convulsions and stripped the life from the bodies left lying in piles in the domes. There were Gray Ones among the dead. The shadow power of the birdmen was like a spear that struck the wolves through their bonds with the humans. Loneliness . . .

Rezs shuddered and wrapped her cloak more tightly around her body. The graysong had swollen into a tide that beat against her skull, drowning out the sense of the camp and fire. Gray Vlen's voice had become a lifeline, pulling her back to her own thoughts.

Wolfwalker—His yellow eyes gleamed in her head.

"Gray One," she whispered. She could feel his need to be near her, and in spite of Bany's caution, wanted Vlen close to herself. She wanted his scruff under her fingers and his howl in her ears. She wanted to hear his soft breath in the darkness before the next dawn approached.

The cub seemed to spring up. *Wolfwalker—I come!*

No, she told him firmly, more with her mind than her voice. She had to push down her need to feel him close and fight the tension she felt at her own actions.

But Vlen was already running. She could feel the speed gather in his limbs. *Wolfwalker!* he sent.

Vlen, no, she sent more urgently. *There could be danger here to you—or to me because of you.* She felt her fists clench, and she couldn't stop the shiver that crawled down her arms.

I feel your need as my own, the cub returned firmly. *We den together tonight. I will hunt instead in the morning.*

"No!" Rezs almost shouted.

Touvinde, startled, was on his feet in a second, grabbing up his bow. With the same instant reaction, Elgon leaped up and faced the other side of the forest, his own arrow notched in his bow. Welker was poised with her sword in hand, and Gradjek had lunged for Bany's bow, which was closer than his own.

Bany barely breathed the words, "What is it—"

"Nothing," she returned quickly. "It's nothing." She flushed as the scouts still stared into the darkness. "I was talking with Gray Vlen," she said more steadily. "It's nothing. Really. I just . . . forget sometimes to keep our words to myself."

Bany studied her for a long moment. "Well," Touvinde remarked, as he set down his bow, "that was good for a little excitement."

Welker lowered her sword. She eyed Rezs warily. "Won't be hard to keep a sharp watch tonight," she agreed.

Rezs said nothing, but glanced at Coale and found the middle-aged woman watching her back closely. Abruptly, Rezs reassured Vlen and closed down as tightly as she could on her link. The other woman flinched almost visibly. Rezs stiffened.

"What is it?" Bany asked sharply, his voice still low.

Rezs hesitated. "It's just Vlen," she said finally. "He's hunting."

The old man gave her a sharp look. "How far away is he?"

"Far enough," she returned shortly. She got up and moved to the fire, where she took the coal stick and stirred the fire so that it flared, sparked, and died back down. She couldn't help the look she shot at the older woman. When the thin smoke shifted, she took the excuse to move to the other side of the firepit.

The older woman was still awake. Rezs glanced at the other wolfwalker over her shoulder, noticed Elgon watching her closely, and felt her jaw tighten.

"He's worried, Rezsia." Coale's voice was quiet, and Rezs doubted that the other scouts heard it. She felt herself that she heard it more through the link to the gray fog than through her ears.

"About what?" she forced herself to answer.

"That you're getting into something you don't know enough about."

You're gutsy—the words echoed in her head—but you have no idea what you're doing . . . Rezs stared at the woman for a long moment, then slowly, she twisted to look at Elgon. The tall man had lain back, and was staring at the stars, seemingly oblivious to their conversation. But even without Vlen beside her, Rezs could feel the man's awareness of her. Had it been he who held that knife to her throat two ninans ago? Had she been traveling with the blader the whole time, and not recognized Grayheart beside her? Did he cling to Coale because she was all he had left?

She turned back to Coale abruptly. "And you?" she asked quietly.

"I am worried," the woman admitted softly. "But I have a confidence in you that my grandson lacks."

Rezs thought about that for a moment. "You know," she said deliberately, "I don't trust you."

"I know it."

"It doesn't bother you?"

For a moment the older woman didn't answer. When she did finally speak, there was a strange note in her voice, that made Rezs think of Ukiah, not Elgon. "If running and riding with you for two ninans, showing you what I know—letting you see me through Shona's eyes—does not teach you something about who I am, and what I can be to you, then there is little more I can do about it."

She stared at the woman. It matters to you, Coale, Rezs thought. Admit it. "Sometimes," she said out loud, "what is visible is not the truth of the person." She touched her chin where the white scar of new skin had not yet faded. "Sometimes the invisible is more important."

"Sometimes it is," the woman agreed. "But usually, what you can't see has always been there, part of the person from the beginning. It's just another piece of information. It doesn't change the person at all; it only changes the way you look at him or the way you want to relate to him."

Rezs snapped off a piece of the twig and tossed it in the fire. "Coale—" Her voice was casual. "Is Elgon Grayheart?"

"No." The other woman closed her eyes. "His hands were never made for music."

Rezs couldn't help the glance she shot at Elgon, nor the examination she gave to her own two hands. Her slender fingers could have been made for music, but she never had the talent. She could hold a tune, but her voice wasn't pure; she could play a few instruments, but she didn't really feel the music as one who truly loved it would. More than playing, she had loved to listen—to close her eyes and let the music roll through her mind with that fog of gray, lupine voices.

Rezs let her mind drift into the fog until she found the thread of the music that had haunted her since that night in neGruli's warehouse. Yellow eyes gleamed in return, and the old threads of youth and grief and that solid wall of gray formed clearly out of the howling din. She touched Gray Vlen, and the yearling's voice became a single snarl, cutting under both music and din, and bringing the Ancients' ghosts with it. Older images shifted over new ones: people moving, talking, running with the wolves ... People growing sick and feverish. People and Gray Ones dying. White domes and lighted doors; long hallways and frozen rooms, and rows and rows of cabinets ... Heartbeats, strong and steady, pulsed through the tide of images until the waves of life began to slow, and Rezs blinked to clear her thoughts. "Coale?" she asked softly. "Who are you?"

The woman didn't answer, and for once, Rezs didn't push it. Instead, she waited for a long moment at the fire, then moved back to the watch position while she listened to the scouts fall asleep. Gradjek was first, but his soft snore faded quickly into a nearly silent breathing. Touvinde was next, then Elgon and Welker and Coale. And then it was only Rezs and Bany, staring at the forest night and waiting for the dawn.

XXI

She woke sluggishly when Bany touched her arm through the sleeping bag. She had thought to sleep lightly, but she felt drugged and bleary-eyed when she tried to sit up. There were echoes of dreams of falling—nightmare feelings that she used to get as a child—that left her mind exhausted, as if she had been working, not sleeping all night. She blinked, breathed in, and shivered. The cold air made her want to huddle back in her sleeping bag.

"Are they still asleep?" she whispered, gesturing with her chin at the others.

The old man nodded. "You can speak normally—it won't wake them."

She blinked again, then rubbed clumsily at her eyes before she realized that the fog in her sight was not fog at all, but a gray sky, still half covered in puffy clouds. "It's dawn," she said stupidly.

He pointed. "There's tea on the fire."

Abruptly, the tension clenched her stomach. Without another word, she rolled from her bag and into the chill, where she took little time to get ready. Cold as she was, she had a hard time swallowing anything but the tea that Bany had made. She tried not to look at the others—the sleeping figures were somehow eerie: Gradjek still wasn't snoring, and Welker, who usually murmured at night, was as silent as a stone. Elgon had sprawled as usual, but his long arms and legs didn't even twitch to shift position. Only Coale had shifted once or twice as she slept, and even her breathing was slow.

It was still dark gray when Bany motioned for them to hit

the trail, and Rezs hesitated. "Are you sure they're all right?" she asked as she eyed the drugged forms.

"You can see their chests rise and fall, Rezs. They're fine."

"But left here, alone . . ."

The old man's voice held a trace of impatience. "There's no other way to do this, Rezs. Are you coming? Or has this whole trip been wasted?"

"It isn't wasted," she returned sharply. "I'm just . . . nervous."

"They'll be fine," the old man said shortly. "We're far enough up the ridge that it's too high for worlags, and too cold for nightspiders, and this isn't badgerbear country. The only threat is lepa, and even if they flew right overhead, they won't see anything with the tree cover this thick."

She nodded reluctantly.

"Now, can you tell where the Gray Ones are—are they far enough away?"

She nodded again. In spite of the distance between them, Vlen had woken with her, and she could feel him stretching his limbs even now. "They only ran three hours before dark, but they went about thirty kays, I think. They're around the eastern side of the ridge."

"Good. Keep them there. You don't want them coming back and smelling Coale—or any of the others here. A drugged body smells differently to a wolf, and Gray Shona would get upset. You won't need your sleeping bag," he added as she stooped to roll it up. "You have everything?"

She shrugged, straightening. "If I don't need my bag, everything I brought is ready to go." She slung her pack over her shoulders and tightened the straps, and Bany nodded. He strode out of camp without another word, and Rezs had to hurry after him.

They paused at the rude corral where they had left the dnu—Bany never failed to feed his riding beast a tuber—but he didn't bridle his animal. Rezs looked up from rubbing her own creature's nose. "We're not taking them with us?"

"Dnu leave deeper tracks than humans," he said shortly.

Rezs would have thought they could make better time with the dnu than without, but once they left the dnu behind, the old man hiked like a runner. Rezs was sweating within minutes and breathing hard enough that the cold air made her teeth ache.

It didn't take long to reach the first shelf of the ridge, and Rezs let her mind wander back to Vlen as she hiked. She could feel the yearling as he dug in the distant meadow for rodents, and his mental howl was a constant snarl inside her head. Between them was the family group she had met the day before. That wolf pack was still close to Rezs, but moving slowly east, following the same trail that Vlen and Shona had taken last night—and their mental voices made a soft din beneath Vlen's young tones.

Rezs and Bany were only twenty minutes along the trail when the wolf pack found Ukiah's camp. Their howling changed—as if they recognized the scout as one of their own, and Rezs felt the music of the blader thread its way into the gray din. Yellow eyes were wary as they followed the movements near a tiny breakfast fire. The human voices that floated on the memories of the wolves were not old, but new and sharp.

Ukiah was not alone.

He'd found them—the ones who followed her party. They were not clear images with square jaws or decorated tunics; they were merely shadow shapes who moved near the scout. Where Ukiah's voice was overlaid with gray, one of the others' was sharp—like a breaking stick—and the other one's voice was quiet. Rezs could feel her interest sharpen the eyes of the wolves. Gray howls pierced the packsong, and Vlen, running with Shona, halted. Ukiah's voice became a murmur of tone, punctuated with the gray music, but the more she concentrated, opening herself to the gray din, shutting out the images of the Ancients in exchange for the new visions, the more the fog brought her father's voice, not the words of the other riders, to her ears.

She shook herself to clear her mind. Bany glanced back, but she waved him on. This wasn't the time to dwell on her father or how to resolve his anger. It was ironic, she thought, that the wolves followed her father so closely, while he rejected them like Grayheart; and she, who was bound to Gray Vlen, sent the yearling away to run trail alone.

Vlen felt her voice in the packsong, and howled a greeting, but there was a pang of anxiety in his tone. Rezs frowned. *Gray One,* she returned. *Stay with Shona—away from the camp.*

But Vlen snarled, low in his throat. *The hunter stalks you like a lepa, and you run up the cliffs to meet him.*

Rezs paused at his tone. *Vlen?* she sent uncertainly.

Shona needs you, Wolfwalker.

Wolfwalker! Shona's voice rang out from behind Gray Vlen's. *I cannot hear my wolfwalker—*

The older female's image of Coale was still as death, and Rezs couldn't help clenching her fists against her sides. Sometimes, said Coale, you have to lie ... But the image in her own head was of the bodies back at camp, eerily silent in sleep, sprawled inside their bags. She closed her own link abruptly. "I'm sorry," she whispered, unable to send the words to Vlen. She could feel the instant snarl of the cub as he tried to reach through to her mind. She kept herself cut off, even though she felt the yearling's panic pull at the cord between them. She had to force herself back onto the trail to follow Bany up the ridge.

Dawn climbed into the sky as they ascended the ridge, but the forest around them was still dark with shadows and cold with the altitude. The light that hit the opposite side of the valley wouldn't touch this side of the mountains till noon, and each time Bany stopped at a fork to examine the tracks in the trail, Rezs became chilled from her own cold sweat.

Even without consciously reading Vlen, Rezs knew they were moving in the right direction. She recognized the path from the memories of the Ancients, and when she let herself look into the gray lupine fog, old images began to blend with recent ones, so that a constant line of dnu shadows moved along the trail. NeGruli's party had ridden here, but so had other riders. When she concentrated, she could see Ukiah at a distance, blurred in the sight of the wolves near his dnu. When she reached, she could hear her father and Cal, overlaid on the gray threads of music. The closer to the domes she hiked, the more the graysong grew, and Rezs's head began to ring with the howling of the pack.

Within half an hour she steered them away from the outer ridge, into the shallow valleys. They crossed a stream on an ancient stone bridge that had collapsed and left a rocky passage from one narrow bank to the other. Rezs slipped near the far bank, and Bany grabbed her arm, so that she banged her knees on the stone. Her instant fear of falling tightened the cord between her and Vlen, so that the yearling snapped into her mind.

Wolfwalker—

The gray voices howled. For a moment Rezs stared into yellow eyes instead of the white, rushing stream. Then Bany hauled her up and she scrambled to regain her feet.

She didn't clear her eyes immediately, and the gray shadows shifted oddly where she had grown sloppy holding herself separate from the cub. The shadows, she thought, were wrong for what she expected—the light was hitting her eyes from the right. It was Vlen, she realized. He and Shona had turned back to the camp, and now the two wolves were running north. Heartbeats merged, two fast, one slow; and Rezs could hear the worry in the Gray Ones' voices. Shadow images flickered between the trees; a figure lay in the middle of her mind, silent and still. She bit her lip as she recognized the other woman.

Wolfwalker . . . Shona's cry was as haunting a howl as Grayheart's.

Bany still gripped her arm. "You're okay?"

She nodded abruptly. "Fine. Let's go on."

On the other side of the mountain stream, there were three draws that led east, farther into the mountains. Two of them pointed almost directly at the Ancients' domes. One ran parallel, but south. Each spewed forth a white, rocky stream that joined the one they had just crossed, and the low mountain mist that crept along the base of all three cuts made Rezs blink. She could have sworn, for a moment, that the fog was made of wolves—shadow wolves—who ran in packs of hundreds.

She gripped Bany's arm. "We're close. I can feel it—"

"Which way?"

She hesitated. Then she shook herself. Coale was right: The packsong was still getting stronger, the closer she got to the domes. It pulled like Vlen until she wanted to swim in that shadow pack. She wanted to see what they saw; take in what they tasted. She wanted to know how far back the memories went. A hundred years? Eight and a half centuries? To the day the wolves first breathed the air of this world and touched the soil with their noses? She concentrated and felt the passing of the dnu a month ago, and realized that they rode, not in one of the first two valleys, but up the third.

"That way, I think. The one to the south."

But Bany gave her a sharp look. "Something wrong, Wolf-walker?"

She stared at the farthest canyon entrance, partly obscured by the trees and the edge of the second valley. The sharpness that had hit her gut was not anticipation, but disappointment: The third draw did not lead directly to the domes.

She wanted neGruli's party to have gone to the Ancients' dome, she realized. She wanted some kind of vindication that, on top of every other action, he had violated the quarantine of the Ancient domes and brought the plague—not worlag attacks—on his people to get them out of the picture. No hidden crimes. No believable setups. She wanted—

A visible enemy, she realized with a tightening of her lips. She wanted some kind of action she could point to and say, This is wrong; he is evil. Without that, it was no more than a debate of one ethic against another. NeGruli's gathering of power—he had the right to move his money as he wished. But the smaller picture, of each person he controlled or stripped of house or livelihood—those were the hidden wounds he left behind. The science he stripped from the Ancient sites—that was what Rezs wanted to find. She wanted to be able to stand up in the council and say, Look, here it is—now you see what he is stealing from us. He trades lives for his profit; homes for his pocket change. The tiny good that he returns to our county—it's nothing compared to the blood he sucks from our people.

In her head, she felt a mental howl break from her lips into the fog. Gray Vlen heard it and snarled, latching onto her voice and forcing the link between them. In an instant the wolf pack surged in, smothering her thoughts. She could feel their feet against the ground; see them as they ran the trails beneath the domes. She stared at the three canyon entrances as if she could see through the solid rock of their rims to the white, stone roofs beyond them. But in the tide of rising gray, only one trail held the memory of the man.

She looked at her hands and found them clenched, and she had to force herself to relax them. Then she looked back at Bany and shook her head. "No," she said flatly. "Everything's fine. He went into that one there."

Bany studied the ground before they went into the draw,

and as usual, the old man led. The trail twisted abruptly, twice, to avoid stands of burned-tip shrubs, then skirted one side of the canyon. Rezs let Vlen remain in her mind, but his voice made her shiver when he echoed Shona's howl into her skull. There was a growing anxiety in the voice of the older wolf—a feeling that had begun to border on panic. When Bany paused to verify the safety of the trail ahead, Rezs let herself blend into the gray. Her own heartbeat was quick and deep and steady; Vlen's was quicker but still strong. Gray Shona's pulse, more toughened from long running, was almost as slow as Rezs's. And then there was Coale. The slow beat of the woman's heart was mixed with a growing numbness. It was as if, each moment the pace slowed further, some set of nerves shut down. And Shona, shut out of her wolfwalker's mind, was beginning to howl in fear.

"Bany—"

The old man looked over his shoulder. "What is it?"

"Coale and the others—you're sure they're all right?"

"They're fine, Rezs." He squinted. "And since this canyon ends at that wall up there, I suspect we're close to that source of yours. We'll be back to camp in no time, and you can check on Coale yourself."

Rezs hesitated. "Her heartbeat is slowing."

He gave her a sharp look. "I thought you sent Vlen away, and that he took Shona with him."

"I did," she said quickly. "They're tens of kays from here. But that doesn't mean that Shona can't still link to Coale, or that Vlen won't project Shona's images to me." She bit her lip. "I'm worried, Bany. She's not a young woman, and her heart is far too sluggish."

The old man studied her for a long moment. "We can go back now," he said quietly. "And it will take us an hour to get there. Or we can go the last hundred meters up this draw, and find the source you've been riding two ninans to locate. And it will still take us an hour to get back to camp. It's your choice, Wolfwalker."

She stared at the rim of the canyon and fingered the belt pouches she wore. She could feel the call of the Ancients' domes—she could hear it in the packsong. Shona's voice, haunting her mind like the echoes of the ancient ghosts—that snarling panic ate at her mind, so that she could not focus her thoughts. Bany watched her for another moment.

Finally, he gestured shortly. "Then let's get this over with."

Soon. She projected the word through her mind at Shona's distant howl. *I hear your worry, and I'll reach Coale as soon as I can.*

The growling voice snapped its urgency, and Rezs almost spun on her heel to go back. She clamped down on her muscles. *Soon,* she sent firmly. She hurried after the scout. Bany had stopped up ahead, and she could see already, over his shoulder, the dark slit in the wall. The echoes surged; the gray tide washed over her mind. Clearly, then back in the fog, the shadow figures moved.

"This is it—" She hurried forward. "I can see it in Vlen's mind. The cave—the opening." She looked over her shoulder. "Bany—" Her voice cut off. "Bany?" She half turned, but froze as he gestured abruptly for her to keep her distance. "What is it? What are you doing?"

He had notched an arrow, and now he lifted the bow as he spoke. "I'm aiming this at you."

The chill that gripped her stomach was hard and tight in its hold. Vlen's howl merged with Shona's until both wolves ignited the lupine fog with a blast of dread that deafened her. "For moons' sake, why?" she barely managed.

"Because once you get inside, you'll understand. So you'll stay where you are now, and we'll talk out here."

"At bow point?"

He shrugged. "Your sword, Wolfwalker. Unbuckle it and toss it down."

"First tell me what's going on."

"Your sword, Wolfwalker," he repeated harshly.

She stared at him for a long moment, then slowly unbuckled her belt and shoulder strap, dropping the blade into the rocky mud.

"Now your bow and quiver."

She complied.

"The pack," he directed. "And the belt pouches."

She shrugged out of the pack, then unsnapped her belt pouches and dropped them in the growing pile. "And now you're going to tell me what you're doing," she suggested.

"Look around you, Rezs. But look through your bond, not

with your eyes." He gestured with his chin at the cave entrance. "There are memories—old memories—here in the minds of the wolves. Even with Vlen at a distance, you should be able to feel them. Wolfwalkers can always feel these places."

Rezs stared, but the point of the bow didn't waver. She looked back at the cave opening. It was a tall entrance—more like a crack than a cave, and it looked like it led into a tall, shallow cavern. But in the back, hidden by a rockfall, a thin passage turned to the left and disappeared into darkness. She couldn't see it, but she knew it was there. The fog that filled her skull was full of images of people. They moved and carried things and shifted around, and disappeared in that cavern. But the thing that made her jaw tighten and her lips thin out with realization was that the memories were not recent at all. They were as old as the wolves on this world.

"It's part of the domes of the Ancients," she whispered. "This cave—it *is* one of the old exit points."

"Not an exit point, but close enough."

"You knew this."

"I've been here before."

"With neGruli." She stated it more than questioned, and the old, skinny man nodded. It wasn't Coale, she told herself. It wasn't Elgon or Ukiah. It was Bany who had betrayed them. She could almost see him distancing himself from what he was about to do, and she heard her voice ask harshly, "So, is that arrow to keep me out or force me in?"

"In, Wolfwalker."

"To a place of the Ancients. To a place that must be crawling with plague."

He shrugged, but the movement of his narrow shoulders didn't shift the point of that bolt. Rezs lifted her eyes from the arrow to his face. The old man's jaw was tense—she could see the muscle jumping along the bone—but his eyes were almost hard—as if he didn't see her anymore, but viewed an object he simply had to get around.

"How did you find it—the cave? Were you looking or was it an accident?"

"Accident—but not ours. It was late summer, and my son and I were traveling through this range. We found a man who had escaped a lepa attack. Everyone else was dead, and this man, too, was dying. There was nothing we could do, but listen to him as he choked on his blood and fell in and out of coherence. We had to swear, he said, to protect his family secret—to take up the job that would otherwise die with him."

"And of course, you swore."

"I'm not a monster, Wolfwalker."

Her jaw tightened.

"We swore. He told us that he had come here every two years, and his father before him, and his great-uncle before his father, and back eight hundred and sixty-two years, to the time of the Ancients themselves. Four times, the job he himself had sworn to do had jumped family lines, when one line died out or was killed. And now it would jump family lines again, to me and my son."

Her voice was far too quiet and calm, she thought, for the pace of her heart. "What was the job, Bany?" she heard herself ask.

"To protect what's in that cave." His blue eyes glinted. "That cave doesn't hide an exit point for the domes, Wolfwalker. It holds something far more important." His knuckles seemed to tighten on the bow. "The rumors of technology caches—of places that the birdmen couldn't reach with their plague—those rumors, it turned out, were true. And this is one of those places. It's hidden. It's protected. It's close enough to the domes that the Ancients would have access to the cache room to add things or take them out. And with the domes practically overhead, they could never forget the location if they were driven from the Ancient sites."

He motioned with his chin at the crack in the rocks. "In the back of that cavern is a room. You press your hand against the door panel to release the lock and allow the room to warm up to a temperature you can survive for a while. When the inner room is warm enough, the door to it will open. And inside are walls racked with cabinets—an ancient collection of what you would call samples. Plant tissues, seedlings, molds—they're all in there. Tubes and cubes and slides and dishes of things we don't even recognize anymore. There's a small library that matches the one in Ramaj Kiaskari, and copies of the maps that are etched out in Ariye."

Rezs was already shaking her head. "Libraries and maps— that I believe. But seedlings and molds—there's no way beneath any of the nine moons that they would have survived nearly nine centuries."

"Yes." He nodded. "There is."

"No—"

"They're in a stasis field, Rezs."

She stared at him.

He nodded again. "Just like the ones that used to protect parts of the domes—before the martyrs went in and deactivated them. A stasis field, and it protects the samples of everything the Ancients wanted to develop for this world. Rootroad hardeners, bacteriums that can splice new genes into old species, bioluminescent fungi . . . It's all in there."

Rezs forced her lips to work. "And you're stripping it out." She was amazed at how matter-of-fact the words sounded. "That man asked you to protect the field as he'd done for decades, and as his family had done for centuries; and instead of protecting it, you're raiding it."

"What good does any of it do us in stasis? It's only useful if we take it out and turn those things into products."

"So you really sent people in there to die." Her tone was still flat, and Bany watched her carefully. "You and neGruli— you traded lives for gold. Those people died horribly, didn't they—of the plague."

"Some," he admitted. "We left their bodies for the lepa."

"And the others?"

"We killed them later, when we were closer to your city, and left them for the worlags."

"Once you told neGruli about the chamber, why didn't he take everything all at once? Why risk coming back every six months, to be found out by someone who saw or trailed him? Someone who was suspicious of what he was suddenly producing?"

"You mean, someone like you?"

Her back tensed to bend to her knives; hand itched to grab the handles and throw. Gray Vlen howled deep inside her head, and the ancient ghosts moved past. She felt them walk toward her from Bany's position, then through her, into the cave. She didn't flinch; she didn't move. "Someone like me," she said.

"Samples rot and seedlings die. There's only so much work you can do at a time. The first time, neGruli took what he thought he could use and still lost sixty percent of those samples to decay. He has a better idea now of what he can develop in a certain amount of time. He takes less and loses less."

"The trade-off, of course, is that you have to make more trips and kill more guards. Anyone who goes into the chamber dies of plague, but anyone who helps get rid of those bodies is a liability."

The old man shrugged.

"And all the money he's been stripping from the council programs—it's funding the stealing of this technology—and its development. It's paying for cold-blooded murder. Gods, Bany, you can't believe that what you're doing is right."

"What I'm doing?" The old man raised his thin eyebrows. "Wolfwalker, it's not a question of right or wrong. It's a question of values—"

"Values? What kind of values can you have without good and bad—right or wrong? Greed over ethics?" Her voice sharpened, and it almost trembled with her growing anger. "Gold over life? I thought you were a good man, Bany. Those aren't values I associate with you."

"I'm glad you believe that," he said simply. "But what I mean is that it's not a moral question at all. It's a question of what I value over what you value. Take the man who values his ethics and won't compromise anything for them. He'll sacrifice everything—including his life—for the sake of a principle."

Rezs felt for the rock behind her. "Is that how you see yourself?"

Bany almost smiled, but there was no humor in it. "No. Your grandparents—Dion and Aranur—fall in that category. That's why they're so hard to live with. Your own father always felt second to his mother's duty to heal, and his own father's duty to his people. The visible need of the people for your grandparents' skills was always greater than the unseen needs of their children."

Invisible wounds . . .

Bany nodded, and Rezs realized she had spoken out loud. "You should have more compassion for them," he said softly. "Your own wounds are far from hidden."

"I have no wounds," she returned shortly. "At least until you shoot."

His faded blue gaze pierced hers. "You don't have as many wounds as a century warrior, but you've one single wound as deep as any a fighter's borne." He shook his head at Rezs's instant rejection of that idea. "Everything you do is designed to make your father proud of you or compete with your grandma's reputation. You talk of ethics and politics, but you took this job to make yourself feel as if you'd done something worthwhile. Something as good as Dion. You're the one who values approval above safety."

Rezs's jaw tightened. "There are other values, too, Bany."

"There's beauty," he agreed. "The man who values that above all else will do anything to possess it. He'll work himself to death to be able to afford something—or someone—beautiful. He might steal—he might even kill to hold something in his possession." He stepped carefully closer, but his feet were solid on the uneven ground, and the point of the bolt did not waver. "Then there's the man who values power. He looks at the world as if it was filled with resources, not with living things. Some of those things will help him gain power; some will prevent his acquisitions. He'll use the former; kill or destroy the latter."

"Like neGruli."

He inclined his head slightly in acknowledgment.

"And you." She swallowed stiffly. "Which are you?" She didn't recognize her own voice anymore. It was coarse and rough, as if she had screamed all clarity from its tones and left only snarls in its place. "What do you value? Gold? Power? Loyalty—like Ukiah? He'll do anything for you now, just because you saved his life. He won't question it, he won't disagree. He'll just do it."

"Ukiah values risk and debt. I risked myself to save him, and by that act, I did for him what he could not do for his own family. He owes me himself and his heritage, because there are no others besides him to continue it."

"And you?" she repeated.

"Love, Rezs."

"Love?"

"Yes."

She stared at him.

"You see, among all men—those who value beauty, money, success, prestige—those of us who value love are the

most dangerous of all. More than any others, we will compromise morals, ethics, our lives, and the lives of those around
us—all for the sake of love.”

He was calm, she told herself. He showed no hate or need to
kill her. She tried to force her eyes to look for hesitation—a
wobble in his arm, a weakening of his grip on the bolt—but
she couldn’t take her eyes from his face. She heard herself ask,
“What do you love, Bany?”

“Wolfwalker,” he said gently. “My name is Banir Gruli
neMunyu. I love my son, and my son is Rioci Banir neGruli.”

Rezs felt the words go in her ears, but something seemed to
interfere with the way they sat in her brain. His son . . . Bany—
neGruli’s father. Gray Vlen whipped across a meadow, and
Rezs’s muscles bunched as if her legs would take her across
that clearing.

Bany motioned ever so slightly with a shake of his gray-
haired head. “Wolfwalker,” he said softly, “I have no quarrel
with your beliefs.” He stepped carefully forward, lessening the
distance between them. “I don’t do this because I disagree
with what you say about my son. I do it because I love my son,
and I won’t let you take him down.”

“He’s a murderer, Bany.”

“And so am I.”

“You could have killed me anytime. Why wait till now to
do it?”

“I gave my word to the elder that I would see you safely
here.”

His voice was still calm, she noticed in some abstract part
of her brain. It seemed wrong—as if her death would be somehow diminished by the lack of emotion he showed. “And all
this,” she managed, “was because of your word to her? Why
give her your word at all? She didn’t ask for it.” Something
flickered across his face, and Rezs stared. “You didn’t give
your word to her to reassure her at all, did you? You gave your
word to her for me.”

He nodded almost imperceptibly.

“Why? Is it because I’m a wolfwalker?”

“No,” he said heavily. “It’s because of your brother Cal.”

“Cal.” She shook her head. “I don’t get it. What has he to do
with all this—” Her voice broke off. “It’s not Cal, either, is it?
This has to do with his mate’s death—the death of Tegre’s

mother." Rezs saw her answer in his eyes. "She worked in the labs with Lit and me—or she did until two years ago." She took a half step forward, ignoring the arrow point. Her voice rose sharply. "You killed her?"

Gray Vlen, in her mind, howled sharply, and his lips curled back from his teeth. Rezs clutched at the link between them.

Bany didn't speak for a moment, but when he finally did, his own voice was quiet. "I didn't plan to do it, Rezs. We were setting the worlag attack scene—we couldn't kill our people here because it would look too odd to have them all die in the same spot. We told them about the dome and that we'd have to bring our samples back to the elders, but that we'd have to do it quietly to avoid panicking anyone about the plague. They believed us. So we rode back together, traveling fast enough that they had no chance to talk to the townspeople in the villages we passed through—no time to tell anyone where we'd been or what we'd done. Then, when we were two days out from my son's city, we poisoned them all. Your brother's mate—she had ridden off the trail to follow a line of blackrope growth. She saw my son and me with the bodies of his party. I called to her. She stopped. And I shot her."

Even though she had already suspected that Tegre's mother was dead, the words seemed to break open a pocket of grief, so that her throat tightened and her voice came out more like a sob. "And she died."

"In my arms, Wolfwalker."

"And her body?" Rezs had trouble forcing the words out. "Did you leave it to the . . . the worlags?"

"I took it to Chameleon Cliffs. It was scavenged by a badgerbear within two days."

Rezs stared at him. "Goddamn you, Bany—you barely even feel guilty."

"What would be the point? I am guilty, Wolfwalker. I was careless, and your brother's mate paid part of the price for that."

"So you made your son leave our business alone ever since then—as payment for her death."

The old man shrugged. "He will eventually take over your labs as he's done with the others in your city. But because of my mistake, he has given you two years to see what's coming—two years to find another line of work."

"Dear moons, Bany, do you hear what you're saying? You killed my brother's mate, then made a business decision to let us use the next two years to abandon our labs to your murdering, greedy son—"

"It could have happened sooner."

"Not without a fight."

"Like this one?" He nodded at her expression. "Wolfwalker, I don't argue that what I'm doing is wrong. I merely state that it won't change my actions. I killed Tegre's mother, I killed my own scouts, and soon I'm going to kill you. Eventually, my son will take over your business as he has taken over the other labs. He's wrong. I'm wrong. But he is my only son."

"What about Welker and Gradjek and Touvinde?" She heard her voice rising, and she couldn't even stop it. "You'll kill them, too—just like the other scouts?"

He shook his head. "The other parties rode here specifically to raid the chamber in that cave. Welker and the others—they don't know what you're looking for or why you're out here. They're drugged, but the drug won't kill them for another three or four hours. Your decision here will determine whether or not I give them the antidote."

"And Coale and Elgon?"

"Like the others, their systems are slowing, little by little, but their hearts haven't stopped, and their lungs are far from not breathing."

"Then you've got them," she snarled, "and you've got me. Why in any of the nine hells are you giving me the lecture? You want me to agree with your philosophy—to say, 'Why, yes, Bany, love *is* more valuable than ethics. I'll gladly give my life so that your son can take over more businesses and put more people out on the streets.' "

"Your agreement or opposition is not the point, Wolfwalker."

"Then what is? You want some kind of absolution *before* the act of murder? That's goddamn optimistic."

"Wolfwalker." His voice was soft. "You base your self-worth on your actions and ethics, so I hold out for you a choice. You can go into the dome and bring out another batch of the samples for my son; and I'll give you the antidote to the poison I gave the others. I have it here, on my belt. I give you my word that before I kill you, you can go with me back to camp and administer the antidote so that you see you have indeed saved their lives. By the time they recover, you'll be a day dead. But you'll have saved them—by preserving their ignorance of what you did, and by trading your life for theirs. Or"—and he paused significantly—"you can die now, from this bolt."

"You're taking a risk, Bany." Her words were tight. "Those samples, which you think to give to your son for his business, are the evidence I need to convict him. You know the elders are already suspicious; if I don't return, they'll go after your son with everything they've got. And how will you counter that?"

"I won't. It's spring. The lepa are flocking thickly enough to dispose of any bodies, and the rains are hard enough to wipe away all footprints. By the time anyone else comes here looking for evidence, all traces will be gone except for the bones, and they will simply corroborate my story."

Ghost bones shifted in her head as the Ancients died in the domes. Figures rode by on the trail, with ghost wolves running beside them. The gray din rose, and Bany's figure blurred. *Vlen!* she screamed.

Wolfwalker!

His voice was sharp, snapping out of the gray howling, and Rezs clenched her fists to touch his mind. She could feel her heart pounding as fast as his. *Help me— Link to the pack, Vlen. There are wolves near Ukiah— I need him. Hurry!*

The yearling howled, and the wolf pack responded. Their voices meshed in the fog. Sworls of sound seemed to whip through her mind, and then the yellow eyes trebled her sight. She could feel Ukiah's voice in another wolf's ears; see the shadow shapes of others. Cal's words drifted past, as if caught in a current, and her father answered the man. She called out, shouting into the bond for the sense of the scout, Ukiah, and what came back was music, filtered through the packsong. The link stretched tight, and yellow eyes gleamed. The gray tide rose in her head like a wave, rushing into her mind with the sound of a dozen snarls. Feet and paws, hooves and claws blended into a din of racing movement. Rezs gripped the rock behind her.

Bany caught the unfocused look in her eyes as she tried to

contact Gray Vlen. "Your wolf is too far to help you, Rezs. You sent him away yourself."

Her voice, in return to Bany, was little more than a vicious growl. "You think he won't know who did this? Are you prepared to kill him, too, when he arrives?"

The old man shrugged, but his hands never wavered. "If I must. But a wolf who loses his wolfwalker won't bond with another human. His memories pose no threat to me."

"He'll come after you."

"I don't think so. Your bond is barely six ninans old—not deep or strong at all. He'll grieve for your death, but he won't follow you into it. Gray Shona would, however—come after me for Coale's death. I'll have no choice in killing that one. Unless you let Coale live."

Rezs tried to swallow, but something coarse seemed caught in her throat, and it choked her like a rock. "Neither of us is stupid, Bany. You can't think I will meekly submit to death, no matter what kind of deal we make for the others."

"No," he agreed. He didn't smile. "You're desperate, and that will give you strength and cunning. And when you come out of that cave, you'll come out thinking and fighting for your life." His voice was quiet. "And all you'll have to overcome is a hundred and thirty years' experience, gathered in these hands."

Rezs had no response.

"You can't just run from the cave and leap on your dnu to escape me by riding—we left the beasts at camp. And if you think to make a break for it on your own . . ." He shrugged. "I can track a wolf across a sea of stone. You might be more comfortable now than two ninans ago running trail, but you still leave tracks like a clumsy dnu. You wouldn't get a hundred meters without feeling my bolt in your back."

Rezs's stomach twisted until it forced the bile into her throat.

"An hour has great value, does it not? I'm offering you three."

She didn't answer, but she knew Bany could read her expressions as if she flung her words out like banners.

He nodded. "The stasis chamber can be opened for no more than a couple hours at a time. After that, the entire thing will deactivate, and all the samples and materials inside will begin growing or dying or decaying at their normal rate. What's left inside won't survive another four years. But what's left inside can still help us bring the advances to our science that the Ancients wanted on this world to begin with."

"It hasn't been six months. Your son won't have time to develop anything I bring out."

"It will have been six ninans by the time I reach him again. He will know by then which samples are unviable. He'll be ready to take some new ones by the time I get back."

"The plague—"

"Won't kill you immediately," he said flatly. "You won't even feel the first chill or convulsion before you come out of the chamber. You'll have plenty of time to help your friends." His voice became suddenly cold. "That's what you really want, isn't it, Rezs? A chance to become a legend like your grandmother?"

"What are you talking about?" she croaked.

"Your options, Wolfwalker. The one thing you want more than anything else in this world. 'Rezsia, the Wolfwalker. I knew her before she was a hero.' That's what you want to hear. You want to be important. You want an epitaph you can carry onto the path of the moons. Before you faced this warbolt, your desire to be a hero was worth more than your life, Rezs. Check your values now. Are they changing?"

Rezs knew she tried to speak, because the ice that had frozen across her jaw cracked when she moved her mouth. No other sound came out.

Wolfwalker . . . Gray Vlen's voice rang out, then was swallowed by the roiling gray. Yellow eyes flashed in and out of the lupine tide, and teeth bared, then sank into the images of the Ancients. Yellow eyes met a brown-black gaze, and Rezs felt the shock of Ukiah's voice in her head.

Ukiah! she screamed. *Help me* . . .

I'm coming!

"Wolfwalker," Bany said softly, "it's time to decide."

He gestured—a tiny motion—and Rezs felt her feet rip themselves from the ground. Somehow, like a puppet, she turned and moved toward the entrance to the cave. In her head, she screamed at herself to stop, to turn, to leap across that space and risk that arrow and the ones she knew would follow. Fight him now, she shouted. *Stop!*

But her feet kept moving, lifting themselves one after the other until her hands pressed against each side of that ragged, rocky slit. Blindly, she stared into the cave. It was black, and yet she could see shadows. It was still, and yet she saw motion. Caught in the memories of ancient wolves, ghosts carried small boxes and lights shone before her, and in her head, a single howl rang out.

Wolfwalker!

The rock was gritty beneath her fingers, but she didn't notice. The gray din in the back of her head had risen with that solitary howl, so that it swamped her thoughts, but the one thing it couldn't hide was the image in her own memory of the bodies, so weirdly still, lying in a ragged circle, dying beneath the dawn.

She didn't look over her shoulder. "No torch to see with?"

"You won't need one."

She stared at the dark. Were there roofbleeders in there? There was something in the cave, because she could see the dull white of the bones along the floor. "I can't do this," she whispered.

"Wolfwalker," Bany said softly.

She half turned.

The old man had relaxed his bow, and now one hand held a small, blue vial. Abruptly, he threw it onto a stone. The glass shattered and the fluid sprayed out like blood.

Rezs gasped and spun, lunging toward him. He grabbed up his arrow and drew it back, and she froze, halfway across the clearing.

"That," he said, "was one life. Now, Wolfwalker." He indicated the cavern. "Bring me back the samples."

And she felt her feet take her back to the cave and move her body inside.

XXII

The cave was dark and rough, but there was just enough light to stumble a few meters in. It was narrow; one side of the cavern had collapsed, so that she had to climb around the boulders through that narrow slot in the rocks. Overhead and along the walls, the roofbleeders clung, and as they felt her motion they began to extend from their nubbins and drop down like weaving tendrils. She grabbed for her knife, but it wasn't at her belt.

Bany.

Shuddering, she swatted at the worms, forcing them to whip back to avoid her fists until she tripped and fell against a rock, cursing as the stone smashed into her shin and knee.

"Goddamn you, Bany, to the seventh hell—"

Wolfwalker . . .

Vlen! But the voices of the wolves rose with Vlen's howl, drowning out the cub. Each time she and Vlen stretched along the bond between them, Gray Shona brought in the other wolves. Finally, Rezs squeezed her eyes shut and pressed her hands to her temples. And realized she could see.

The ghost figures—the lights—they were still in the cave. The yellow eyes that gleamed from the entrance—wider so many centuries ago—saw and remembered, and now they projected those memories to Rezs. She opened her eyes. Gray, faded memories showed her the shape of the cave. She pushed herself to her knees, then to her feet. She *could* see the path through those rocks.

Bany had known this—that she would be able to see through the wolves. The old man had expected her to be drawn to this cave. And she was. The memories of the wolves pulled her like a magnet to the back of the twisting cavern, where the patch of roofbleeders thinned to bare rock, and the floor of the cave became smooth as a rootroad. Twenty meters in, the tunnel turned abruptly to the left, and Rezs hesitated. She could barely see the entrance to the cave; there was only a thin sliver of light still visible through the rough rock cavern. Then she stepped around the corner.

Even with the wolf memories guiding her, she walked with her hands out in front: one chest-high; the other up, in front of her face. She moved slowly, and struck a rock only once. It bruised her upper forearm and tore her left sleeve where she had mended it, but she didn't even curse. She just switched arms, ducked beneath the slab that had half fallen across the increasingly cold tunnel, and eased her way past the rock that littered the floor. There were turns—three more. And the cold was growing with her dread. The ghosts . . . She walked behind one, then another as they moved more quickly through their lit cavern than she did through the dark. And then, as she followed the last curve around, she felt the lupine voices howl. She came slowly to a halt.

The thin light was faint at first, but like a line of rootroads that mark the edges of town, it delineated the doorway clearly. It was not a big door—rather like the kind of door one would build to a small shed. It was barely one and a half meters tall, and half a meter wide. If Rezs had not been familiar with the style of the Ancient buildings, she would have said it was not even made for humans.

Gingerly, she moved forward. There was a panel beside the door—flat, without buttons or language. She stared at it, then pressed her hand against it. The panel was ice-cold, and the door didn't move. She pressed harder. And realized that the panel had begun to glow.

The print of her hand was clearly visible on the flat screen, and it was becoming brighter. Gently, she touched the panel again. Where the glass-smooth surface had been frigid before, it now was becoming warm, and the faint line that outlined the door was becoming brighter.

In the back of her head, the gray din seemed to surge, and distant memories boiled beneath the yearling's urgent howl. Finally, Rezs projected back the sense of where she was. The dark images spun out. More gray memories triggered. Gray shapes drifted up. Voices, figures—walls that were themselves made of light . . . Shadow shapes that spun to the left, down into her mind. And winged forms that spoke not in her ears, but through the bond with the wolves . . .

Rezs pressed her fists to her head and cried out, but the sound was swallowed by the hungry walls, deadened by the rough, black rock. She took a ragged breath and deliberately shut herself off from the yearling. The panic that beat back at her mind made her stagger. She lost her footing, fell against the door, and screamed.

The door shimmered into a clear panel, sparking across her skin with tiny jolts of current. Then the panel dissolved completely, and Rezs fell through.

She landed on the floor, staring down at her hands, then jerked back with her arms instinctively over her face. She froze. She couldn't help holding her breath, as if that would keep the plague that inhabited this place from her lungs. She couldn't close her eyes. She simply crouched, frozen and staring, while the cold pierced her body with time.

The first thing she noticed was the sliver of vision that showed her the floor. There were no tiles; no swirling growth marks on the floor. The surface was a blue-white layer of ice with tiny bumps and swells where the ice had accumulated. She shifted infinitesimally and the ice crackled with her weight. There was no other sound but the heartbeat in her neck. And there was no darkness in her sight. Abruptly, she looked up.

It was not the memories of the wolves that made the room as light as it was. There were no lamps, but only patches of light on the ceiling. It wasn't an even lighting—there were dim patches and places where it looked as black as the tunnel outside, but there was enough light to see the area. It was different—very different from the buildings she knew. It was clearly a place of the Ancients.

And she was not alone.

Three pairs of eyes stared back at her.

For one moment of horror she thought they were moonwarriors, sent by the Ancients to guard the stasis chamber. In that instant the graysong boiled through her mind. It stripped away the shards of her thoughts and left a chaotic sense of being trapped. Her body tensed; her lips curled back, and her teeth ached with the cold air. Then some part of her brain kicked in and began to work again: moonwarriors were just another legend that grew out of the Ancients' landing. Guards wouldn't be frozen in place. The eyes that, unblinkingly, watched her were open and dead. The bodies were not posed to view anything—they were twisted and bent against the cabinet walls as if they had died in the middle of one last convulsion of plague. The chill that rose from their frozen flesh created a mist that clung to their bodies and was gently sucked away by some sort of flow of air.

"Not moonwarriors," she whispered. "Ancients."

Two ghosts walked through one of the bodies. The gray tide swelled as one of the ghosts looked up. The man called back to a Gray One so long dead that the wolf's voice was barely a ripple in that fog. Rezs pulled a tentative breath into her lungs, then, cautiously, looked over her shoulder at the door. It was once again a shimmering panel, locking her inside.

"Vlen?" she called out.

A rage of howling answered her. The memories of the wolves behind the Ancients ran side by side with Vlen and Gray Shona. The packsong was so thick it seemed to roll through her head, crushing her thoughts before it. She began to tremble.

The cold, she told herself harshly. "It's just the cold," she repeated out loud. She got to her feet and rubbed her hands to get the circulation back in them. When she had touched the dry, frigid floor, her fingers had stuck for an instant to the ice. Now they were red and pale from the cold. She wrapped her arms around herself as she studied the room and the bodies.

The closest body was half-arched against the wall. Like the others, its eyes were open and frozen in place; its skin patchy and pale from the ice crystals; its hair stringy and hard from the cold. There was almost no sense of decay. Rezs took another bare breath, afraid to breathe in, and the cold air almost cut her lungs. She couldn't help taking a step forward. The clothes, she noted, had a two-toned sheen like silk. There was no jewelry outside a single stud, which glinted dully from the dead man's left temple. She forced her feet forward again until she could squat beside him.

Deliberately, she touched his hair. The frozen strands were

like fragile glass—they snapped as she moved her fingers. She jerked her hand back; the hair pieces fell to the floor with a thin clatter. She didn't even know how she backed away; she just found herself pressed against the narrow back wall, beside the door to the room, where the ice on the walls clamped onto her clothes and forced her to jerk away.

"Vlen—" She couldn't help the panic in her voice. *Gray One . . .*

The echo that rang off her skull was chaotic, and Rezs clenched her fists against her temples. She tried to focus her thoughts, but the thread of her link to Vlen, strong as it had grown, could not compete with the memories the Gray Ones sent. Like a storm, the ancient images kept coming. They chilled her thoughts and froze them in place, so that all she could do was lean into the ghosts and let them walk through her mind.

Wolfwalker! Vlen's voice sang out between the memories.

She caught that thread and clung to it. She was afraid, she admitted, not only of this place or of the Ancient plague, but of those frozen Ancients. There was something terribly lonely about eyes that could not close. She shivered, and the chill reached deeply into her bones until she had to rub hard at her arms to keep warm. She pulled the collar of her tunic up over her mouth to protect her teeth from the algid air she breathed.

She forced herself to examine the room with her eyes. It was a huge, frozen chamber, twenty meters by forty, half-filled with a mix of cabinets. Some cabinets were tall and twice as wide as a coffin; some were a meter square and stacked in rows to the ceiling. They were slightly unmatched colors—from whites to light, dirty grays, with three facades a pale, light blue—and had different types of handles and doors, as if they had been made by different people. There were gaps between some of the clumps of cabinets, and Rezs could see that the walls, not just the floor, of the freezing room were also coated with ice. Near the base of some of the cabinets, the ice had built up to form tiny slopes. In lines that angled away from the hinge side of four, floor-level cabinets, she could see where the ice had been chipped or broken away so that the doors would open.

Each cabinet had, on its door, its own flat access panel, which was clear of any ice and looked the same as the panel that held her handprint outside. Beside each cabinet access panel was a smaller panel of text; and beside that was a patch map or grid, which, up close, looked like a cube composed of a skinny lattice. Reluctantly, she was drawn to the first cabinet, where she eyed the cube grid warily. "Some kind of map to what's inside," she breathed. "Some kind of inventory . . ."

Over half the grids in the room were white. Some had a few tiny squares of amber or red. Perhaps an eighth of them were mostly green, and the rest were black. All four of the floor-level cabinets that had been opened in the last few years had black grids.

Tentatively, she touched the access panel for a small cabinet whose grid was completely black. It was cold, but not frozen, and she pressed her hand against it with more confidence. She waited. Like the door panel to the chamber, when the panel warmed enough to trigger the latch, there was a hum of energy, and the seals gave way with a small, sucking sound. It was keyed to her hand, she guessed, and chemically triggered by heat or some other signal that her skin gave off. "So simple," she breathed as she watched the door release. "The cold to preserve them; the seals to keep them isolated . . ."

Cautiously, she pulled open the first door. It seemed to be another freezer chamber, but the smaller cabinet inside fit the freezer completely, so that only the facade of the inner cabinet was exposed when she opened the outer door. She pulled her sleeve over her hand and touched the handle warily. But like the outer access panel, it was not frozen. She took a breath and pulled that door open as well. It was not half as big inside as she expected: The walls of the inner cabinet were so thick with shielding that all that was left in the center was an inner box, oddly shaped, barely as long as one hand. The chill that rose from the shielding around the box made Rezs cringe, but she reached in anyway and, with her hands protected by her sleeves, grasped the box by its outer handle and pulled it free. Then she set it on the icy floor and opened the lid. Inside was a simple rack, empty as a winter stomach. Whatever it had once held was now gone—stripped away by neGruli's men. Thoughtfully, she put the box back in the shielding and closed the inner door, then the outer one, and watched the cabinet reseal. Then she turned to the next cupboard.

Methodically, she checked the next ten cabinets. Six of

them were empty. Black grids indicated empty racks; white indicated full. She guessed that green meant organic, and brown some kind of nonorganic material; she assumed that the amber and red shades indicated growth or decay. The notepad on each door was in the same kind of code that she used in the lab—LT for living tissue; SD for seeds; and SP, spores; C for colloids; and O for osmolites—but the names at the base of each panel were unfamiliar. "Edard, Lachute, Yogya . . ." She halted. "Kurnu."

Lightly, she touched the panel the Ancient had signed. She had an ancestor by that name—on her father's side. Kurnu Brantun neDeaglan. And he had died of the plague eight hundred and fifty-six years ago.

"Ah, gods," she whispered.

The sob that flashed into her chest caught her unprepared, and she choked. She didn't notice the shiver that had begun to remain in her flesh. She didn't notice the chatter of her teeth. She saw only the Ancient ones, frozen for all time, with their eyes wide open as they watched her loot their grave.

She threw back her head and screamed, and the sound was harsh and dulled in the small room. Only the tiny thread that linked her to Vlen kept her focused through the ghosts of the wolves. Rezs's jaw clenched, and she felt her teeth grind together. When she finally rose, her violet eyes had a steely glint, and there was no longer a tremble in the hands that reached for another cupboard to continue searching the room.

There were sixty-one cabinets in the room, and forty-two of them were empty or contained near-empty racks. After a while she stopped pulling the inner boxes out of the shielding and began simply opening them in place. Five hand-sized boxes with seeds; four of spores and fungal tissues; eleven with cubes of gelatin that contained dark specks in their cores. One of the empty cabinets was a body-sized chamber, and after watching the gray ghosts as they worked, Rezs leaned in to study the surface of the walls.

Abruptly, the sense of the wolves was cut off. An isolation so cold that it seemed to cut through her skull bone hit her like an ax. She jerked back, banging her shoulder against the outer door. "Vlen?"

The yearling howled in her head, his voice ringing out of the emptiness and bringing with it the snarling, gray fog. Rezs clung to the frigid door. The sense of the wolves was thick and filled again with ghosts, and she stared at the inner stasis chamber as she tried to feel that loneliness again.

It wasn't there. Tentatively, she stretched her hand back into the stasis box. Then leaned forward again. The gray tide cut off just as shockingly fast. She had to force herself to remain with her head in the chamber. It felt as though the back of her head had been sucked empty of thought and emotion. She tried to reach for Vlen, but the yearling wasn't there. There was no howling din, no snarling sounds low in the back of her head. There were no yellow eyes that floated, watching her like guardians. There was nothing.

She leaned back out, and as soon as her head cleared the shielding, she felt the wolves return. It was not a gradual lessening of isolation; it was abrupt and clear—like crossing a threshold. And Gray Vlen's panic at her absence was strong enough to overshoot the gray din and cause her neck muscles to tense.

Rezs shivered and backed away from the cabinet. Outside, the wolves were clear and strong. Inside the stasis box, there was no sense of the Gray Ones at all. The emptiness it created—she had never felt that before, she realized. There had always been some sort of gray fog behind her thoughts—some pair of gleaming yellow eyes to watch over her dreams, or a tiny distant mental growl to keep her company at dawn.

She had never been alone.

The thought was so novel that she stood stock-still. All her life, the wolves had been with her—as a child, as a girl, as a young woman. . . . Even when she cut herself off from Vlen, there was still the sense of the Gray Ones in the back of her mind. A sense of age in the gray din that watched with some sort of patient acceptance for her to recognize it in the fog and call it by name.

She looked at the bodies frozen to the floor of the room. The ghosts that moved from one cabinet to another still stepped through the dead Ancients as if they weren't there. The cabinets filled up one by one. Time passed in the minds of the wolves, and the graysong threaded itself with years for every second she listened. And then the graysong began to sound with the death howls of abandoned wolves. The sickness came, and wolfwalkers died. The packsong thinned like a fraying thread. Time passed like wind. More and more, the wolf packs ran the heights alone, while their numbers dropped each decade. She saw pups born still and cold, and felt the noses of their mothers nudge them in hopeless grief. She heard the lepa cry as they flocked in spring and felt the talons tear into her body. Time moved forward, and the packs survived, and the Gray Ones buried their grief in the years since the Ancients landed.

"And now," Rezs whispered, "I've brought it back."

The absent bonds between the Gray Ones and their human partners; the deaths of the wolfwalkers, which, with grief, isolated their Gray Ones from their own packs. She stared at the Ancients' bodies. In less than two hours she would be nothing more than a few pieces of tissue waiting to be torn from the bone. In less than two hours Vlen would add his own voice to that ancient lonely cry.

Bany.

He was waiting.

The first full cabinet she found contained racks of clear cubes with dark lumps in their centers. She took one cube out of the rack to examine it, but finally put it back on the rack and went on, stepping over the Ancients' bodies. More spaces; more empty racks; more cubes. It took her an hour, perhaps, to check all of the cupboards, and when she was done, she stood in the middle of the room and wrapped her arms around herself as if the cold had frozen her into the ancient tableau. It was time to think. Time to plan.

The panic took her suddenly. It filled her head and flung her body at the cabinets, so that she tore at the doors. A shield—a cutting edge—anything. She wrenched at the cupboard doors, but they were on solidly, and she couldn't budge the hinges. She tried to break a side off one of the oddly shaped stasis boxes, but it was like trying to break a metal plate. She looked at the bodies of the Ancients, but even if she could break one away from the floor, she wasn't strong enough to carry it, nor hold it up as a shield. Finally, she threw back her head and screamed.

The sound was swallowed by the room as if it, too, were dead of emotion. Rezs leaned her forehead against the cabinets and let the frigid touch of the cabinet doors seep into her skull. Her skin was dangerously cold. Her teeth had begun to chatter incessantly, and she understood more clearly Bany's confidence. Cold as she was, she would not even be able to run when she left the cave of the Ancients. All she would be able to do would be to give him what he wanted, and stand, near frozen, waiting for her own death. She clenched her fists, feeling the sluggishness of their response. Then, carefully, she began to jump, pumping her arms up and down to get her circulation going while she tried to keep her balance on the icy floor.

Then she selected a shirtful of cubes, closed the cabinets that had been left open, and resealed them one by one. Finally, she let herself out of the chamber, leaving only the dead behind.

When she stepped this time through the shimmering door, Gray Vlen howled and jerked at the tingly sensation. The tide of gray that swept with him into the back of her head threatened to drown her, and she staggered as it hit her. She found herself on her hands and knees on the floor of the cave, her arms and legs tight as if to leap. The sample cubes bounced and scattered among the rocks like marbles.

"Vlen!"

Wolfwalker, we are close.

She could feel him, racing up the trail. The camp was in his sight, and human scent and wolves in his nostrils. "The pack," she whispered.

They watch the hunter like lepa on the heights. He seemed to turn and snarl suddenly, and Shona's voice was shockingly hard.

Wolfwalker, the older wolf snarled in her mind. The image she projected was of the bodies, still and silent, with Coale like a corpse among them.

Rezs forced herself to her feet. "I know, Gray One. I'm doing what I can."

She could see now, through her eyes, after the lightness of the chamber, the cave was blacker than before. Her pupils widened as they tried to see any edges of definition, but behind her, the door shimmered, turned opaque, and began to dull into darkness. It took perhaps ten minutes to turn completely dark, and after finding as many of the cubes as she could, Rezsia just sat and watched it. Eventually, only the faintly lit edge of both door and panel were left floating in the blackness.

She was still shivering, and the air of the cave, cold as it was, seemed warm to her skin. She pulled her collar from her mouth and breathed in deeply, then carefully ran in place for a few minutes until she felt the sweat begin. When she stopped, the sweat cooled instantly like a layer of ice, and her flesh felt no warmer than before. She couldn't help the chatter of her teeth. When she tried to clamp her jaw shut, she bit her tongue instead.

Gray One! she called finally.

Wolfwalker—we come!

I need you now, Vlen. Help me. She projected the need for warmth, and the yearling blasted back a shaft of motion and heat that seared her thoughts. She gasped. Gray Shona clamped onto his mental voice and added her own energy to the cub. What flowed into Rezs was a warmth akin to fire. Everywhere the fog curled, the flames followed like snakes, touching her head, then her neck and down into her body. Her bones stopped shivering. Her jaw relaxed as her teeth stopped clacking together. And she felt powerful as an Ancient herself. She touched her face. It was warm now, not cold, and the sweat that still clung to her skin was no longer icy, but sticky and hot.

"Moons," she whispered. She touched the samples tucked into her shirt. Her mind seemed to crystallize.

Swiftly, she made her way back out the way she had made her way in. The ghosts lit the path, and this time she didn't even slam into the widowmaker that hung halfway down in the tunnel. By the time she approached the slit of light that marked the cave exit, her eyes were so adjusted to the light that she paused inside the entrance—well back from the cave worms, and waited. She could feel the weight of the wolves outside—neither Vlen nor Shona was with them, but the song of the Gray Ones rose in a howl that echoed out on the rocks. She could smell Bany through the Gray Ones; sense Ukiah with him. At her side, her fists clenched. Their words floated to her clearly, not through the cave entrance, but through the ears of the Gray Ones who slunk closer outside.

". . . looting their tomb for technology?" It was Ukiah.

"Been doing it for a couple years now," Bany answered. "She's been working for neGruli all along."

Rezs's lips thinned. "Dik-dropped worlag," she cursed under her breath. She tried to focus her sight through the wolves, but it was still blurred. She could see the figures of Bany and Ukiah, but she couldn't see her gear. The old man had probably gotten rid of it as soon as she went inside.

"So all this reading the memories of the wolves—"

"Was a show to make us think she was searching for a site, when she knew it was here all along. She led me along like a dog on a leash, and I, like a well-trained mutt, followed her without question."

"We'll have to take her back to the elders. Stealing from the domes, betraying her family to work with neGruli, drugging the others at the camp . . ."

Bany's voice was flat and hard, and in the cave, the warmth of the wolves seemed suddenly distant. Rezs shivered at his tone. "I know her parents, her grandparents—her whole family in Ariye. If she stood trial, before everyone in the county, I think they'd die of shame. And the terror of plague we'd unleash—that isn't something to take lightly, Ukiah."

"So what do you suggest?"

"No reason for a trial block when it's as clear-cut-and-dried as this."

There was a pause, as if Ukiah was thinking. Then the wolf-song in her head tightened with his steady words. "So we kill her here."

"When she comes out of the cave," the old man agreed.

Did the old scout shrug? She couldn't tell; her eyesight was blurred from the ghosts and the Gray Ones, and the only thing real to her was the chill that crawled again over her skin. Outside, the gray wolves shifted in the shrubs, and both scouts listened closely.

"It's the wolves," Ukiah said flatly.

"But not hers."

"How can you tell?"

"She sent Gray Vlen and Shona away. Said she didn't want to risk them getting the plague, but I think the real reason was that Shona would smell the chemicals in Coale's body and rouse the rest of us to the fact that we were being drugged." The old man gestured. "I'll stay here, where she can see me;

you move near the rocks—get behind her if she tries to run back in the cave once she's seen me."

"What about the Gray Ones?"

"They won't attack—her bond isn't strong enough to provoke them." Bany's voice was confident, but his sweat to the wolves was stronger suddenly, as if fear had entered his body.

Ukiah hesitated, then moved toward the rocks. He moved like a wolf himself, and the Gray Ones nearby watched him with gleaming eyes. Rezs could feel his presence like music in the packsong. His wall of gray reserve was tight. The ghosts moved through the cave to the light outside, and Rezs felt others come closer. Through the forest, racing like Vlen, gray shadows of humans moved. And she couldn't tell if they were real or not, only that they blinded her to the cave and left her with only Bany's voice in her ears.

Then the old man raised his voice. "Wolfwalker."

Rezs steeled herself. Deliberately, she moved forward. She batted her way through the roofbleeders, then eased through the crack in the cliff. Her eyes cringed closed, and her arm went up over her face. Tearing, her eyes cleared slowly. Then she lowered her arm and looked at the old man.

He was steady as if time had never touched his muscles. His age-seamed face was expressionless, and his sharp blue eyes piercing as they judged her chill. Then a Gray One growled behind him. The old man didn't stiffen; he merely tightened his fingers on the arrow. But he looked suddenly tired. "It's time, Wolfwalker," he said quietly. "Put the samples down and step away from them."

"Does Ukiah know that you forced me in there at bow point?" Her voice was as calm as his. No sign of tension trembled its tones, and no fear tightened its pitch. "Does he know that you're neGruli's father? Or that you've been killing people in this area nigh onto two years now?"

Bany didn't smile. "Wolfwalker, Ukiah knows everything. You can't hide behind your words. The samples, Rezs. Now."

She dumped out the samples on the rock. Behind the older man, the gray wolves rustled. A massive shape slunk into the shadow of a boulder.

"Don't do it, Rezs," he said sharply. "Ukiah—"

In a flash, the other scout was at her side, his knife out and pressed against her throat. She didn't move. She didn't even flinch at the touch of the steel. It seemed fitting that it lay its icy line on her flesh along the same angle that the blader in neGruli's warehouse had used. Except this time it was death, not a lesson that the steel would give her. She tensed, as if to move, and Ukiah's eyes flashed a warning.

"Don't try it," he said coldly. "This steel will take the blood from your throat faster than you can call out for your wolf."

Rezs stiffened. Wolves howled in her head as she stared at the scout. Ghosts seemed to creep up behind him. The pack snarled, and their teeth were suddenly gleaming in the light. The old man's sweat was as hot as his blue eyes were cold. "Stand aside, Ukiah," he ordered.

"I owe her," the man returned. He didn't take his eyes from Rezs. "Besides, the one thing I've learned is that you never hesitate in the kill."

Rezs felt the howling shatter with a memory so clear it was like looking through time. She didn't have to nod; she sent a shaft of acknowledgment through the wolves, and felt the scout's hand shiver as the Gray Ones snarled back in his mind.

"The result," he added harshly, "would be like this—"

His arm snapped out. Rezs grabbed the blade and twisted it out of his willing hand, following the motion into a throw and snapping the blade at Bany. The instant it left her hands, Ukiah hit her, throwing her clear of the cave. A wolf lunged at Bany, catching his attention, and he staggered as the knife sank into his thigh. His fingers released; the arrow flew like a shot. Then the bolt caught Rezs on the biceps and tore through her flesh as if it was silk. She must have screamed, because she could hear the Gray Ones howling. The old man didn't even curse. There was already another bolt on his bow, and the bowstring snapped, sending the warbolt deep into Ukiah's shoulder as the other scout lunged across the clearing. Ukiah staggered back, falling to the ground. Rezs couldn't move. Wild-eyed, she stared at Bany. The old man lifted his bow again. His two fingers tensed. The string drew taut.

"Bany, *no!*"

The old man arched his chest and released. A dark spot blackened his tunic front. And then the arrow flew, straight as eyesight, across the clearing to Rezs.

XXIII

She threw up her arms, and the warbolt tore through her biceps again, just below the other wound. She screamed and grabbed at her arm. The Gray Ones snarled as they leaped from the brush, forming a rough circle in which their black pupils seemed to focus their yellow eyes into lenses of the moons. Rezs waited for Bany to raise his bow again, but the old man simply stared.

He had missed.

He had been aiming at Rezs's heart, and he missed. He took a step forward. Rezs tensed, and caught her breath in a sob. Bany hesitated. Then he fell slowly to his knees. One hand reached inside his jerkin and pulled out the glass vials.

"No!"

The old man threw the vials against the rocks, and the tiny bottles shattered. Shards of glass flew out in a spray of blue fluid. And the antidotes dripped off the rocks like rain. The old man looked at Rezs. "He is . . . my . . . only son."

He collapsed on his front. The arrow that protruded from his back stuck out like a stiff flag, and the Gray Ones didn't go near him, but snapped at his figure as they lunged toward it and jerked back.

Gray Vlen leaped across the clearing from the forest behind the old man. He was at Rezs's side in an instant, snarling and sniffing her arm. She scrambled to her feet, and ran, stumbling, to Ukiah. But the man thrust her away, and she pushed back at his arms, trying to keep him down. Then she froze again. The men running through the wolves from behind where Bany collapsed—the tall men, with black hair and square jaws and eyes as gray as winter skies—

"*Father!*" she screamed. "Cal!"

They sprinted to her side. Her father hauled her up like a child and crushed her to his chest. "Rezs . . ." He set her away and yanked a belt pouch open, pulling a bandage from it. She didn't speak as he wrapped her arm quickly and competently. Instead, she simply stared at his face. He looked up once and met her eyes, and his hard gaze softened for an instant, then closed up again. She opened her mouth to speak, but couldn't say anything. The sense of the grim man, of his voice, of his scent to the wolves—it had been in her head for two ninans, and she only now recognized it as him.

She turned to Cal and touched his arm as he knelt at Ukiah's side. The other scout had already broken off the feathered end of the arrow, and now Cal slowly eased the other side through. Ukiah's gray face went deathly pale, but the man ground his teeth together to keep from crying out. Her brother handed Rezs the bloodied shaft.

"How is he?" she asked, worried.

"I'll live," Ukiah retorted through clenched teeth. But a surge of blood had followed the arrow out of his shoulder, and there was a smear of it across his cheek where he had wiped it after breaking off the arrow.

"We're controlling the bleeding," Cal told her. "How's the arm?"

"It hurts." She dug her free hand into Gray Vlen's scruff and stared at her brother. Riders, following . . . Voices in her mind . . . "Father   Cal   " she began. "Why were the riders you?"

Cal gave her a humorless grin. "Well, that's at least different than asking what we're doing here."

She didn't smile. Bany's body lay on the ground fifteen meters away, and it drew her eyes like a magnet. She forced herself to look at her brother. "That, too. What are you doing here?"

Olarun looked at his daughter. She was pale, and one sleeve was torn and stained with blood; one hand had red, cracking runnels where the blood that had dripped from her fingers was already drying. She wasn't wearing a warcap, and her hair was loose and tangled. There was a faint mark on her chin—like a new scar—and her violet eyes were still glinting with fear. And something else. He felt his jaw tighten as he recognized the depth of the hold the Gray Ones already had on his daughter. He knew that look as well as he knew himself. "We're here," he said quietly, "because you needed us."

"The shadow shapes on the trail . . . Your voices—"

"That was us."

"You've been following me all along."

Cal caught the flash in her eye. "Don't get angry, little Lunki—"

"Don't call me that," she said shortly.

Cal glanced at Ukiah. "By the time you were gone five days," he explained, "even Lit was squirming as a rast in the jaws of a wolf. The more we thought about neGruli, the more we wanted to put a few more bodies in your riding party. Then Father rode in, and nearly blew the roof off when he heard you were gone. He didn't want to intrude, but he didn't want you out riding. It was spring, the lepa could flock, and . . ." He shrugged.

Rezs glanced at her father's neck where a childhood scar stretched white against his spring-tanned skin. She understood. "But why hang back so far? Why didn't you just join us? You made Bany jumpy as a wolf in a pit."

It was her father, Olarun, who answered. "We didn't want to intrude, Rezs, because of . . . Coale. So we hung back, a day away mostly."

"Oh, moons. Coale . . ." Rezs's eyes flashed to the broken glass. She broke away from the two men and hurried to the rocks. She stared down at the scattered glass, then touched the wet spots on the stones. Slowly, she knelt. There was a tiny pocket of fluid in the end of one broken bottle, but that was it.

Cal knelt beside her. "What was it?"

"An antidote. Coale and the others—they're drugged down at the camp. Bany said they'd die if they didn't get the antidote in time."

Olarun and Ukiah moved to join them, and her father put his hand on her shoulder, urging her up. "It's all right, Rezs. You don't need it anymore."

She jerked her arm away and stared at him in horror. "They're dead? They're gone already?"

"They're not dead yet," Olarun said sharply. "There's still time—"

"Time? If they're not dead yet, they're going to be dead shortly," she returned. "Four hours ago they were lying down there like corpses. They don't need me to take more time up here. They don't need another hour while their hearts slow like a tired drum. What they need is right in front of us, all over the rocks, soaking into the dust."

Her father gripped her arms, turning her to face him. "Look at me, Rezs. There is time. The antidote—you don't even know if that's what it was, or if it was more of that drug. NeGruli doesn't exactly have a good track record of bringing back his men, and if Bany was working for him, he'd probably use the same tactics."

She stared at him. Finally, she gestured helplessly. "Then what do I do?"

"Keep the other wolves nearby so they can follow us down to the camp." He glanced at Ukiah. "You, Ukiah—can you ride?"

The other man smiled without humor. "Don't know if you'd call it riding, but I can always stay in the saddle. Just get me to a dnu."

Olarun nodded. Cal drew Rezs away from the rocks. For a moment they looked down at Bany's body. Rezs didn't touch him. When Gray Vlen sniffed at the old man's body, snarled, and trotted away, he left no sense of Bany's life in her mind. "Do we leave him here?" she asked tightly.

"We'll come back." Her brother motioned for her to follow him down the draw.

"You rode?" she asked.

He nodded. "The dnu are back here, by the stream—we didn't know how far up this draw you were, and we didn't want to give ourselves away to Bany. Dnu aren't known for quiet riding. As it was, without the wolves, we would never have gotten this close." He cast her an approving look. "You're getting good, Rezs. The Gray Ones brought your message clearly and guided us like scouts. And up here, you used them well as a distraction."

Rezs was sober as she followed him down the trail. "I sent the message to Ukiah, yes; but up here, it wasn't I who did it, Cal. I didn't know you were this close."

He glanced back, studying her face. "But Vlen was running beside us, leading us up here. Surely you can see now through his eyes."

"I saw ghosts. I saw Ancient ghosts moving and running and riding along the trails. And your ghosts were just more images in the packsong. I heard your voices, and didn't even know it was you with Vlen. I'd been hearing you for almost two ninans—I thought it was some sort of echo from home, through some other Gray One's ears."

"Lucky for you we were nowhere near home."

Rezs didn't look back. "Lucky for me," she murmured.

Gray Vlen snarled and trotted ahead of her, and she nodded at the yearling. The sense of the pack was heavy as the other wolves slunk through the bushes. She caught glimpses of them as they trotted onto the path ahead of her and Cal, and their mental howls were loud. In the distance she could feel Gray Shona, but the wolf was snarling almost constantly, and the gray wolf's frustration was tinged with worry. The image of the other wolfwalker's body was still as death. Rezs clenched her hands.

They were at the mouth of the draw when the trembling hit. All of a sudden her knees got weak, and her breath came to her in a sob. She clamped her jaw shut, but Cal heard it. Swiftly, he turned and grabbed her arm.

"Rezs—"

"I'm . . . all right." She forced the words out. "I think . . . it's just hitting me . . . now."

But her eyesight blurred, Gray Vlen snarled, and all of a sudden she was sitting on the ground with Cal's arms around her shoulders, rocking her and holding her close as if she was a child. She let him hold her—she didn't mind the throbbing where her torn arm was pressed against his chest. She felt Gray Vlen's comfort as the yearling shoved his nose into her face. The pack that had been nearby seemed to pause and turn back on the trail, and Rezs couldn't send them the reassurance to continue. Her breath began to come in tearing sobs, and Gray Vlen, worried, began to nip at Cal.

"Back off, Gray One," he snapped back.

Vlen gave him a baleful look and growled low in his throat.

"Give her a minute," Cal said firmly to the cub. Vlen snarled once more, then shoved his face into their hug as if he could find by sense of smell what was wrong with his wolfwalker. Rezs tried to calm her breathing, gulping air. Cal didn't say anything; he just held her until she was again controlled, while Gray Vlen pushed his rancid, worried breath into their faces and nudged them with his cold nose. Finally, she pushed away.

Cal released her, helping her to her feet. "Okay?"

She wiped at her eyes and nodded. Her eyes were still so blurred she could hardly see.

"Good." Her brother's voice was dry. "Then you can tell the other Gray Ones to go on down the trail."

She looked behind him. Two of the males and one of the female wolves from the other pack were standing on the trail, watching her and Cal. Their bristles were half-raised and their teeth almost bared as they linked to her through Vlen.

"It's all right, Gray Ones," she told them. "Please, go— down to the camp where Gray Shona waits."

The biggest male met her eyes, and his bristle slowly smoothed. *Wolfwalker.*

"You honor me, Gray One."

The three wolves turned and disappeared.

By the time Rezs and Cal reached the dnu, her cheeks had dried of tears and her voice was more calm. It took little time to retrace their steps and return up the draw to Ukiah, and by the time they got there, the scout was completely bandaged up. Olarun had packed his wound with a temporary poultice and made a sling for his arm. The other scout was sitting on a boulder, gesturing with his good arm as Rezs and Cal rode up.

Immediately, Ukiah slid off the rock. His eyes went straight to Rezs, and she met his gaze steadily. He was still pale, and the blood that stained the front of his jerkin had soaked into a large patch. His face was unsmiling as ever. Rezs dismounted and handed the reins of her father's dnu to Olarun, then moved to greet Ukiah. "Grayheart," she said softly. "All those days I could hear you in the packsong, and I never knew it was you."

Wolfwalker. His voice seemed to float out of the gray fog in the back of her mind. He touched her chin, letting his thumb rub the one fading scar that marked it, then shifting to lightly touch her lips. He didn't speak. But she could feel the strength in his hands, as before. She could feel the calluses and the line of his fingers; she could see the thin stubble along his chin.

And in the packsong, the thread of music that haunted him was strong and close, while the gray wall that separated him from the wolves was now as solid as the thread between Vlen and her.

Cal leaned on the saddle horn as he eyed the bandaging job. "Looks tight, Ukiah. Ready to ride?"

The scout nodded, but didn't take his eyes from Rezs. Finally, he took the reins of his dnu from Cal and mounted awkwardly. Cal shifted his dnu closer, as if to give the other man a hand, but Rezs didn't offer to help. "He's fine," she told her brother. "He smiles at arrow holes and broken bones. You can worry when he starts laughing. He probably only does that when he's mortally wounded."

Cal gave her a thoughtful look.

She looked up at Ukiah. "Why didn't you shoot them—my brother and father? How did you know they were family?"

"Loyalty goes only so far, Wolfwalker. And much as I'd worked to get into Bany's good graces, I wasn't going to give him that much of my soul. Murder is still murder, no matter how you trade it."

"Much as you'd worked ... You knew Bany was with neGruli?"

"No." He shifted in the saddle, winced, and straightened. "But I knew he was somehow involved. I let him save my life so that he'd think I owed him. Then all I had to do was wait. Eventually, he'd need help with something, and he'd ask me to do it."

"Like kill my father and brother."

"And you."

She glanced at Olarun. "Did you tell him who you were?"

The older man shook his head, but his eyes were as thoughtful as Cal's as he watched the two of them together. "He told us," he answered.

Rezs took Cal's hand and slid up onto his saddle behind him. She glanced back at Ukiah. "How?" she demanded.

"The shape of your eyes," he said softly. "They're the same. Your noses, your cheeks, your chins. And"—he pointed to the bridle on Cal's and her father's dnu—"your bridle ornaments."

She followed his gesture. The tooled ornaments on Olarun's and Cal's dnu were leather, not the metal that she had used, but the intricate design was the same. "Your ornaments belonged to my mother when she was a child," Olarun said softly to his daughter. "And to her mother before her. I gave them to you when you were six. It was fitting."

Then Cal wheeled his riding beast and they began to lope down the draw.

It took no time to reach the camp. As before, going downhill was faster in some ways; where oldEarth horses had always been awkward on the downhill stretches, dnu were smooth as water. Gray Vlen had gone on ahead, then doubled back to see Rezs before going on to the camp. The gray tide of the Ancients that ebbed and flowed in her head grew fainter the farther from the cavern they rode, until, as they made their way into the camp area, it was only a dull echo in the back of her head, nearly swallowed by the other, closer voices. The Gray Ones who formed a rude circle outside of camp waited without entering the area. Gray Shona, lying beside Coale, had rested her head on the other woman's chest, and her low snarl was constant with worry.

Rezs slid from Cal's dnu as he came to a stop. Instantly, Gray Vlen was beside her. He nudged her hand, and she gripped his scruff. Ukiah dismounted and went to Touvinde, then Welker and Gradjek. "They're still alive," he reported.

Olarun nodded. "Cal?" he asked his son.

Cal looked up from Elgon's side. "Still breathing."

The older man moved to stand over the other wolfwalker. "Help her first," he said softly.

"How?"

"Vlen and Shona will show you. This woman first, Rezs."

Rezs got to her feet and moved to stand beside him. His jaw was tight, and a muscle jumped along it. She looked at him, then down at the woman. "Why her? Because she's a wolfwalker?"

"Because she's a healer. She can work then with the others."

Rezs looked up at him sharply. "A healer—Coale?"

"No." He looked down at the older woman with a peculiar look on his face. "Your grandmother, Ember Dione."

XXIV

Rezs stared at the still figure. In sleep, without the weight of the wolves blurring Rezs's eyesight, Coale's face was relaxed and clear in line, her profile a more delicate copy of Rezs's. Slowly, Rezs knelt and touched the woman's face. It was like looking into a mirror of time, she realized. The lines, the weathering of the pale skin . . . "Ember Dione maMarin," she whispered. "Here. Not Coale, but my grandma—Dion."

"Your grandmother," Olarun agreed. "I named you after her—your middle name: Monet-Marin. Marin, for your Grandma—not just Monet, after your mother. It broke tradition, but I—" His voice broke off. "It needed to be done," he finished.

"She called herself Coale—like Ember." She looked up. "She chose a name that was still her own. Elgon tried to tell me. I just didn't know how to listen."

"Elgon is your cousin, by my oldest brother, Tomi."

"The boy adopted during the refugee years."

He nodded. "More so than any of your blood relations, Elgon could travel with you safely—you wouldn't have recognized his features."

Cal knelt beside her. "She looks like us," he said softly. "We look like Father and Grandfather, but somehow, we also look like her."

She touched the faded line that ringed the woman's warcap. The thinned circle marked the spot where the healer's band had been worn, she realized. "Why was she here, Father?"

He dropped to his knees at her other side. "I sent her."

"You've not spoken to her since you left Ariye."

"The day you became a wolfwalker," he answered heavily, "was the day I rode back home."

Her own voice was low as she said, "I thought you were angry with me."

"I was. The wolves never give up their own, Rezs, and I'd kept you out of the forest for most of your life. You knew nothing. You wouldn't survive a ninan without a teacher. Who else would I ask? Evans can't ride a kay since he crippled his leg—he'd be useless in protecting you while you learned to stay out of trouble. Sulani's lost three babies to miscarriage; she wasn't about to risk losing her fourth just to teach you how to run trail. Bunairre will bed anything with two legs—he'd have been my last choice of a wolfwalker to take you out, alone, in the wilderness."

"So you went to Dion."

He touched his mother's limp hand. "I went to the wolfwalker, Ember Dione."

"How did she take it? You just showing up and telling her to teach me? You've never even let her see me before this."

"I hurt her, Rezs."

His voice was tight, and his grip on the wolfwalker's hand was tighter. Rezs placed her hand over his. "Father—"

"I told her that she had never had time for me. Time for the wounded; time for the wolves; time for every task the elders asked. But not for me, her son. I told her that even if she never bothered to spend her time with me, she could at least take a few days away from her work and spend that time with you."

"And now she's here, dying, and it's my fault."

"It isn't your fault, Rezs."

She looked up, and her face was tight. She could see, without looking, the bodies that lay around the cold firepit. She could feel their slowing heartbeats and the muffling of their lungs. "No," she agreed, "it's not my fault. And yet—like a catalyst—I'm responsible for everything."

"Not everything."

"Enough of everything to carry guilt like a wagon on my back. Oh, moons, Father—I think I've killed them all."

"You've done nothing, Rezs," Olarun said sharply.

Rezs caught her breath. Her voice was suddenly quiet. "Exactly," she said. "I've done nothing. I merely provided the setting for all of this to happen. I stood aside and watched Bany drug these people and didn't lift a finger to stop him. Did you know that Bany was neGruli's father?" Only Ukiah didn't look surprised, and she nodded at their expressions. "All along, I was suspicious of Coale and—Dion," she corrected, "and Elgon. I looked for extra motives and distrusted their reserve. Gray Vlen told me I was being hunted. But it was Bany, not Co—Dion all along. I just didn't know how to interpret Vlen's wariness. Now Bany's dead, and these five will die." She stared down at her hands. "With the speed of the second moon, in a few days, I'll be dead myself."

Her father gripped her wounded arm, and she flinched. He didn't let go. "You're alive, Rezs. And no plague is going to take you from me."

She caught her breath. "Oh, Father, none of the Ancients, with all their technology, could beat the plague. How do you expect me to do it?"

"Because—" He looked down at the still face of his mother. "There is a cure for the plague, and Dion found it long ago."

"I'm not Dion," she cut in, suddenly harsh. "I'm not the healer—she is. Look at her, Father. She's dying right here, in front of us. She can't help me, any more than I can help her."

Olarun looked up, meeting her gaze, and she was shocked by the steely glint in his gray eyes. "You're wrong, Rezs. You can help her, just as she, in the end, will help you. Look at her. There is no finer scout, Rezs. No finer wolfwalker. No healer that can come close to this woman's touch. She is Ember Dione, your grandmother, a master healer and wolfwalker. She is dying," he agreed. "But you can help her. Believe this, Rezs. You are the one who can save her."

Rezs felt Shona's eyes flash through the fog. She shivered. "She's dying," she repeated in a whisper. "I can't help her by trying some forgotten technique that only a healer would know."

"Rezsia, she's taught that technique to you already—I can feel it in the way the wolves perceive you."

"You're not a wolfwalker," she said sharply. "You can't know what she has or hasn't taught me."

"I could have run with the wolves any year of my life. They've always been there in the back of my head, but I pushed them out of my life. And now I can't push them any farther, because I need them. I need what they can do for my mother. And I need for you to do it with them. I can feel your growth, Rezs, and I know what you can do."

"The energy transfer . . ." Rezs felt a flash of light. A word that meant spin to the left. A dizziness, and a healing touch . . .

He nodded. "Ovousibas," he said flatly.

Cal sucked in his breath. "The healing art of the Ancients?"

"Ovousibas . . ." Rezs looked up and met Gray Shona's eyes, and the yellow gaze split the fog in her mind and left her jaw tight with the Gray One's pain. "It's supposed to be legend," she said. "It's supposed to kill any Gray One that helps a human do it." But Dion's words echoed in her head: Never take energy out of the wolves—only from another human . . .

"It's no legend," Olarun stated flatly. "And it kills the wolf only if the Gray One is used as the channel for the energy. Dion's been doing Ovousibas for decades, Rezs, and she's taught it to a dozen others."

She stared down at their hands. Dion's hand was slack and pale, the slender fingers twisted and crushed in Olarun's grip; the back of her hand scarred in ridges that made ragged seams across her bones. Olarun's hand was wide and tanned, his knuckles white, and his fingers long and thick with strength. And Rezs's hand, with her own slim fingers, unscarred, barely weathered, and unlined by age, clenched slowly around her father's.

Her voice was matter-of-fact when she answered. "I guess I knew it all along—that it wasn't just an energy transfer. Ukiah's leg was broken, but Dion healed it for him to ride, and she hid that healing in my bond with Vlen. And the dizziness I've felt—that was Dion using the internal healing on the wolves. I could feel it in the packsong—the pain, then the easing of it, and always accompanied by the dizziness."

Olarun released Dion's hand. "Gray Shona will guide you, and Vlen will protect you."

"I'm not a healer."

"Doesn't matter. Your grandmother knows what to do, Rezs. She just can't pull herself out of the grip of the drugs. That's all you have to do. Reach her mind and give her the focus to heal herself. She'll do the rest. She always does," he added, more to himself than to her.

Cal looked at her. "She's family, Rezs."

Slowly, she nodded. "I can feel it now. All that time, riding and running with her, and I never knew who she was because Gray Shona just called her Wolfwalker. She kept the wolves' image of herself so hidden in the graysong—she blurred my eyesight with the weight of their senses so I couldn't see her face."

"Can you do it, Rezs?" Cal said quietly. "Can you keep her alive?"

"I don't know." She was silent for a moment. "I've wanted to meet her, to know her, all my life, and now that I've found her, she's already halfway along her path to the moons." She looked up at him. "I'm afraid, Cal. I've got the plague—I have to have it. I went into the place of the Ancients. I breathed the air; I touched the walls—I brought the Ancients out with me in the form of their work. And now I sit here and hold my grandmother's hand. I know I have to help her, but all I can think is that she's going to die, and I'm going to be right behind her."

Cal's rough hand covered hers, but it was Olarun who spoke. "You can do this, Rezsia Monet-Marin maDeiami. You have the will; you have the strength. The only thing you lack is a guide to take you in. But look around you. There's an entire pack of wolves here to show you what to do. How do you think Dion found out about it? She was younger than you when she asked the wolves, and they told her without hesitation." He paused and studied her face. "Now," he said quietly, "it's your turn."

"My turn . . ." She had wanted to be a hero, she thought, but heroes don't kill their wolves; and heroes don't kill their family.

"She's already dying, Rezs. The worst you could do is nothing."

She stared down at her grandmother. Her father's hand gripped Dion's, and Rezs could see his knuckles whiten as he tried to reach his mother by the pressure of his flesh alone. She looked up at Gray Vlen, who had come to sit across from the woman. Shona scrambled up and sat beside the yearling. The two yellow gazes seemed to pierce her mind, and she could hear the howling start. She barely noticed when Olarun and Cal stepped back.

"Vlen?" she asked.

His yellow eyes met hers, and she felt the snarl of Gray

Shona rise up with his voice until it swamped her. *Run with me, Wolfwalker. Run with us.*

Coale—Dion. Her grandmother. She could feel the woman's heartbeat through Gray Shona. She could feel the slow wind of air that moved through Dion's lungs. When she looked into Vlen's eyes and let the links between all of them merge, she could feel the cold knot of the other woman as it slowed and chilled into an icy block of nothing but will.

Wolfwalker, Gray Shona sent. *Help us.*

She clenched her fists and closed her eyes. Then she laid her hands on Dion's sternum and let the sense of the other woman filter through the lupine fog.

Deep in her mind, the gray fog swirled. Other gray voices joined the packsong, and around her, Rezs felt the wolf pack gather. The massive male that had met her eyes before—he was a deep, strong snarl that focused the voices of his mate and yearlings. The female with the scarred shoulder—she was a soft, melodic voice that echoed under his. The packsong swelled with strength until it became again that gray tide, rising and swamping her mind and drowning out her thoughts.

Gray Ones! she cried out.

Wolfwalker . . . In her mind, their voices were the roar of an ocean.

Show me how, she told them. *Take me in where I need to go.*

Wolfwalker!

The waves rolled over her, tumbling her thoughts, and she felt herself falling. If she cried out, she didn't know it. She didn't notice that her ragged fingernails cut her own palms. Heartbeats, slow and fast, mixed like untimed percussion. Lupine lungs filled and emptied so unevenly that she could not breathe . . . Ukiah put his hands on her shoulders, and she couldn't feel him. Only the gray waters rising and dragging her down, in a clockwise spiral. Down into the minds of the wolves. The swirl became a curving path. The path became a line of sight. Gray Shona was like a spear, shooting to the center of the other woman, and Rezs merely followed it like a line attached to the bolt.

Hard and solid, Dion's will had condensed as if it was all the woman could do to hold it in one place while her body slowed and began to stop. Where her grandmother had before focused onto the blood and bones of Ukiah, Rezs focused only on the other woman's will. She touched it and felt it shiver with the force of energy she used. Gray Shona howled and latched onto that kernel as if she used her gleaming fangs to sink her lupine mind into that of her wolfwalker. And the energy flowed. From Rezs to Dion. From Ukiah to Rezs—she could feel him now, and his hands, digging into her shoulders, created a pain that kept her from falling completely into the fog. Thicker, stronger, that kernel of will grew until Dion's heartbeat began to speed up and her breathing began to deepen. The woman's thoughts began to gel. Rezs felt the gray fog boil as her grandma's consciousness entered the packsong. Gray Shona howled. Vlen, echoing the other wolf's joy, clamped onto the thread of their bond and forced Rezs behind the gray wall that flashed into her mind. Energies suddenly snapped back and forth. Sparks of heat and light flashed through her mind. There were images of lightning balls that rolled together and broke apart, molecules that seemed to form before her mental eyes. She couldn't go closer; she couldn't break away. Not until the gray wall frayed and faded, and the yearling drew her back himself, did she begin to hear through her own ears again, or see light through her own violet eyes.

Rezs sagged into Ukiah's arms and, wounded as he was, he caught her. She stared up at him. "Did I do it?" she whispered.

He nodded. And smiled.

XXV

Rezs gave the samples she had brought back from the place of the Ancients to her father. He examined them and, with her help and Cal's, tested them. They weren't the same samples that neGruli had used before, but they were close enough, he said, to take before the elders. If nothing else, Bany's confession would help take neGruli's funding and put it back into the programs that had been stripped. There was enough evidence for that, her father said.

Olarun had time to examine everything: They didn't leave the camp for three days. Even after Coale-Dion—Rezs still had a hard time distinguishing the names—treated the other scouts, they were groggy, and their muscles full of twitches. Touvinde was the worst—he'd either had more of the drug than the others, or his metabolism had taken it badly. As for Rezs, she kept waiting for the plague to hit her. Dion had used Ovousibas, the ancient healing, to take her into her own body, and since then, there had not been a semblance of fever or the twitch of a mild convulsion. Still, her sleep was uneasy, and the slightest sign of a shiver at night made her tense up like a wire.

"How can you be sure?" she asked the older woman as they sat together that second afternoon with Vlen and Shona beside them.

Dion rubbed absently at Shona's shedding fur. "Because I, too, once had the plague—as did your great-uncle Rhom, and my mate, Aranur. I did to them and myself what I've just done to you. It worked then, and it's worked on others since then. There's no reason it won't work for you."

Rezs studied her face in the light. It was still strange to see the other wolfwalker with her eyes, as though seeing the wolves' impression of Dion so often had permanently distorted her view of the other woman. Her voice was sober when she asked, "If you can cure the plague, why have you kept this secret? Why do you hide this when it could help us return to the domes? When it could help us relearn the science of the Ancients—even grow better, stronger houses which would keep more families out of the streets?"

Dion stopped petting Shona, and the gray wolf got to her feet. "What I did is not a cure," Dion returned flatly. "It's a healing, nothing more. You gain no immunity by having the plague once—or twice or five times or even more than that. I've gone back to the domes, and every time I got the plague again, as did my mate and the others who went with us. And the longer we stayed, the sicker we got." She stared down at her hands as if they held a secret she could wrench from her own flesh. "Can you imagine what would happen if it became known that you could reenter the domes? Hundreds of people would try it. They would sicken within a day of stepping into those rooms. Within three days, they'd be dead."

Gray Vlen snarled in Rezs's head, and she looked at the yellow, gleaming eyes. There was a memory in his mind now—one of his own, of that spin to the left that allowed their heartbeats to merge. She could follow it like the cord that stretched between them. The gray shield wall, the sparks of energy—they were set as much into his mind as hers.

Rezs looked back at her grandmother. "You could heal them again," she said. "Olarun says you've taught this technique to others. You've even taught it now to me."

"Think, Rezs." Dion's voice was sharp. "The healing technique drains you like a seven-day flu. I've learned my limits over the years, and what I've found is that the limits are severe. A simple healing—I can do several of those in a day if I have certain foods to sustain me, and do nothing but sleep in between. A detailed healing costs me a complete day of recovery—sometimes more."

Rezs watched her face. "That's why you always rode into camp and went straight to bed. Those healings you were doing on the wolves as we traveled—that drained you enough to need that kind of sleep?"

"That, and when Elgon rode with me in the afternoons, he not only hunted and gathered extra food, but he stayed with me so that I could sleep in the saddle if I needed it." She smiled faintly. "I've gotten rather good at that lately."

Rezs glanced up the ridge to the place where the white domes hovered. "So you couldn't heal the number of people who would return to the domes?"

"No. If even one man went back to the domes to stay, it would take all my energy just to keep both him and me alive. I could never do more than that—never explore the domes with him, never examine the rooms, never speculate about the Ancients. I would be nothing more than a healing machine."

"And if others knew about Ovousibas?"

"The same thing would happen. Everyone with any injury or sickness would crowd my door, demanding that I heal them."

"You can't heal everyone . . . Grandma." She hesitated over the word, but as she said it she realized that it felt good. "No one could possibly expect you to do that."

Dion looked suddenly tired. "You're wrong, Rezsia. Every man thinks that his wound is more important than the next man's wound. His son's injury more critical. His mate's labor more difficult. His daughter's sickness more serious. I would be forced to make thousands of choices every ninan: who would lose or keep his arm or leg, who would recover from this sickness or that, and who would end up dying. People would travel when they have no business doing that—they would risk killing or worsening themselves when they should have simply stayed home and let their own healers work. Ovousibas can't heal everything, nor should it be used all the time just to accelerate a healing."

"You did it with Ukiah."

"I did," the dark-eyed woman agreed. "But that was not only for him, but partly to protect myself. Had Grayheart gone into shock, I would have had to work on him as a healer. Healing skills are as obvious as those of any other field: Bany would have known instantly who I was. By using Ovousibas instead, I limited Grayheart's injury to something that Bany or any of us could have treated. Used discreetly like that, Ovousibas can make the difference between life and death, between a farmer whose arm is crippled or healed enough to work. But if I wasn't discreet—if word got out that that is what I was doing—I would be hounded to death by every desperate person in all nine counties." Her lips tightened. "The hospital in Ramaj Ariye is the best in all nine counties, but Ovousibas or not, we still lose patients. People die. It's part of life. And I could work on the injured till my own heart didn't have the energy to beat, and I'd still not heal them all." Her voice grew tight. "Who lives, who dies ... I can't take the guilt for those kinds of choices. I just can't do any more, Rezs. There has to be something left for my family. There has to be something left for me."

Rezs gripped the other woman's hand. Dion stared down at their hands, their fingers twined together. Then she looked up. Their eyes met. The two wolves were suddenly on their feet. Shona's howl merged with Vlen's. In Rezs's mind, the gray fog tightened into a wall of solid rock which then shattered into the packsong.

Rezs touched the hilt of the knife that she wore in her belt. "I'd like to keep this," she said quietly. "And I'd be honored, Grandma, if you kept mine with you."

Slowly, Dion nodded.

The fourth day found Rezs and Elgon up the trail, watching the dawn cross the valley. They stood for a long time without speaking while the dawn colors lightened, then began to glow on the distant range that marked the other side of the wide land. Gray Vlen was beside them, lying in the trail with his head on his paws, and through him, Rezs could feel the gray fog softly in the back of her head.

As the dawn glow grew to a golden color, Elgon said, "I should apologize."

Rezs glanced at him. "For what?"

"For being so hard on you."

"It's understandable, Elgon."

"Is it? I could see you, getting close to her," he explained. "Beginning to rely on her—putting her in a role that wasn't real to you. To you, she was just a teacher. Just another scout—a wolfwalker who was willing to show you a little bit about the trail. To Dion, you were her flesh and blood—the child of her own son. Her granddaughter. And I hated the thought of you turning your back on her when you found out who she was."

"My father's feelings are not necessarily my own."

Elgon smiled without humor. "If you had met Dion on the trail and known who she was right away, can you truly say that you'd have ridden with her from day one with an open mind and heart? You wanted to meet her, but you weren't going to come to her with an open mind. She needed that—for you to get to know her yourself, not through the eyes of guilt and resentment. After all, you never once tried to see her on your own—how could she not think you resented her like your father did?"

"Ariye is so far away," Rezs said softly, almost more to herself than Elgon. "And there was always so much to do in Randonnen."

"She came to Randonnen nearly every other year to see you and your brothers. She never spoke to you or came to the house—she had promised Olarun she wouldn't. But he told her where you'd be so that she could see you, playing as you grew up; working at the schools; riding between the hubs of the cities."

"And when she wasn't here, she watched us through the wolves."

He nodded.

"Biran was sick once—for ninans. He just kept getting worse and worse. Nearly died as the fevers burned through his body. Then a healer came from out of town. The fevers broke that night; the delirium went away. He was weak, but he was with us again. The healer—she came in the night, and left before dawn. Only Mother and Father saw her." Rezs looked out over the valley. "That was Dion, wasn't it?"

He nodded again.

"Ukiah said Coale didn't walk like Dion—that she limped the wrong way to be Dion, and that her feet were too small."

Elgon's lips twitched, and suddenly he grinned. "That was on purpose. When Dion was in camp with the rest of the scouts, she wore boots that were too small—cramped her feet and made her walk with a different kind of limp. When you went running, she changed into her real boots. That's partly why she didn't spend much time with the whole group. Too many chances to be recognized; too awkward to keep those small boots on for long."

Rezs felt the gray fog stir in her mind, and Vlen perked

his ears. "She's coming. With Grayhe—with Ukiah," she corrected.

He nodded.

"You can feel them, too?"

"I'm no wolfwalker, but I've been around the Gray Ones all my life. One thing I do know is how to read the wolves. Vlen just told you that someone's coming, and right now there's only two people who would seek you out at dawn. Dion and Ukiah."

She looked down the trail. There were two figures who climbed up: one limping—differently now, and more easily, she noted with a faint smile—and the other tall and careful still of the swing of his wounded shoulder. Elgon touched Rezs's shoulder, then made his way down the trail, passing Dion and Ukiah on their way up. The other scout gave Elgon a sharp look, but said nothing, his eyes going to Rezs as she stood on the rim of the path with Gray Vlen beside her.

Grayheart and Dion joined Rezs silently. For a long while none of them spoke. As the sun rose and the air warmed, the moons paled in the sky. Tiny popping sounds filled the air as the grass pods opened, and Rezs let her ears fill with the scream of the dawn hawks who hung over the valley. Finally, Ukiah looked at her for a long moment, then turned and strode away.

The morning light stretched into the valley, and the dark, sparse canopy became suddenly bright. In the distance, the mountain range that dropped down into Ramaj Ariye was just visible above the ridge.

Rezs's voice, when she finally broke the quiet, was soft. "He is Grayheart."

Dion nodded.

"Did you know that the whole time he rode with us?"

"I knew."

"You didn't tell me—even when I asked you about him."

Her grandma smiled wryly. "I thought, since you were riding to meet him, and since you were sensitive enough to feel his reserve, that you had already discovered that for yourself. Until you asked if Elgon was Grayheart, I thought you knew it was Ukiah. After that . . ." Her voice trailed off, and she shrugged. "It was up to him to tell you, not me."

"I met him in the dark, when I couldn't hear his voice or see his face. I was so scared that all I remembered was the feel of his hands and the chill of his steel on my throat. I never made the connection to Ukiah. I kept thinking it was Touvinde."

"They've ridden together for a long time." Dion studied her for a moment. "He wants you, Rezsia."

"He needs me," Rezs corrected. "Or he needs what I represent. It's that—not me—he's afraid to lose."

"And you?"

"He saved my life," she said simply.

"And you're grateful. Nothing more?"

Dion's voice had been carefully casual, and Rezs gave the other women a sharp look. She remembered the way her heart had seemed to stop when Ukiah helped her up on the rocks and held her for that instant close to his body. In the lava tube, the way, even with his broken leg, that he'd pulled her close to protect her as she slept. The way her eyes always seemed to follow him, and his voice seemed to float in her thoughts. "If I feel more for him," she said quietly, "it needs time to become defined."

"But now?"

"Fear and gratitude make for a lousy relationship."

"Need can hide love, Rezs. And gratitude—it can give you the patience to help someone bring out the whole of himself. You have to look beyond the scars, Rezs. Sometimes, what's obvious it not what's real."

Unconsciously, Rezs touched her chin. Visible scars and invisible wounds . . .

Dion nodded, as if she had caught Rezs's thought. "There's a lot more to you two than fear and gratitude. You watch each other like hunters. You're aware of each other like two wolves circling in a mating ring. Right now you're testing each other—like checking the water for depth."

Rezs began to smile. "Now, that's the way I've always thought of finding my mate—by hunting him as he hunted me and then testing him when I found him."

The other wolfwalker's eyes glinted with quiet humor. Without her own eyesight blurred, Rezs could see that Dion's smile was too much like her own. It felt strange—as though she were watching herself, not Dion, talk and smile and move. "Testing your lover is part of learning to live with him: How does he think? How do you feel? What is important to both of you? What do you need from and what can you give to each other?"

Gray Vlen growled, low in his throat, and the woman didn't speak for a long moment. When Dion did speak again, her voice was so low that Rezs had to listen through the yearling's ears, not her own. "Life and death," she said painfully. "They're the only things I was ever able to give to my family."

"Grandma . . ." Rezs began. Her voice trailed away. "When I was twelve, you gave my brother Biran his life. We all thought he'd die. Father—he didn't sleep for days, sitting at Biran's side and riding out at all hours to check the ring messages that came in on the birds. And Momma, she lived for Biran's breathing. You gave us back my brother, and then left, and I never even knew it was you. Father never even told us you had come; and you never even said hello."

"I made a promise."

"To Father? Yes—I know that now. But what about us? Didn't we deserve to meet you ourselves?"

"Don't—"

"Ah, Grandma." Rezs fumbled for the older woman's hand, and Dion, after a moment, gripped her fingers tightly.

"I'm sorry," Rezs whispered. "Much as I want to accept you fully, I still resent growing up without you. Yet at the same time, I feel as if I've always known you. I always saw the Gray Ones' eyes in my mind, watching and protecting us. I could always feel them nearby when I was riding. I'd see them at dawn in the commons." She looked down at their hands. "Gray Vlen is your gift to me, isn't he? We're bound together now, through the wolves."

Dion didn't deny it.

"I've never really been alone," Rezsia realized out loud. "You've always been there—with the wolves, in my mind." She glanced up the ridge. "Even when you were drugged, I could feel your heart, slow in my mind. Only once—in the place of the Ancients—there was a chamber that cut you off. When I put my head in it, all sense of the wolves disappeared. My head felt empty—as if there was nothing but a void in my mind. It was . . . terrifying. I couldn't find Vlen. I couldn't find the packsong. I couldn't find you. And for the first time in my life I was truly alone. Oh, don't be sad, Grandma." She touched Dion's weathered cheek where a trace of moisture glistened. "I realize now that since the day I was born, you've been there for me. You might not have bounced me on your knee, or taught me to sing or swim, but you've watched over me like the moons. Olarun knows that. For all that he hates the part of himself that rejects you, he loves you."

The dark-eyed woman didn't answer for a moment. "In time," she said finally, "perhaps he'll come to accept me again. Right now his guilt is still too close, and there are forty years between us."

"But are those decades of time or decades of pride?"

Dion studied her for a long moment. "Ukiah had best watch out," she said softly. "He might be able to hide his truths from himself, but not from you for long." She wrapped her cloak around herself as if the morning had suddenly grown chill. "I can heal the bodies of everyone else, but I've never learned how to heal the wound between myself and my son."

Rezs looked down at Gray Vlen, and the yellow eyes that gleamed back caught her up in the packsong. Deep in her head, the gray fog roiled. Memories, old and ancient, mixed and merged into a solid thread. Gray wolves leaped through the forest, and shadow shapes of two boys raced side by side with Dion. Rezs could feel Olarun's presence in the packsong, and with it, was Dion's voice. "Maybe you don't have to," Rezs said quietly. "Maybe it's already healed, and all you have to do is find a way to tell him that."

Dion's smile held no humor.

Rezs hesitated. Then slowly, she said, "Grandma, my full name is Rezsia Monet-Marin maDeiami."

Dion's jaw tightened, and for a moment she couldn't speak. "Monet-Marin," she breathed finally. "Rezsia Marin."

Rezs nodded.

The older woman eyed her with an almost lupine hunger. Then the woman nodded, touched Rezs's arm, turned, and walked away. Rezs looked after her, but the woman seemed to fade into the stone as easily as she faded into the forest. Only Vlen heard Dion's steps as the woman moved back down the path. But in the fog that filled the back of Rezs's mind, the gray tide rose like a smooth wave, and Rezs felt her lips curl back like a wolf. But it was no expression of aggression or hunt; it was, instead, a smile.

* * *

By the time they were ready to start back across the valley, Ukiah's limp was less pronounced than Dion's, and Welker's bihwadi bites were merely new scars on her arms. The last day on the ridge, Rezs took Olarun, Cal, and Dion back up to the site of the Ancients. The cave, the ice, the bodies, the chambers—they were all the same. They made some drawings to take back with them to the elders, then resealed the room. And by the end of the day Dion and Rezs did the healing again to rid them all of the plague.

Rezs wasn't sure it had been a good idea to have Olarun go in with them. It seemed that, when her grandmother did the healing on her father, Olarun closed off even further from his mother, so that, when they did begin the journey home, they never rode together. If Olarun was at the head of the line, Dion was near the end with Touvinde. If Dion was near Rezsia, her father rode with Gradjek. For three days this continued. Then, on the fourth day, Rezs, riding beside Olarun, deliberately called Dion up to her position, then left the woman alone with the man. For a while neither one looked at each other except through silent glances. As Rezs joined Welker near the back of the line, the tall scout raised her eyebrows. Rezs shot her an almost guilty look. But Olarun and Dion rode together for kays. And on the fifth day, mother and son sat beside each other at the campfire. That night, they talked. Long into the night, when the coals had become nothing more than a bed of flashing, glinting, orange-black eyes, they murmured to each other the things that neither· had been able to say for nearly forty years.

Muddy trails and steep ridges; valley floors and ponds— they rode steadily back to the east. They stopped only once, when Gradjek's dnu went lame and had to be walked back to the last village.

Rezs, waiting with Touvinde by the dnu, watched Gray Vlen nudge the older man's thigh. The man tried to shove the cub away nonchalantly, but Rezs stopped him. "Why does he do that?" she asked slowly, feeling the eagerness in Vlen's mind. "He comes to you when he'll come to no one else."

To her surprise, Touvinde flushed.

And then Rezs knew. "You've been feeding him," she accused. "Scraps and bits of meat."

The scout tried to shrug, then gave up and awkwardly patted the gray cub's head. "I could deny it, Wolfwalker, but your mutt would take *my* meals at this point if I forgot his evening treats." He jerked his head to the side to indicate her father. "Looks like Olarun wants you to join him."

"You've been doing this the whole ride?" she demanded, ignoring his gesture.

"Pretty much." His expression softened. "Always had a weak spot for the Gray Ones. Olarun's waving again, Wolf-walker."

She went obediently, but when she glanced over her shoulder, she caught a glimpse of the scout dropping something into Gray Vlen's mouth, and the sudden satisfaction that the gray wolf sent made her own lips twist with a smile.

Five days out from the city Rezs and Ukiah reined in, leaving the others to make a noon camp. When Rezs glanced at the other scout, Ukiah nodded, then motioned Cal off the trail. In the distance a wall of stone rose roughly and abruptly from the floor of the valley, and a game trail wound through the trees toward it.

Cal followed Ukiah's gesture. He cleared his throat. "Chameleon Cliffs?"

Rezs nodded silently. She started to rein her dnu back, but Cal stopped her. "Stay with me," he said simply.

She glanced at Ukiah.

"You also," Cal added. "Please."

Ukiah glanced at Rezs, and she nodded. They rode together toward the cliffs.

Rezs and Ukiah searched for the signs; Cal couldn't seem to move once they reached the rocks. But it took less than an hour to find Cal's mate. At the base of the cliffs, as Bany had said, the bones were bleaching in the sun. Scattered, splintered, half buried in the detritus two year's winters and springs, they were mute testimony to Kairyn's death.

Cal sat in the saddle for a long moment before dismounting to join Rezs and Ukiah. When he did finally slide off the riding beast, Rezs took the reins and let him kneel, alone, by his mate's bones. The man touched them, then brushed aside the leaves and soil until he found a crumpled bracelet, dingy with two years of dirt packed into its delicate design. The remnants of a hair ornament that had held her light brown hair. And finally, the sternum bone.

The ribs were cracked off the bone, leaving its sides sharp and jagged; and the shards of those edges made Cal catch his breath as he held it. But in the center of the white, flat sternum were the two gems, still rooted in the bone. One purple, for the year they had waited to be Promised together. And one blue, for the Promise itself . . . The simple cut of the studs told him more clearly than anything else that he held his mate's remains. Then Cal threw back his head and let out a harsh cry that rang off the cliff and lost itself in the forest. Again he screamed, and his throat convulsed as he pressed the bone to his forehead.

Rezs clenched her fists. Ukiah reached across to grip her hand. They waited until her brother was finally silent. Then Cal took his knife and pried the studs loose from their setting. He pressed them to his own chest, where the two studs he wore were hard and sharp against his hand. Then he put the gems in his belt pouch. He said nothing as he returned to his dnu.

Rezs leaned across and touched his arm.

Cal looked at her once. His voice, when he spoke, was harsh. "Gather them. Burn them. She's been gone too long to sing a new path for her to the moons."

Rezs nodded. She said nothing as he rode away.

Ukiah helped her gather up what was left of the bones. There was something macabre about handling the bones of her brother's mate. She had to force herself to pick up the hand bones and skull. Then they built a deep firepit, lined it with stone, and torched the bones until the brown-white pieces glowed. After a while Rezs couldn't watch, and Ukiah pointed to a boulder back in the forest, where she could sit but not see the cremation.

She didn't know how long she was there. Gray Vlen lay down at her feet, and let her rub her toes along his belly. Gray Shona joined them for a few moments, watching the fire in the distance. There were blue ettivinion flowers at her feet and a ragged carpet of yellow lilies, which stretched away through the forest. Rezs could hear the crackling of the fire; through a faint link to Ukiah, she could feel the heat of it—as though it were she who was close enough to really feel it on her skin. She could hear the noise of the trees, shedding their winter bark, and the peeling, whining sounds were like a faint crying that made her shudder. She could feel the peltstone, sharp in her pocket, pressing against her side, and the promise it reminded her of made her eyes grow sober and thoughtful.

Finally, as the shadows grew, the smoke died down, and Ukiah came to stand near her. "It's done," he said flatly. But he didn't move toward their dnu.

She glanced at him. He seemed wary, as if he was waiting for her to do something. "What is it?" she asked quietly.

He didn't touch her, but the sudden hunger and fear in his eyes made the lupine fog in her mind start to boil. Gray Vlen sat up and flicked his ears at the scout, snarling low in his throat. Ukiah ignored the yearling, but Rezs felt him warn the cub away. Then the tall man stooped and gathered a handful of blue flowers, holding them out to her.

Rezs looked into his brown-black eyes. Slowly, she took the bouquet. She held it to her nose, letting the faint, sweet scent of the flowers fill her lungs before she spoke. Her voice was quiet as she asked, "Why did you do it, Ukiah—risk your life to help me? You didn't have to move that close to the cave. You could have stayed back and thrown your own knife at Bany."

"No." Ukiah's voice was almost absentminded—as if he spoke an afterthought while watching Rez's reactions. "Bany was too good. He thought I was loyal to him, but he still didn't trust me; the slightest movement of mine to point a weapon at him, and he'd have killed me as I stood. I didn't know how long it would take Olarun and Cal to get into position—without the wolves brushing through the grasscs and snarling to cover the noise, Bany would have felt your brother and father creeping up like screaming schoolchildren. You—you were the unpredictable one. By forcing you to act, I gave Bany two targets at once instead of one. Even the split second he took to make his decision cost him his aim on you. By then, Olarun and Cal had their chance to find a shot."

But Rezs shook her head. "I saw your eyes, Ukiah. You didn't care if you died or not. You could have turned and pretended to aim at me yourself, then turned to shoot at Bany. He'd still have had to react, and you'd still have shoved me out of the way. Instead, you *made* him shoot at you."

He didn't answer for a moment. When he did finally, there was a tightness to his voice that made Rezs stare. "Bany was good, Rezs, and he wanted you dead. No matter what I did, I didn't expect you to live. And if you were going to die, I wanted it to be in my arms, not alone in the dirt like . . . Your brother's mate." A muscle jumped in his jaw. "I didn't want you to die alone."

Rezs studied him carefully. What she saw was not the man before her—the one with the shuttered eyes and the smile that held no humor. She didn't see the lines that had begun to stretch along his forehead or out from the corners of his eyes. Instead, she saw through her bond with Vlen that, behind that gray voice, was a ghost image of a boy, then a man, then a boy again. Lost, lonely, shut off from what he loved, and abandoned by life. Coale's words, soft in the back of her head: You accumulate grief as you go through life . . . And that wall of fog that kept the Gray Ones separate from his mind.

"You can hear the wolves as clearly as I," she stated in wonderment.

"No. But I can hear them."

"In the dark, at neGruli's warehouse, you could hear Vlen even then. You knew it was a wolf, not a dog that was following me. But you still put your knife to my throat."

He didn't smile. "You were about to be caught, Rezs. What else was I to do?"

"You could have simply said something."

"Would you have believed me? Or asked for proof and tried to discuss it? There were guards on their way. Had we hesitated, we'd have been shot."

"Did you know who I was?"

"I knew you were important to me. It hit me the moment I touched you—when I felt you in the packsong." He stared up at the canopy, and the glimpses of sky that flashed between the trees. "I've lost too many people, Rezs. I couldn't afford to lose any more."

She looked down at the small bouquet. "I think," she said slowly, "that it's not me you need, but the wolves. By Promising to me, you get the Gray Ones through my bond, and you don't have to open up to them yourself. You want me to give you what you don't allow yourself to have."

Ukiah shook his head. His eyes glinted with dry humor. "It's love, Rezs." He pointed to his arrow wound. "Cupid struck."

"That's not funny," she said sharply. "How is it, anyway?"

"Sore. And I'm not laughing, and you've said that before."

"I'll probably say it again, if I ride with you much longer. Why is it you only make jokes when you're in pain?"

"What better time to do it, Rezs, than when you're weakest?"

"Is that how you think of yourself—only in terms of weak or strong?"

"You can make a show of cunning, Rezs, but it's still strength that carries the blade in the end."

"That's a platitude, not a truth, and there's no real belief in your voice when you say it."

"Maybe I don't believe it. Maybe all I believe in is you and me."

"No . . ." She shook her head slowly. "It's not a question of belief. It's easy for you to say those things—from you, the words mean nothing."

He raised his eyebrows.

"You can talk like that—without emotion—because the words hang out like forgotten laundry. They're unattached to your self. You've hidden your heart behind so many layers that no mere word can pierce those weavings." She wiped irritably at her blurring eyes. "You locked yourself up when you were sixteen, and you've never allowed your heart to feel or age with your emotions. It's never been exposed to anyone. It never really felt the grief. You're still so young inside, you don't even know what you are."

He watched her soberly. "I was never young," he said.

"But once, long ago, you had the joy of a child in you. I heard it in the packsong. It's been your music all along, that I've listened to in the howling. You might have hidden your heart from yourself, but you never could hide it from the wolves. No matter how sternly you rejected them, they've been faithful to you like a mother."

She looked down at the bouquet. She had to clench her hand to keep it from shaking. Then, deliberately, she took one flower from the clump, and handed the rest back to him. "Listen to your heart, Ukiah. You'll need me, but you won't really love me until you accept yourself first." She forced her voice to remain steady. "There's a teacher you need to talk with, and a piece of yourself to free before you can Promise with me. When you come back, I'll be here. I'll be waiting."

He looked at the bouquet, but she held it out, unmoving. Finally, he took it, his face set like stone.

"I want no other man to ride with," she said softly. "But I want the whole of you, not just the part you're willing to look at, yourself. And you must take the whole of me, not just my bond with the wolves."

The tall man didn't move, and Rezs got up and stepped away. Vlen nudged her hand, and she gripped the Gray One's scruff, then she mounted her dnu in a single movement and reined the beast away. She hesitated once, but didn't look back as she rode into the woods. Only the set of her shoulders and the howl he heard in his head told Grayheart she was crying.

EPILOGUE

The moons rode the sky as if they raced each other. Neck and neck, they paced across the dark expanse. Their light cast deep shadows between the trees, and left the open amphitheater stark white and gleaming. In the center of the stage below, the speaker's podium stood alone, and on that was a long, round-edged box that cast its own night ghost on the stones. The outer fabric of the box was worn with the age of centuries, and the strap by which it was carried had frayed and been replaced more than a dozen times.

Up on the steps of the amphitheater, two dozen people sat. The others had gone home already, to meetings or dinners or bed, and all that were left were the ones who waited or those who simply watched the stars and moons. Sometimes the scrape of a boot against the stone was unnaturally loud. Occasionally someone murmured to his neighbor, but no one spoke to the old man in their midst. His aged shoulders had begun to bend with the weight of two centuries, and his face dragged down with the years. He sat on the stones and stared at the podium. Waiting. Breathing. Never moving from his seat.

An hour passed, and three people left. Another hour, and another went. Dusk was long gone when the last woman shifted uncomfortably from her seat and made her way up the steps. She looked at the old man, but didn't speak. And when she reached the top of the amphitheater, a boy made his way down in her place and tugged at the old man's sleeve. "Aestro, please," he said steadily. "It's late. You're cold. There's no reason to wait any longer."

"He'll come." The old man shook him off. "It's tuned. It's

ready for his hands—and no hands like his have touched it since he put it down. He cannot help but come."

"It's been eighteen years, Aestro."

The old man's voice was sharp. "He'll come."

The boy hesitated, then sat beside the old man. He didn't speak again. The moons crawled by in the bowl of the sky, and the stars washed out as the white orbs passed. An hour seeped away. Then another, and the amphitheater was dark and cold. And finally, when the old man's arms were rough with goose bumps, the boy got up again.

"It's time, Grandpa."

The old man did not speak.

"You have to let him go."

The old man did not move for a long moment. Then, finally, as slow as time, he nodded. The boy helped him struggle to his feet. It could have taken them hours to move up the seventeen steps. It could have taken years. The old man didn't see his feet move on the stone; instead, he saw the shadows, heard the ghost music he had lost so long ago in blood.

They were at the top of the stairs when the old man stiffened.

The boy looked up with worry. "Aestro?"

There was a sound from below. A clicking sound, as if metal had snapped across metal.

The old man's grip was suddenly hard on his grandson's arm. "Hanult—do you hear?" He turned, stumbled; and the boy staggered under his weight. They both stared.

In the amphitheater, under the moons, a single man stood. He had unlatched the case, and now did not move, his hands resting on the fabric of the box. The boy looked down at the tall man, then up at his grandpa, then back at the woods around them. Yellow eyes gleamed from the dark. He felt a chill.

"Grandpa," he whispered. "There are wolves . . ."

The old man didn't move.

Down below, shadows shifted, and the tall man opened the case. The moons glinted dully off the varnish of the violin, and the man's hands caressed it. Soft varnish, to keep the sounding board pliable. Old wood that almost breathed its age . . . He picked the bow from the lid of the case and tightened it with infinite care. When he lifted the violin, his hands trembled.

Ancient wood, ancient tone ... Slowly, he tucked his chin over the wood. Then he drew the bow across the strings and let them simply sound.

The perfect fifths rang in his head just as they reverberated off the stone. He let the last note simply fade away, but he didn't drop the bow from the string. And suddenly it moved. By itself, the bow seemed to sweep across the strings. The man's fingers, rusty, fumbled with the notes. Even at that, the tones were nearly true. He played a scale, then a complex scale, then half an étude that swept up into the higher notes and brought back a sense of confidence to his fingers. He let the violin fall silent as he bowed his head.

Moons shifted. Yellow eyes glinted from the rim of the amphitheater. Down below, the tall man took a breath and let it out. Then he began to play. No song at first. Just one note. Then another. Then a sound that seemed to spill from his chest. His heart seemed to crack, and the gray fog seeped into the space inside, flooding then into his mind. When he raised his head and cried out, the violin answered. And above, on the stones, the old man began to cry. Slowly and silently, the tears fell across the age-seamed cheeks as the instrument below gained life. No single melody rang out, but the music of years—of grief and death, of loneliness, of guilt and regret and anger. Every emotion that had been bolted for years into the tall man's heart rushed out in a flood of music.

Up on the rim of the amphitheater, the slender woman watched. Her hand was buried in Gray Vlen's scruff, and her violet eyes locked on the scout. Gray wolves gathered in her shadow, and the howling they projected in her head was an orchestra to the solo she heard in her ears. Around her, in the village, lights sparked on. Doors and windows opened, and people, murmuring, began to thread their way out of their homes, drawn to the speaking place.

Beneath the moons, the tall man played. Blind to the people who gathered on the steps. Blind to the Gray Ones who filled his mind with their howling. Blind to the woman who watched from the rim. He saw nothing but music; for at that moment that's what he was. The hands that had gripped the woman so hard were light on that ancient wood. The haunting melody that played in her head—it now sang roughly in her ears.

She stirred as the people began to gather. Then she found

herself moving silently down the steps until she sat beside the old man. When she reached for the old man's wrinkled hand, he fumbled for her own. They sat like that, in the dark, together, while below them, the tall man played.

AUTHOR'S NOTE

Wolves, wolf-dog hybrids, and exotic and wild cats might seem like romantic pets. The sleekness of the musculature, the mystique and excitement of keeping a wild animal as a companion . . . For many owners, wild and exotic animals symbolize freedom and wilderness. For other owners, wild animals from wolves to bobcats to snakes provide a status symbol—something that makes the owner interesting. Many owners claim they are helping keep an animal species from becoming extinct, that they care adequately for their pet's needs, and that they love wild creatures.

However, most predator and wild or exotic animals need to range over wide areas. They need to be socialized with their own species. They need to know how to survive, hunt, breed, and raise their young in their own habitat. And each species' needs are different. A solitary wolf, without the companionship of other wolves with whom it forms sophisticated relationships, can become neurotic and unpredictable. A cougar, however, stakes out its own territory and, unless it is mating or is a female raising its young, lives and hunts as a solitary predator. Both wolves and cougars can range fifty to four hundred square miles over the course of a year. Keeping a wolf or cougar as a pet is like raising a child in a closet.

Wild animals are not easily domesticated. Even when raised from birth by humans, these animals are dramatically different from domestic animals. Wild animals are dangerous and unpredictable, even though they might appear calm or trained, or seem too cute to grow dangerous with age. Wolves and exotic cats make charming, playful pups and kittens, but the adult creatures are still predators. For example, lion kittens are cute, ticklish animals that like to be handled (all kittens are). They mouth things with tiny, kitten teeth. But adult cats become solitary, highly territorial, and possessive predators. Some will rebel against authority, including that of the handlers they have known since birth. They can show unexpected aggression. Virtually all wild and exotic cats, including ocelot, margay, serval, cougar, and bobcat, can turn vicious as they age.

Monkeys and other nonhuman primates also develop frustrating behavior as they age. Monkeys keep themselves clean and give each other much-needed, day-to-day social interaction and reassurance by grooming each other. A monkey kept by itself can become filthy and depressed, and can begin mutilating itself (pulling out its hair and so on). When a monkey grows up, it climbs on everything, vocalizes loudly, bites, scratches, exhibits sexual behavior toward you and your guests, and, like a wolf, marks everything in its territory with urine. It is almost impossible to housebreak or control a monkey.

Many people think they can train wolves in the same manner that they train dogs. They cannot. Even if well cared for, wolves do not act as dogs do. Wolves howl. They chew through almost anything, including tables, couches, walls, and fences. They excavate ten-foot pits in your backyard. They mark everything with urine and cannot be housetrained. (Domestic canid breeds that still have a bit of wolf in them can also have these traits.) Punishing a wolf for tearing up your recliner or urinating on the living-room wall is punishing the animal for instinctive and natural behavior.

Wolf-dog hybrids have different needs than both wolves and dogs, although they are closer in behavior and needs to wolves than dogs. These hybrids are often misunderstood, missocialized, and mistreated until they become vicious or unpredictable fear-biters. Dissatisfied or frustrated owners cannot simply give their hybrids to new owners; it is almost impossible for a wolf-dog to transfer its attachment to another person. When abandoned or released into the wild by owners, hybrids may also help dilute wolf and coyote strains, creating more hybrids caught between the two disparate worlds of domestic dogs and wild canids. For wolf-dog hybrids, the signs of neurosis and aggression that arise from being isolated, mistreated, or misunderstood most often result in the wolf-dogs being euthanized.

Zoos cannot usually accept exotic or wild animals that have been kept as pets. In general, pet animals are not socialized and do not breed well or coexist with other members of their own species. Because such pets do not learn the social skills to reproduce, they are unable to contribute to the preservation of their species. They seem to be miserable in the company of their own kind, yet have become too dangerous to remain with their human owners. Especially with wolves and wolf-dog hybrids, the claim that many owners make about their pets being one-person animals usually means that those animals have been dangerously unsocialized.

Zoo workers may wish they could rescue every mistreated animal from every inappropriate owner, but the zoos simply do not have the resources to take in pets. Zoos and wildlife rehabilitation centers receive thousands of requests each year to accept animals that can no longer be handled or afforded by owners. State agencies confiscate hundreds more that are abandoned, mistreated, or malnourished.

The dietary requirements of exotic or wild animals are very different from domesticated pets. For example, exotic and wild cats require almost twice as much protein as canids and cannot convert carotene to vitamin A—an essential nutrient in a felid's diet. A single adult cougar requires two to three pounds of prepared meat each day, plus vitamins and bones. A cougar improperly fed on a diet of chicken or turkey parts or red muscle meat can develop rickets and blindness.

The veterinary costs for exotic and wild animals are outrageously expensive—if an owner can find a vet who knows enough about exotic animals to treat the pet. And it is difficult to take out additional insurance in order to keep such an animal as a pet. Standard homeowner's policies do not cover damages or injuries caused by wild or exotic animals. Some insurance companies will drop clients who keep wild animals as pets.

Wild and exotic animals do not damage property or cause injuries because they are inherently vicious. What humans call property damage is to the animal natural territorial behavior, play, den-making, or child-rearing behavior. Traumatic injuries (including amputations and death) to humans most often occur because the animal is protecting its food, territory, or young; because it does not know its own strength compared with humans; or because it is being mistreated. A high proportion of wild- and exotic-animal attacks are directed at human children.

Although traumatic injuries are common, humans are also at risk from the diseases and organisms that undomesticated or exotic animals can carry. Rabies is just one threat in the list of over one hundred and fifty infectious diseases and conditions that can be transmitted between animals and humans. These diseases and conditions include intestinal parasites, *Psittacosis* (a species of chlamydia), cat-scratch fever, measles, and tuberculosis. Hepatitis A (infectious hepatitis), which humans can catch through contact with minute particles in the air (aerosol transmission) or with blood (bites, scratches, etc.), has been found in its subclinical state in over 90 percent of wild chimps, and chimps are infectious for up to sixty days at a time. The *Herpesvirus simiae*, which has a 70 percent or greater mortality rate in humans, can be contracted from macaques. Pen breeding only increases an animal's risk of disease.

Taking an exotic or wild animal from its natural habitat does not help keep the species from becoming extinct. All wolf species and all feline species (except for the domestic cat) are either threatened, endangered, or protected by national or international legislation. All nonhuman primates are in danger of extinction; and federal law prohibits the importation of nonhuman primates to be kept as pets. In some states, such as Arizona, it is illegal to own almost any kind of wild animal. The U.S. Fish and Wildlife Service advises that you conserve and protect endangered species. Do not buy wild or exotic animals as pets.

If you would like to become involved with endangered species or other wildlife, consider supporting a wolf, exotic cat, whale, or other wild animal in its own habitat or in a reputable zoo. You can contact your local zoo, conservation organization, or state department of fish and wildlife for information about supporting exotic or wild animals. National and local conservation groups can also give you an opportunity to help sponsor an acre of rain forest, wetlands, temperate forest, or other parcel of land.

There are many legitimate organizations that will use your money to establish preserves in which endangered species can live in their natural habitat. The internationally recognized Nature Conservancy is such an organization. For information about programs sponsored by the Nature Conservancy, please write to:

Nature Conservancy
1815 N. Lynn Street
Arlington, Virginia 22209

Special thanks to Janice Hixson, Dr. Jill Mellen, Ph.D., and Dr. Mitch Finnegan, D.V.M., Metro Washington Park Zoo; Karen Fishler, Nature Conservancy; Harley Shaw, General Wildlife Services; Dr. Mary-Beth Nichols, D.V.M.; Brooks Fahy, Cascade Wildlife Rescue; and the many others who provided information, sources, and references for this project.

SATISFACTION GUARANTEED

We at Del Rey believe in our books. In fact, not a single Del Rey book is published unless somebody here loves it and believes in it. We are so sure that you'll agree with us that we guarantee your total satisfaction! If you are not 100% satisfied with this book, fill in the form below, then return it, together with the entire book, to us at the address below. (Be sure to send in the completed form and book before the expiration date noted below.) Photocopies of forms or forms submitted without books (or submissions after the expiration date) will not constitute acceptance of this offer. *Please note that you should not return the book to the store where you bought it—you must send it directly to us together with this form in order to take advantage of this offer.* We'll send you a list of alternate Del Rey titles to choose from—and you can pick any book from the list. Your new book will then be sent to you completely free of charge!

Name:_____ Age:_____

Street:_____ Apt. #:_____

City:_____State:_____ Zip Code:____

I did not like this book because:
[ ] of the plot or story line   [ ] of the characters
[ ] of the wolfwalker world [ ] of the writing style
[ ] other _____

Number of books you read per month: [ ] 0–2 [ ] 3–5
  [ ] 6 or more
Preference: [ ] fantasy [ ] science fiction [ ] horror
  [ ] other fiction [ ] nonfiction
I buy books at: [ ] superstores [ ] mall bookstores
  [ ] independent bookstores [ ] mail order
I read books by new authors: [ ] frequently [ ] sometimes
  [ ] rarely

Send completed form and book to: Del Rey Guarantee
                                 201 E. 50th Street
                                 New York, NY 10022

[Expiration Date: 8/31/97]

DEL REY® ONLINE!

The Del Rey Internet Newsletter...
A monthly electronic publication, posted on the Internet, GEnie, CompuServe, BIX, various BBSs, and the Panix gopher (gopher.panix.com). It features hype-free descriptions of books that are new in the stores, a list of our upcoming books, special announcements, a signing/reading/convention-attendance schedule for Del Rey authors, "In Depth" essays in which professionals in the field (authors, artists, designers, sales people, etc.) talk about their jobs in science fiction, a question-and-answer section, behind-the-scenes looks at sf publishing, and more!

Internet information source!
A lot of Del Rey material is available to the Internet on our Web site and on a gopher server: all back issues and the current issue of the Del Rey Internet Newsletter, sample chapters of upcoming or current books (readable or downloadable for free), submission requirements, mail-order information, and much more. We will be adding more items of all sorts (mostly new DRINs and sample chapters) regularly. The Web site is http://www.randomhouse.com/delrey/ and the address of the gopher is gopher.panix.com

Why? We at Del Rey realize that the networks are the medium of the future. That's where you'll find us promoting our books, socializing with others in the sf field, and—most importantly—making contact and sharing information with sf readers.

Online editorial presence: Many of the Del Rey editors are online, on the Internet, GEnie, CompuServe, America Online, and Delphi. There is a Del Rey topic on GEnie and a Del Rey folder on America Online.

The official e-mail address for Del Rey Books is delrey@randomhouse.com (though it sometimes takes us a while to answer).